The

BUTTERFLY'S
DAUGHTER

Also by Mary Alice Monroe

Time Is a River

Last Light over Carolina

The

BUTTERFLY'S
DAUGHTER

MARY ALICE
MONROE

G

GALLERY BOOKS

New York   London   Toronto   Sydney

Gallery Books
A Division of Simon & Schuster, Inc.
1230 Avenue of the Americas
New York, NY 10020

First Gallery Books hardcover edition May 2011

GALLERY BOOKS and colophon are trademarks of Simon & Schuster, Inc.

For information about special discounts for bulk purchases, please contact Simon & Schuster Special Sales at 1-866-506-1949 or business@simonandschuster.com.

The Simon & Schuster Speakers Bureau can bring authors to your live event. For more information or to book an event contact the Simon & Schuster Speakers Bureau at 1-866-248-3049 or visit our website at www.simonspeakers.com.

Designed by Renata Di Biase

Manufactured in the United States of America

10   9   8   7   6   5   4   3   2

Library of Congress Cataloging-in-Publication Data

Monroe, Mary Alice.
    The butterfly's daughter / by Mary Alice Monroe.
       p. cm.
    1. Monarch butterfly—Migration—Fiction. 2. Voyages and travels—Fiction.
3. Self-actualization (Psychology)—Fiction. 4. Mothers and daughters—Fiction.
5. Female friendship—Fiction. 6. Psychological fiction. I. Title.
    PS3563.O529B87 2011
    813'.54—dc22

                                                                    2010045544

ISBN 978-1-4391-7061-8
ISBN 978-1-4391-7102-8 (ebook)

To Lauren McKenna,

who understands the chrysalis will become a butterfly

ACKNOWLEDGMENTS

I have had an amazing education into the marvelous monarch butterfly and the unique phenomenon of its migration, and I owe a debt of gratitude to many people for helping me on this journey.

For riding as my navigator and for expanding my vision of the novel and the characters with grace and wisdom, I thank my sister Marguerite Martino. Loving thanks to Gretta Kruesi for reading drafts and for sharing delightful anecdotes of her adventures on the road.

I'm indebted to Linda Love for her mentorship and an education on raising monarchs. Linda was also a source of information on the topic of equine therapy for drug addiction, which made her a gift from the gods for this novel.

Heartfelt thanks to Lauren McKenna, my editor, for her excitement and support of the story since the book's inception and for the patient and inspirational editing that gave me and my novel wings. Thanks also to Louise Burke, publisher of Gallery Books, for her continuing support of my work. And to my agents Kim Whalen, who loves butterflies as much as we do, and Robert Gottlieb—I'm fortunate to have your advice and support. I also send my thanks to the enthusiastic team at Gallery Books/Simon & Schuster.

I warmly thank Angela May for her endless and cheerful support and encouragement in every aspect of this business of writing a novel, Lisa Minnick for keeping track of the books so I can look after mine, and Ruth Cryns and Diana Namie for countless kindnesses. Many thanks to Barbara Bergwerf for spending hours chronicling the metamorphosis of butterflies with her beautiful photographs; to Leah Greenberg for reading an early draft and for talking through story points; and to Patti Callahan Henry for a memorable retreat for revisions. A special thank you to Suzanne Corrington for her support and the use of her name.

Thank you to Billy McCord of the South Carolina Department of Natural Resources for an education on tagging monarchs; to Carlos Chacon and Natalie Hefter of the Coastal Discovery Museum for their generosity and time (and monarch eggs); to Sally Murphy for her expertise; and to Bill Russell for pointing me in the right direction for monarch research.

I'm beholden to Trecia Neal and Susan Myers of Monarchs Across Georgia for a truly memorable trip to the butterfly sanctuaries in Michoacán, Mexico, that was both educational and spiritual. Thanks especially to Trecia for reading an early draft of the manuscript for content on butterflies and the Day of the Dead. We were a hearty bunch climbing more than nine thousand feet, and for all their support and camaraderie I fondly nod to Ellen Corrie, David and Mozelle Funderburk, Dave and Audrey Harding, Sharon McCullough, Mary Moyer, Raina Neal, and Cindy and Kathleen Wolfe.

In Mexico, I came to appreciate the threats facing the monarch sanctuaries and am indebted to Jose Luis Alvarez, the head of La Cruz Habitat Protection Project, an amazing organization dedicated to forest restoration in Michoacán. Thanks also to Estella Romero in Angangueo, and to Guadalupe Del Rio and Ana Maria Muniz, founders of Alternare, for their efforts to educate local

ACKNOWLEDGMENTS

farmers about alternatives to logging for the protection of the sanctuaries.

I am indebted to Maraleen Manos-Jones and her wonderful book, *The Spirit of Butterflies,* for inspiration and education about Aztec myths and legends. I read many books and journal articles that educated me and piqued my interest in the subject. Though there are too many to list here, I especially note the following books: *The Last Monarch Butterfly,* by Phil Schappert; *Four Wings and a Prayer,* by Sue Halpern; *Chasing Monarchs,* by Robert Pyle; *An Obsession with Butterflies,* by Sharman Russell; *My Monarch Journal,* by Connie Muther and photographs by Anita Bibeau; and *Through the Eyes of the Soul, Day of the Dead in Mexico,* by Mary J. Andrade. I'd also like to acknowledge the many websites that educate us all about the monarchs—their biology, current status, migration, and rearing—especially Journey North, www.learner.org/jnorth; and Monarch Watch, www.monarchwatch.org.

Love and thanks to Zachary Kruesi for the backbreaking effort of creating my butterfly garden, and to Claire and John Dwyer for a constant stream of support and for giving me Jack and Teddy, my great joys. And as always, I'm grateful to my husband, Markus, for his expertise in fine-tuning the personalities and problems of my characters, for helping me understand car maintenance, and for his constant support and love throughout this book and others all these many years. I am blessed to be traveling this journey with you.

"We delight in the beauty of the butterfly, but rarely admit the changes it has gone through to achieve that beauty."

—MAYA ANGELOU

The
BUTTERFLY'S
DAUGHTER

The Fall Monarch Migration

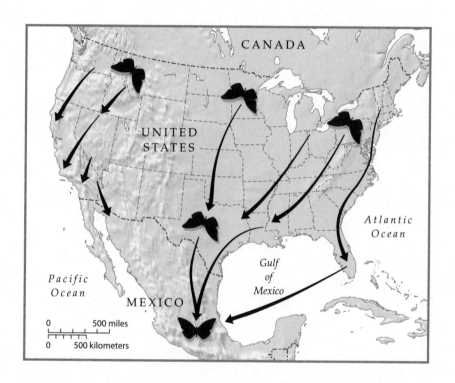

This map represents the routes taken by migrating monarchs
to Mexico during the fall migration (September–November).
The route reverses during the spring migration as monarchs
leave the mountains and follow the milkweed north.

PROLOGUE

ong, long ago, before time began—can you imagine so far
back, *querida*? The world was plunged in darkness. There
was no dawn. No dusk. It was always night. So the gods
journeyed from all points of the compass to gather in Mexico at
the Sacred Circle to create a sun. One among them would have
to sacrifice herself to the fire and become the new sun that would
endure for all time.

The gods called out the challenge: "Who will light the world?"

The gods were silent. Then one god, Tecuciztecatl, stepped
forward. He was a proud and vain god. He thought by sacrificing
himself he would win immortal fame and glory. While the gods
created a great bonfire, Tecuciztecatl painted his body in brilliant
colors, put on flame-colored feathers, and adorned himself with
gold and turquoise. When the blaze was roaring the gods called
out, "Jump now into the flames!"

Tecuciztecatl stood before the inferno, felt its great heat, and
lost his courage.

Then the gods called out again, "Who will light the world?"
Again the gods were silent. Only Little Nana, the smallest and hum-
blest of the gods, stepped forward. She was ugly and covered with
sores. "Little Nana," they said to her. "If you sacrifice yourself, your
wretched body will be transformed into the glorious sun and you
will bring light and warmth to the people of the world till the end of

time." Little Nana did not want to die, but she thought of the light she would bring and stood at the precipice of the inferno.

The gods commanded her, "Jump now into the flames!"

Little Nana closed her eyes and bravely jumped into the heart of the fire. The red flames shot high into the heavens; Little Nana rode a fiery path to the sky and was transformed into the resplendent new sun.

Then the gods saw that the world had no color. They called out to the gods, "Who will bring life to the world?"

Xochiquetzal, the goddess of all things beautiful, called out, "I will do it!"

The gods loved Xochiquetzal and cried, "But you will die!"

"No, I will not die," the goddess replied. "I will fly into the sun and when I fall back to the earth I will transform into new life. I will be the mother of all to come."

It was as she said. Xochiquetzal gave herself the plumed wings of a butterfly and flew high into the heavens to be filled with light. When she fell back to the earth she was transformed into flowers and butterflies of every color.

Since then, every year when days grow short and a cold wind blows, the butterflies fly from all points north to the Sacred Circle in memory of the goddesses who stood at the precipice and bravely jumped, sacrificing themselves to bring light and life to the world.

"So, *querida,* do you understand that in every life there is death and rebirth? Life cannot be renewed without sacrifice. Now I ask you, my daughter, *mi preciosa.* My young goddess. Will you bring light to the world?"

One

Each fall, millions of delicate orange and black butterflies fly more than two thousand miles from the United States and Canada to overwinter in the mountains of central Mexico. The annual migration of the monarch is a phenomenal story—a miracle of instinct and survival.

Esperanza Avila had told the story so many times over the years that it was accepted as truth—even by herself. She'd meant only to blanket her granddaughter's frightening loss, not to mislead her. She saw the story she'd created as a safe, happy cocoon for her to grow up in.

But in the end, she'd created a lie. Now she was caught in her own trap of deception. The only way out was to tell Luz the truth, no matter how painful that truth might be.

Esperanza counted the strokes as she brushed her long, white hair in front of the bureau mirror. Morning light fell in a broken pattern across her room. Her gaze fell upon an old sepia-toned photograph of herself and her second husband, Hector Avila. She paused her brushing as she gazed at his brilliant smile, his hair that waved like the ocean he loved, and his eyes that were as impossibly blue.

Hector Avila had been the love of her life, taken too soon from her. When she was a younger woman her raven hair flowed down her back to swirl around her hips. Hector had loved her hair, whispered to her how it was like a waterfall at night that captured the reflection of the stars. He used to wind her hair in his hands, wrap himself up in it when they made love. Even after all these years, closing her eyes, she could remember the feel of his skin, and her hair like silk pressed against her body.

Opening her eyes again, she saw that her long hair was no longer the lustrous skein that Hector had relished. So many seasons had passed since those halcyon days, so many joys, and so much sadness. Her hair was a blizzard of snow falling around her shoulders. She pressed the brush to her heart as it tightened. Where did the time go?

Suddenly the room felt like it was tilting. Esperanza closed her eyes and grasped the bureau for balance. She was tired, she told herself. She didn't sleep well the night before. Ever since she'd received that phone call from her daughter Maria, old memories and worries had plagued her. They spilled over to her dreams, haunting her, and lingered after the pale light of dawn awakened her.

Her troubled gaze traveled across the other photographs on her bureau, resting on a small silver frame that held the treasured photograph of her daughter Mariposa, aglow with happiness. In her arms she carried her baby. Luz couldn't have been six months old but already her pale eyes shone as bright as the sun. Tears filled Esperanza's eyes as her heart pumped with love for this child, who'd been a gift to her in her later years, after Mariposa had vanished.

"Hector," she said aloud. "I need your wisdom, now more than ever. I could bear this hardship alone. But Luz . . . she is twenty-one, no longer a child. Still, I can't endure to see her hurt. I've told Luz so many stories about her mother. But now *this*! What words can I say to make her understand this truth?" She shook her head with grief. "How will she not hate me?"

She finished gathering her long locks in fingers that were gnarled from age and hard work. While she methodically wound the hair like a skein of wool, her mind reviewed her plan to tell Luz the truth about her mother. She needed uninterrupted time and a safe place to tell her granddaughter the story from beginning to end.

Her hands trembled as she finished pinning the thick braid of hair securely at the base of her head. Taking a steadying breath, she opened her drawer and pulled out the amber plastic medicine bottle she kept hidden behind socks and underwear. She didn't tell Luz about the pills that kept her heart from skipping its beat. Luz already had to worry about too many things for a girl her age. There was a fine line between being responsible and being burdened.

That thought strengthened Esperanza's resolve. She pried open the bottle and shook out the last pink tablet into her palm, then sighed. She needed to get the expensive prescription refilled. How would she pay for it after today? She placed the pill on her tongue and washed it down with a glass of water. Tomorrow she'd worry about that. Today her course was clear.

With great care Esperanza applied smudges of rouge to her cheeks and dabbed on some lipstick. The ruby color added fullness to her thinning lips. She cast a final, assessing glance in the mirror. There were times when she looked at her reflection that she caught a peek at the girl she once was, trapped deep inside of her, barely visible behind the wrinkles and sunken cheeks. That young girl shone bright in her eyes this morning, excited for the task ahead.

Sitting on the edge of her bed, she put on her tennis shoes, then slipped down to her knees. Usually she'd pull out her rosary for her morning prayers, but today she reached her arm under her mattress all the way to her shoulder and began groping. The mattress was heavy and Esperanza panted with the effort. At last, her fingers clutched the small leather pouch and pulled it out.

She sat cross-legged on the hardwood floor, catching her breath, and then gingerly opened the worn, hand-sewn purse that had traveled with her from her small village in Mexico all the way to Milwaukee so many years before. Her fingertip traced the image of a butterfly etched into the golden leather. Without hesitating further, she opened it and pulled out a thick wad of bills. She counted the dollars in her lap, smoothing each bill. Her ruby lips spread into a satisfied grin.

She had enough.

Esperanza put on her black trench coat and slipped a triangle of red silk scarf over her head, a gift from Luz. Before leaving, she made sure the coffee machine was turned off and the iron was unplugged, then made a fervent sign of the cross in front of the framed portrait of La Virgen de Guadalupe in the front hall. With a puff, she extinguished the candle and pulled the door closed behind her.

A north wind hit her face and she tugged the collar of her coat higher around her neck. Fall came early in Wisconsin and spring took its time. She made her way down the stairs to the cracked cement sidewalk.

"You off?"

Esperanza turned toward the throaty voice of her neighbor, Yolanda Rodriguez. She was dressed for the weather in a thick black sweater and gloves as she raked leaves from her tiny front

6

yard. Yolanda stood with her head cocked and her dark eyes gleaming, like a crow at the fence line.

"Yes," Esperanza called back with conviction as she walked closer to the chain-link fence that divided their front yards.

At the sound of her voice, two small black-and-white mixed-breed dogs rushed to the fence, barking wildly. Yolanda hushed them, then paused to lean on the rake. "This is a good thing you're doing," she said, nodding her head for emphasis. "Luz is not a little girl anymore. She should know."

"She will know soon."

"You should have told Luz the truth long ago. I told you so!"

Esperanza held her tongue but felt her heart squeeze in anxiety.

"You still planning on driving to San Antonio?" Yolanda's voice was filled with doubt.

"Yes."

Yolanda shook her head doubtfully. "I still think you should fly. It's faster. Not so much trouble. Not so dangerous."

"It's better this way. And I did it before, don't forget. I have it all planned. It will take only three days to drive to San Antonio. It's perfect, don't you see? That will give Luz and me enough time to talk, where it is quiet and safe."

Yolanda snorted. "And Luz won't be able to bolt like Mariposa."

Esperanza frowned and looked off into the biting wind. She thought how sharp words could sting when they held the truth. "Perhaps. I must go now."

"Do you want me to come with you?"

"No, no, that's kind of you. I want to do this on my own."

Yolanda caught a note in her voice and reached out to gently pat Esperanza's shoulder in commiseration. "It's a good plan. I will say a prayer to the Virgencita that it will succeed. *¡Buena suerte!*"

she said with a farewell wave, then returned to her raking, muttering curses under her breath at the gust of wind that brought a fresh torrent of leaves to her yard.

Esperanza hurried to the street corner to catch the bus she saw cruising up the block. She found a seat and looked out the window at the familiar scenery of bungalow houses, brown brick buildings, and fast-food restaurants. There were so many people, she thought. In cars, on foot, in the windows—all strangers and all with their hands rammed into pockets and their faces set in hard frowns. Her mind flitted back to the small village in the mountains where she'd grown up. Everything was green and she knew everyone's name. Esperanza shivered and tightened her coat. Even after all these years she couldn't get used to these cold northern winters. No coat was warm enough. She longed for the warmer climate and the simple tranquillity of her home.

Stepping off the bus, she felt the chill of the winds off Lake Michigan clear to her bones. It took her a minute to get her bearings. She consulted the small piece of paper on which she'd written the directions, then began to walk. After a few blocks, she sighed with relief at seeing the enormous sign: NICE USED CARS.

It wasn't much of a car lot. It was an old filling station surrounded by a long line of wire tethered between buildings, affixed with colored plastic flags flapping in the breeze. Beneath was a small collection of random cars, some with new coats of paint that didn't do a good job of covering rust. The salesman didn't see her walk onto the lot at first. She knew the moment he spotted her, though, because he instinctively fixed his tie.

"Are you in the right place, dear?"

"I'm where I need to be," she replied. "Are you going to show me some cars or do I have to look myself?"

The salesman was a short, beady-eyed man in an ill-fitting suit. He smiled and led her to a midsize sedan. After looking at the sticker, Esperanza shook her head. "Oh no, I can't afford this car. Please, something more . . ." She didn't want to say *cheap*. What was the better word in English? "Affordable."

"I can do that," he replied cheerfully, though his smile was more forced now.

He led her to the far side of the lot, where the prices dropped significantly. She peered into the windows of a Ford Taurus.

"That's a nice car there. You've got good taste."

"I don't know anything about cars."

"May I ask why you're looking for a car now?"

She looked at the man as though he was addled. "I need one!" she said, then turned to move down the line of cars.

"Are you really here to buy, ma'am? Or just kicking tires."

Esperanza didn't know what he meant by that, so she didn't reply. She walked down the first line of sad-looking cars, feeling her heart drop into her shoes. Each looked worse than the next. When she turned to the second row she saw the car she'd come for.

The battered orange Volkswagen was very much like the one that her first husband, Luis, had found abandoned on the side of the road. He'd spent hours repairing it, then he'd taught her how to drive along dusty roads as she ground the gears.

"You like that one?" the persistent man asked as he approached again. "I dunno. Maybe you shouldn't be looking at a manual transmission."

"No," she said, feeling as though fate had just smiled on her. "This is the one."

Luz Avila looked out the wall of grimy industrial windows at the foundry to see thick, gray clouds gathering in the sky. She reached up to tug at the elastic of her ponytail, then shook her head to free her long mane of black hair. Then, slipping into her brown corduroy jacket, she took her place in a long line of employees waiting with vacant stares to enter their numbers into the employee time clock. One by one they moved forward, but she felt they were all really just stuck in one place.

"You wanna go out tonight?" the young woman behind her asked. Dana was only a year older than Luz but already married and divorced. Her short, spiky hair was an unnatural shade of red and she liked to experiment with varying shades of green and blue eye shadow. "We thought we'd hook up at O'Malley's."

Luz shook her head. Dana wouldn't understand that she was saving every dollar she could to finish college. Or that her conservative Mexican grandmother didn't approve of freewheeling single girls who went out to bars alone.

"Sully and I have plans. But thanks."

Dana shrugged. "See you at the grind tomorrow, then."

"Yeah," she replied dully. The foundry paid a good wage but Luz felt trapped inside its walls, unable to see a brighter future for herself. The best part of her day was clocking out.

Luz stepped out into an October wind tinged with acrid industrial scents. She wrinkled her nose and walked quickly toward the parking lot, where she knew her boyfriend would be waiting for her.

Sully's face burst into a grin under his baseball cap when he spotted her. Sullivan Gibson was a traditional midwestern boy of German-Irish farming descent, evident in his six-foot-three-inch height, his broad shoulders, his penchant for basketball and beer, and his polite manners toward a lady. His long arm pushed the truck door open for her as she approached, and she climbed into the warm compartment just as an icy northern rain began.

"God, I hate this rain," she said.

"At least it's not snow."

The air in the truck was close and reeked of stale cigarette smoke—she couldn't get Sully to break his habit. She leaned across the seat to meet his lips. Sully's brooding blue eyes sparked to life when they kissed, like his truck when he fired the ignition.

Beneath Sully's rough exterior beat the steady, generous heart of a gentle man. He worked at an auto repair shop in Milwaukee. It was a small garage but it had a sterling reputation and a waiting list for appointments. Sully felt lucky to have been offered a job there, but Luz knew that his diligence, reliability, and honesty meant that the garage was the lucky one. Sully already had his own roster of clients. He made a good living with the promise of raises, promotions, and if his dreams were realized, his own shop someday. He was a man ready to settle down with a wife and raise a family. They'd been dating for three years and Sully was her rock. She felt safe when he slipped a possessive arm around her shoulders and drew her close as they pulled out from the parking lot.

Every day after work Sully drove Luz to her home on Milwaukee's south side. He pulled to a stop in front of her unassuming A-frame bungalow, one of many identical houses bordering the narrow street. It was a modest neighborhood, mostly Hispanic. A neighborhood where the residents couldn't afford improvements to the houses and the city didn't bother to improve the streets. But there were pots of brightly colored geraniums on front porches, well-tended shrubs, bicycles chained to a railing, and soccer balls lying in the yard. This was a close-knit neighborhood of families.

Sully let the engine idle and bent to deliver a slow, probing kiss that took Luz's breath away. She pulled back, blinking in a daze.

"What was that for?"

His lips curved shyly, cutting deep dimples into his cheeks. "I was going to ask you. You're awful quiet today."

Luz's grin slipped and she looked out the windshield. "It's Abuela," she said, referring to her grandmother. In her mind's eye she saw Abuela as she was early that morning. She hadn't been in the kitchen humming over the stove as usual. Luz had searched and found Abuela shivering outdoors in the damp chill, her nightgown billowing at her ankles and her long, white hair streaming tangled down her back. She'd stood motionless, like a stone statue in the garden.

"What's the matter with her?"

"I'm worried about her," she said, and immediately his gaze sharpened with concern. "She wasn't herself this morning. She seemed so distracted and her face was chalky and tired, like she didn't sleep a wink. I know she's upset about something but she won't talk about it."

Sully's dark brows immediately gathered over a frown. "Maybe I should drive her to the doctor."

Luz's heart softened. Sully loved Abuela and in turn, Abuela doted on her granddaughter's tall and tender-hearted boyfriend. The two shared a bond that endeared Sully to Luz. Abuela was always asking Sully to drive her to the grocery store or the mall or to pick something up because they didn't have a car. Sully was gallant and never refused her. In exchange, Abuela invited him to dinner regularly, knowing he lived alone, and always had a bag of leftovers or cake for him to take home.

"I don't think it's her health," Luz replied. "Something happened yesterday."

"What?" he asked, and shifted the gear to Park.

The big engine rumbled loudly, rocking them gently, and Luz could at last confess the worries she'd carried all day. "When I came home from work yesterday she was on the phone. But she got off real quick when I came in, like she didn't want me to overhear. When I asked her who it was she said it was my *tía* Maria, but she wouldn't look at me, and her look was kind of guilty, you know the kind I mean? She just went out to her workroom and began sweeping. I tried to find out what happened but Abuela brushed me off, saying we'd talk about it later."

"Sounds like it was just a fight."

"Maybe. Abuela and my aunt are always fighting about something. But this was different. It's big, whatever it is. I've never seen Abuela so . . ." She stumbled for a word, trying to put a name to the sullen expression she'd seen in Abuela's eyes.

"Upset?"

"Worse. Shaken." She saw Abuela's face again, so pale and drawn, and unbuckled her seat belt. "I better go in and check on her."

Luz moved to leave but Sully tugged at her elbow, holding her back.

"Uh, Luz," he began, and cleared his throat. "There's something I should tell you."

Luz heard the seriousness in his tone and she grew alert. She settled back against the cushion. "Okay."

"You know how your grandmother asks me to run a few errands for her?"

"Yeah."

"Well, for a while now she's been asking me to go to the pharmacy to pick up her medicine."

"Her medicine? What medicine?" Luz asked, alarmed. She hadn't known Abuela was taking any prescriptions and was seized with a sudden fear. Her grandmother was her world. After her mother died when Luz was only five, Abuela had raised her single-handedly, giving Luz the only home she knew. "She never told me she was taking medicine. Sully, if anything ever happened to her, I don't know what I'd do. I can't even think about it without getting teary-eyed."

"See? That's why she didn't want you to know. She asked me not to tell you, but you're worried about her, and well, I thought you should know." He looked at her anxiously. "I hate to break a promise."

Luz took a shaky breath and exhaled. "No, Sully, you did the right thing to tell me. Especially if . . . I won't tell her I know." She looked out anxiously at the house. "I better go in and check on her."

"Do you still want me to pick you up tonight? Maybe you should stay home."

She shook her head. "I'm probably making too big a thing out of all this. I'll be ready." Luz leaned in for a quick kiss, then climbed from the truck. She heard the sudden roar of the engine as Sully pulled away. A light rain chased her up the stairs to her front door.

Her grandmother's brown brick bungalow appeared dreary and dull from the outside, but once she was inside, the little house pulsed with life. Abuela's vibrant spirit breathed in every brightly painted room. Metal and ceramic icons from Mexico hung on the walls and in a place of honor in the living room was a large, framed painting of the Virgin of Guadalupe.

Luz set her purse down on the small tile-topped hall table. She heard sounds of children's laughter and, lifting her nose, caught the unmistakable scent of maize. An involuntary smile eased across her face.

"I'm home!" she called out.

"*¡Aquí!*"

She followed the voice to the kitchen, where the rich smells of dark roasted coffee, maize, and cumin embraced her. A wooden bowl overflowed with limes, oranges, and the avocados Abuela adored. She told Luz tales of enormous *aguacate* trees growing on her family farm in Mexico, ripe with avocados she could pick by the bushel. Fragrant steam rose from a pot on the stove, rattling the lid. Abuela was surrounded by two girls and a boy around seven years of age. Looking up, Esperanza caught Luz's eye, then with a quick smile she clapped her hands.

"Time to go, *mis niños*! Your mothers will be calling you for dinner," she sang, herding the children toward the door. "No, no, the butterflies are gone. They flew off to Mexico. *Lo siento.* I'm sorry. But don't worry. They'll be back in the spring, eh? *Sí, sí, yo prometo.*"

Luz leaned against the doorframe, relieved to see her *abuela* back to her normal self. She crossed her arms and watched the hectic scene unfold. Abuela was called La Dama Mariposa, the Butterfly Lady, in the neighborhood because she raised butterflies. Monarchs in particular. For as long as Luz could remember there had always been children hovering near Abuela, especially during the summer, when the monarchs were bursting from chrysalises or being released into the garden.

At last the door closed and Abuela turned to face Luz, clasping her hands tightly. Her dark eyes sparkled with mysterious excitement.

"I have something to show you! A surprise!"

Luz dropped her arms and straightened, alert. "A surprise? For me?"

"For us! Come!" Abuela laughed with the enthusiasm of a child. She reached out to pull her black shawl from the back of a chair.

Luz couldn't help the ear-to-ear grin that spread across her face. She'd thought it was such a rainy, gloomy day, but now Abuela was laughing and talking about surprises. She laughed to herself as she followed Abuela outdoors.

The rain had slowed to a faint drizzle, more a mist that fell soft on her face. She tucked her arm under Abuela's as they made their way down the six cement steps to the front sidewalk. Abuela detoured across the short expanse of city grass to stop before an old Volkswagen Bug at the curb. Dropping Luz's arm, she dug into her pocket. Her face beamed in triumph as she pulled out a key.

"Surprise!"

Luz's mouth slipped open in a gasp. "*A car?*"

"Come, take a look!" Abuela exclaimed, placing the key in her hand and nudging her toward the curb. "What do you think?"

Words failed Luz as she took in the small burnt orange car at the curb.

Abuela clasped her hands together near her breast. "You were surprised, right?"

"Ah, yeah," Luz sputtered.

"I knew you would be. I could not wait to see your face."

Luz walked across the soggy soil closer to the car. Under the yellow glow of the streetlight, she could see that the old VW Bug had lived a hard life. Multiple small dents and spots of rust were like a pox across the faded orange metal. When she peeked in the window, everything looked more spindly and less plush than in newer cars. She shook her head, wondering to herself what surprised her more: that Abuela had actually bought a car, or that Abuela had somehow managed to unearth the ugliest, sorriest car on the planet. And yet, something about it was utterly vintage, and she had to admit she liked it.

"You bought a car!" she said, and knew a moment of giddiness.

Abuela cocked her head at Luz's hesitation. "You wanted a car, right?"

"Oh, yes," she agreed with a shaky smile. She'd had a savings account for several years, just to buy a car, but it never seemed to get past a thousand dollars. "I wanted a car. But . . ." Luz bit her lip and hesitated.

She didn't want to appear ungrateful, yet niggling worries about money dampened the fire of her enthusiasm like the cold rain. Luz was frugal and knew to the penny how much—or how little—was in their family checking account and how much they currently owed on their credit card. Since she was the only one employed, the responsibility for paying those bills fell on her shoulders. How could Abuela just go out and buy a car? she wondered, feeling her shoulders stiffen.

"So, what do you think?"

"Abuela, where did you get the money for a car?"

Abuela waved her hand in a scoff. "It's not so much."

Luz looked at the ancient VW with dents in the fenders and patches of touched-up rust and hoped her sweet grandmother wasn't fleeced. "How much did you pay?"

Abuela sniffed and lifted her chin. "It isn't polite to ask how much a gift cost. This does not concern you."

"I'm sorry. But, Abuela, it *does* . . ." Luz took a deep breath. "Did you charge it on the credit card?" She had to ask. The credit card company had just raised its rates and she was already wondering how long it would take for her to pay it back.

"No. I had money."

Luz's brows rose. "You did? From where?"

Abuela's gaze diverted. "I have a secret place . . ."

Luz imagined a sock filled with dollar bills, coins hidden in a coffee can. She suppressed a chuckle at her grandmother's old-fashioned ways. "How much do you have?"

Abuela put out her hands toward the car with pride. "Enough for this!"

Luz struggled to find words that were respectful and wouldn't hurt her grandmother's feelings. But she had to be practical and think of their future. "Abuela, you know we're cutting things close to the bone. We could've used the money to pay off our debt. Those interest rates are killing us. And besides, Sully always says buying a car is like buying a puppy. The purchase price is the cheap part."

Abuela tugged at the ends of her black crocheted shawl. "I thought maybe Sully could look at it."

There it was. Poor Sully, Luz thought. "That car is a beater. It might take more time than he has to offer." Not to mention money that he'd never bill them for. "How many miles does it have?"

"I don't know."

"You don't know? And you bought it?"

"It is a good car. I can tell."

God help me, Luz thought.

Abuela's back straightened and her smile slipped. Once more Luz saw the cloak of anxious worry slip over her grandmother's usually serene expression. Abuela clasped her small hands before her, like a woman in prayer, and when she spoke her voice was grave.

"Luz, we need this car."

Luz felt the morning's anxiety stir again. "Why?"

"We must go on a trip."

"A trip? Where?"

"To San Antonio."

"Does this have to do with that phone call?"

Abuela's eyes widened with surprise that the phone call was mentioned, then her eyes shifted and after a pause, she delivered a quick, tentative nod.

Luz thought as much. "Is there an emergency? Is Tía Maria sick?"

"No. Not that."

"Then why the hurry?"

"You must trust me, *querida*. We just have to go to San Antonio."

"Oh, Abuela . . ." Her grandmother had always planned to take Luz to visit her daughter and family in San Antonio. Unfortunately, money was always short and trips were as unrealized as Luz's dreams. "I'd love to go. But right now, we just don't have enough money." It was the truth, but as soon as she said the words she saw Abuela's face fall. "But if we're careful and save our money, we can go next year."

Abuela clutched Luz's hand. Her dark eyes flamed and her voice broke with emotion. "No, not next year. This year! Right away!"

Luz rushed to wrap her arms around her grandmother. Abuela was barely five feet tall, slim in the shoulders and barrel-waisted. Luz was only four inches taller but she had to lean over her.

Closing her eyes, she smelled in her hair the scents of corn and vanilla and all things safe and secure.

"Okay, Abuelita," she said reassuringly. "I'll find a way, I promise. Don't worry. I'll get a second job. But let's go inside now. It's starting to rain again and you're shivering. Your hands are like ice."

With one arm wrapped around Abuela's shoulders she shepherded her back to the house. Luz didn't know how she was going to keep her promise, but she'd figure that out later. Now she had to bring Abuela back inside, where it was warm.

"I'm cold," Abuela said. "I must go home."

Two

The Rocky Mountains divide the migration pattern. Generally, monarchs west of the Rockies travel to small groves of trees along the California coast. Monarchs from the central and eastern Canadian provinces and the eastern and midwestern United States fly south to the oyamel forests in the mountains of Mexico. But they are the same species.

The walls of Abuela's kitchen were painted the rich, sun-kissed color of oranges; the chairs and table the color of limes. It was Luz's favorite room and the heart of the house. Abuela went to her bedroom and reappeared looking composed in her long, black skirt and a voluminous flame-colored sweater that curled high around her neck, setting off her white hair and shining dark eyes. Luz carried cups of hot coffee to the table and poured in thick cream and sugar. The cinnamon smelled delicious, but Luz watched anxiously as Abuela listlessly stirred her cup.

"Are you feeling okay?" Luz asked, thinking of Sully's warnings. She searched Abuela's face. "You look pale. Maybe you should go see the doctor."

"I don't need a doctor," she scoffed as she relinquished her spoon. It clanged against the rim of the cup. Abuela laid her fingers against her sallow cheek and began tapping. "I hardly slept last night. I had so much to think about. I am tired, this is all."

"Why don't you lie down for a little while?"

"I can't," she said with emphasis. "There is much to be done! So much to plan for our trip."

"Abuela, please," Luz said, alarmed by her urgency. "Tell me what's going on. Why must we go now? What's the hurry?"

Abuela adjusted her seat and her eyes appeared troubled. "I have my reasons, Luz," she said, turning her head and lifting her chin in a gesture of hurt pride. "I am not some old woman losing my mind."

Luz reached out to lay her hand over Abuela's. It was small but firm, her fingers bent from a lifetime of labor. When she was young, Esperanza had raised two children alone on a farm in rural Mexico while her husband toiled in the United States. Years later she traveled alone to Milwaukee and worked as a cook in a restaurant to provide a home for her granddaughter. These strong, beautiful hands had created the only home Luz had ever known.

"I know that, Abuelita," Luz said, her heart pumping with love as she bent to kiss her knuckles.

Abuela's face relaxed into a smile and she turned her wrist to hold Luz's hands. "*Mi preciosa,* it will be a good thing for us to take this journey together. It will give us time to talk. I thought long about this. First, we will go to San Antonio. But then, together, we will go to Mexico. It is time for you to learn where you are from."

Luz pulled away and folded her hands under her arms. "I'm *not* from Mexico. I was born here, in Milwaukee. I'm American."

"Mexico is where your family is from. And . . ." Abuela took a breath. "You must meet your family," she said firmly.

"Family? There's always been only you and me."

"Why do you say that? There is Tía Maria and her children— your cousins—in San Antonio. And your *tío* Manolo in Mexico. And others . . ."

"I don't even know them." Luz frowned and stared at the murky coffee in her cup. How could Abuela expect her to care about relatives she'd never met or who never cared enough to come visit?

Abuela had two children by her first marriage. Her elder daughter, Maria, lived in San Antonio with her two children, cousins who never wrote or called. Abuela's only son, Manolo, had returned to Mexico to take over the family store. They were all strangers to her. Luz wouldn't recognize them if she passed them in the street.

"Besides, what would we talk about? I can barely even speak Spanish."

"*Sí,* I know," Abuela said with a sorry shake of her head. "This is my fault. You do not want me to talk to you in Spanish. Only English." She sighed. "You can be so stubborn."

"It's no one's *fault,* Abuela," she said, looking away. "I just don't see the point. I don't speak German either. Or know my father's family."

"*Him.*" Abuela's lip curled. "He is nothing to us. We do not even know his family name. I will never forgive him for abandoning your mother."

Luz's voice was soft. "Maybe he didn't abandon *her.* Maybe he just didn't want *me.*"

"Ah, no, *querida*! Who wouldn't want you? You are the only thing that is good from that union."

Luz looked at her short, unkempt nails, feeling unsure.

"Your family—*tu familia*—comes through your mother. Through *me,*" she said in a tremulous voice, bringing her clenched fist to her heart. "*Mi niña,* have I taught you nothing? Have I given you nothing? *¡Mira!* Look around you. These colors, the food you eat, and the music you hear—all these things are Mexican. The stories I tell you are so you know who I am. And who you are." She bent her head and said more softly, "And who your mother is." She looked up, renewed conviction ringing in her voice. "Mexico is in your blood. You should be proud of your heritage."

Luz glanced under lowered lids at Abuela sitting across the heavy wood table, idly fingering the thick braid that fell like a heavy rope over her shoulder. Sometimes she felt as tightly bound to her culture and its expectations for her as a woman as her grandmother's long, traditional braid. She *was* proud of her Mexican heritage. Yet Luz didn't want to be defined by it. She wanted the freedom to discover herself.

Abuela brought her hand up to cup Luz's cheek. Her fingers felt papery and cool and her dark eyes pulsed with meaning. "We must talk about Mariposa, your mother."

"I don't remember her," she said softly. "She's been dead so long she's becoming some vague memory, more a feeling than someone real. I'm forgetting her and it makes me sad."

Abuela's brows gathered over troubled eyes. "Luz," she said, stumbling for words. "There is much you don't know about Mariposa."

"I know she was beautiful."

"*Sí*," she replied, arching her brow in memory. "Very."

"Am I at all like my mother?" She heard the pleading in her own voice.

Abuela hesitated. Luz felt the heat of her gaze on her, searching for traces of family resemblance. She knew Abuela worried about her American granddaughter who did not know her family traditions and did not speak her native language.

"Not so much in looks. You have her beautiful skin. So creamy and smooth. Mariposa was taller, and so thin a gust of wind could blow her away. And often did," she added with a bittersweet smile. "You and I, we are made of more sturdy stock, eh?"

Luz cringed. *Sturdy* in her mind meant strong bones, oxen, hardly what a young woman wanted to hear. Luz was full-bodied with rounded breasts and curvy hips. *Plump,* mean girls might say. *Curvaceous,* Sully said.

Seeing her reaction, Abuela tsked and shook her head, frustrated with the English language. "No, maybe I use the wrong word. I mean steady, eh? We have both feet rooted on the ground. Your mother"—Abuela paused and her eyes grew sad—"she had both feet planted firmly in the air."

Luz's eyes widened with surprise. Abuela had only ever spoken of her mother as a princess in some fairy tale, using superlatives and terms of praise. She'd never heard Abuela criticize her perfect daughter.

"Sometimes, I think that's better," Luz said. "You have more fun."

"No! More trouble, that is all." Abuela shook her head slowly, exposing a weary sadness. "My poor, foolish daughter. For all that she enjoyed life, she made it hard, too. Mariposa was a flighty creature. Like the butterfly I named her for. You could never pin her down. I used to think that was her gift." She shrugged and regret flashed in her eyes. "But it was also her flaw."

Luz wiped a strand of hair from her forehead, pausing to take all of Abuela's words in. She saw deep lines carved into Abuela's face, more obvious today with her fatigue. A new grief seemed to weigh heavily on her, causing her shoulders to droop. Most important, these words of criticism and despair came from a dark place in her heart she'd never revealed to Luz before.

"Perhaps if I had been more strict," Abuela continued. "I never should have allowed Mariposa to go to the university."

"Why wouldn't you want her to go to college?" Luz asked indignantly. She'd give anything for the chance to go to college.

"What does a beautiful woman need with school, eh? Mariposa should have stayed at home and married a good man. Her life would have been so different. She might have—" Abuela stopped herself, closing her eyes for a moment with a sigh. "But her father was an educated man and insisted."

Luz knew the end of this story as well. Abuela had been deeply suspicious of the idea of sending her beautiful daughter—the only child of her second marriage—away to the university. Abuela could read and write in both English and Spanish, but for her, these were necessary skills, not ones used for pleasure. Cooking, gardening, sewing—these were skills she valued as a woman. Abuela's worst fears were realized. Mariposa had been at the university for less than a year before she ran off to America with a German student, a young man she had never brought home to meet her father and mother. Years later, when Luz had wanted to go to college, Abuela didn't forbid her, but neither did she support her. She wanted Luz to marry Sully and to settle down as a wife and mother. "What do you want with all those books?" she'd ask when she saw Luz squirreled in her room reading.

Abuela looked deeply into Luz's eyes, her face softening with affection. "Mariposa was impulsive. But you are *fortaleza,* eh? Strong and dependable. You have a special light in your eyes that comes from your soul. I saw this the moment you were born."

Luz looked away, disturbed that she couldn't see that light shining in her own eyes. "Maybe my mother wasn't impulsive," she said, feeling a sudden urge to defend her dead mother. "Maybe she was like the goddess Little Nana. She had courage. She wasn't afraid to jump into the flame."

"Listen to me, Luz. I am old enough to know I do not have all the answers. But I know this. Impulsive is not the same as courage. True courage comes from the heart. *Tu corazón.* Sometimes, it takes more courage not to jump and to stand strong. When each of us looks into the fire, we must decide for ourselves whether to jump."

Abuela leaned back in her chair, her eyes bright with resolution. "But you and me, we must jump now." Her wizened face softened and she reached out across the table, wiggling her fingers, luring her granddaughter to place her hands in her outstretched ones, as she did when Luz was a little girl. Luz obliged.

"I see in your eyes your doubts. Do not worry. This journey will answer many of your questions," Abuela said. "We will go to San Antonio in our fine car. We will see our family there. Then, we will continue on to Mexico. To Angangueo, where Manolo and my family live. What a reunion we shall have! Then finally, we will go to the mountains to see the butterflies. Together, as we always planned we would. Soon you will stand at the precipice of the Sacred Circle, as my mother stood with me, and I stood with your mother. As we have done for generations. You will dance with the butterflies. You will take your place with the goddesses."

Luz sighed with resignation, having heard this story many times before. Other children heard fairy tales about Hansel and Gretel, Sleeping Beauty, or Jack and the Beanstalk. Abuela had told Luz myths about the Aztec gods and goddesses and the monarch butterflies in the mountains of Mexico. But that's all they were to Luz—childhood stories.

"Last I looked," Luz said with a self-deprecating smile, "goddesses didn't work for minimum wage in a factory."

"Oh, yes they do!" Abuela said with a squeeze of her hands. "Goddesses are everywhere, if you look for them."

"Even if I wanted to go, I don't think that car can make it all the way to Mexico."

"That little car has great heart. I have faith. And so should you. I dream of going all the way home to Mexico. But in truth, all that car has to do is get us to Texas. After that . . ." She shrugged. "We will hope for the best." Abuela brightened and in a burst of enthusiasm rose from her chair. "I have studied the map. Wait!"

A few minutes later Esperanza came hurrying back into the kitchen carrying sheets of paper and maps. She spread out a map on the table and pointed a gnarled finger at a spot she'd circled in red.

"Here is Milwaukee, see? First, we go to San Antonio. Today I called Jorge Delgado. He owns the taqueria on Greenfield. Jorge made this drive a few months ago. He said if we have no problems, we can make it to San Antonio in three, maybe four days."

"If you return the car tomorrow and get your money back, you can buy a plane ticket to San Antonio and get there in one day. And you can visit with Tía Maria for as long as you like. Wouldn't that be easier?"

"But that would not include you. I also called the airlines today. To fly is very expensive. And," she said, wagging her finger for emphasis, "when we get to Mexico, we would still need to drive a car to get to the mountains where your uncle Manolo lives. Look," she said, pointing again at the map. "This is Morelia airport and this"—her finger moved several inches across the map to where the terrain was mountainous—"is where I grew up. See? We need a car." She said the last in a manner that implied her logic was flawless and couldn't be argued with.

Luz's lips twitched. "You've been busy today."

Abuela nodded her head with conviction. "*Sí*. I plan and plan.

We must arrive in Angangueo by November first, for the Day of the Dead. This is very important. It is when the monarchs return to our village on their way up the mountains."

Luz couldn't deny the flurry of excitement she felt at the idea of making this trip with Abuela. She yearned to leave on some adventure, to see the world. Yet, her stomach also clenched at the thought of all the bills waiting to be paid, and now the added expenses of the VW.

They put away the maps and enjoyed a leisurely dinner of chicken tamales with a verde sauce that was Abuela's own recipe. While they ate, Luz listened patiently as Abuela talked about the journey and discussed their route, which would chase the monarch butterflies as they migrated south across the country.

When dinner was finished and they began washing up the dishes, however, the harsh realities of their finances took root in Luz's mind. It was fun to dream together, but she couldn't let Abuela go on believing that in a few days' time they would actually pack up and drive off on this adventure. She dried the last of the heavy green pottery plates and put it away in the cabinet. Abuela was rinsing the suds from the sink.

"Abuela," she began hesitatingly, folding the towel neatly in thirds. She set it on the counter. "I know how important this is to you. But . . ."

Abuela's hands stilled at the sink and she slowly turned. Her beautiful dark eyes turned wary as her smile fell.

"Let's think about the timing, okay?" Luz continued in a cajoling tone. "First, I have my job. I can't just take off on a trip tomorrow. Then there are the bills. We really have to finish paying off our credit card debt. I won't be getting a raise this year. But I'll get a second job on the weekends." She put on a brave smile. "We can do this, I know we can. But I really can't see how we'll be able to leave this week. We just can't. Unless we win the lottery." She laughed at her little joke but it fell flat. Abuela's face crumpled with distress and disappointment.

From outside the house they heard the blare of a car horn. Luz glanced up at the clock. "That's Sully. It's raining cats and dogs, so I'll run out."

Abuela brightened. "Ah, Sully! Tell him to come in. I will make him a plate." She turned to grab a plate from the cabinet. "I want to show him the car. He will tell you it is good." She nodded her head in emphasis.

"Oh, Abuela, I wish he could. He has to work late tonight. But I'll bring him a plate."

"Work will always be there," Abuela said quietly, and turned to the stove.

Luz reached for her jacket and put it on while watching Abuela scoop mounds of tamales, beans, and rice onto the plate. Abuela had Mexico's sense of time. There, time was considered circular. There was always more coming later. Unfortunately, Sully worked for an automotive repair company run by Germans who believed time was shot from an arrow to get from point A to point B in as short an amount of time as possible. Clients were always in a hurry to get their cars back.

"Well, I'd better go."

Abuela wrapped the plate in foil and handed it to Luz. "Here, give this to Sully. A man can't work on an empty stomach."

"You spoil him."

"He's a good man. Why you two don't get mar—"

The truck's horn blared again.

"Got to run," Luz exclaimed, relieved to be spared another of

Abuela's grillings about getting married. She grabbed her purse and headed to the door, but paused to cast a final glance back.

Abuela stood with a natural dignity beside the kitchen sink. A mountain of pots and pans lay washed and drying on the counter behind her. She was looking down, wiping her reddened hands on her apron. Her long braid fell over her shoulder. When she looked up again, Luz's breath hitched at the sight of the deep creases of worry she saw carved into Abuela's face. When she met Luz's gaze, Abuela smiled again. But it was a sad, defeated smile.

Luz felt a twinge of worry. "Will you be okay? I can stay home with you if you want. Sully will understand."

"I'll be fine. Go to your young man before he blasts that horn again and riles Mrs. Rodriguez's dogs. I'll never hear the end of it."

"If you have any trouble or don't feel well, call me. I have my cell phone."

The horn sounded again. As though on cue, Mrs. Rodriguez's dogs began yapping hysterically. Luz and Abuela's eyes met and they shared a commiserating laugh. Luz rushed back to wrap her arms around Abuela and kiss her cheek.

"That was impulsive," she teased.

"*Sí*. The good kind. From the heart."

"Thank you for the car, Abuelita. You're right. It's a fine car. I love you."

"*Mi preciosa* . . ." Abuela reached up to pat Luz's arm. "Now go."

Luz released her but lingered, her hands resting on Abuela's thin shoulders.

"You won't fly off to Mexico with those butterflies while I'm gone, will you?" she asked jokingly.

Abuela smiled, her dark eyes shining, but didn't reply.

Three

*Monarch butterflies that emerge in the fall are unique. Butterflies
that emerge in the spring and summer live two to four weeks. But
the fourth-generation monarchs that emerge in the fall do not mate.
They follow their instincts and migrate south. Called the Methuselah
generation, they live for six or seven months.*

Morning light flowed freely through the window, its brightness poking her from sleep. Luz curled away from the light, eager to go back to sleep. Back to her dream where butterflies of all colors—the tawny, spotted fritillaries, the yellow swallowtails, the iridescent blue morphos, the magnificent orange and black monarchs—were spiraling and swirling in luminous light, coming together to form the wavy visage of a woman. The sight filled Luz with unspeakable joy. The butterfly goddess had no face, but Luz instinctively knew that she was her mother, Mariposa. She reached for her, eager to touch her. Instantly, the butterflies scattered and the goddess was gone.

Blinking in the harsh morning sun, Luz no longer felt like a brave or beautiful goddess. Rather, her heart was filled with yearning for her mother.

Luz wrestled with her sheets and dragged herself to her feet. Yawning, she looked around the small bedroom she'd slept in all of her twenty-one years. Ghostly, early morning light dappled the lavender and pink floral wallpaper, the white provincial dresser with its matching mirror, and the shadow boxes filled with butterflies on the wall. It was the room of a little girl, outgrown long ago. This room with its frayed ruffled curtains and peeling paper had been decorated by her mother and held all the dreams of her childhood.

Luz crossed the hall to the cramped bathroom she shared with Abuela. She bent over the sink to wash her face. Slowly she lowered her hands and saw her eyes emerge from behind the thirsty towel. They were pale gray, a mercurial color that changed to green or blue depending on the light. Moody eyes, her boyfriend, Sully, called them. Gringo eyes, her *abuela* called them. The eyes of the German father she never knew.

She may have inherited her blue eyes from her father, but her skin was the same creamy tan color of her Mexican mother. Her hair was as black as the tip of a monarch's wing, and her strong cheekbones and straight nose she inherited from Abuela and their Mayan ancestors. Luz turned from the mirror, tossing the towel into the basket. Pretty, some said . . . but hardly the stuff of a goddess.

In a hurry now, she quickly brushed her thick mane of hair, so much like her grandmother's and her one point of vanity, and tied it back with an elastic band. She didn't need to primp for her job at the foundry. She slipped into a sweatshirt and old jeans, then pulled on her tennis shoes and walked down the darkened narrow hall, flicking on lights. It was odd that the house was so quiet. She didn't hear Abuela's ranchero music blaring from the kitchen radio or kettles rattling. Sniffing, she didn't catch any of the usual tantalizing scents of maize.

"Abuela?" she called out. The kitchen was dark and the stove was cold. Luz shivered as a sense of dread swept over her. Was

Abuela in the garden again? she wondered, and hurried to the porch. The small screened porch was cluttered with her grand-mother's tools. A row of empty aquariums perched on a low wood shelf. During the summer, these were filled with fresh milkweed leaves alive with hungry yellow and black monarch caterpillars. Bright, jade green chrysalises hung by the dozens from the screen tops like delicate lanterns. Caterpillars moved fast and Abuela didn't always catch them all as she cleaned the habitats. Luz re-membered how, as a child, she'd spent hours hunting for the hid-den chrysalises, finding them in niches, hanging from the porch rafters, the shelves, the curtains, even the terra-cotta pots.

This late in the season, however, the caterpillars had trans-formed to butterflies and migrated south. The aquariums sat empty save for a few milkweed leaves that lay curled and dry; chrysalises hung from the screened tops like shredded bits of transparent paper.

Luz pushed open the creaky screen door. The air was chilly and ripe with scents of autumn. Squinting, she stepped out onto the first step under the awning.

"Abuela?" she called out, and was met with silence.

The house and garden occupied a narrow city lot wedged be-tween two tilting stockade fences. Abuela had bought the bunga-low with her life savings soon after Luz was born. A few years later Luz's mother, Mariposa, died. Abuela had rolled up her sleeves and raised both a garden and a girl.

But she wasn't here. The porch door squeaked as it slipped from Luz's hands. She wrapped her arms around herself for warmth. The empty kitchen, usually a place of refuge, frightened her now as a deep unease chilled her blood.

It was a small house. The only room she hadn't checked was

her grandmother's bedroom, but Luz couldn't imagine her tidy, disciplined grandmother lying in bed in the morning. Unless she was sick. Luz's feet felt like lead as she made her way down the hall. The silence now was oppressive. Abuela's bedroom door was open but the room was dark. The only light was from the streetlamp outside her window, casting pewter stripes through the blinds across the floor.

Luz paused at the threshold. Each minute seemed a lifetime. She took a ragged breath, then bent forward to peer into the darkened room. In the shadowy light, she saw Abuela lying on the bed, one arm across her chest, the other flung out across the mattress. She looked like she was still sleeping.

Except something inside of Luz, something raw and primal, knew that she was not. She began to shiver uncontrollably and her heart pounded so loudly she could hear its tympanic beat in her ears.

The door whispered a sigh as Luz pushed it wide. Details of the room loomed large as Luz gazed at everything except her grandmother. On the bureau a brush held a few long, white hairs. Abuela's wooden rosary beads rested on the bedside stand. Beside it, a common plastic pill jar lay on its side, empty. Abuela's black, sensible shoes sat neatly on the floor by the bed. Slowly, by degrees, Luz lifted her gaze to her face.

"Abuela . . ." Luz's heart constricted as her cry caught in her throat.

Her grandmother's eyes were closed and her mouth, which had told Luz so many stories, was slightly ajar. In one hand she clutched a photograph to her heart. It was of Abuela and Mariposa holding an infant Luz. It had always been Abuela's favorite photograph, the one she called *the three goddesses*.

"Abuelita," she cried, slumping to her knees. She reached out to hold her grandmother's hand, so cold and lifeless. "Please, don't leave me."

Luz didn't remember calling Sully but suddenly he was there, holding her tight while she clung to him. Nor did she remember her grandmother's body being carried away. Snippets of conversations from the EMT crew came back to her: *A heart attack. Massive. Nothing could be done.* She vaguely remembered an ambulance with a flashing red light. And the curious neighbors standing in the street: old men standing straight, young men leaning against cars, women in tight clusters, whispering, holding wide-eyed children.

She remembered clearly Abuela's words: *I must go home.*

Death, Luz learned, was complicated.

There were countless legal forms to be completed, information to gather, papers to be signed, an obituary to write, and people to inform. Abuela had left a will giving the small bungalow and all her worldly possessions, such as they were, to Luz. She had been a woman who lived by her senses. She didn't plan for the future or dwell in the past. She had made decisions based on what was right in front of her at that moment. So she'd never discussed with Luz what she'd wanted done in the event of her death, and Luz had never imagined a world without her beloved Abuela in it.

But now that horrible possibility had become a reality. Abuela was dead. Luz had to face it and grow up fast, to set aside her grief and assume responsibility for Abuela's sake. With no family in town, it fell to Luz to make all the arrangements. A week passed in a blur of activity. Sully was at her side as she went through the motions, and she found some comfort in tending to the myriad details of Abuela's funeral.

She'd tried calling her *tía* Maria in San Antonio immediately after Abuela's passing. Since Maria was Abuela's only surviving daughter, Luz thought it was her rightful place to make the funeral decisions. Luz had searched through the rolltop desk in the living room and found her grandmother's leather address book. Fifty years of names and addresses were stored in its slim, dog-eared pages. Many of the entries had been crossed out and replaced with new addresses and phone numbers. Several had the word *muerto,* dead, written beside them.

Luz dutifully dialed the number listed for Aunt Maria in San Antonio. Her hands shook as she listened to the phone ring—she'd only talked to her aunt a handful of times—and she stood still with shock when she learned the number had been disconnected. Luz followed up with operator assistance, but to no avail. She had worse luck for Uncle Manolo in the remote village in Mexico. In the end, it was Father Frank at St. Anthony's who helped Luz decide on a mass and cremation.

It was a simple but tasteful funeral at her parish church, and Luz felt her *abuela* would have approved. Abuela had never been ostentatious. The choice of Our Lady of Guadalupe holy cards and her favorite psalms and hymns came easily. Flowers of all kinds filled St. Anthony's, more than Luz could ever afford, all brought from the many friends and neighbors who came to pay their respects to La Dama Mariposa, the butterfly woman who had shared the gift of flowers all her life. The Mexican men stood silent while the women wept openly and made exclamations to the Virgencita.

And so many children! Every day after the funeral the mailbox was filled with hand-painted pictures of butterflies. Luz wept as she read each sweet note.

For several days after Abuela's death, friends of her grandmother had come to clean the house. Now the floors smelled like vinegar, the garden was weeded, and Abuela's refrigerator had been cleaned and stocked with casseroles, vegetables, fruits, and cakes. They were good women who'd hugged Luz, cried with her, told her how much Abuela had meant to them. A cry stuck in Luz's throat for days. It held tight, like a wad of cotton that made it hard for Luz to breathe or do more than utter a short yes, no, or thank you. She'd managed to hold herself together during the daytime hours when she was busy and people surrounded her.

Nights were lonely. After the funeral and the reception at the house, the little bungalow felt so empty and cold. Luz felt utterly alone and longed to hear Abuela's voice calling to her, *Mi nene, come to dinner, eh?* The house and everything in it was a reflection of Abuela. Her colorful kitchen redolent with smells, her garden filled with host and nectar plants and countless butterflies. It was a home where children had come to play, women shared secrets, and a granddaughter was loved.

Luz was only five years old when her mother died. She only remembered the sudden emptiness she didn't understand and a darkness where there had been light. For a long time afterward she'd wept inconsolably for her mother and looked for her everywhere. Eventually Luz found solace in the constant nurturing of her grandmother. She'd clung to Abuela and felt panic flutter in her chest whenever Abuela left the house, thinking she wouldn't come back.

But she always did. In the years that followed, though she might not have fully understood the murky concept of death, Luz knew that her mother was never coming back. In all those years Abuela had seen to it that she'd never felt unloved or unwanted.

Now, as darkness fell after the funeral, Luz understood that Abuela was never coming back.

Luz walked through room after room, switching on lights in the empty house. *Her* house now. Outside, traffic moved. She was amazed how life went on around her when her own life felt over. Her gaze lingered on the folk art from Mexico that Abuela had loved. She remembered how Abuela's heart broke when the huge, brilliant green ceramic pineapple made in Michoacán arrived in pieces, packed poorly by family. Abuela had spent days with glue and tweezers, piecing it back together again. Luz traced the barely visible veins of cracks in the glaze.

Beside it was the intricate ceramic Tree of Life, a favorite of Luz's growing up. She remembered Abuela pointing to the different colorfully painted people on the tree and naming the family members they represented. Though she'd never met them, hearing their names made Luz feel part of a bigger family.

She paused at the large painting of the Virgin of Guadalupe. A snuffed red votive candle sat cold. Tears filled her eyes as she remembered how Abuela lit the candle each evening to say her prayers.

The only place she couldn't look was the fireplace. On its mantel sat a small cardboard box. Inside that box were Abuela's ashes. For a flash Luz regretted not picking out one of the fancy, pricey urns. But she'd held back because she believed that she'd find her *tía* Maria and allow her the opportunity to make that important, intimate choice for her mother. Still, to think of Abuela in that plain box . . . She shuddered.

"You okay?"

Luz sucked in her breath and turned to see Sully leaning against the wall, arms crossed, his long sleeves rolled up over muscled forearms. His sharp cheekbones appeared more pronounced in his fatigue. Behind his stoic expression of support, his eyes seemed at a loss as to how he could help ease her pain; he was searching, she knew, for signs that her fragile hold on composure might snap as silence and darkness took hold of her spirit.

"She's really gone," she said, her voice breaking. "I feel so alone."

In two steps he was at her side, holding her. "You're not alone. I'm here. I'll always be here. You know that, don't you?"

She tightened her lips and nodded. His arms felt so safe, but his words didn't fill the void. "I know, but this is a different kind of alone. I lost my grandmother. I don't have a mother or father, no sisters or brothers. Not even aunts, uncles, or cousins that I know. I don't have a family. You can look around the dinner table and see people who have the same nose as you, the same eyes, the same laugh. What about me? I'm not connected to anyone who shares my DNA. Maybe Abuela knew she was going to die and didn't want to leave me all alone. That's why she wanted me to meet my family. But she did die, and I feel like I'm in the dark."

"I'm here," Sully said again. "And I love you." He squeezed her tight. "Come on, babe. Let's get you to bed," he said, slipping his arm around her shoulders and guiding her to the familiar comfort of her bedroom. The frilly lavender lamp offered meager light—neither of them had had the time or energy to change the overhead bulb that had burned out after Luz had slept with the light on every night the past week.

Luz felt beyond tired. She felt unwashed, overwhelmed, and

utterly spent. She moved with sodden lethargy as he helped her out from the now despised black A-line wool dress and lifted one foot, then the other, from black pumps she'd purchased for the funeral. She stood slack shouldered as he unhooked her bra, then she lifted her arms as he slid a long flannel nightgown over her head.

She'd never known a fatigue so total it made her want to dissolve into tears. Sully knew just what to do. He gently led her to the lavender chair and seated her as if she were made of glass. He removed the clasp from her hair and watched as it fell like black water down her shoulders and back. Sully loved her hair. He'd made her promise that she'd never cut it short. He picked up her small brush with his big hands, more accustomed to heavy tools and machinery, and with steady, even strokes ran the soft boar bristles from her scalp down to the ends. Rhythmic. Intimate. Luz sighed heavily, a sound like steam released from a valve as she cried silent tears. She'd loved this man for three years, known him to be gentle, but never had he done anything so precious to her as this tender caring when she could not care for herself.

When he'd brushed her hair till it felt like silk, Sully pulled down the comforter and turned off the light. She gratefully lay in bed in the velvety blackness, eyes wide and seeing nothing. A moment later she felt the mattress sag with his weight as Sully stretched out beside her, scooping her close to lie like spoons. His chin rested on her head and she caught the scent of soap and axle grease as coarse fingertips skimmed her forehead, smoothing strands of hair from her face.

How long they lay together she couldn't guess, but at some point she felt Sully's familiar warm breath on her cheek followed by a soft kiss.

"Sleep now," Sully said in a low voice by her ear.

Luz knew that someday she'd have to find the words to tell Sully how much she appreciated his knowing just what she needed, when she needed it. But speaking was beyond her now. Luz heard the door click shut and slipped into oblivion.

Luz waited for the dream of the butterflies. She longed to hear her mother's voice, to feel some connection to her mother and grandmother. But the dream didn't return. Despair bloomed larger in her chest as she began to fully grasp the profound depth of her isolation. Luz pushed back her blankets and walked directly to her grandmother's bedroom. Clutching the doorframe, she peered inside. The room was exactly as it always had been while Abuela was alive. Everything was tidy and in its place. Luz wasn't afraid. She'd welcome her grandmother's ghost, even prayed she'd come. With an impulsive rush Luz ran into the room, pulled back the coverlet, and climbed under the wool blanket. The sheets were crisp and ironed, cold as death, and she shivered, desperate to feel some spark of warmth, some connection to her grandmother.

Maybe it was Abuela's scent still lingering on the sheets, but the fragile thread that held Luz together during the past week suddenly snapped. Clutching her pillow, Luz felt a rush of emotion.

"Abuela!" she called out into the darkness. "Are you there? Do you hear me? Why did you leave before I got to say good-bye?"

She was crying so hard she had doubled up, and her throat burned like she'd been screaming at the top of her lungs. She wiped the tears from her face with the sheet and took a deep, shuddering breath. Her emotions, so mercurial in grief, quickly turned to self-loathing.

"I didn't get to tell you I'm sorry. I'm so very, very sorry. You gave me everything I needed and you never asked me for anything. Not once in all those years. And what did I do when you asked me to do one thing? To go on this trip with you? I said no. I always say no!"

She squeezed her pillow tighter and brought her knees closer to her chest. She repeated "I'm sorry" in a litany, over and over, counting apologies as a child would count sheep. In time her grip loosened from the pillow, and she felt her muscles slowly relax and her ragged breathing grow more even. Before falling into a fitful sleep, Luz murmured a final prayer.

"Abuela, won't you send me a sign that you hear me? Some signal that you're still with me. I don't need to hear your voice or see a ghost or anything like that. I'm not asking for much. It's just . . . I don't know what to do. I feel so alone. Please, Abuela, just some small sign that you're still with me and I'm not alone."

Luz awoke to the sound of tapping against her window. She licked her dry lips and rubbed her eyes, grainy from tears, then pulled herself up on one elbow and looked around the room. She caught the scent of vanilla and maize and thought Abuela's death had been a dream. Then, waking fully, she recognized Abuela's dark wood bed, the crucifix on the wall, her bureau and mirror adorned with photographs. Abuela was gone. Luz squeezed her eyes against the fresh wave of grief.

She heard the tapping noise again. Lifting her head, she followed the sound to the windows that opened up to the back porch—Abuela's workroom. She felt a chill travel down her spine when she spied the unmistakable shadow of tiny wings frantically beating against the glass.

A butterfly!

Abuela had told her many times that a monarch butterfly was the soul of the recently departed. She felt her heart quicken—this couldn't be a coincidence. She threw back the blanket to run to her grandmother's closet. Opening it, she was assailed again by her grandmother's scent, more powerful here than on the sheets. She slipped on Abuela's ruby flannel robe and, tying it around herself, felt wrapped in her grandmother's arms. Then she hurried down the hall, through the kitchen to the back porch.

The early morning light played tricks with the lush green plant leaves, dappling the floor with shadows. Her first smile in over a week played on her lips as she spied a magnificent monarch butterfly perched on the windowsill. Coming closer, she stretched on tiptoe to study the gorgeous burnt orange wings separated by thick, black veins in a pattern Abuela had always compared to stained glass. It was a female.

"Hello, beautiful," she whispered.

Luz leaned against the wood worktable and patiently waited, watching, while the monarch's wings hardened in the morning light. Eventually the butterfly became more sure-footed and climbed steadily to the top of the window frame. There, like a triumphant mountain climber, she flapped her wings exuberantly. Luz climbed atop a bench to slowly put out her hand toward the butterfly. The young, untested butterfly delicately stepped onto her finger. Luz felt the tickle of minuscule feet on her skin.

"Come meet the world," she said as she carried the butterfly into the garden.

The long rain had finally ended and the morning sun seemed to say, *Enough of lying in bed feeling sorry for yourself. The rain is over! No more tears!*

Luz breathed in the newness of the air and lifted her face to the sun's warmth. Maybe it was because there'd been so many days of rain, or because this one butterfly lifted her spirits as nothing else had since her grandmother's death, but Luz felt almost giddy as she watched the delicate creature perched on her finger flutter her wings like a coquette would her lashes.

For the next hour Luz played with the monarch in her grandmother's garden. She'd never in her life held such an endearing butterfly. This monarch didn't immediately fly away, as they were wont to do. This one lingered to walk up her arm, flutter to her shoulder, her head, tickling her as she landed on her nose. It seemed reluctant to leave, even when Luz gently nudged the butterfly to her fingertip. The monarch remained and let the morning sun shimmer on her wings.

"Don't worry," Luz whispered to her. She lifted her hand over her head toward the sun. The monarch fluttered her wings. "It's time. Jump!"

On a whisper of breeze, the butterfly flew off.

Luz watched the butterfly glide around the garden and return to circle her once, then again, before flying higher over the fence. Luz watched until she could no longer see the graceful flicker of orange against the brilliant blue sky. From a place deep in her heart Luz heard her grandmother's voice. *I want to go home. To the mountains of Mexico.*

Luz went still. She'd prayed for a sign and her prayer was answered. Her grandmother told her that sometimes she had to listen with her heart rather than her mind. She listened now and in that miraculous instant, Luz knew what she had to do. For once she would silence her doubt and ignore her shivers of fear.

For once, she would be brave and say *yes!*

Four

In all the world, no butterflies migrate like the monarchs of North America. Their migration is more the type we expect from birds or whales. However, unlike birds and whales that make the round-trip, it is the monarch's great-great-grandchildren that return south the following fall.

L uz took a final look around the quiet house. She'd given a key to Sully, who promised to water the plants. Mrs. Rodriguez would keep an eye on the house. She fingered the soft, worn leather of her grandmother's wallet. Luz had nearly a thousand dollars from her savings account, plus another four hundred and change from Abuela. It had to be enough.

Turning, she faced the deep rose sky of a dawning sun. Leaves scattered in a sudden gust of cool wind and an empty Coke can rolled noisily down the street. She loved this time of year with the changing colors and the scent of ripeness in the air. In Wisconsin, winters were too harsh and summers too hot. It was fall that stoked nostalgia and prompted reflection. She sighed with the heaviness of all the changes she'd suffered in the past week. She wondered whether, from this year on, she'd come to cherish this season as the one that had changed her life, or hate this season and always associate it with death.

Luz tucked the plain cardboard box that held her grandmother's ashes securely under her arm. It was still hard for her to believe that all the bones, flesh, contours, colors—everything that she recognized as her grandmother—was in a box this small. Part of her felt that nothing meaningful of her grandmother was here. Her soul was gone.

And yet . . . Luz moved one hand to stroke the top once, twice. In a strange, indefinable way, she sensed Abuela's spirit still lingered here, with her ashes.

The Volkswagen was parked in its usual spot at the curb. Thankfully, the enormous red sedan that had wedged her in like a sardine had left, so there was plenty of room for her to load the trunk. She nestled the box securely in the backseat with her pillow.

She brought only one suitcase, filled with a few pairs of jeans, some sweaters, heavy socks for hiking the mountain, a few sundresses, and her rain slicker. She was wearing her brown corduroy jacket. At the last minute she'd tossed in the despised black dress and shoes that she'd bought for Abuela's funeral, just in case. In the front seat she laid out in arm's reach her grandmother's maps of Mexico and the United States with the route highlighted in yellow, Abuela's address book, bottles of water, a bag of mixed nuts, and her cell phone. Finally, she dug into her jacket pocket and pulled out Abuela's rosary beads. She kissed the crucifix, then hung the beads on the rearview mirror.

All was ready. She took a deep breath, feeling excitement bubbling in her veins. She looked down the street, tapping her foot. Where was Sully?

A few minutes later she saw the familiar silver pickup truck round the corner and roar up her quiet, dimly lit street. The tires skidded to a halt as Sully maneuvered it into the only open spot, conveniently in front of her. The bed of the truck was sticking conspicuously into the street as he leaped out. When she'd told him two days earlier of her plan to drive to Texas he'd been shocked first, angry second, and finally, when he listened and understood her reasons, supportive. His tousled hair, stubbled cheek, and sleep-rimmed eyes spoke of the night they'd had. They'd spent most of the night talking, making love, then talking some more. She breathed deep, remembering the feel of his skin against hers, the sound of his voice husky with sleep against her ear.

"Luz, think again. Just wait till I can go with you," he had told her. "Maybe next month. Two at the latest."

Luz had known in that moment how her grandmother must have felt when Luz had suggested they wait till spring. There wasn't any concrete reason she could offer Sully why next month was too late.

"I have to leave *now*, Sully. I know it sounds crazy, but it makes sense to me." She took a deep breath, looking directly into his eyes. "In Mexico on the Day of the Dead the families gather to greet the monarchs when they return to our village. You see, we believe that the monarchs are the spirits of our recently departed."

Sully's expression shifted to reflect his appreciation of her use of the word *we*.

"Do you remember what I told you about the butterfly that emerged after Abuela died?" Luz asked him. "The night before I prayed to Abuela to give me a sign of what I should do. I believe—I *know*—that butterfly was my sign. The Day of the Dead is November first. I have to be in my grandmother's village by that date." She paused, gauging his response. "I have to be there because I want to greet my grandmother when she returns to her village."

He scrubbed his face with his palms, as though he were waking up from some bad dream. When he dropped his hands, she saw the resignation on his face. "Just remember you're putting everything we have at risk. Not just your life, but mine, too."

They'd awakened early and to his credit, he'd not voiced another word of worry, though she knew he had many. Now she watched him walk briskly to meet her at the car, carrying takeout coffee and a bag of donuts.

"I went as fast as I could, but there was a line," he said, handing her a Styrofoam cup.

She peeled off the top, inhaling the aroma before taking a sip. "Mmm, tastes so good. I needed this. You're an angel of mercy for getting it."

"I don't want you falling asleep at the wheel."

"No chance of that. I feel wired up. Besides, El Toro will take good care of me."

"El Toro?"

"I named the car El Toro. It means 'The Bull.'" She chortled. "I thought the little car needed all the encouragement it could get."

"Yeah, all right," Sully said with a laugh, then reached out to pat the hood of the car. "You take care of my girl, hear? And you," he said, pointing his finger at Luz, "don't take any chances. Just follow the map and call me if you run into trouble."

Luz wondered why men liked to sound so macho and firm at such tender moments, like a gorilla beating his chest. She smiled, thinking how sweet it really was. "I will. I promise."

He handed the donuts to her. "For ballast."

"No, you keep them. I'm too excited to eat."

"Take it," he said firmly. "You'll get hungry on the road."

She took the bag, knowing it would make him feel better. "Well, I better go before rush hour hits."

He walked her to the car and waited till she loaded her coffee, donuts, and purse. When she came up again he wrapped his long arms around her. He cupped her head in his big hand and rested his cheek against the top of her head.

"Call me if you run into any trouble," he said in a thick voice. He lifted his head and his eyes pulsed with meaning. "No place would be too far."

"I will."

"I'll be right here, waiting for you to return."

He kissed her with a fierce possessiveness that spoke to her of all his pent-up worry. She kissed him back, matching his intensity, absorbing his strength. She climbed in and he closed the door after her, pushing down the lock in a last gesture to make certain she was safe. Luz felt as though all the millions of butterflies that were flying on this same journey south were fluttering in her stomach.

Luz started the engine, patting the dashboard when it roared to life. She shifted into gear, then took a last glance at the brown bungalow with its bright blue door and trim before pulling away from the curb. Sully walked to stand in the road, his arm lifted in a silent wave. She tapped the horn. It sounded a funny, nasal beep that made the neighbor's cat leap from the porch and Sully shake his head with a wry grin.

Luz shifted her glance from the rearview to see the road ahead. "Okay, Abuela," she said. "I'm doing what you asked. It's you and me now." She took a deep breath and hit the gas. "Let's jump."

When Luz was a child she grew sad each autumn when the monarchs began leaving the garden to fly south. Abuela would wrap her arms around her and explain how it was the nature of the monarch to abandon its home when the milkweed grew scarce and the daylight dimmed, to journey to a faraway place it had never been before.

Such courage, eh? This is what makes the monarch special among all butterflies. They have such character. Such determination. People wonder, how do they know where to go? It is a mystery! But querida, *do you know what I think? I think the monarchs listen to the call of the goddess. Xochiquetzal calls out to each butterfly to follow the light.*

Luz remembered these words as she began her journey from a simple, working-class neighborhood in the northern United States to strange forests in the mountains of Mexico. She told herself that she was following the light.

As she drove through Milwaukee, she breathed in the heady scents of different sections of the European-like city—bread from the Italian bakery, cocoa from the chocolate factory, and the pungent smell of hops from the brewery. She'd always loved the city on the lake that she'd grown up in. But she'd never done anything adventurous in her life. She thought again of her mother, who had taken off on a whim with her German lover. My God, it had to have been scandalous, she thought. That one decision had changed the course of Mariposa's life, and Abuela's as well. How many other lives had been changed? Maria's? Manolo's? She thought of Abuela's warning against impulsiveness. Luz didn't think what she was doing today was impulsive, no matter what Sully might say. To her mind, she was fulfilling a promise.

She looked around the compact interior of the VW Bug.

Everything in the cozy space—the worn seat fabric, the metal dash, what was left of the carpet—was a dull gray, the color of granite. The radio didn't work, nor did the air-conditioning, but Sully had declared the little car sound.

She drove out of Milwaukee onto I-94 past Racine, then Kenosha, on her way to Chicago. The engine strained to match the speed of the cars rushing past her, rattling her little Bug, but she buzzed along noisily at a steady fifty-five miles per hour. She smelled the odd scent-mixture of oil and rubber the car emitted—not bad, just its own, unique perfume. She chuckled at the quirks of El Toro and felt a surge of excitement at the beginning of this epic journey.

Luz drove past farms dotted with grazing cows, an amusement park with a spectacular roller coaster, and acres of open fields. An hour later the open fields grew scarce and soon changed to chockablock houses, shopping malls, and office complexes. Closer to the city of Chicago, lanes doubled and traffic grew congested. An elevated train line zipped past, sparks flying from the wheels. Horns honked angrily at the poky Bug, and people cut into lanes without warning.

She wasn't used to this kind of traffic and her heart pounded in her chest as she maneuvered her way through the downtown framed by skyscrapers and walls of cement. She'd just breathed a sigh of relief as she made it onto the outgoing expressway when she felt the car losing power. Her gaze darted to her speedometer and she watched helplessly as it slipped below fifty miles per hour.

Her heart rate zoomed as she flicked her turn signal and began looking in a panic over her shoulder for a break in the traffic. She grabbed her first narrow opening and darted into the exit lane, earning a chorus of angry honks. El Toro limped off the exit, sputtering like a speared bull. She clutched the wheel so tight her knuckles whitened as she leaned forward and scanned the streets for a gas station.

It was a seedy area with grimy brick buildings and signs for pawnshops, Western Union, and liquor stores. Iron bars covered most of the street-level windows. Please, God, don't let me break down here, she prayed. A little farther along the street the building windows weren't boarded, and instead of pawnshops, she spotted small groceries and shops with signs written in Spanish. Luz's fingers relaxed their clutch on the wheel.

"Thank God," she exclaimed when she spotted a modest, cinder-block garage with a bright red sign advertising AUTO REPAIR. She pulled in and turned off the engine. While El Toro shuddered, Luz laid her head against the wheel and practically wept with relief. A mechanic promptly came out to greet her, wiping his hands with a rag. He was an older, wiry man, unshaven, and dressed in an oil-stained mechanic's uniform. But when he smiled it went straight to his eyes. He introduced himself as the owner, Mr. Vera. He listened to her story, then chuckled, putting her at ease. "You came to the right place. I know these old Vochos. I'll take a look right away."

Luz sat at the edge of a dented metal chair in the cramped waiting room. The room oozed grease from the old magazines, the car accessories, even the peanuts in the machine. How could this happen to her? she wondered as she slipped her head in her palm. Only two hours into her epic journey and already she had car trouble. How could she hope to make it to San Antonio, much less Mexico, if she couldn't get out of Cook County? She reached into her purse, pulled out her cell phone, and started punching in Sully's number. It was like an automatic reflex. Then she stopped. She recalled the long argument she'd had with Sully the night before about the car being safe enough to drive cross-country.

What was all her talk about being able to take care of herself? she asked herself. One of her goals for this journey was to discover her inner courage. To make her own decisions. Did she want to be proven wrong so quickly? Did she really want to be rescued?

With a flick of her wrist she closed her phone, then put it back into her purse and vowed not to call for help at every wrong turn. After half an hour the mechanic came back.

"Well, I have some good news and some bad news," he began.

Luz cringed. She hated that opening because it always meant bad news.

"The good news is it's not serious and the part won't set you back much. It'll be mostly labor. The bad news is we don't have the part in stock. We can get it, but we won't have it in until maybe tomorrow."

"Tomorrow?"

"Maybe. Maybe two, three days. I called around but no one had one."

"But . . . I can't stay here for two or three days!"

The old man wiped his hands again with an old, ragged cloth. "You could haul it somewhere else, but for this old Vocho . . ." His shrug spoke of his doubt she'd get a different answer.

Luz felt the blood drain from her face and took several slow, deep breaths. She was stuck here waiting for a car for two or three days? Hotel rooms were costly in the city. Then again, what choice did she have—other than picking up the phone and calling Sully?

Luz walked on watery legs to the Volkswagen. She yanked her

suitcase from the trunk, then retrieved the box of her grandmother's ashes from the backseat. Her shoulders, heavy with worry and disappointment, felt as if they were carrying another bag, weighing her down. She looked around, bewildered. Inside her heart, she felt all her earlier excitement and resolve wither.

Five

Monarch caterpillars eat only milkweed. Adult monarch butterflies sip nectar from flowering plants using a sucking tube that resembles a soda straw and is called a proboscis. You can see it coiled under the monarch's head when not in use.

L uz felt small and insignificant against the overwhelming vastness of a great city. Everything was so loud! She was engulfed in the raucous sounds of engines revving and backfiring, sirens wailing, and voices shrieking, as well as the ubiquitous blaring of horns.

Carrying her suitcase and the box of ashes, she began walking. Mr. Vera had told her if she walked a few blocks south she'd run into a bus stop that would take her near Union Station. There she could catch a train back to Milwaukee. It seemed the logical thing to do, even if it felt to her like running back home with her tail between her legs. She turned the corner and stopped in her tracks. There, dominating the stone wall of the garage, Luz saw an enormous, brilliantly colored mural of La Virgen de Guadalupe.

Luz's mouth slipped open. She didn't know whether to laugh or cry.

It was a magnificent mural. The Virgin Mary was resplendent, enshrined in a brilliant gold aura that rained down upon the earth. Gold stars floating in her robe caught the sunlight and sparkled.

Abuela had lit a candle every night before the icon of La Virgen de Guadalupe to say her prayers. She'd told Luz that Mexicans were more devoted to this beloved image of La Virgen than to the national flag.

"It's a sign," Luz whispered, and held the box of ashes closer to her chest. She imagined what Abuela would have done at this moment. Or her mother. They wouldn't have stopped now. Not even a monarch would turn back at its first obstacle. She had to have faith. But just in case, she made the sign of the cross.

Luz walked several blocks but didn't see the bus stop. A few men in open shirts leaning against a black iron fence eyed her but she ignored them, veering away to follow two women pushing strollers, heads bent toward each other in conversation. Then, like an unexpected gift, there appeared a small taqueria. Outside the door was a welcoming terra-cotta pot overflowing with cheery red and yellow flowers, and above it was a hand-painted sign with a colorful rendering of an iguana and crude letters spelling out EL IGUANA. She recalled how Abuela always said you couldn't think on an empty stomach.

"Perfect," she whispered.

One step inside and the scent of chilies, corn, and spices carried her back to her grandmother's kitchen. Even ranchero music was blaring. On the long wall to the left was a colorful, primitive mural of a mountain village in Mexico with farmers working the soil, women doing laundry at a cistern, and children teasing a dog. Here and there throughout the mural fluttered monarch butterflies.

Feeling more at ease, she took a place in the long lunchtime line.

Behind the counter a harried young woman was scurrying at a mad pace to write down the orders shouted out by the customers. Her wild, curly hair was loosely held back by a hot pink headband and elastic. Though very pregnant, she managed the orders with a combination of tough-girl attitude and wise-ass humor.

One look at the cooking area and Luz knew why the little taqueria was so popular. It was what she imagined a taqueria in Mexico would look like. The black iron grill was surrounded by baskets brimming with fresh green heads of cabbage, big yellow and orange peppers, and the ever-present avocados. Beside these were trays of thinly sliced onions, tomatoes, and beef. The cook was a burly man standing wide-legged over the steaming grill, a sagging, grease-stained apron double-wrapped around his paunch. But he could flip tortillas with the finesse of a matador.

Luz's mouth watered and she thought of the bag of uneaten donuts in the car. She hadn't been hungry since Abuela's death a week earlier, but looking at all the foods Abuela used to cook, she felt suddenly starved. Most of the people in front of Luz were ordering takeout, so she was able to find a free table at the rear of the restaurant.

Luz had no idea where in the city she was, but embraced by the familiar tastes and sounds of her Mexican heritage, she felt strangely at home. The Spanish language that she'd never wanted to speak at home was comforting to her now. She ate slowly, in no hurry to come to a decision. The lunch rush was ending. Only a few people lingered in the taqueria. Luz stirred her soda with a straw, mulling over her options, which at the moment seemed to hover between calling Sully immediately and calling him after he finished work.

"Hey, miss?"

Luz looked up at the woman calling her in a slightly annoyed tone from behind the counter. She was wiping her brow with one hand, tapping her fingers on the counter with the other. A few curly tendrils managed to escape the thick ponytail to hang loosely around her flushed face. Her heavily lined, almond eyes looked at her with cool regard.

"You deaf or something? I said, miss?" she called out again. "You want anything else? If not, I'm gonna sit down a minute. My dogs are barking."

The cook turned his head from the stove and called out in a gruff voice, "Whassat? I didn't say you could take a break. If you're done with customers, we gotta clean up."

"Aw, come on, Mr. Cordero," she said in a soft whine that mimicked a sob. "If I don't take a break I'm gonna have this baby right here on your floor."

Mr. Cordero looked fierce with his acne-scarred face and short, steel gray hair. "You always say that. That baby's not coming for a month."

"I dunno. I'm feeling these pains . . ." She rubbed her back meaningfully.

Mr. Cordero waved his hand dismissively in the air. "Aw, go on. You rest. I'll clean up. I'm only fooling with you."

Luz caught a small, smug smile escaping from the girl's full lips. Then she called to Luz again, jutting her chin out. "So, you want something more or not?"

Luz shook her head. She'd been thinking about the flan, but didn't dare ask the exhausted pregnant girl to get her anything else.

She watched as the young woman stretched her arms behind her back to untie the long, white apron and slip it off, revealing a hot pink spandex top that clung to her very pregnant shape. Then she reached up and, with one yank of the elastic, released a shower of brown curls heavily streaked with gold down her shoulders. She walked from behind the counter with her hand still rubbing the small of her back. She slumped into a chair at a table near Luz.

Luz slanted a glance her way, thinking the girl couldn't be older than she was. Maybe she was even younger, but flashier, with heavy brown eye shadow and several colored stones climbing her ear like a sparkling crescent moon. A tiny diamond studded her nose.

"So, how far along are you?" she asked in a friendly manner.

The girl slipped off her shoes and bent at an awkward angle to rub her arches. "About eight months," she replied, not looking up.

"Well, good luck."

The girl sat back in her chair and said with a derisive laugh, "I don't need luck. I need a miracle. That no-good Carmen up and quit on us. And now I have to do the work of two people. Hey, Angel says if I do the work of two people, I should get the pay of two people!" Turning her head, she called out in a louder voice to Mr. Cordero, "*¿Me oyes?*"

"Yeah, yeah, I heard you," Mr. Cordero mumbled, his back to them.

"It would help, you know? Especially with the baby coming!" she called back. "They need so much," she said, turning around in her chair. "Those teeny things are expensive."

"You should've thought of that before you got knocked up," Mr. Cordero called over his shoulder.

"Who was thinking? If I was thinking, I wouldn't have a belly the size of a beach ball, would I?"

Mr. Cordero turned, smiling, and they shared a laugh. Luz noticed how when the woman smiled, her full lips slipped back over a mouth full of large, straight teeth, revealing bits of pink gum. The smile lit up her face and seeing it, Luz couldn't help but smile, too.

Luz held out her hand when the girl turned back to her. "Hi, I'm Luz."

The girl narrowed her eyes and looked at Luz like a dog about to bite. She turned in her seat, giving her back to the hand, and took a sip from her water. "Never seen you before. Are you from around here?"

Luz withdrew her hand, stung. She knew the drill. No one had to ask her to leave twice. "Uh, no. Milwaukee," she replied, bending to pick up her purse.

"Visiting?"

"Nope. Just passing through."

"Uh-huh," she said with suspicion. "Where to?"

Luz stopped fumbling for her keys and thought about saying San Antonio, but thought again. What did she have to lose by telling a complete stranger where she wanted to go, really, in her heart of hearts? There was safety with a stranger, no consequences.

"I'm on my way to Mexico."

Hearing this, the girl's wariness slipped from her face like a mask removed. "Really? That's cool." She paused, considering, then said simply, "I'm Ofelia."

Mr. Cordero ambled toward them, drying his hands on a towel. "Hey, did I hear you say you're going to Mexico?" he asked with sudden interest. "Where?"

"A little town called Angangueo. It's in the mountains," Luz explained, not expecting anyone to know it.

He lifted his arms exuberantly. "Sure, I know where that is!"

"You do?"

"Yeah. I'm from Zitácuaro. Not far from Angangueo." He tossed the towel over his shoulder, crossed his arms, and rocked on his heels, warming to the subject. "That's where I was born. It's beautiful there. Man, I miss being in the mountains. Well, whaddya know. You got family there?"

"Uh, yes."

He beamed at her. "What's their name? I might know them."

"Gimme a break," Ofelia said with a roll of her eyes. "Everybody says something stupid like that."

"No, no, it's a small town," Mr. Cordero argued.

Luz had to think for a moment of the family name in Angangueo, since Manolo was the son of Abuela's first husband. "It's Zamora," she replied. "My uncle is Manolo Zamora."

He rubbed his jaw, then shrugged. "There are lots of Zamoras."

"Told ya," Ofelia chimed.

Luz noticed that Mr. Cordero took Ofelia's incessant teasing in stride. "My grandmother's family is from there," Luz continued, and found it comforting to be talking about Abuela. "She moved to America with her first husband. To San Antonio. But after he died, she married my grandfather, Hector Avila, and moved back to Morelia. Then after I was born she came to Milwaukee to take care of me. She was a cook in a restaurant, too," she added, pleased to see Mr. Cordero's brows arch like two woolly caterpillars over his eyes. "She always talked about going back one day."

"Yeah, we all do. I go back and forth when I can."

"This is my first trip. I'm taking her ashes home."

Ofelia shrank back in her chair as she pointed to the box on the chair beside her. "Is that her?"

Luz nodded, thinking that Ofelia was acting like a child as she shifted in her seat to scoot farther from the box.

"*Acepte mis condolencias.* You're a good kid, you know?" Mr.

Cordero said as a pronouncement. "Not everyone would go through the trouble."

"Yeah. I'd use FedEx," Ofelia said.

"Oh, shut up," said Mr. Cordero, but there was a laugh in it.

"I'm just saying," Ofelia said in mock defense. "It'd be easier."

"If you knew my *abuela*," Luz said to Ofelia, swallowing a lump of indignation, "you'd understand why I'm doing this. She was pretty amazing. And she raised me all by herself. She meant everything to me."

Luz looked over to see the monarchs painted on the mural. "Abuela loved the monarch butterflies. She used to tell me stories all the time of what it was like when the butterflies returned to the mountains near her village in the fall. She always wanted to take me to the sanctuaries to see them. We talked about it all the time. But . . ." She felt the sadness bubble up in a spurt.

It was the way it was with grief. One moment she was fine, and the next, a comment, a thought, something trivial would waft by to spark a memory and grief would surge. She didn't want to cry in front of these strangers and struggled to pull herself together. "She passed away before we got the chance. So I'm taking her home."

Mr. Cordero seemed moved. He cleared his throat and stared at his boots. They were thick soled, worn at the heels. "Yeah, well, your *abuela* was right about them butterflies," he said. "I remember them real clear. Man, I tell you, the way they shoot through the villages on their way up the mountains. Thousands at a time!" He shook his head as though to emphasize the point. "When I was a kid, just a schoolboy, eh? We went up to the mountains to see them high up there. You never forget it, you know? Millions of them, roosting so thick they look like clumps of brown leaves hanging on the trees. It's the kinda thing that stays with you." He pounded his chest near his heart. "Right here."

He tugged the towel from his shoulder and began walking back to the counter, then stopped. "You're doing a good thing, taking your *abuela* back to Mexico. Shows duty. *Fortaleza,* eh?" he added, nodding with his encouragement and approval.

Luz cast a glance at Ofelia to see that she had stilled in her chair and was listening to the exchange intently. When she met Luz's gaze, she shrugged indifferently and went back to rubbing her feet.

"You gonna be there for El Día de Los Muertos, right?" asked Mr. Cordero.

"I hope I make it."

"You gotta be there for that!" he exclaimed, hands out. "I mean, you gotta be there when *las monarcas* fly in. That's when her spirit flies with them. You know that, right?"

To see the hefty man speak with such sweet sincerity was moving. Luz nodded. "Yes, but I'm having car trouble. That's why I'm waiting here."

"Car trouble? You take it to Vera's?"

Luz nodded again.

"They're good people."

"They have to order a part so I've got to wait till tomorrow. Maybe the next day or two. I don't know what to do. I'm thinking of calling my boyfriend to pick me up. I can't afford just to hang out."

Ofelia perked up. "Hey, you know what I'm thinking, Mr. Cordero? We need somebody to take Carmen's place, right? Why not hire Luz?"

"I'm only going to be here for a day or two at most," Luz reminded her.

"But that would help us out till we find someone new."

"You ever been a waitress before?" asked Cordero skeptically.

"I worked for a while at the restaurant where my grandmother worked. Just part-time after school."

Ofelia sat straighter in her chair.

"You said your *abuela* was a cook. What'd she make?" he asked, testing her.

"Classic Mexican, mostly, for the restaurant. But she could make anything. And you've never tasted mole sauce until you've tasted hers. It was earthy dark and sprinkled with melted cheese." She remembered cooking with Abuela, an apron tied around her waist, standing in front of four or five pots bubbling on the stove. Abuela would wag her fingers to draw Luz close, then she'd hold out the herbs and spices, one by one, under her nose and make her sniff—coriander, cumin, chilies, cilantro. Luz could still smell them in her mind.

"Sometimes she'd cook up special recipes from her village. People would flock to the restaurant, eager for a taste of home. She taught me everything she knows. I could prepare every dish you cooked today."

Ofelia snorted. "Then you know everything, 'cause it's the same every day."

"If your *abuela*'s from Michoacán, then she knows my style," Mr. Cordero said after giving it some thought. "I guess it could work. You seem like a pretty smart girl. Do you speak Spanish?"

"I understand it but I don't speak it so well."

"*Lo suficientemente bueno como para tomar un pedido?*"

"*Sí.* Good enough to get an order," Luz replied.

"I gotta tell you, this isn't the way I like to do things. But I will do this because your *abuela* is from my home." He shrugged. "And my girl Ofelia is getting tired. It's no good for her baby to work this hard and no good for me if she gets any slower, eh? So maybe this is a good idea after all. You work a few days, maybe longer if you like. Earn a little money for your car. Then everybody is happy. Okay?"

Luz held her breath and wondered if this wasn't another push from Abuela. She could hear her voice. *Fortaleza.*

"Okay," she replied, and for no reason laughed.

Ofelia clapped her hands. "This is, like, so great. I mean, really, *chica,* I can't believe it. And don't you worry none, you'll catch on quick." She went to Mr. Cordero and gave him a quick hug. "My feet thank you, Mr. Cordero!"

"Yeah, yeah," he said, unconvincingly feigning a frown.

"There's still the problem of where I'm going to sleep tonight," Luz said. "Do you know of some hotel that's clean and decent and won't cost me an arm and a leg?"

"There's a Holiday Inn near the expressway," Mr. Cordero said.

"That's not cheap," countered Ofelia. "What about Las Damas?"

Mr. Cordero scratched his jaw. "It's nothing fancy, but it's clean. And cheap. I know the woman who runs the place. I'll give her a call. Find out if she has a room."

"It's where I stayed when I first got here," said Ofelia. "It's kind of a boardinghouse for women who come to the city and need a safe place to stay for a few days. A lot of women from Mexico stay there when they first get here."

What Ofelia was describing sounded to her like a halfway house. "I don't know. Maybe the motel is better."

Ofelia caught the worry in Luz's tone and said reassuringly, "I know what you're thinking but this is better. Really. It's nice."

"So, why did you move?"

"I live with Angel now."

Mr. Cordero began clearing a few tables. "He's no good."

Ofelia waved off the comment. "And Suzanne Corrington—she's the lady who owns the house—only lets girls stay till they get a job or find another place to live. It's a safe place for them when they get to town. I figure that's because she had such a hard time. I heard stories about what happened to her and, girl, you don't want to know."

"She's a saint in my book," Mr. Cordero said.

"I can take you there to meet her and check it out, okay?"

Luz puffed out air, considering. It sounded like a good offer and she wouldn't have to turn back. Then she thought of the mural. It had to be a sign. "Okay. Yes," she said, deciding. "Thanks."

"Well, if you two are finished yakking, grab an apron and let's get started before the dinner shift rolls in," said Mr. Cordero with a swing of his arms. "*Vámonos.*"

For the next few hours Luz learned how to hustle. Mr. Cordero's system of taking orders, serving them, and cleaning up was strictly short-order business—no flourishes. The menu was simple and displayed on a big board behind the counter. Most people were regulars and knew what they wanted. Mr. Cordero was pleased that she caught on so quickly. Ofelia was loud and boisterous, a know-it-all who was always correcting. But she was also open and friendly. When they left El Iguana for the night, Ofelia's enthusiastic personality overflowed.

"This is so great!" she said, linking arms with Luz. Ofelia had let down her hair and put on a fresh coat of coral-colored lipstick, a gold cross around her neck, and several bracelets on her arms. They jangled and clicked sexily when she moved. "I thought I was going to end up giving birth to my replacement."

They walked down the street, past a mural that dominated the side of the two-story brick building. It came alive with the faces of heroes from the history books of Mexico. More brick apartment buildings lined the sidewalk. Most of the street-level windows had bars across them and the paint on the sills and doors was peeling. Dilapidated cars were parked in front along the curb. One building stood out like a tangerine in a basket of potatoes. Freshly painted a bright orange with shiny black shutters, Las Damas punctuated its statement with flower boxes filled with cascading ivy and lipstick pink geraniums exploding in the final flush of summer.

"It looks like my old Barbie house," Luz exclaimed.

Ofelia giggled and tugged at her to keep walking.

What the house lacked in subtlety it made up for in security. There was a tall, heavy black iron fence enclosing the house that made it appear impenetrable and safe. They rang the bell. Minutes later a pretty, petite blonde with short, spiky hair answered the door. She wore thick black glasses through which her gaze scoured every inch of Luz. Then they rested on Ofelia and with the speed of shooting fireworks, her smile exploded in welcome.

"Ofelia! It's about time you came back to see me!" The woman engulfed Ofelia in a hug.

"How're you doing, Suzanne?" she replied, suddenly sheepish.

"Look at you!" Suzanne exclaimed, eyeing the belly. "Last time I saw you I couldn't tell you were pregnant and now . . . that baby looks like it's ready to come out and play."

"Not till next month, so don't give this baby any ideas. I'm counting on a paycheck for a few more weeks."

Her cell phone rang and Ofelia immediately dug it out from her purse. All her earlier bravado fled and Luz thought she saw her physically draw into herself. She clutched the phone tightly to her ear.

"I'm at Las Damas," Ofelia said into the phone. There was a pause and her expression grew haunted. She turned her back, huddling over the phone, and spoke in a softer voice. "But I told you I was going to take Luz. I did, Angel, really. Okay. I'm sorry. I didn't know. I'm sorry, it's my fault. Yeah, okay." Ofelia was nodding her head and her voice rose in forced cheerfulness. "I'll be right there."

Luz cast a quick glance at Suzanne, who stood scowling with her arms crossed.

"What was that about?" Suzanne asked.

Ofelia made an effort to shrug it off. "Oh, I was stupid. I guess I didn't tell Angel to pick me up here. He's waiting at the restaurant."

"Do you realize how many times you just said you were sorry?" Suzanne asked.

"Hey, it was my fault, okay?" She slanted a nervous glance at Luz. "Suzanne, this is Luz, the girl I told you about. I'm, like, so sorry, but I gotta run. Angel is waiting. I'll see you tomorrow." She hugged Luz, then turned to Suzanne. "Take good care of my girl, okay?"

Ofelia raced down the stairs so fast that Luz was afraid she'd fall.

After the door closed Suzanne shook her head. "That Angel keeps her under his thumb, wants to know wherever she goes. And he has a dangerous temper. You heard how he intimidates her? She'll never admit it, but I'm sure he slaps her around. Sometimes I see her with a bruise that she covers with makeup."

"Why doesn't she come back here?"

"I wish she would and she knows my door is always open. But

bottom line—she won't leave him. There's nothing I can do unless she asks for my help. And now with the baby coming"—she shook her head again—"it's not likely. I've seen it over and over. Battered women are made to feel like the problem is their fault. In the end, they lose their self-esteem."

"Ofelia doesn't strike me as someone with low self-esteem."

"You mean her attitude? Don't let that fool you. Underneath that tough-girl exterior, she's really a pretty insecure kid." She sighed in resignation and lifted her hands toward the stairs. "Anyway, let me show you your room."

Suzanne led Luz to the converted attic on the third floor. The bedroom across the hall from hers was empty so she didn't have to share the bathroom. Hers was a spare room, clean, and painted a daffodil yellow with a pale blue trim that matched the cotton bedspread on the twin bed. Under the steep dormer sat a small painted desk.

Luz closed the door and crossed the room in a few steps. She looked around the spartan space. Her suitcase sat on the painted wood floor, her coat on the narrow bed. Suddenly her decision to go to San Antonio felt very real. She was twenty-one, alone in the world, she'd left her home in Milwaukee, and for the next day or two, this was home.

She scrubbed her face, changed into warm pajamas, then, exhausted and road weary, climbed under the thin blanket on the narrow bed. Noise from the street poured in through her window: a drunken man was shouting something unintelligible, car doors slammed, dogs barked, garbage cans clattered, and the wail of the police sirens was as persistent as the song of cicadas in the country. Luz brought the cotton blanket higher up to her neck and shivered with a cold that felt more like fear.

She turned to her side and reached for her phone, cradling it to her chest. It felt like a lifeline to Sully. Suddenly it rang, startling her. She wiped her eyes and looked at the number. It was Sully. She flipped open the phone.

"Hi. I was just thinking about you."

"Hi," he replied, and she heard his relief at hearing her voice. "You okay?"

At the sound of his voice her heart squeezed. "Yeah. I miss you."

"I miss you, too. It's weird not having you here."

He sounded sleepy. She imagined that he'd eaten some takeout dinner and was lying in bed, like she was. He lived in a modest apartment in a brick two-flat in the city. It was a typical guy's place with sparse metal and wood furniture collected from home and garage sales, a bicycle parked against a wall beside other athletic equipment, and a kitchen filled with mugs for coffee. She'd stayed there often, telling her grandmother that she was staying with a girlfriend. It had felt ridiculous to be a grown woman with a job and still have to lie about where she spent her nights. But her grandmother had been old-fashioned and Luz didn't want to upset her, so the ruse continued.

"So, how far did you get?" he asked.

Luz curled her toes. "Not far, actually."

"Like, where? St. Louis?"

"Chicago."

There was a silence. "*What?*"

"Well"—she took a breath—"I had a little car trouble."

"Shit."

"It's nothing bad. A fuel pump."

"Why didn't you call me? Luz, I'da come down to fix it. Where is it now?"

"It's at a good mechanic here in town. He's ordered the part. So you don't have to worry. It's all taken care of."

There was a long pause and she imagined him counting to ten. He cleared his throat, a sure sign he was upset.

"Where are you now?" His voice was determinedly level.

Luz took another breath, looking around her spare room. "I'm at a . . . bed-and-breakfast."

"Luz, I could've come down to get you. You don't need to be staying in a hotel."

"I'm okay. And I didn't want to bother you."

He sighed, and she envisioned him putting his fingers to the bridge of his nose as he thought. She could almost hear the gears in his brain grinding as he worked out his rescue plan.

"Okay . . . I've got a few cars coming in first thing in the morning but I'll come pick you up at noon, latest. Hell, I can come get you right now."

Luz moved to a sitting position, tucking her legs tightly beneath her. "I don't want you to pick me up."

"What do you mean?"

"I've got it under control. I'll get the car fixed and keep on going like I planned. This doesn't change anything."

"Wha— You're serious? You're still planning on driving that heap of tin to Mexico? After this?"

"No. Just to Texas. I'll see what happens there." She could feel the seed of tension take root in her chest. "Sully, we talked about this already."

"That was before you broke down. It's gonna happen again."

"Then I'll get it fixed again."

"Just tell me where you are." He ground out the words.

"Sully," she said firmly, pulling her shoulders back. She felt her heart pounding in her chest. "I don't want you to come pick me up. It's okay. I'm okay."

There was another silence. The last thing she wanted to do tonight was fight with Sully. "You know how much this means to me. You just have to have a little faith. I can handle this." She wanted him to understand. To take her side. "I'm afraid if I don't do this, I'll be lost forever. Does that make sense?"

"No. It isn't safe, Luz. I can't stand the thought of you traveling cross-country in that car all alone."

She took a deep breath, trying to remain reasonable. She knew Sully was a traditional guy who believed in traditional roles. The man married, settled down, took care of his family. It was hard for him to understand, much less accept her notion of going off alone across the country.

"I know you're worried, but I've thought this through. My car will get repaired and I'm going to continue my trip. This is just a glitch."

"A glitch . . ." She heard a derisive snort. "You're just being stubborn. Listen, I know what I'm talking about and I'm telling you it's not safe. If you continue on this crazy trip the next call I get will be from some policeman telling me he's found your body on the side of the road."

"Nice," she snapped. Luz stood up and looked out the window. The moon was barely visible behind the buildings, a sliver of hope in a sea of black.

He started arguing with her then, his voice growing louder and more strident as he told her over and over what a bad idea this was. She held the phone away from her ear. In her heart, she knew it was just his fear for her talking, but she didn't want to listen anymore. His words were wearing her down.

"I'm going to say good-bye now, Sully."

"Don't hang up on me. We're not finished talking."

"We're not talking. You're yelling and I'm waiting for it to be over. That's not a conversation."

"Then we just keep talking. Hey, look, I know I'm being bull-headed, but your grief is making you irrational."

"Sully . . ."

"You're a smart girl. You're not some flake. So don't start acting like one now. Be the levelheaded girl I love and come home. Or I'm coming down to get you."

Luz took the phone away from her ear and stared at it in her hand. She knew he was worried and his heart was in the right place. But she didn't want him discouraging her now when she needed his support the most. She brought the phone back to her ear with a sigh. "I'm tired," she said in a voice hoarse from fatigue. "It's been a tough day and I have to get up early tomorrow. So good night, okay? I'll talk to you in the morning."

There was a long silence.

"Okay? Good night, Sully. Sully?"

"So, you're still going then." It wasn't a question but a statement of fact.

"Yes."

There was another long silence.

"Sully, try to understand. I have to do this."

"I don't understand. But it doesn't seem to matter."

"It *does*."

"What do you want me to say?"

"I don't know. Something supportive. Like good luck."

He laughed, but there was a bitter sound to it. "Sure. Good night and good luck."

She heard a click and the dead silence of disconnection.

He'd hung up on her. Luz's mouth dropped open in a silent gasp. They'd had arguments before, but no matter how hard they fought they'd never been so rude as to hang up without saying at least "Gotta go." She closed her cell phone with a snap, then crawled back under the covers. A moment later the phone rang again. She scrambled to grab the phone and bring it to her ear.

"I shouldn't've hung up on you," Sully said.

Luz sighed with relief and rolled onto her back. "No, you shouldn't have," she said, but there was no scolding in her tone. "You never did before."

"I guess I'm just scared. For you. For us."

She was about to say "Don't be," but thought better of it. He didn't need to hear platitudes now. He was telling her how *he* felt, which for Sully was a big deal. He was good at being strong and supportive for her, but rarely revealed when he was feeling insecure about something and needed support. Instead she said, "I'm scared, too."

"I'm glad to hear it. That means you'll be careful."

She smiled inwardly. He was beginning to accept her decision. "What are you most scared of?"

"I'm scared I won't see you again. I'm scared you'll change. I'm scared of all the bad that can happen."

She'd thought of all those same things and they scared her, too. "When I get scared, I try not to think of all the bad that can happen. Instead, I think of all the good things. Like I'm going to meet my family. I'm already meeting some really neat people. I'm going places I've never been before. I'm thinking for myself, making decisions for myself. It's all good."

"Yeah. Okay. I'll hold on to that."

Outside she heard the police sirens blaring, but on the other end of the line she heard the soft and steady sound of Sully's breathing, and she felt safe. She yawned.

"You should go to sleep now," Sully said.

"Okay. Good night, Sully."

"Good night. Sleep tight. And call me in the morning."

This time the click was soft and she didn't feel disconnected. Luz curled her legs higher into her chest and tucked her arms tight. Hearing his voice made her miss him all the more and she felt torn again between her decision to keep going and the fear that Sully was right and she was taking too many risks.

Then she remembered the butterfly in her garden, how she'd fluttered her wings and without hesitation lifted herself into the air, fearlessly beginning her journey south to a place she'd never been before. No one was telling her to stay home. She had to fly or die.

Such courage, eh?

Luz closed her eyes, feeling as small and fragile as the butterfly. What was courage? She didn't know. Maybe courage was listening to one's own voice rather than the opinions of others. Paying heed to the call of one's instincts, no matter how small and weak the voice sounded in her ears.

Before sleep overcame her, Luz wondered if maybe courage was nothing more than taking wing and staying the course.

Six

The journey south is difficult and filled with danger. Often the monarchs' wings get torn and damaged, but they persevere.

The iron mantle of winter loomed in the daunting gray clouds over Lake Michigan. Luz found the appeal of her journey south growing with every gust of wind. She woke early on her third day in Chicago, eager to pick up her car and get back on her journey. In the back of her mind she ticked off the days of the calendar. She was in the second week of October, and if she was going to find her aunt in San Antonio, then head off to Mexico in time for the Day of the Dead, she needed to hustle.

The lunch rush was over at the taqueria. Luz scrubbed the last pot till she removed every bit of baked-on grime. Then she took a cloth and wiped the stainless steel counter with the fervor of a sailor on deck, not settling till it gleamed.

"Hey, *chica. ¿Estás loca?*" Ofelia leaned in to tell her, elbowing her gently in her side. "You want to make the rest of us look bad? We don't want Cordero to get used to this."

"I'm just trying to leave everything clean. It's my last day and all."

"Still, girlfriend . . . *slow down.* I'm still working here when you go, you know?"

Luz leaned back on the counter and blew out a plume of air. Her hands were chapped from the bleach cloth she used to wipe the tables, and her feet sore from hours running food and refilling beverages. Yet, she'd enjoyed the past few days at the taqueria. The banter with Ofelia kept her mind off the gaping hole in her heart that grieved for Abuela, and the pace of taking orders for tacos, tamales, and beans was so fast that she didn't have time to be self-conscious about her Spanish. Table by table she butchered the language, but the orders somehow managed to come through.

"Have you called your boyfriend back yet?" asked Ofelia. She joined Luz and leaned against the counter, tossing her towel over her shoulder. "What's his name, Sammy?"

"Sully. And no, I haven't." She felt the sting of pride again. She'd checked her phone messages a dozen times but he hadn't called. Not once in three days. At night she sat alone in that small room and gazed out the grimy, bolted window at the street below, keeping her cell phone close.

"I think he's trying to make me call first." Luz tossed the towel on the counter with a sigh of frustration. "I know he doesn't want me to go on this trip. What is it about men that they're so reactionary? All I asked him was to let me take care of myself and he's like beating his chest with his fists."

"Tell me about it! *Ay,* Angel has such a temper!"

"He can call me first," Luz said, crossing her arms.

"Yeah, but what if he doesn't? I know if it was me, I'd be calling Angel before some other girl caught his eye."

Luz never thought of herself as the jealous type. Sully had never given her reason to be. Yet the thought of Sully going after another girl so quickly after she left town made her skin clammy. "He wouldn't," she said summarily.

"I don't know," Ofelia said in a singsong voice. "When the cat's away . . ."

"Maybe *your* cat," she replied. "Not Sully. But if he does cheat on me, then I don't want him!"

"You got it, girl," Ofelia said, leaning in to bump shoulders.

"I'll call him tomorrow, when I'm back on the road."

"Nothin' he can do about it then, right?" She wiggled her brows.

Luz's lips twitched in commiseration. That was her plan. She wanted to talk to Sully, but she was nervous enough about heading out on the road. She didn't need to hear his doomsday scenarios.

"So, do you love him?" Ofelia asked.

Luz looked at her, surprised by the bluntness of the question. "Sure I love him. We've been dating for a few years." She paused as she mentally counted the years from the day she met Sully as a freshman at the Milwaukee Area Technical College. "I was studying for an associate's degree in social services and he was almost finished with his automobile mechanics program. He was this tall, broad-shouldered grease monkey with stick-straight brown hair and a shy smile. Every time I see it, I melt. We had lockers next to each other, and though we'd see each other every day, it took him two weeks to work up the nerve to ask me for coffee."

"Sweet. Kinda high school, though."

"I don't know. Guys can be shy like that no matter what age."

Ofelia laughed. "Not Angel. He was born forty."

"God, is it three years already?" Luz muttered, more to herself. Her face softened. "Sully's a great guy. Very thoughtful."

Ofelia made a face. "Thoughtful? I'm talking about *love*. Passion! Check it . . . the kind where your heart leaps every time he walks in the room. When he kisses you, he makes your bones melt."

Luz shifted her weight, wondering how long it had been since she'd felt her heart leap when Sully drove up to the house. "Don't get me wrong. Sully's sexy. He's brooding and muscled, in a working-class kind of way. More Marlon Brando than James Bond."

Ofelia scrunched her nose. "Who are they?"

Luz rolled her eyes and laughed, not knowing how to explain. "Sexy working-class versus sexy money."

"My Angel's a little of both," Ofelia said archly.

Luz thought that she *was* always happy to see Sully, but did her heart flutter? Did that bone-melting tingling dissipate over time, replaced by something stronger and more sure? Or was something lacking? "What we have is comfortable."

"My old sofa is comfortable. That's not love."

"No?" Luz asked, feeling suddenly defensive. She absently reached up to tug at the silky hair that fell from her ponytail over her shoulder. "Then what do you call it?"

"That's . . ." Ofelia tugged the towel from her shoulder and gathered it in her hands. "I don't know what to call it. Friendship, maybe? With benefits?"

Luz choked out a short laugh, shaking her head no. That definitely wasn't it. Her relationship with Sully wasn't so trivial.

"He *is* my best friend," she said, trying to explain her strong feelings. "That's true. I can tell him anything. Things I can't even tell my girlfriends. And it's like he knows what I need and when I need it." Her eyes softened as she recalled his strong arm around her in the funeral home, and his gentleness in holding her while she wept.

"When Abuela died, he was always there, looking out for me. He made sure I always had something to eat, and that I slept. He even brushed my hair." She glanced quickly at Ofelia to see her bewildered expression.

"Sounds like your mother," she said.

"No, it was cool," she added with a short laugh. "You see, after Abuela died I didn't remember to do basic things like eat, sleep . . . and my hair is so thick. It was all knotted up, a real mess. So one night he just picked up my brush and started brushing my hair, real gentle-like, stroke after stroke. It felt so good, like I was being hypnotized." A small smile escaped as she remembered the feelings that had coursed through her. "He was so tender. I felt taken care of. Safe."

Ofelia's sarcasm fled from her face and in its place Luz saw a yearning so fierce it embarrassed her. She averted her gaze.

"I think maybe you're the one who has it wrong," Luz said. "What you were describing earlier sounds to me like that first gush of attraction. That's fun, sure. But that's lust. Easy come, easy go. What I'm talking about is real love."

Ofelia wiped her hands on the towel, then pointed a long, painted nail at Luz. "Whatever. Girl, if you've got a man with clean teeth and feet, *and* he brushes your hair, marry him! It don't get better than that."

"Abuela thought I should marry him. She was afraid that at twenty-one I was getting too old. That's not the way it is today, though. I'm too young to get married and I'm sure not ready to start a family. But hey, that's just me," she said, acknowledging Ofelia. "I know Sully is ready. He'd get married today if I said yes. But honestly, there's a lot I want to do, to learn, before I settle down. Maybe go back to school. Something, you know?"

Ofelia made a face. "Not really. I couldn't wait to get out of school! You've got a good man who wants to marry you and you're walking away? *Chica,* what's the matter with you? All I want is to settle down and have my baby and be a family." She laughed and affectionately patted her belly. "And I'm on my way."

"Are you and Angel getting married?" Luz asked.

Ofelia's smile slipped. "Oh, sure," she said with forced bravado.

"I hope it's soon, or your little bambino there won't have his last name when he or she pops out."

She'd meant it as a joke but Ofelia paled and stared at her hands. Luz immediately regretted her facetiousness. "Ofelia, I didn't mean—"

"Angel tells me we don't need to be married for when the baby's born," she said in a hurt tone. "That it's just a piece of paper. The baby won't know. But he promises we *will* get married. He just wants to wait until he has enough money saved up so we can do it proper. I want a big wedding with a white dress and my parents coming up from Mexico." Ofelia idly scraped at something on the counter. "But we gotta wait, that's all. It's not his fault he's marrying a girl with no papers, right?"

It occurred to Luz that Ofelia was using words that Angel had put into her head.

"Family is everything," Ofelia said with passion. "My mom and my dad, they got sent back to Mexico. So I went to live with my aunt in Kansas. She's a good woman, but she's not my mother, you know? I was only thirteen and I cried and cried, so hard I thought I was going to die. You don't know what it's like to be alone in a strange country with no family."

"I might have an idea," Luz said softly.

Ofelia arched and rubbed the small of her back. "My aunt didn't have no children or husband and she treated me okay. She tried. But it wasn't easy. I had to go to school in the day and when I came back I worked at the garden center where my aunt worked. When I got to be a senior my aunt had this new boyfriend." Her lip curled at the memory. "He drank a lot and wanted me to call him uncle.

As if. He was no good so I went out a lot. I started hanging with a bad group and my grades were dropping. It was a bad scene. I just had to get out. I wanted to go back to Mexico. I missed my mother and my father and my two sisters. *They* got to be a family. But what about *me*?"

She let her hand drop and straightened her apron. "That's why I'm going to marry Angel. He's all I got. I know he might not be the most handsome man and he has a terrible temper when he's drinking, but he's my baby's father and I'm gonna make it work. Angel *will* marry me and he'll be a good father to our baby." She put her hand over her belly. "*That's* what love is," she said, convincing herself as much as Luz.

Ofelia marched off with intent to the radio and, with a wink, cranked up the ranchero music. "Come on, *chica*! It's your last day, eh!"

Ofelia loved to dance and her condition didn't slow her down. She lifted her arms and began waving the dishcloth in the air, around and around over her head, while rocking her hips, her belly straining against the apron. Throwing back her head, she belted out the lyrics to the popular ballad by her favorite singer. Luz burst out laughing and whirled around, joining in. They formed a line dance, swinging their hips in unison and slapping towels in time to the music. Luz remembered how she and Abuela used to dance together in the kitchen as they stirred the sauces or washed the dishes, giggling like girls.

"Hey, you girls go *loca* or something?" Mr. Cordero called out over the singing. He came out from the back room, stopping to turn down the radio.

"We just love our job so much it makes us so happy," Ofelia said with a lilt. "And it's Luz's last day so we should party a little, eh?"

Mr. Cordero waved his hand at her in dismissal while his eyes scanned the tables, counters, and floors of his restaurant. He put his hands on his hips and pursed his lips in satisfaction. "Looks good," he said. Luz had cleaned out corners that had never seen steel wool.

He came closer to Luz and spread out his hands magnanimously. "You sure you don't want to stay on? I could offer you a little more per hour."

Ofelia swung her head, eyes hopeful.

"Thanks, that's a nice offer," Luz replied. "But you know I made a promise to Abuela."

"Yeah, yeah, I know," he said, nodding. He hadn't really expected her to accept. He handed her an envelope of cash. Then, looking over his shoulder to be sure he wasn't overheard, he said in a low voice, "I put a little something extra in there for your trip. To tell the truth, I wish I was going with you." He saw her about to protest and shoved the envelope toward her. "No, no, I wanted to. Take it! Consider it an offering for your *abuela,* eh?"

Luz smiled and gave Mr. Cordero a hug. The move surprised him and he awkwardly patted her shoulders. "Thank you, Mr. Cordero."

"Let me know how it goes, eh? A postcard maybe? Not that e-mail stuff. Or you could call Ofelia. And, if you have a minute, look up my family, eh? I put a note in there for my mother. Could you see that she gets it?"

"I will. *Yo prometo,*" she added, already feeling more at home with the language.

"Go on, then. Get your car before the shop closes. And if you want a job when you come back, let me know."

Luz thanked Mr. Cordero again. She went to hug Ofelia,

whispering in her ear, "Good-bye, sweet friend. I'll come back to see your bambino."

Ofelia's eyes filled with tears as she hugged her fiercely. "You better."

Luz took a quick look around the restaurant, dropped her dirty apron in the bin, grabbed a peppermint candy from the dish near the register, and tugged open the door.

"Good-bye!" The little bell over the door rang as she left.

She immediately walked to Vera's to pick up her car. Mr. Vera charged what he said he would. Luz laid out the twenties, spreading the worn paper on the counter. She was used to paying bills, to seeing most of her meager paycheck disappear in a day. But so much spent on one car repair hurt. The mechanic thanked her, then told her the old Volkswagen was good to go for another hundred thousand miles.

"Or not . . . ," he added with a crooked grin.

She felt a rush of affection for the battered orange car when she saw it looking clean and raring to go in the lot. When she turned the ignition, El Toro roared to life. It was a beautiful sound.

"Thank you!" she exclaimed to Mr. Vera. Then, with a final glance at the mural of La Virgen, she said, "And thank you, Abuela." She'd thought the car breaking down was the worst thing that could happen. For a stop that hadn't been planned, it turned out to be an empowering experience. Instead of turning and running back home and letting Sully solve the problem, she'd handled it on her own. She'd discovered strangers could be kind, and that there was something to learn from every job. Most of all, she'd discovered a new confidence in herself.

She pulled her maps from her bag and laid them across the passenger seat. Her plan was to spend a last night at Las Damas, then head off tomorrow at first light for another full day's drive to make up time. She was on her way again!

Unfortunately, the repairs didn't help the car's speed any. The car roared but advanced slowly along the side street.

"That's okay, El Toro," she said, patting the dashboard affectionately. " 'Slow but sure' works for me. I'll make you a deal. I'll fill you with fuel and promise not to push you too hard if you promise not to break down again. Okay?"

That night Luz was awakened by the ringing of her cell phone. She rose up on her elbows and looked around the darkened room, disoriented. Her phone rang again, and waking more, she lurched across the bed to grab it from the nightstand, thinking it was Sully.

"Hello?"

"Luz?" The voice was muted and high-pitched. "Sorry to bother you. But I had no one else to call!"

"Ofelia?"

"Yes. Can you come get me? Please."

"Now?"

"Yes . . . wait!" she said in a panicked whisper. There was a pause, during which Luz sat bolt upright, tossing back her covers. Her heart pounded and the adrenaline awoke her fully. She sat clutching the phone, tense and in the ready.

"Please come," Ofelia said in a hoarse whisper. "I'll meet you downstairs. Don't ring the bell. Hurry!"

"I'll be right there."

Luz flicked on the bedside lamp. Jeans, a clean T-shirt, and her jacket were draped over the chair. She dressed quickly. While sticking her feet into her boots she glanced at the small alarm clock by the bed. It was nearly three in the morning. What could be wrong with Ofelia? she wondered as she grabbed her suitcase and the box of ashes. Everyone was sleeping so Luz tiptoed down the stairs, leaving an envelope filled with money and a note to Suzanne on her desk. By the time she reached the front door, she knew. She closed the door quietly behind her.

Outside, the city was asleep. The air hung cold and dank in a fog. Luz knew it was dangerous to be out alone at this time of the night in this part of the city. She shivered and zipped up her jacket while eyeing the street. The traffic light turned green and two cars passed. The sedan slowed in front of her building. From the corner of her eye she spied a male driver checking her out, music slamming against his closed windows and plumes of smoke covering his face. Luz hunched her shoulders, put her keys between her knuckles like someone once told her to do for self-defense, and began walking purposefully toward her car farther down the block.

She climbed in and couldn't lock the doors fast enough. Looking up, she noticed the same sedan passing by again. El Toro sprang to life and she drove off. When she reached Ofelia's apartment she double-parked in front, then leaned across the seat to peer through the side window. A moment later, a door opened and Ofelia emerged wearing a flamboyant, vintage emerald green satin coat and dragging a small carry-on bag. There was something about the way she was hunched over and gripping the railing that propelled Luz to sprint from the car to help her. As she approached, Ofelia looked up.

In the yellow light of the building's light fixture, Luz saw Ofelia's face and gasped. Ofelia's left eye was a slit in her swollen face and her lip was split. She grabbed Ofelia's arm.

"That son of a bitch."

"Come on, let's just go!" Ofelia urged, breathless and in a gar-bled whisper. She continued plowing down the stairs in a single-minded focus, one labored step after the other.

When they got to the car, Luz rushed to open the door. "Give me your suitcase."

Ofelia handed it to Luz, then stiffened and swung her head to look in a panic behind her. "Wait! Where's Serena?"

"Who?"

"*My dog!* Oh, *Dios,*" she cried. "She was right behind me! I've got to go get her!" She turned and began walking slowly up the stairs.

Luz grabbed her arm. "What are you doing? You can't go back up there. Let's get out of here!"

Ofelia jerked her arm away. "Lemme go! She's in the hall. I just gotta open the door."

"Where's Angel?"

"Passed out. But when he wakes up, he'll kill her. I know he will. For spite."

Luz silently groaned. "*Okay!* I'll get your dog." But she was ter-rified of going into that building with Angel in there. "Are you sure he's passed out?"

"Yes! The dog is just inside. Here." She plunged into a pocket of the voluminous coat and dragged out the key chain. It clanged noisily in the quiet night.

Luz grabbed it, wrapping her fingers tight around it to silence the keys. "Just leave the suitcase and get in the car. I'll be right back." She started off but then spun on her heel. "What kind of a dog is it?"

"A Chihuahua. She won't bite."

"Oh, good," she said faintly. At least it's not a pit bull, Luz thought as she went up the stairs. She unlocked the door and opened it slowly, expecting the dog to charge out. Or worse, Angel. But the front entry was empty. Luz opened the door wider, squinting in the dark foyer. What was that dog's name? Was it Sally? She pursed her lips and made soft smacking noises.

"Here, Sally," she said softly. "Here, girl."

She heard soft growling farther up in the darkness. She moved to enter the unlit hall. It was dank and smelled of cooking grease. She took another step and heard the soft whoosh and click of the door closing behind her. Instantly, she was plunged into darkness.

Her heart began pounding. "Sally, come!" she called in a stage whisper. The sound of nails click-clacking up the stairs made her grind her teeth in frustration. Luz gripped the railing and stumbled up the stairs like a blind woman. The higher she climbed, the louder the growls grew. When she reached the third floor she spied something huddled in front of an apartment door.

"Come here, Sally. It's okay, I won't hurt you, you little rat," Luz said as sweetly as she could. But the Chihuahua wanted nothing to do with her. She cowered against the door, lifting one paw and showing her teeth, growling louder. Luz took a step closer.

It was too much for the frantic dog. It erupted in high-pitched, relentless yaps. Luz froze in a panic. Angel would have to be dead not to hear it. Sure enough, a loud crash sounded from inside the apartment, like a chair falling back on the floor.

"That's it." Luz lurched forward to grab hold of the dog with one hand and grip the railing with the other. She took off down the stairs as fast as she could. Her heels reverberated in the narrow hall but she was beyond caring. As she reached the bottom landing she heard Angel's voice shouting in a sleepy slur from above, "Who's there? Ofelia?"

Luz pushed through the front door as the dog wriggled in her arms to escape. With her free hand she grabbed Ofelia's suitcase and raced toward the car. Ofelia opened her door and Luz tossed the dog into her lap, then slammed the door shut. She ran to the trunk, jerked it open, and crammed Ofelia's carry-on into the cramped space, pounding on it to push it in.

Suddenly the building door swung open. Angel lurched out and stood with his arms wide, rocking on his heels and staring at her in drunken confusion, weaving from left to right as he tried to figure out who she was. Then he spotted Ofelia in the car.

"Hey!" he bellowed. "Where the hell do you think you're going? Get outta that car." He took a step down. The front door slammed shut behind him, angering him more. He raised his fist. "Don't make me come down there and drag you out."

"Start the car. Start the car!" Ofelia cried in terror.

Luz clenched her jaw, grabbed the tire iron, and swung it high into the air. "You stay away!" Fury tore at her throat. "Do you hear me? Don't go near her again or I'll call the cops!"

Angel drew back. He staggered, lost his balance, and then fell back on the stairs.

Luz slammed the trunk shut and ran to open her car door and jump in. She tossed the tire iron in the backseat. Her hands were shaking so badly she had a hard time getting the keys from her jeans pocket and into the ignition. Next to her, Ofelia was clutching the shivering dog in her lap. Her eyes were trained on the man struggling to his feet.

"Hurry! Lock the car!" Ofelia said.

Luz turned the key in the engine. The engine cranked but didn't fire.

"No, no, not now!" She tried again. The engine strained again, weaker. Angel was coming down the stairs, yelling in Spanish.

"Go, go, go . . ." Ofelia careened, rocking back and forth.

Luz pumped the gas pedal twice, her hands tightly gripping the wheel. She nearly jumped from her skin when a loud thump pounded on the roof.

Luz jerked her head around and saw the hulking figure of a man at the door, his muscles bulging as he tugged at the handle while viciously hammering the roof and shouting obscenities in a drunken slur. The little dog went crazy, barking and jumping from Ofelia's lap to the floor and back. Ofelia was screaming at him in Spanish.

Time stood still while Luz thought, Is this how my journey will end? Beaten up by some drunken asshole? "Hell, no!" she said, and gripped the keys again. She pumped the gas pedal and turned the ignition. "C'mon, c'mon . . ." She never heard a sweeter sound than the roar of the engine at that moment and swore her devotion to El Toro forever. She rammed the gear into place and took off with Angel still gripping the door handle. Next to her, Ofelia was hysterically screaming, "*¿Sabes qué? ¡Ya me voy!*"

Halfway down the street, Luz glanced at the rearview mirror. Angel was flapping his arms like a bird about to take flight as he fought for balance, before he fell, face-first, onto the street.

A victorious grin creased Luz's face as she spun around the corner.

Seven

Migrating monarchs journey throughout their extensive breeding range. However, over half of the monarchs breed in the corn belt of the Midwest. Thus, most years, large numbers of butterflies can be seen migrating through that region in the fall.

D awn tore at the seam of night, pulling the blackness back a little farther with each passing minute. Luz had left the sharp and jagged cityscape behind and drove through a seemingly endless tunnel of darkness, the only light a cold glare from the highway cobra fixtures and the narrow beams of her car.

She cranked open her window and let the moist freshness of morning air roll over her, reviving her senses. Her hair fluttered behind her like a flag. She released a long sigh, the kind that came from deep within and completely emptied her lungs. Bad air out, good air in, she thought, then ran her fingers through her hair, scratching her scalp vigorously. Lowering her hand, she held it before her eyes. She'd been driving for over two hours and her hands had only just stopped shaking.

What a night, she thought. She still couldn't believe all that had happened. It felt like it was all some horrible nightmare. Or perhaps she was in shock, the suspension of natural reactions after trauma. She had to confess it was nice to have some company as she drove these long, lonely miles. But never when she planned her trip did she include a woman in her eighth month of pregnancy. It was crazy to take Ofelia along, but what choice did she have? She shook her head. "Well, Abuela, this certainly wasn't part of our plan."

After they'd escaped Angel, she had driven directly to Las Damas and double-parked in front, thinking Ofelia would want to stay there. When the car stopped Ofelia jerked up and looked wildly out the window, searching the street as though expecting to see Angel come roaring down.

"We can't stay here," she said in hysteria. "He's *loco*. He's got a gun. He told me he'd use it if I left him. And he will. I know he will!"

Luz felt the fear tightening her chest again. "You'll be safe here. Suzanne won't let him in."

"No! It's the first place he'll come. He's probably on his way now."

Luz froze in indecision.

"Luz, please," Ofelia shouted. "Get us out of here!"

"I'll take you to the police," Luz said, and shifted into gear.

"Police can't do shit. He has to shoot me first." Ofelia wiped her eyes and pulled her dog closer to her chest.

Luz glanced nervously at Ofelia, then took off down the street, not sure where she was headed. Her only goal at the moment was to get as far from Angel as possible. "Do you know a shelter nearby?"

"That's no good either."

"Ofelia . . ."

"No, listen," she said in an urgent whisper. "A woman I knew came here from Florida. Her husband was beating her, real bad. But when he pulled a knife, she ran. She went to a shelter. I don't

93

know how he found out she was in Chicago but one day she was walking home from work and this car pulled up and it was him. He dragged her screaming into the car and nobody stopped him. They found her body a week later in some ditch. Nobody did nothing." She sniffed and looked back out the window. "Sometimes, a girl just disappears forever."

Luz wiped her damp palms on her jeans. "Where can I take you?"

"Take me with you!"

"To Texas?" she blurted in disbelief.

"Yes! He won't follow me there."

"But . . . you don't know anyone. And what about your job? Mr. Cordero?"

"No job is worth my life, and he can't protect me. Nobody can. I'll call him. He'll understand. It's not safe here and I got nowhere else to go!"

"But . . ." Luz swallowed thickly. "What if you have the baby?"

"I'm not due for another month," Ofelia rushed to say.

"You'd need your passport."

"I have it. I stuffed it in before I left." She bent over to get her purse, dug through it for a moment, then pulled out her passport. "And I have money. Look." Ofelia opened an envelope to show a thick wad of bills. "It's almost five hundred dollars. I hid it. Just in case."

Luz couldn't speak. Common sense warred with her emotions. This was crazy. It wasn't part of her plan. Then Luz imagined Ofelia so afraid that she was sneaking money, some clothes, her passport, hiding them from Angel in her apartment, just in case she had to flee.

"Luz, please," she said, her usually upbeat voice now low in defeat. "I'm scared. I don't know anything about having a baby. I've got no one. Oh God, Luz, I want to be with my mother. Please. Just get me to San Antonio. That's all I ask. I can catch a bus there. I'll find my way to my mother on my own. I just want to go home."

Seeing the tears streak down Ofelia's bruised face, Luz realized she'd come to the end of her argument. Bubbling in her veins was a primal fierceness she'd never experienced before. No matter what, she was *not* going to leave Ofelia to go back to that creep who'd hurt her, and would again.

So here she was, driving south on this highway most of the night with her runaway friend and her soon-to-be-born baby, a runt of a dog, and her grandmother's ashes.

A soft moan caught her attention. Luz stole a quick glance at the passenger side. Ofelia was curled up against the door, her head on Luz's pillow and her outrageous satin coat serving as a blanket. Over the collar Luz caught a glimpse of bruises that were turning an ugly purple. In the rearview mirror she saw the small, thin Chihuahua snuggled up like a waif against the box of Abuela's ashes. Luz frowned, thinking that rotten little dog that had almost got them killed was always in the wrong place. She considered pushing the dog away from the box, but the poor skinny thing looked so peaceful after such a harrowing night, she didn't have the heart. Then she remembered how much Abuela had loved animals, little dogs especially. Luz released a reluctant grin. Her grandmother might even be enjoying the company in the backseat.

"Where are we?"

Luz startled at the sound of Ofelia's voice, gruff with sleep. For so many hours all she'd heard was the hum of the wheels on the road and a low, soft snoring. The inside of the car was dim with the soft, gray light of dawn.

"Southern Illinois, heading for St. Louis."

Ofelia grunted, then shifted in her seat, pushing the satin coat to the floor. She moved slowly, muffling her groans as muscles complained.

"You okay?" Luz asked.

Ofelia sighed. "No . . . yeah. I dunno. I'm stiff all over, like I got hit by a truck."

"You look like it, too."

"Ha-ha," she replied dryly. When she didn't find a mirror on the back of the visor, Ofelia reached up to turn the rearview for a peek at her face. She gently touched her left cheek and let her fingertips graze the scab over her eye. Then she pushed the mirror back into place and slumped back in her seat, her head against the window. "Why does he always go for the eye?"

"He hit you before?"

Ofelia nodded. "When he starts drinking, it can get bad," she said in a low voice. "One time, I tried to make him stop. But that made it worse."

Luz tried not to let her imagination go there. "What made this time different? Why'd you leave?"

"I was afraid for my baby. Oh, Luz, if he hit the baby . . ." She hugged her belly, rocking back and forth. "No way I'm gonna let him hurt my baby."

"He didn't—"

"*No!*" She took a breath. "No. He only hit my face. He was so drunk, he passed out pretty quick."

"Why did you stay with a guy like that?"

"I love him," she said in a small voice. "You only saw his bad side. He can be real sweet, like your Sully, and he's always sorry. After he gets mad he spends good money and tries to make it up to me."

"Hey, don't defend him to me," Luz said with heat. "And don't

ever compare that bastard to my Sully. They're nothing alike."
She shook off the revulsion at the idea of Sully hitting a woman.
"Angel's a big guy, with big muscles, but he's no man. He's a brute.
He could've killed us both. I thought he was gonna try." Her voice
trembled. "I was scared."

Ofelia sniffed, wiping her face with her palms, and said, "No.
You were so brave."

Brave? No one had ever called Luz brave before. She shook her
head. "You were the brave one to get out."

"Big deal. A phone call," Ofelia said with sarcasm. "I'm a cow-
ard. I couldn't even help myself."

"You made the call."

"Yeah? I talk a good game," Ofelia said. "But do you know what
I was doing while you were standing up to Angel? I was locking
the doors, crying like a baby. I should've stood up to that scum
long ago. But I just take it. Over and over. If it wasn't for you"—her
breath hitched and she reached out to grab Luz's arm tight—"you
maybe saved my life. My baby's life. I'm nothing to you but you
came to help. You're my hero."

Luz didn't think she was a hero. That seemed such a grand
word for what she'd done. She used to wonder what she'd do if
she saw a stranger get hurt. She read in the paper a story about
how a man got beaten on a city street and, even though people saw
it happening, no one came to his aid. And there was also a girl who
was jogging through the park and murdered in full daylight while
people watched.

"It all happened so fast," she tried to explain. "I guess it's not
something you can prepare for. I just knew that I couldn't let him
hurt you. It's like, you and me, we were one and the same."

Ofelia's face crumpled with emotion and, closing her eyes, she let her head drop back against the cushion. After a minute she said in a thick voice, "Well, one thing's for sure. A lot of people wouldn't have bothered."

They drove for a while in silence as the wheels hummed beneath them, each passing mile a hymn of safety. The dim light of the snug car made the atmosphere intimate, like a confessional. Beside her, Luz heard the soft, muffled sound of crying.

"It's okay, Ofelia. You're safe now."

In a broken voice Ofelia said, "He wouldn't stop hitting me. Even when I begged. I *loved* him! I tried so hard to be what he wanted me to be. But he never loved me." She sniffed loudly and reached up to wipe her nose. "Sometimes, the way he looked at me . . . made me feel like nothing."

Luz didn't respond.

The intimacy of the night had tapped into Ofelia's already waning strength. She leaned forward to rub her back, groaning softly. "My back is killing me."

Luz looked at her nervously, focusing on her huge belly. "Like a backache or cramps?"

"Kinda both." Ofelia stretched her spine and moved from left to right in her seat while her facial muscles pulled into a grimace. "*Maldito,*" she swore. Then she looked at Luz, her dark eyes limpid with fear. "I don't know if I'm gonna make it to Texas."

Luz's heart raced. "You mean, you think you're in labor?"

"I don't know! I never had a baby before. But this lady told me that a backache is the first sign the baby's coming."

The news slammed into Luz. "Jesus, Ofelia, what should we do? Go back to Chicago? To Suzanne? She'd help us."

"No! You know I can't go back there."

"Then where?" Luz felt panic rising in her chest.

"Let's just keep going. I'm not gonna have the baby now. Just, well, maybe sooner than I thought."

"We need to think a minute," Luz said, gathering her wits. She needed a plan of action. "One thing's for certain, you can't have the baby in my car. I'll take you to the nearest hospital," she said decisively.

"I can't just go to some hospital! I don't have insurance and I'm not legal."

Luz leaned back in her seat and with a free hand rubbed her temple. Did being legal make a difference? Her mind was working on only one cylinder. Her tired brain went over and over what choices they had, and whether the services she'd thought she could count on were available to Ofelia. It scared her that she didn't know.

"What are you thinking?" asked Ofelia anxiously. "Are you, like, planning to just dump me at the hospital and shove off? I guess I couldn't blame you if you were."

"No, I wouldn't do that," Luz replied, shaking her head, though in truth the thought had briefly crossed her mind.

"Thanks, Luz." Ofelia's voice was very small.

Luz's fatigue hit her like a brick wall. She mopped her face with her hands and tried to come up with a solution to this new problem—and it was an enormous problem—but her brain felt like it was made of cotton. Why was this problem hers? she asked herself for the tenth time. And for the tenth time she told herself the answer. She had inherited the responsibility for Ofelia the moment she'd agreed to take her along on her journey.

"Okay," she began slowly. "First thing you need to do is get checked out. There's got to be a hospital or clinic we can go to in St. Louis."

Ofelia swung her head around to peer out the window, squinting as though searching for something to identify on the horizon. "Is that where we are? St. Louis?"

"Pretty close. Why? Do you know someone there?"

"Not in St. Louis. Near Kansas City. That's not too far."

"Who?" Luz asked with hope.

"My aunt."

"Wait," Luz said. It took her a minute to process the startling admission. "You have an aunt in Kansas City?"

"My *tía* Luisa, the aunt I told you about. She lives in Lawrence."

"Why didn't you ask me to take you there in the first place?"

Ofelia picked at her nail. "I wanted to make it to Mexico, to be with my mother when the baby comes." She looked up and her face was without guile, easy to read. "I know you lost your *abuela*. I know you want to bring her ashes home and you want to be with your family. After everything that's happened, I guess I wanted that, too."

Luz thought of how lonely and frightened Ofelia must be now that she was on the verge of giving birth. She couldn't even imagine how much Ofelia must want to be close to her mother. "I only wish I could take you all the way to Mexico."

Ofelia reached out to pat her arm. "Hey, girl. You've done plenty."

"Right now, I just want to get you to Lawrence before the baby comes. How far is Lawrence from St. Louis?"

Ofelia grimaced as she rubbed her back again. "Not too far. It's a straight shot from here to Kansas City and from there, I dunno, maybe an hour more. If you take me there, I'm sure she'd take us in. We could spend the night, get some food. I mean, she has to. She's family, right? You could leave me there and I'll be out of your hair."

Luz felt her shoulders sag with relief. "I don't want you out of my hair. I just don't want your baby born in my car, silly." With one hand steering the car, she reached far into the backseat, blindly rummaging through bottles of water, trail mix, and an umbrella to pull maps out of her canvas bag. Ofelia spread the map of the United States over her lap and found St. Louis. She traced west to find Kansas City. Just like she'd said, it looked to be a straight shot down I-70.

"I don't think it'll take more than four hours, plus however much extra time it's going to take to find your aunt's place." Luz looked anxiously at Ofelia. "Can you make it?"

Ofelia nodded. "I'll make it. Can you?"

Luz exhaled and thought to herself that with lots of coffee, she could make it, too. She had to try. Ofelia's aunt was a lifeline. At least now they had someplace to go.

"Try to rest," she told Ofelia, whose lids were drooping again. She was still in obvious discomfort. "Do you want anything? Should I stop at the next exit?"

"I just want to sleep."

"I'll wake you when we get near Kansas City."

Ofelia obliged, tugging the voluminous coat up over her shoulders and curling against the pillow. It wasn't long before Luz heard the soft, guttural sound of her snoring.

Narrow shafts of pale yellow and pink light stretched across the sky, brightening the horizon and revealing the vast, rolling farmland of southern Illinois. Luz thought of Ofelia's desire to be with her mother, and her thoughts drifted to her own mother, as they often did when she let her mind wander. Was it possible that Mariposa felt like Ofelia did when she found herself pregnant and abandoned with only very little money? Mariposa had been eighteen, like Ofelia. Still a girl, yet about to become a mother. And her father . . . All she knew about him was that he was a German student studying in Mexico when Mariposa met him. They'd run off together and soon after, Mariposa discovered she was pregnant. Did they even talk about getting married? Or did her father simply do the cowardly thing and run off? What name fits a man who would leave a girl pregnant and penniless in a foreign country, utterly alone? Luz was ashamed to be the daughter of such a man. Would Ofelia's child feel a similar humiliation?

A new thought dawned as Luz's fingers tapped on the wheel. Was it possible that her mother had been physically abused, too? What if her father hadn't just abandoned her? What if he'd beaten her mother, and she'd fled, like Ofelia?

It could have happened like that. It would explain why her grandmother came running. Abuela would never have told Luz such a story about her mother. She'd only told stories of how clever and beautiful Mariposa was. Until the day before she died . . . Abuela had been intent on taking this trip with her. Luz now knew that Abuela had planned to tell her the truths about her mother that Luz, now an adult, could accept. *There is much you don't know about Mariposa.*

Now she might never know the truth. The only hope she had was to find her *tía* Maria.

The early hours after dawn were always a time of hope for Luz. The sun was an enormous red ball in the gray sky hovering over miles of shadowy fields. Luz yawned and looked out over the highway that stretched long and flat for miles. She was beginning to see life as a long highway with a series of stops. She hadn't made many choices before, but now she was in the driver's seat. She saw the road with a new perspective. What the stops were in the future, she didn't know yet. But in her heart, she knew they would be important.

Eight

How do the great-great-grandchildren of the butterflies find the overwintering sites each year? Is it instinct? Genetic memory? The mother-daughter cell? How their homing system works is one of the many unanswered questions in the butterfly world.

A woman in a pale suede jacket sat astride the palomino horse, overlooking a vast expanse of rolling hills and valley. She sat very still, closing her eyes in concentration as the wind whistled, rattling the leaves of the trees and rippling her black hair like waves down her back. She shivered and, tilting her head, leaned forward in her saddle.

"Mariposa? Is something wrong?"

She startled at the sound of Sam's voice and jerked back on the reins. Her concentration snapped and her horse snorted and tugged at the bit. She loosened the reins and steadied herself in the saddle. She'd thought she'd heard someone calling out to her. Of course it was her imagination, or perhaps a bird call carried in the wind. But sometimes, out here in the hill country of Texas where the horizon was so vast that the line between earth and heaven seemed to blend, the line between what was real and surreal grew fuzzy, too.

"No," she replied, her eyes on her horse's long, golden mane. "I'm fine."

She heard the crunching of hooves in the rocky soil as he rode closer. Her hands tensed on the reins, causing her horse to paw the ground. Mariposa settled her, then looked up to see the distinctive black and white rounded markings of Sam's Texas Paint, Tank, as it halted beside her more delicate palomino. Sam Morningstar loomed over his large quarter horse, sitting like he was molded to the saddle. He reached up to tip back his cowboy hat, revealing a proud face the golden color of the Texas prairie grass. Moisture beaded his broad, tanned forehead and soaked the edges of the thick, black hair that framed his face.

"Well," he began in his slow drawl. The leather from his saddle creaked as he leaned toward her and searched her face with his piercing dark eyes. "Your horse doesn't seem to agree. She says you're nervous about something." A slow smile added another crease to his leathery skin. "And I've never known a horse to lie."

Mariposa released a shaky, reluctant smile. There was no use arguing with him. She could lie to Sam, but she couldn't lie to her horse. Opal was finely attuned to her emotions and sensed her disquiet. There were no secrets when Mariposa was on her back. On cue, her horse shook her head and her hooves struck the soil, raising dust. "Traitor," she murmured with affection as she reached down to gently pat the palomino's neck. "I'm okay. I can handle her," she said to Sam.

"I know you can. But I don't want you to feel spooked. We can wait a while, if you need time. We're in no hurry."

She slanted a look at Sam Morningstar. He owned this 140-acre ranch on which he raised his prize Texas Paint quarter horses. She'd come here for a year to do equine therapy, and after she finished, she continued taking riding lessons from Sam. He wasn't her therapist, a point he was clear to make from their first session.

Sam had told her that he was simply someone who wanted to help her connect with the "four-leggeds" and the energy that surrounds them, so that in time she could connect again with the "two-leggeds." He'd laughed and referred to himself as a "six-legged," as ancient warriors of his Native American tribe were called because they were so connected to their horses. In the past year, Sam and Mariposa had become more than teacher and student. She didn't know quite what to call their connection, but it was at least friendship.

Mariposa thought it fitting that Sam raised horses, since he was a lot like them. He didn't talk much, and he was alert to body movements—especially the language of the eyes. He was watching her now, assessing her mood.

"I'm fine. Really."

"Okay, then. Let's follow the trail a while longer." Sam made a soft clucking noise with his tongue and his enormous Texas Paint began walking.

Mariposa settled in the saddle, then guided Opal to turn and follow Tank on the trail. In the past four months, Mariposa had developed a bond with Opal. During her first sessions she'd spent time grooming her, feeding her, and cleaning her stall. Sam said she had to learn the body language of a horse before she could put one boot into a stirrup. Now she rode with Sam through the rolling Texas Hill Country, and coming here was the highlight of her week. Everywhere she looked it was beautiful. Today the wind blew soft waves over hills exploding in golds, scarlets, and bronzes.

They rode in a companionable silence along a wide stone trail that wound around clumps of mesquite trees, pines, and rail fencing that held in pastures. The loudest sound was the crunch of gravel as hooves hit the ground in a steady gait. It was a perfect day for a ride—sixty degrees, breezy, and with a sky so bright it hurt to look at it without sunglasses. Not a single cloud dared to mar the vast blue, though she knew farmers and ranchers alike were praying for rain. Mariposa prayed, too, because the monarchs would be migrating through here soon and a good rain would guarantee a plethora of flowering plants for nectar.

She looked over at Sam. They'd been riding for almost an hour and he'd said nothing. He just kept on riding, Tank's hooves kicking up the dry earth in clouds of dust as Sam pointed out a deer or a turkey. Nothing seemed to be on his mind but the beautiful day. After a while the path split. One path led back to the ranch house and the barn where they'd say the usual perfunctory good-bye before he went to his next client and she returned Opal to her stall. The other path went north.

He surprised her by heading north. They climbed a steep hill, then rounded a bend, and suddenly, there was the lake. She sucked in her breath, captivated by the small body of crystalline water that reflected the sky, shining in the light like an aquamarine.

"We can sit and rest here a spell," said Sam.

He'd said "sit and rest," but what he really meant was *talk*. Sam wasn't nosy and didn't pry or ply her with questions like her therapist did, but he was good at finding out what he wanted to know.

Sam dismounted, then came to her side. She swung her leg around the saddle, then felt his large hands grip her hips and guide her to the ground. She tensed beneath his palms. No sooner did her boots hit the ground than Sam cleared his throat and dropped his hands. He took a few steps back, creating a respectful space between them. Mariposa's chest eased when he let go and she leaned a moment against Opal, pressing her palms against the damp hair, comforted by the heat emanating from Opal's body. She closed her eyes and breathed deep the heavy scent of sweat mingled with leather.

Mariposa was more skittish than a wild mustang and still tensed whenever touched. Three years in jail had taught her to keep rigid boundaries. She'd been out for two years but she still maintained a distance from most people. Truth was she preferred to be alone or in the company of critters. That was why when she finished her time at the rehab house and was offered a spot in a horse therapy group, she'd leaped at it. Horses were big, powerful animals, as definite about their boundaries as she was. There were no pretenses with them. When she entered their space they weren't concerned about what happened in her past. They lived only in the moment. They didn't ask for anything from her but to be calm and relaxed.

And her trust.

That was the hardest part. It had been a long time since she'd felt she could trust anyone or anything. Even herself. Especially herself. But she was trying hard to change all that. If she could learn to trust herself with horses, she hoped, in time, she could trust herself with people again. Mariposa had lived mute and guarded for too long. Sam—and Opal—were trying to help her open up. She had to, if she ever hoped to have a relationship with her daughter.

She straightened and stepped back from her horse, patting Opal's hide gently. She reached out to hand Opal's reins to Sam. With a nod, he took the reins and walked on ahead, guiding both horses across the scrubby grass to a cooler area of shade under a cropping of mesquite trees. Mariposa followed to join him at the intricately carved wood bench.

Sam eased down onto the bench with a low sigh and stretched his long legs out before him. He took off his hat and wiped his brow with his sleeve. Mariposa stole a glance at him. Sam was born on the Alabama-Coushatta reservation, and though he lived on his own place, his ancestral ties to the tribe ran deep. His profile was that of an eagle's, with his serious black eyes and proud, curved nose. His hair was the color of an eagle's wing, black interspersed with slender streaks of gray. It was thick and coarse and formed a ragged line over the edge of his pale blue denim.

Sam was more striking than handsome, not that she was interested in attractive men. She wasn't interested in men at all. She'd been celibate since she'd been released from jail, another line of defense, and she aimed to remain so. Sam was a good man of character, and in her experience, those were few and far between. She didn't want to screw up their relationship by crossing boundaries.

Sam patted his cowboy hat back on his head, then leaned back, stretching his long arms over the edge of the bench while he surveyed the lake with a proprietary air. "You ready to tell me what's troubling you?" he asked, his gaze on the lake. "You seemed a million miles away back there."

She held back her smile, not at all surprised that he'd hit his mark. "Not quite that far. More like a couple thousand."

"Ah," he said, turning his head to look at her, pinning her with his gaze. "You were thinking of your daughter."

"My mother."

"What's got you upset?"

She tilted her head. "You know I called her. Or, my sister did."

"I know."

"That was three weeks ago."

"Uh-huh."

Mariposa stiffened. "She hasn't called back! Not even to tell Maria that she doesn't want to see me. Or that she doesn't care about me and how I should leave her alone and never call again." She clenched her hands till the knuckles whitened. "Not that I'm worthy of anything more. But I'd hoped . . ." She stopped, taking a breath when her voice shook. "It hurts, Sam. Not a word!"

"Hold on now," he said, calming her rising voice. "Are you sure Maria even called your mother?"

Mariposa's brow furrowed in thought. She'd wondered the same thing herself. "She told me she did. She wouldn't lie. That's not Maria's style. She's very straightforward. If she says she will, she will. If she won't, she'll tell you that, too. To your face."

"But if I recollect correctly, you said you and your sister don't get along. That she was jealous of your relationship with your mother. Are you sure she wouldn't try to keep you and your mother apart by not calling?"

"First, she's my half sister. We were never close, that's true. But I don't think she hates me. Maria is a lot older than I am so we didn't grow up together. You couldn't say she knew me well enough to hate me. If she didn't like me, it was more a by-product of her ongoing war with my mother."

"Sounds to me like Maria has trouble getting along with a lot of people."

"Well," Mariposa said, choosing her words carefully, "let's just say Maria is very opinionated. But this goes way back. Maria didn't approve of my mother getting married again after her father died. I think she expected Mami to wear the long, black dress and shawl and remain celibate for the rest of her life. But Mami wasn't even forty when Luis died. She was still so young. Hardly ready to throw herself on the funeral pyre."

Sam looked down at his boots and smiled. "Hardly."

Mariposa half smiled at his retort. She was forty and guessed

109

Sam to be a few years older. Neither of them would consider themselves old—hardly! In fact, Mariposa was hoping she was still young enough for a new beginning.

"And what's more, my mother is a striking woman. She's small, but she looms large in personality. She has beautiful eyes, warm and inviting like melted chocolate. And her hair. You've never seen such long, thick hair. When I was little she'd let me brush it. I still remember the feel of it in my hands, like raw silk."

He watched her expressions as she talked as his own, hard-hewn features remained placid and impossible to read. But she saw his eagle eyes glimmer with interest.

"Do you enjoy talking about your mother?" he asked.

"Yes. I miss her terribly. She's very old-world and traditional. She cooks and gardens, skills she believes a woman should have. But that doesn't mean she's a dim bulb. Just the opposite. She was wise beyond her years—an old soul, I think it's called. And generous to a fault. Everyone who met her loved her."

"Including you."

She turned her head to smile at Sam. "Especially me. Anyway, it was only natural that someone with her zest for life would find love again. Hector Avila and my mother fell in love quite quickly and, from what I heard, quite passionately. But Maria didn't like Hector. He was a good, kind man. A professor at the university. So it was a step up for my mother. But I don't think Maria would've liked *el presidente* if he'd come calling. To her mind, no man measured up to her father. She had a fit when Mami married Hector. Then when I came along . . ."

Mariposa rolled her eyes. "I think even my parents were surprised when she got pregnant. Hector took us back to Mexico. They tried to convince Maria to join them but she was stubborn and refused to go. She stayed in San Antonio, married the boy she'd been dating, and that was that. I grew up in Morelia and never saw much of her. Only the obligatory family visit to San Antonio or when she'd come to Mexico. She was always critical of my mother and complained bitterly that she loved me best."

"Did she?"

A wry smile crossed Mariposa's face as memories rushed back. Maria hadn't been an attractive girl. She'd had her good points— her mother's beautiful hair and skin. But she also had her father's round, flat face and small, beady eyes that always reminded Mariposa of an armadillo and made her glad Luis was not *her* father. In contrast, Mariposa had been an exceptionally pretty child and grew into a beautiful young woman. Mariposa had discovered early how beauty gave her power over males. She'd been a terrible flirt, young and foolish, without a clue about the pain of heartbreak. That harsh lesson she'd learned later, and learned well.

"Did Mami love me best? I liked to think so." She leaned back and crossed her arms, remembering the fireworks between her mother and half sister that eventually fizzled out to cold noncommunication. "Their rift went deeper than that, though. Maria was furious when Mami came to Milwaukee to live with me. She felt it was selfish of me to ask her to come. But the truth is, I never did. I didn't have to. Mami just showed up when I needed her most."

"That's when you were pregnant?" Sam asked.

Mariposa tightened her lips and nodded, feeling suddenly the same shame now, so many years later, that she felt when her lover had skipped out on her, leaving her as if she were a pet he'd grown tired of and left by the side of the road.

"Mami never meant to live in Milwaukee permanently, just until I had the baby and was strong enough to travel. But she got a job as a cook at a nice restaurant and made good money, more than she ever could back home. She needed a job. She was a widow at this time. My father died a few months before."

Mariposa looked up at the sky. Soft, white cumulus clouds floated by like masts on a sailboat. She'd always wondered if her running away from college with Max had caused her father's sudden heart attack. Her mother said he'd been hurt, of course, but no, it wasn't her fault. Mariposa didn't believe her, and it was yet another guilt she'd have to carry.

"So she stayed," Sam prodded.

Mariposa looked back sharply. "Yes. Mami sold her house in Mexico and with that plus some money she'd saved, she bought a little house in Milwaukee for us to live in. Maria went through the roof. She'd wanted us to move to San Antonio. By staying in Milwaukee with me, I think she felt Mami took sides. Things fell apart between them."

"Maybe she felt abandoned," Sam said.

Mariposa's face clouded at the word, which elicited a world of guilt in her heart. She struggled to keep her voice even. "Maybe. I don't know . . ." She looked off in the distance. "It was a long time ago."

"But when you came out of rehab, when you felt ready to make that important first contact with family, you called your half sister, who you felt estranged from. Not your mother."

Mariposa nodded slowly.

"Why? Why not your mother, if you were close to her?"

"It's *because* I was so close to her," she exclaimed in a heated tone. She stood up and walked a few paces to stand beside the trunk of the nearest tree. "When I left, I hurt her. Badly. And it's been such a long time."

"How long? Fifteen years? Twenty?"

Shame shut her down. She felt the old coldness slide over her. Her face was impassive and her voice empty. "Sixteen. I left when my daughter was five."

"After all that time, why didn't you want to call her yourself?"

"I thought"—she felt her back stiffen and she turned to meet his gaze—"I hoped maybe it would come easier for her to hear from Maria first."

"To hear what?" Sam's dark eyes held hers, unyielding.

Mariposa looked down at her boots. They were scuffed and dusty and the heel was worn low. She said nothing.

"To hear that you were alive?"

Mariposa cracked. "Yes! Okay? Yes!" She turned her back to Sam, unable to face him. "She didn't know if I was alive or dead. I'd called a few times at first, just to let her know I was okay, but later I got in with a bad group. I . . . I couldn't call. Or write. After a while, I was too ashamed. I couldn't bring myself to tell her what I'd become. Better that she thought I was dead."

There was a long silence. Sam knew her history. Knew she got caught up in the world of drugs—using and selling. It was a vicious circle that was near impossible to break from without dying or being killed. For her, landing in jail turned out to be a blessing. Hard time and rehabilitation had led her to this moment of reconnection. But first she had to own her history. To accept it and talk about it. No more running or escapes. Sam wouldn't allow her to hide any longer in her silences.

"So," he said in a soothing voice, "it was easier for you to contact Maria because she meant less to you than your mother did."

Mariposa swallowed the emotion rising in her throat and shook her head. After a minute she said vacantly, "I didn't think of it that way. I don't try to make things easier for myself anymore. It just made sense to call Maria. She was here in San Antonio. I could talk to her face-to-face." She stopped, rubbing her arms in thought. "In a way, it was like a practice run. To see if I was strong enough."

"Strong enough to confront your mother."

Mariposa nodded and closed her eyes. "And my daughter."

There it was. Sam didn't have to reply because they both knew this was the crux of it. Her daughter, Luz.

"And are you? Strong enough?"

"I thought I was. Now I'm not so sure. Maybe it was too soon."

"But you met your sister. How did that go?"

Mariposa recalled the day she took the bus to Maria's house. She'd been extremely nervous. They'd only talked a bit on the phone, largely because Maria was shocked speechless to hear from her sister after so many years of thinking she was dead. Likewise, Mariposa was shocked to see Maria. The years had not been kind to her sister. Maria had gained a lot of weight after her divorce and her eyes were now gleaming slits in her face with dust-colored smudges beneath. But when she smiled her face lit up and they hugged spontaneously. Maria's fleshy arms held Mariposa tight and she smelled of vanilla, a scent reminiscent of their mother. In that moment all the disagreements of the past had dissipated into the ridiculous.

"It went well. She was kind and considerate. Gracious, even. I was surprised by that. She's divorced and her children have moved off. After all these years, after all our differences, we both ended up alone and in San Antonio." She shrugged in a manner that spoke of the irony of fate.

"So you asked her to call your mother for you," Sam said.

Mariposa took a breath and leaned against the tree trunk. "Yes.

And she did. Maria told me she called the next day. She said Mami had broken down in tears when she heard I was alive." Mariposa looked off at the lake. She couldn't think of that scene without getting choked up.

"What happened next?"

"Maria and my mother talked for only a few minutes more when they were interrupted by Luz coming in." Hearing the name of her daughter cross her own lips gave Mariposa pause. She pushed her hair from her face, feeling the moisture gathering at her brow and lip. "Mami didn't want Luz to find out about me like that, so suddenly and unprepared. So they got off the line quickly. She told Maria she'd call back."

Mariposa swung her head around. "But she never did! Why wouldn't my mother call back?" she demanded to know, straightening to stand with her fists at her sides. "Could she be so angry with me that she wouldn't want to see me again?"

"Yes," Sam said evenly.

Mariposa's eyes flashed with pain. Sam's calm suddenly infuriated her.

"You don't know her!" she shouted back at him. "You don't know anything!"

At the sound of Mariposa's high-pitched shouting, Opal immediately jerked up her head and eyed her with worry.

Once again, Sam gave her time to collect herself. She didn't look at him. She picked up a stone and tossed it into the lake. It made a soft, plopping noise as it fell into the water. Mariposa watched the ripples spread out, farther and farther. The effect was, she knew, like her decision to leave her daughter. She had to face the consequences of so many ripples from that one selfish, irrational decision.

"I'm sorry," she said, still facing the water. "I didn't mean to yell. I was taking out my frustrations on you. But you're wrong."

Sam didn't reply.

She looked over her shoulder at him. His face was as brown and weathered as a well-worn saddle. When he squinted in the sunlight, as he did now, long lines carved his skin from the corners of his eyes to his jaw.

"It's pretty here," she said calmly.

"Yep," Sam replied, his gaze shifting from her face to the lake beyond. "I do believe this is one of the prettiest spots in the Hill Country," he said without boasting.

A gust of wind stirred the dust around them and lifted the ends of Mariposa's long hair. She blinked and turned her head. Her attention was caught by the sight of a single monarch flapping its wings against the breeze to reach the blue sage a few yards away.

"Look!" she exclaimed, heartened. "A monarch!"

Sam turned his gaze to where she was pointing. "We should be getting a lot of them passing through soon."

She nodded.

He smiled. "That's right . . . you raise monarchs, don't you?"

"It's no big deal. It's just something I'm interested in."

"Your name . . . Mariposa. That means butterfly in Spanish, doesn't it?"

"Yes. So? You think that's why I like the butterflies?"

Sam smiled again. "Just curious, is all. Did your mother love butterflies, too?"

Her face softened at the memory. She could still see her mother in her mind's eye, out in her beloved garden, searching for caterpillars, bringing them indoors to raise in her habitats, teaching Mariposa how to clean the cages, watching with her the metamorphosis in wonder. Over the years she'd witnessed the cycle hundreds of times and never grew tired of it. "Oh, yes. She taught me everything I know about butterflies."

"Ah. The mother-daughter cells at work."

"The *what*?"

"The mother-daughter cells. Basic mitosis. Each time a cell divides, the mother cell passes on genetic material to the daughter cells."

"Are you implying I'm like my mother? I'm not a fraction of the woman my mother is."

"Don't be so sure. The cells are not exactly alike. It's complicated, and I'm sure I can't explain it very well. But I've always found the passing on of information from one generation to the next fascinating. A great mystery. Just look at the butterflies you're so fond of. If I remember correctly, in the spring the female monarch mates, then leaves the sanctuary to travel north, to right here in Texas. She lays her eggs on milkweed leaves, then dies. It's the next generation, the daughter, that follows the milkweed north to lay eggs again, then her daughter continues the cycle, leapfrogging north to repopulate. There's no map handed down, no powwow to discuss the plan. Just knowledge, instinct stored deep that guides the butterfly north. That's the mother-daughter cells at work." He looked off into the distance. "Nature is so beautiful."

Mariposa thought that somehow, the cells got screwed up in her. Where was the genetic link motivating her to love and care for her child? She couldn't bear to talk about anything that had to do with the connection between mothers and daughters. What was Sam doing with this mother-daughter cell discussion, anyway? Falling into an old habit, Mariposa put on a blank face and looked out at the lake.

Sam spoke again. "Why don't you try calling your mother yourself?" he asked. "Today?"

She shook her head brusquely.

"Why not?"

"For all your talk about genes, I'm not like my mother. I'm not that strong."

"Yes, you are. You've gone through rehab and stayed clean. That takes plenty of strength. And courage."

"Don't praise me, Sam. I can't bear it." Her voice was low and trembling as she fought for control.

"So now you're beating yourself up again?"

Her fragile hold on composure broke. "Sam, I let my mother and daughter think I was dead. I left my child!" she blurted, furious with herself for the tears burning in her eyes. "My little girl. She was only five years old and I left her for some man I can't even remember. He was just a link in a chain, who promised me a new life, away from the drudgery of the foundry and the machines. And the cold. I hated the cold."

"And, of course, there were the drugs."

He said the words plainly, with the cool precision of a surgeon, and they cut like a scalpel, leaving her raw and exposed. She turned to stare straight into his eyes. They were like two deep, dark pools of water, without judgment or condemnation. She wanted to shock him. To see his placid face stiffen with disgust. To make him hate her, like she deserved.

"Yeah, there were always drugs. That's how it was for me," she told him bitterly. "One man after another. One worse than the other. But I didn't care, as long as I got my fix." She felt so cold and rubbed her arms. She cast a sidelong glance at his face. He remained as impassive as stone.

"I hate myself for what I did. What kind of woman does that?"

"An addict."

Mariposa choked back a cry and put her face in her palms. "I'm so ashamed. I don't deserve to ask their forgiveness."

"That's in your past. Mariposa, you have to let the past go. It's a bad place of guilt and self-recrimination. You have to live for now. In the moment."

"I can't. I keep thinking of them. Wondering why she hasn't called back."

"What's so different today than three weeks ago when you made the decision to call your mother? You were ready to communicate."

"But they don't want to communicate with me!"

"You don't know that."

"Then why doesn't my mother call Maria back?"

"As you pointed out, I don't know her well enough to answer that. But you've put a lot on her shoulders. She's probably in shock, struggling with her emotions. And she needs time to prepare your daughter."

Her tears subsided as she took in this possibility. "Luz," Mariposa said in a soft voice. She sniffed and wiped her eyes. "Of course."

"Be patient, Mariposa. Have a little faith. They gave you sixteen years. Give them a few more weeks. Trust me. One way or the other, you'll hear from them."

Nine

Fat in the form of lipid proteins not only fuels the monarch's flight of one to three thousand miles, but it must last until the next spring when they begin the flight back north. As they migrate southward, monarchs stop to nectar, and they actually gain weight during the trip.

The sun was high in the sky on the fourth day of her journey. Luz had driven through St. Louis early in the morning when the sunshine sparkled on the gleaming glass skyscrapers. She'd gawked at the famous St. Louis arch, but as a midwestern girl, she got her biggest thrill from crossing the bridge over the mighty Mississippi River. She thought she and Ofelia were like Tom Sawyer and Huck Finn, on an adventure, riding the highway due west toward Kansas City.

The highway flattened into monotony soon after. While she drove seemingly endless miles, Luz figured she'd got maybe four hours of sleep before Ofelia telephoned the night before, and now she'd been driving for over seven hours. In the past three hours they'd stopped three times for Ofelia to pee while Luz chugged down Red Bulls and coffee.

She opened the window wider, hoping the air would help her stay awake, but the coolness of morning was replaced by warm humidity. Ofelia had moved to the backseat so she could stretch out, at least a little. Luz yawned loudly, wishing for the hundredth time that she had a radio to help keep her mind busy. She glanced at the passenger seat. Her copilot was a Chihuahua, curled up like a cat on the now soiled and wrinkled green satin coat.

"Ofelia?" Luz called to the back. She was feeling a little desperate to stay awake and hoped some conversation would help. "Are you awake?"

"Yeah."

"I'm sorry if the open window woke you up."

"The fresh air feels good. And it stinks in here."

Luz glanced in the rearview mirror. The backseat was littered with empty water bottles, wrinkled magazines, and candy and fast-food wrappers. Her attention was caught by Ofelia's fingers busily working over the box of ashes.

"What are you doing back there?"

There was a pause, then Ofelia replied, "I'm, uh, making a little surprise for you with your box of ashes."

"*What?*"

"Don't worry. It's nothing you can't undo. I just felt sorry for your *abuela* to have her ashes in such a plain cardboard box. It seemed, I dunno, sad."

There was an uncomfortable silence while Luz's face flamed. "I purposely didn't buy one of the more expensive urns or fancy boxes at the funeral home," she explained. "Not because I was cheap or anything. I decided to let my *tía* Maria pick out something nice in San Antonio. She's Abuela's daughter, and she didn't get to come to the funeral."

"She didn't come to her own mother's funeral?" Ofelia said in horror. "That's pretty lame."

"It wasn't her fault. She didn't know. I couldn't reach her. She must've moved or something because her old phone number was disconnected."

"Didn't you try information?"

"Of course I did," Luz said reprovingly.

"Well, I guess that's okay then."

"I just hope I find her."

After a pause Ofelia said, "Wait a minute. You mean you haven't found your aunt yet?"

"Not yet."

"What? Girl, you're on your way to see her, only she doesn't know you're coming?"

Luz shrugged. Ofelia spun off a string of words in Spanish that Luz was just as glad she couldn't understand.

"Don't get too worked up about it," Luz said. "We don't want that baby coming. Besides, when you think about it, it's not so different from what we're doing with you."

"You're crazy. Yes, it is."

"Oh? Did you reach your aunt yet?"

"No, but at least I got her number." Ofelia smiled weakly. "She's just not answering."

"Uh-huh," Luz drawled with a smug smile. Part of what endeared Ofelia to her was that they were both alone in the world. She peered again in the rearview mirror to see Ofelia plucking at string around the box. "So, what *are* you doing to that box?"

"I just thought . . . Well, in my village in Mexico, on the Day of the Dead we decorate the graves to show respect. It's my favorite holiday of the year. All over town there are special flower stands that sell *cempasuchitl.* Those are the bright orange marigolds we use for decorations. It's the favorite flower of the goddess

Xochiquetzal, the goddess of flowers. It's supposed to remind us that life, like the beautiful flowers, quickly fades."

"Where'd you get *those* marigolds?" Luz asked, looking at the four marigold heads that Ofelia was trying to attach to the box with twine. The petals were curling and tipped in brown.

"I found them at the last gas station. They were dying anyway." Ofelia looked up. When their gazes met in the mirror they burst out laughing. Ofelia returned to her craft, made a few adjustments, then lifted the box higher to show off her handiwork with obvious pride. "I don't have any tape so I used that twine you put on Serena. I just tied it around the box and stuck the flowers in. I'll tape it all down later, but it's pretty, isn't it? And look here. You said Abuela liked candy and McDonald's, so I took the breakfast muffin wrappers and my old candy wrappers and made little paper flowers." She plucked at the edges of one, then said, "It'll look better when I get some tape, of course."

"It looks . . ." Luz drifted off. It was so thoughtful of Ofelia. Luz thought the box covered with faded marigolds and fast-food wrapper flowers looked, if not exactly pretty, at least a lot better than a plain cardboard box. It looked *cared for*. Tears filled Luz's eyes.

"Oh, shit, Luz. I'm sorry. It's bad, isn't it? I should've asked you first before I started doing all this. It's your *abuela*, after all. Sometimes I act first and think later."

Luz sniffed and wiped her eyes with a hasty swipe. "No, it's not that. I like it. It's really nice. It's just . . . I should've done it myself."

Ofelia leaned forward to lay her hand on Luz's shoulder and offered her a consoling pat. "She knows you loved her."

Luz felt a big empty hole open up in her heart. Each day since Abuela's death, living was like walking a tightrope with no net.

As long as she kept her eyes straight ahead and didn't look down she did okay. But the minute she lost her step she fell into a vast nothingness. She felt swallowed up now and her voice shook as she spoke.

"I never did anything important for Abuela while she was alive to show her how much I loved her. I was such a kid. I took her being there for granted. That's a big part of why I'm making this trip. It's kind of a memorial to her."

"And this box will be her *ofrenda*."

"What's an *ofrenda*?"

"That's the special altar we build on the Day of the Dead for our family members who died. It's traditional. We put their favorite foods, *pan de muerto,* and drinks and things on the altar as offerings and decorate it with flowers so that when the spirits return to their homes, they'll feel welcomed. My *abuela* used to make the best chocolate cake for special occasions. So when she died my aunts made the recipe for her spirit. Only they made the cake look like a coffin."

"Isn't that kind of creepy?"

"No way! It's what we do. On the Day of the Dead everywhere you look you'll see coffins and skeletons and stuff like that. Not scary like Halloween. It's more respectful. It's a big deal and lasts for days. But every family is different. Every town is different. Some are solemn and some not so much." She laughed lightly at some private memory.

An *ofrenda* for Abuela, Luz thought. Her experiences in Chicago with Ofelia had given her a new appreciation for the Mexican culture—working in the restaurant, speaking the language. When she was a girl she'd studied hard at school to get good grades so that she could go to college. She embraced her American culture and distanced herself from her Mexican heritage. But when she was in trouble in the city, it was her Mexican culture that made her feel like she belonged.

"Abuela would love that I was making her an *ofrenda*. I never would've thought of it on my own. Thanks, Ofelia."

"You don't have to thank me. We're friends, and that's what friends do."

Luz kept her eyes on the road ahead, and her lips shifted into a watery smile. She may not have a family, but she had a friend. After all, friends were relatives you made for yourself.

Hidden Ponds was a jewel of a garden center. They drove over a small, gurgling river on a narrow wooden bridge, then past a wall of pine into a charming enclave of small, rough-hewn outbuildings. Luz parked in the gravel lot and climbed from the driver's seat, grateful and relieved to be out of the car at last. Her legs felt weak while she stretched her arms high over her head, yawning noisily. The sky was impossibly blue, with big, puffy white clouds like balls of cotton. Then she let her sleepy gaze sweep across the nursery. A slow smile spread across her face. This was more like a hidden garden from a time past than a retail nursery. In the distance she got a peek between late-season flowers of shimmering water from a pond. Hovering over them fluttered sweet, yellow sulfur butterflies. Luz felt astonished and even a little awestruck.

"Hey, *chica*! Give me a hand, will ya? I can't get out of here."

Luz hurried around the car and opened the passenger door. The dog leaped out first, made a beeline for a patch of grass, and commenced mad sniffing. Luz pushed forward the squeaky front seat and helped Ofelia through the cramped opening. It was like pushing the *Queen Mary* through the Holland Tunnel. First came her head of wild hair, which sprang open like an umbrella, followed by her belly, which seemed to be getting larger each time she squeezed out of the car.

"God, I'm so fat!" Ofelia put one hand on her back while she caught her breath and looked around, squinting in the sun.

The stark light revealed how the day-old bruise around her eye had become an angry, deep violet and yellow color. A row of thin Band-Aids that Luz had purchased at a gas station bound together a jagged wound that cut through her beautiful arched brow. Ofelia lay her hand on her belly in an absentminded gesture. Luz noticed a purplish band of skin circling her wrist like a bracelet and felt a renewed surge of protectiveness toward her friend.

Ofelia had changed into a clean maternity top trimmed with roses, more demure than the form-fitting hot pink top she wore to dinner the other night. Luz was wearing the same jeans and long-sleeved waffle Henley top she'd hurriedly put on at Las Damas racing to get to Ofelia's. Was that only last night? Luz wondered, stupefied by how long ago it felt. Ofelia pulled out a pair of mammoth sunglasses from her purse. They practically covered the upper half of her face. She'd purchased these, too, at one of the gas stations.

Ofelia slowly looked around. "This place hasn't changed much."

"No?" Luz said, looking out at the picture postcard. "And you left here because . . . ?"

Ofelia smirked. "I was seventeen."

Luz laughed and put her hands on her hips. "Well, it's really nice here. All those gardens and flowers."

"Do you know how much work it takes to care for all those beds of flowers? Huh? Well, I do. And let me tell you, it's lots."

"I'm guessing that had something to do with your leaving? Somehow I can't picture you gardening."

"I dunno. It was hard work, don't get me wrong. Bending over and pulling weeds, lifting plants—that's backbreaking labor. And we didn't get paid much. But honestly? No, that wasn't the reason." Ofelia sighed, and Luz imagined the expression in her eyes as she saw her lips purse in thought.

"There wasn't nothing for me if I stayed here. It wasn't exactly my dream job, you know? Plus my aunt and I were having trouble. I wanted to go out all the time with my friends and she had a new boyfriend. It didn't take a degree to figure out I was in the way. Besides, I was afraid I'd end up like my aunt, thirtysomething and divorced and lookin' old before my time. I was reading all those magazines—you know, like *Seventeen* and *Cosmo*—about what other girls were doing with their lives and I thought, Why not me? So I saved my money and as soon as I graduated I took the bus out."

"To Chicago."

"Yeah. Then I met Angel and . . ." Ofelia's face fell and she looked down at her belly. "When I left I was all about making something of myself, how I was too good for this place. And now I'm back and look at me. Pregnant and broke." She compressed her lips as her face contorted. "Angel was right. I'm such a loser."

"No, you're not. You can't listen to him. He's the loser!" Luz hated to see that Ofelia's usual fight had gone, leaving only this defeated shell.

"I'm scared."

"About what?"

Ofelia flipped her hands up in exasperation. "About what? Everything!" Then she added, more softly, "Seeing my aunt again after all this time—like this." She indicated her belly with her hand.

"She'll understand."

"This is a small town. It's not like Chicago. Here, this is a big scandal."

"Well," Luz sighed, her mind void of any bright new suggestions. They'd come to the end of the road. "Abuela told me that true courage comes from the heart. You're one of the bravest women I know. And your baby needs you now. So here we are."

"Here we are," Ofelia repeated, accepting that reality. "For now. Right?"

"Right."

Ofelia grimaced and put her hand on her back. Shaking her head, she said through clenched teeth, "And I'm glad we're here. The backaches are getting so bad."

"But I thought you said they'd gone away."

"I lied." Ofelia looked at Luz's face and rolled her eyes in acknowledgment of the frustration she saw there. "*Again.* I didn't want you to worry while you were driving."

"Ofelia!" Luz blurted out in frustration. When she thought of what could have happened! Luz realized there was no point in berating Ofelia now; she needed encouragement. Luz shook her head and held out her hands to stop any further pointless argument. "We're here now—thank God. That's all that matters. Let's find your aunt."

"This way," Ofelia said, leading toward a path that led through one of the gardens.

It was surreal following Ofelia, who moved as slow as an old crone, through this fairy-tale garden. All Luz could think was how much Abuela would've loved this place. She'd be out there now, looking for migrating monarchs. A small white Victorian house with a mother lode of gingerbread bric-a-brac was nestled in a prime spot in front of the lake. Ofelia told Luz this was where Mrs. Penfold, the owner, lived. But the house also served as the garden center's office. Luz followed Ofelia until they reached the stairs, then stood back. She was tired, wrinkled, and smelled of fast food. She didn't want to meet anyone.

Ofelia peeked in the front window to scope things out. She looked over her shoulder and said in a loud whisper, "I don't recognize the lady at the desk."

"What did you expect? It's been a few years. Go on. I got your back."

Ofelia reached up to tie back her wild hair. Her numerous colored bracelets jangled as she looped the elastic. Then she smoothed out her maternity top and took a breath to gather her confidence. She looked back at Luz. "Do I look okay? Maybe a little more lipstick?"

Luz didn't think a little lipstick was going to deflect from her obvious pregnancy. "You look fine."

"Okay." Then realizing that Luz was still standing at the bottom of the stairs, she made a furtive wave. "Well, come on!"

Luz groaned inwardly, then hurried up the stairs.

Inside, the house had the homeyness of an old Victorian, with its dark polished floors and tall ceilings with white, filigreed arches. The windows had elaborate floral curtains, complete with swags and jabots. The sweet scent of the beautiful arrangement of seasonal flowers on the front table mingled with the citrus smell of furniture polish. Like the gardens, the interior was immaculate and well maintained. The front rooms had been converted into offices with desks, computers, and filing cabinets.

A woman sitting at a polished desk glanced up when she heard them approach, her hands going still on the keyboard. Her hazel eyes narrowed, mildly surprised, maybe even a little annoyed at the interruption.

"Can I help you?" she asked.

They shuffled closer, feeling unsure. Luz figured the woman at the desk must never get out of the office, because her face was so pale. It was also devoid of any makeup. Her hair was sandy blond and fell in a blunt cut to her shoulders. Even her eyelashes were blond. Luz guessed she was somewhere in her thirties. She was dressed completely in beige, from her khakis to the crisply ironed long-sleeved shirt that bore the green insignia *Hidden Ponds Nursery*.

Ofelia nervously smoothed out her blouse again as she approached. "Uh, hi. I'm Ofelia Alvarez?" She said it like a question, maybe hoping the name would ring a bell. It didn't. The woman's gaze was impassive. "I'm looking for my aunt. She works here."

The woman reached for a black ledger and opened it with a crisp movement. "All right. What's her name?"

"Louisa Alvarez."

She frowned and began going through the names in the book, muttering, "Alvarez . . . Alvarez . . . Alvarez." When she looked up again, her face was blank. "Sorry, there is no Louisa Alvarez on our payroll."

Luz knew the tone of the "sorry" so well. It was the same tone used by the woman at the college admissions office who told her there was no scholarship money available. It was the same nuance of the bank loan officer when she went for a car loan. They said the word, but they weren't sorry at all.

Ofelia was stunned. "But she has to be!" She rushed closer to the woman's desk and began speaking louder, as if somehow that would make the woman understand better. "Her name's gotta be there. I spoke to her just six months ago. She's been working here for, I dunno, at least twenty years!"

"I've only been here since May," the woman replied, "and I don't know anyone by that name. She must've left just before I got here. Did you try her at home?"

Ofelia's face contorted like she was about to cry. "Where's Mrs. P? *She* knows her."

The woman tilted her head, her interest captured by the nickname. "Mrs. P?"

"Yeah. Mrs. Penfold. She owns the place."

"I know who Mrs. Penfold is. How do you know her?"

"I used to work here, too. My name's Ofelia Alvarez," she said again. "She'll know who I am."

The woman closed the ledger and folded her hands over it. "I'm Margaret Johnson, the general manager here. I replaced Lucinda Pfizer."

"Yeah, I knew Lucinda."

"I know the name of everyone who is currently working at the nursery and I don't know a Louisa Alvarez." She looked at Ofelia's crestfallen face and revealed a modicum of empathy. "But let me see if I can find Mrs. Penfold for you. Take a seat, please," she said, indicating the sofa as she rose. "I'll be right back."

Luz watched the slender young woman walk with straight-shouldered grace into the next room.

In contrast, Ofelia paced the floor, chewing her nails. "Ten to one she was a debutante somewhere," she muttered. "You could iron a shirt on her ass."

"How long do you think she'll be?"

Ofelia grimaced and rubbed her back. "Not long, I hope."

Luz's gaze moved to the plush burgundy sofa; she knew she'd fall asleep if she sat on it so she remained standing, staring in a blurry daze out the window. A few minutes later, the door opened and a heavyset, elderly woman in the same beige uniform strode in, wiping her hands with the dark green apron that she wore over generous hips. With her short, white, permed hair and glasses, Luz thought she looked like somebody's grandmother. She walked with the air of authority, and as she crossed the room her pale blue eyes were like searchlights. If she was a grandma, Luz amended, no kids pulled tricks on her.

Mrs. Penfold spotted Ofelia and her eyes widened with recognition. "My goodness! Ofelia . . . is that you?"

Ofelia seemed to fold into herself. "Hello, Mrs. Penfold. It's nice to see you again."

"My, my, my," Mrs. Penfold clucked, crossing the distance between them. She took hold of Ofelia's hands while her sharp gaze swept over her face. The cheeriness ebbed from her voice, filled now with compassion. "Dear girl, what's happened to your pretty face?"

Ofelia's face colored and she looked downward. "Oh, nothing. I just fell."

Mrs. Penfold's eyes narrowed and Luz could see she didn't buy it for a minute. She cast a quick glance at Margaret, who promptly retreated to her desk. Then she studied Luz and she smiled a quick acknowledgment.

"Come, sit down," she told Ofelia, taking her arm and guiding her to the sofa. To Luz she said over her shoulder, "Please, sit anywhere you like." Turning to face Ofelia, she said, "So, you're going to be a mother."

"Yes, ma'am."

Luz put her hands in her pockets and took a few steps closer, listening carefully.

"Does your aunt Louisa know?"

"Uh, no, ma'am. That's why I'm here. To tell her."

Confusion flickered across Mrs. Penfold's face. "But she doesn't work here anymore. I thought you'd know that. She got married, Ofelia. We had the wedding here; it was a lovely affair. Your aunt was closemouthed about your whereabouts and I have to admit, I was surprised that you didn't come."

"That's because I didn't know!" Ofelia brought her hand to her back and began rubbing it while shaking her head in consternation. "Oh, it's not her fault. It's my fault. I should've told her my address when I got to Chicago. I always meant to but I guess I never figured she'd ever leave here."

"Your aunt is a good woman. She deserves her bit of happiness and I don't begrudge her moving to Florida with her husband, though I miss her. She's in Jacksonville now." Mrs. Penfold looked across the room to Margaret, who was still listening from her desk. "Could you get that address for Ofelia?"

Luz brought her fingers up to rub her tired eyes as her stomach fell. Her address? God help her, what was she going to do now? Ofelia's aunt wasn't here anymore and it seemed she was being set up to drive Ofelia to Florida.

"Speaking of marriage, when did you get married, dear?"

"I, uh . . ." Her gaze shot to Luz in helpless appeal: What should I say? Luz couldn't help her on this one. She shrugged and her gaze replied, *You might as well tell her the truth. What have you got to lose now?* Ofelia mumbled, "I'm not married."

"Oh. I see." Mrs. Penfold's icy tone made it clear that she did, indeed, see the picture clearly and didn't approve. "Did you know the young man? You weren't, well, taken advantage of, were you?"

"What? Oh, no, nothing like that."

Mrs. Penfold tilted her head and looked at the bruises on Ofelia's face, her expression curious.

"He was my *novio*. We were supposed to get married," Ofelia confessed, shamefaced.

"But you left him."

Ofelia nodded.

Mrs. Penfold drew back and considered this, furrowing her brow. Then she straightened her shoulders and looked at Ofelia, mustering a sanctimonious air. "You know I don't approve of living in sin. The Bible is clear that even when the partners feel themselves united by a deep bond of love and intend to be married at some point in the future, it is forbidden."

Ofelia's eyes shot lightning bolts, but she held her lips as tight as her clenched hands in her lap. Then the older woman's face softened and a flicker of compassion glowed in her eyes.

"But if that man did to your face what I think he did, then I'm glad you did not marry him."

Ofelia's surprise turned into a choked cry and she slapped her hand over her mouth. Tears filled her eyes and she struggled to compose herself.

Mrs. Penfold appeared flustered by the spike in emotion but she rallied. Putting her hand on Ofelia's shoulder, she said, "You were just a teen when you left here. So young." She tsked. "You still are! And now you're going to be a mother." She raised her hand to gently graze Ofelia's bruised face. Hers was a gardener's hand, with short nails rimmed with dirt that wouldn't come out even after several scrubbings. "Are you okay, child? Have you seen a doctor?"

As though on cue, Ofelia bent over, her face grimacing in pain.

"What's the matter?" Mrs. Penfold said in alarm.

"Oy, these pains!" Ofelia cried, clutching Mrs. Penfold's forearms. "They're so bad!"

"Where are the pains?" Mrs. Penfold's voice became matter-of-fact and calm.

"In my back, down here," Ofelia answered, pointing to her lower back. "Then they move to the front, kinda like cramps."

"How long have you had them?"

"Since early this morning. They weren't so bad then, so Luz and I kept going, but that's why I came to see my aunt instead of going to Mexico, because we were worried that maybe the baby would come early and I needed someplace to go!" Ofelia was babbling hysterically.

"Since early this morning?" repeated Mrs. Penfold, and she showed her first real sign of emotion. "Good Lord, when is the baby due?"

Ofelia grimaced in another burst of pain.

Luz stepped closer. "She's not due for another month."

"Another month? We'll see about that," Mrs. Penfold said. "If these aren't labor pains I'll eat my hat. Margaret," she called out, all business again. "Call Tommy for my car. We've got to get this girl to the hospital."

"No!" exclaimed Ofelia. She panted heavily but her eyes were wild. "I don't have no insurance or money. I can't go there." Ofelia looked to Luz. "Do you think we could make it to Florida?"

Luz's mouth dropped open but no sound came out.

"Don't be ridiculous," Mrs. Penfold said. "You're not in a condition to go anywhere."

"But . . ."

"Child, you're one of the Hidden Ponds family and we take care of our own. Don't you worry one bit about money. You have more important things to worry about, like having that baby! If you are early and this baby wants to come, you need a doctor." She rose and took Ofelia's arm. "A young girl like you," she clucked. "Come along."

"I'm coming, too," Luz said, digging in her pockets for her keys.

Mrs. Penfold held out her hand. "You wait here, dear. It could be a while and you'll be more comfortable here than in some waiting room." Seeing the doubt in Luz's eyes, Mrs. Penfold smiled with motherly compassion. "Now, don't you worry about your friend. I've known Ofelia since she was a little girl. I'm very fond of her and will take good care of her. I'll call you just as soon as we know anything. Besides, you look exhausted. Margaret will make you comfortable." Mrs. Penfold looked across the room. "Won't you, Margaret?" She put her arm around Ofelia, the discussion settled. "Ready?"

Ofelia stopped in front of Luz. Her black eye made her face even paler as she mustered a weak smile. "Don't worry, I'll be okay. But could you do me a huge favor?"

"Sure," Luz replied instantly. At that moment Luz would have done anything for her.

"Take care of Serena?"

Luz held back her groan. Anything but that, she thought. "Of course," she replied.

The heavy silence in the room after Ofelia left with Mrs. Penfold wore on Luz like a heavy, uncomfortable blanket. Margaret stood at the door, watching until the car taking Mrs. Penfold and Ofelia to the hospital drove off.

"Just what the world needs," Margaret muttered, closing the door. "Another child brought into the world without a father and no means of support."

Luz blinked in a sleepy stupor as the words fought through her sluggish brain. Did she hear right? She turned to face the slim, well-heeled woman.

"Excuse me, but do you even know what my friend just went through?"

Margaret appeared surprised by the question, or by the attitude. She crossed her arms and said, "But she put herself in that position, didn't she? The one I'm worried about is that poor baby. People will call it a bastard. It won't be easy for either of them."

"Don't worry about them," Luz shot back. "They'll be fine. A whole lot better than if she married that son of a bitch. Do you think being married would've stopped him from pounding her with his fists?"

Margaret started to respond, but hesitated. She closed her mouth and shook her head in remorse. "I'm sorry. She's your friend. I shouldn't have said those things."

"No. You shouldn't have. You shouldn't talk about things you know nothing about." Luz turned on her heel and stormed out of the house, trying to escape the dark cloud that seemed to follow her no matter how fast she walked with her hands clenched in her pockets. The heels of her boots left indentations in the soft gravel as she rounded the tall hedge. At last she saw her sweet, funny little VW Bug parked in the shade. She could hear Serena barking, and as she drew near, she saw her paws at the window. Luz opened the door and pushed the front seat forward to reach for the dog. Serena crouched back, her head ducked and eyes bulging. Luz paused, hand in the air. She'd never meant to frighten the little dog.

"You're so ferocious for something so small." She softened and patted the dog's head using only her fingertips. Serena shivered so violently that her body shook. Luz stroked her thin body, feeling the delicate ribs and spine. Then, in a soft, gentling voice, she said, "You don't know what's going on, do you? Your whole life's been turned upside down. All of a sudden you get grabbed by a stranger, tossed out of your house, and the next thing you know you're driving somewhere, you don't know where." Luz gave the dog a wry smile. "You know what, Serena? I know just how you feel."

On impulse, she bent to kiss the dog's head, surprised when Serena licked her face. "I think we just bonded," she said with a soft chuckle, scratching under the dog's chin. "Let's take you out, okay?"

She picked up the dog and carried it out into the fresh midday air, then walked Serena to a patch of grass and waited. The tiny dog was staring up at her, one paw lifted in question. Luz released a short laugh that changed into a sob as she bent to pick up the dog. She pressed her face against the soft fur of her back.

"I want to curl up on the backseat of the car with you and cry myself to sleep," she murmured. What was she doing here? She didn't want to take care of Ofelia and her dog. She wasn't sure she could take care of herself.

Luz gently set Serena in the backseat and climbed in after her, scooping up Ofelia's candy wrappers and empty cups into a plastic garbage bag. She cracked the windows open to allow the cool breeze to clear the stale air of the car. Serena was so happy for the company she was jumping all over her, excitedly licking her face and making growly, whimpering noises that sounded like she was talking. Luz's heart melted at the dog's unconditional love when she needed it so badly. She blamed the heaviness she felt in her heart on exhaustion, but she knew the source went deeper. She fluffed up the pillow and curled up with Serena lying in the curve of her belly, her hand resting on the box of Abuela's ashes on the floor.

She desperately needed to sleep. But no matter how tightly she closed her eyes, her mind refused to back away from the words Margaret had flung out so carelessly. One in particular: *bastard.*

Luz had a happy enough childhood. Abuela made her feel loved and the home secure. Yet she always sensed that she wasn't like the other kids at school. Being a child, she blithely assumed it was because her mother had died. But hearing those words this afternoon brought back a memory she'd kept deeply hidden. She was young, no older than ten. Boys from the neighborhood, Luis with his buckteeth and Carlos, a fat boy who always had candy in his pockets, had pointed at her and called out in jeering singsong, "We know what you are. You're a *bastarda.*"

Luz hadn't known what the word meant, so when she came home she sneaked Abuela's English dictionary to her room and closed the door. There were several definitions, and each of them began with the phrase "an offensive term." Shaking, her index finger traced the words as her mouth formed them, sounding the big ones out. When Luz closed the dictionary she knew why the boys had singled her out and not Maria Elena or Carmen.

Abuela had told Luz that her father had left her and her mother before she was born, but Luz knew lots of kids whose parents were separated or divorced. She knew that her mother had died, but everybody knew there was no shame or blame in dying. But that day had been the first time she'd comprehended that her parents were not married.

Offensive term. The phrase clawed its way into her child's heart, scarring it. She hadn't known before then that words had the power to hurt so badly. Those mean boys had rubbed her nose in the word *bastarda* until it had burrowed into her soul. Bad. Dirty. She'd shivered deep in her tummy knowing somehow she was tainted by it.

Weeks later, Luz found the nerve to tell her grandmother about it. She'd been sitting in her favorite easy chair in the living room, a pair of long knitting needles click-clacking as she watched television. Abuela's needles went still. Then she set her knitting on the table, picked up the remote and turned off the television. Her dark brown eyes peered into Luz's pale ones like she was rummaging through her brain, sorting bits of hurt and pain that she could clear away, like debris. Then Abuela gathered Luz in her lap. Luz rested her head against Abuela's breasts. Abuela's voice resonated with fierce love as she spoke to her granddaughter.

Querida, *do you remember how, a few weeks ago, you called me to come hurry and see a chrysalis that had a strange string coming out of it? You knew something was wrong.* ¿Te acuerdas?

Luz nodded her head. I remember.

All chrysalises are beautiful when they are formed. Each is bright and green like a piece of jade with those pretty gold dots. God's own jewelry, eh? But sadly, once in a while a tiny parasite is planted into the caterpillar before it becomes a chrysalis. It is a bad seed that lies in wait until the caterpillar changes into the chrysalis. The poor infected chrysalis is not as smooth and green as the others. It grows brown and mottled, like rotten fruit. This tiny parasite grows until it kills the butterfly before it ever has the chance to fly. Only the lowly worm of the thief tachinid fly emerges.

Mi hija, *all your life there will be those who will seek to hurt you by planting the evil of mean words and cruelty into your heart. Those words are like the parasites. They have the power to destroy all that is beautiful in you. If you let them. But you are strong, my sweet young caterpillar! You will grow and grow and someday you will become a bright and shiny chrysalis, and from that you will emerge a beautiful butterfly.* Yo prometo. *Like your mother before you.*

You remember how we threw that foul larvae of the fly away, eh? That is what you must do. You must discard that horrible word from your mind and not let it fester.

Abuela never brought the topic up again and neither had Luz thought of it. Until today. She felt she was peeling an onion and her eyes began to sting and water. The fact that she was illegitimate was no big deal, her mind told her. That word was archaic, watered down by time and tolerance. It didn't define her. Nor would it define Ofelia's sweet baby when he or she was born.

Why, then, did the word have the power to make her curl up in her cocoon of a car, shivering like she did that day thirteen years earlier?

Ten

Monarchs begin their epic journey as individual butterflies. They are joined by tens, hundreds, thousands, and tens of thousands of other monarchs, all traveling to the same destination. During the day they feast on nectar from favorite flowers, and at night when the light fades and temperatures drop, they roost close together in trees.

Waking to her face being licked was a new experience for Luz. Prying open an eye, she saw two large ears fanning out from a fawn-colored head like butterfly wings. She turned her face from the velvety tongue and moved Serena off her.

"Okay, that's enough kisses. No more. I'm awake!"

Yawning, she raised herself up on her elbows, moving slowly as her muscles complained from being too long in the same position. She mopped her face with her hands, then looked out the window. The sun was beginning its descent in the west. Glancing at her watch, she discovered she'd slept hard, two, maybe three hours. Her mouth felt stale and her head groggy, like she could sleep another eight hours. She needed some fresh air. Stepping outside the car, she noted the dropping temperature and reached for her jacket.

"Come on, Serena. Want to go for a walk?"

She reattached the slender rope to Serena's collar and the two took off along the gravel path. Serena trotted by her side like a filly, her slender legs strutting out before her, delighted to be out of the car on the walk. Caterpillars were the closest thing to a pet she'd ever had. Luz had never known how a skinny, bad-breathed, big-eared dog could help fill the void left by her grandmother.

As she walked through the maze of nurseries, a small burst of orange in the air caught Luz's attention. She stopped short and, swinging her head, spotted a monarch in a dizzying flight pattern. With a start, she spotted another. And another two flying high in the air. Picking up the pace, she and Serena followed them down the narrow path.

In a breath, the path opened to a great field of alfalfa that rolled over hills as far as she could see. She stood facing the vista, feeling the country breeze on her cheeks and drinking in the sight. Again she spotted familiar bits of bright orange floating over the field, monarchs sipping the last nectar of the day before the sunset. She raised her hand like a visor over her eyes and, squinting, she spied several butterflies flying toward a single cluster of trees that sat smack in the middle of the field.

"Come on, Serena," she said with a gentle tug. Her heart pounding with excitement, she took off after them.

The great oaks stood in a majestic cluster, their thick yet graceful branches intertwined, like giant goddesses in a prayer circle. Luz felt a sense of awe as she approached them. She'd heard stories of farmers who knew about certain trees that were sacred and that should never be cut. Driving across the midwestern countryside, from time to time Luz spied a small cluster of trees in the middle of a plowed field and wondered.

Luz slowed her pace as she approached these holy trees.

Stepping under the canopy of entwined limbs she sucked in her breath. Abuela had told her about such things, but Luz had never seen it, nor could she have ever imagined it. She felt like she was walking into a cathedral. She walked slowly, on tiptoe, trying not to make a noise to disturb the settling butterflies. Even Serena appeared hushed and watchful, her ears high and alert.

Nestled in the protective embrace of the mother trees were several hundred monarch butterflies. They clustered close, roosting side by side with their paper-thin wings closed tight, appearing as countless gray-brown leaves on the branches. When a new monarch fluttered in and jockeyed for position on the crowded branch, wings fluttered, revealing bursts of fiery orange color as the others made space.

"So many . . . ," she breathed. Who knew where they all came from? Perhaps one came from Abuela's garden, all the way from Milwaukee. Luz smiled at that possibility.

"Hey there!"

Luz's heart leaped to her throat at the sound of a man's voice. Serena erupted in a warning bark, her small back coiling in alarm. A rush of wings fluttered around her as a hundred butterflies swooped like bats. Luz swung down to scoop up her growling dog, then turned to see a tall, slender man approach. He was dressed in worn field pants, a brown shirt with pens in the pocket and rolled-up sleeves that exposed long, tanned arms, and a faded, broad-brimmed hat. On his back he carried a knapsack, and in his hands a butterfly net. Seeing the net, she relaxed her guard. It signaled a purpose for his being here. And Luz didn't imagine she'd be attacked by a man with a butterfly net.

He approached slowly, his arms swinging in an easy gait, careful not to spook her or the butterflies. As he drew near, he nodded his head in friendly greeting.

Luz saw he had the long, thoughtful face of a scholar and the weathered tan of a man who spent many hours in the sun. His hair was the color of the prairie grass surrounding them, his eyes of the Kansas sky overhead. His mustache and soul patch moved when he smiled.

"My name's Billy McCall," he began by way of introduction. "I'm a biologist with the University of Kansas. This is a favorite spot for me to tag butterflies. I didn't expect to find anyone here."

He tilted his head in a friendly manner but his eyes were shrewd as he took her measure. He was older than she, but not old. His boyish build and his white-blond hair made it hard to speculate, but she thought he was somewhere in his late thirties. Though he continued to smile, his look pinned her, asking her name and right to be at this place.

Luz pushed her hair from her face, acutely aware that it was as thick and tangled as the brush beneath the tree. She shifted her weight nervously and shushed Serena, who growled low in her throat. She hoped they weren't trespassing. "I'm Luz Avila," she answered. "I'm just visiting folks over at the Hidden Ponds Nursery. I saw the butterflies and followed them in here. I hope that's okay."

The corners of his mouth turned downward, indicating his uncertainty as he focused on Serena. "Sure. As long as your little dog there doesn't spook them."

"She won't," Luz replied. "But be careful not to spook her or she might bite *you*."

He gave a short laugh of disbelief, then looked over his shoulder at the setting sun. Shifting his weight, he swung his backpack to his arm. "If you don't mind," he said, walking past her, "I've got to tag a few more before dark."

Luz stepped out of his way, patting Serena to keep her from yapping. Billy approached the lower branches of the tree with the soft-footed stealth of a cat. He was slim but his shoulders were broad like a swimmer's.

She saw what he was after. At the base of a low-lying branch was a small cluster of butterflies. She held her breath as he stopped beneath the branch, motionless but alert. The cat was poised to pounce, she thought.

In a flash, Billy's arm shot out and the net swept over the limb. Luz squelched her yelp of surprise. Billy flipped his wrist neatly and stepped back, bringing the end of the net bag over the handle, closing off the wide mouth. Several butterflies fluttered off to a spot higher up in the leaves, but in the deep of his net, Luz could see at least five monarchs struggling to escape.

He used one hand to hold the net handle and with the other he removed a butterfly using his thumb and forefinger. She admired his speed and technique as he worked with a single-minded focus, as though she weren't even there. Luz's mouth dropped open in a silent gasp when he placed the wings between his lips, reached into his left pocket, and pulled out a glassine envelope. Then he removed the butterfly from his mouth and tucked it neatly into the envelope. He repeated this over and over until all the butterflies were neatly placed in envelopes and stored in the canvas pouch he carried at his side. When he was finished with all five, his eyes searched more of the branches.

"What are you doing with all those monarchs?" she dared to ask.

"What, this?" he asked, indicating his pouch. "I'm tagging them," he said in a tone that implied it was obvious. He saw her face cloud with doubt, and a wry smile creased lines into the corners of his eyes. She figured he'd had lots of success with that lazy grin in his lifetime.

"I don't have time to tag them all now. That sun is fixing to set any minute. So I'll bring these guys home. Each one will get measured and weighed. I'll check out the condition of the wings, determine sex, and tag them. It'll take me an hour at least so I like to do it while watching a football game. I figure I've got over fifty in there. I've already tagged another hundred. It's been a good day."

He looked out over the field and pursed his lips in thought. "This is a prime spot for finding butterflies. One of the few left in these parts. Time was, there were fields like this all across the Midwest—wild butterfly meadows, fields of goldenrod—rich with diverse ecosystems that supported a few dozen species of butterflies. Not to mention all the bees. And now? Like the song says, they put up a parking lot." He paused and she sensed his sadness at the thought. "Every year, I come out to this field and hold my breath, praying it's still here."

"Doesn't it hurt them to put them in those envelopes?"

He shook his head. "Wouldn't do it if it did," he replied easily. "These envelopes protect them from hurting themselves fluttering their wings. I put them in my cooler and it calms them down, kind of like roosting here overnight. They lie all still in the dark, like they're asleep. In the morning I'll release them and they'll go on their merry way, hopefully all the way to Mexico."

"I never understood why you tag them. Their wings seem so fragile to put that sticker on them. Doesn't it slow them down?"

"Nope." He pulled out a sheet of Monarch Watch tags and

showed them to her. "See, these tags are ultralight. And the monarchs are amazing creatures. So fragile yet so strong. They don't have any problem with them. It's kind of like you wearing a shirt when you run. We tag them to get answers to a lot of questions we have about their migration patterns. How do they navigate? What markers do they use? There's a whole lot we don't know about these amazing bugs."

The passion for butterflies she heard in his voice appealed to her; that kind of devotion was attractive.

"So each year we tag them," Billy continued, "and if anyone finds a butterfly with a tag on it, they call in the number. So if, say, a butterfly from Nebraska or Maine made it to the sanctuary and somebody found the tag, it would help us learn more about them. And the more we learn, the more we can protect them and perpetuate the species. Hopefully we'll recover a lot of these tags this year."

She thought of the thousands of butterflies Abuela had raised and how she would have loved to have helped the likable Billy McCall with his study. "Is it hard to learn?"

"Not at all. I teach volunteers all the time." He tilted his head and his smile lifted one corner of his mouth, almost flirtatiously. "Want to tag one? That is, if your dog won't get in the way."

The offer surprised her. "Me? Sure. Wait, let me put her down." Luz settled Serena on the ground and tied the rope around a nearby shrub. To her relief, for once Serena was calm and obliging. Luz made a note to give her a treat later.

Billy walked to a low branch where a half dozen butterflies sat with their wings tightly closed, like sitting ducks. Once again he swooped and captured all six.

This time, Luz helped him bring the butterflies out from the net with her thumb and forefinger, enjoying the familiar feel of the tender wings. Billy showed her where to place the small white dot of paper and as she did so, he recorded the number on his sheet.

They stood so close that his cotton sleeve grazed hers; she felt a crackling tension and wondered if it was one-sided. She scolded herself for being foolish and told herself to concentrate on the delicate task at hand. She completed all six with a dexterity that surprised Billy. They continued to work side by side, Billy catching and Luz tagging and releasing as the sun lowered in the western sky.

She recalled Abuela telling her that if you whispered your wish to a butterfly, then released it, the butterfly would carry your wish to the heavens. So with each butterfly release, she sent her love to her grandmother on the monarch's wings.

In the next half hour they finished tagging all the butterflies that Billy captured.

"That makes another thirty-seven tagged, for a grand total of a hundred and forty-two today." He turned his head and looked at her quizzically. "You've done this before," he said, calling her bluff.

"No, really I haven't." Her lips twitched. "*But* I've handled butterflies before."

"Thought so. Where?"

"My grandmother raised them from the eggs she found on the milkweed in her garden. She taught the children in the neighborhood how to raise them, too, and all about metamorphosis. She believed if you taught a child about nature, you hooked them for life. I was her chief cook and bottle washer, so I've been handling caterpillars and butterflies all my life."

Billy raised his brows, impressed by this. "I don't hear that too often. Usually people are just so surprised to find out how interesting this little bug is, they want to learn more. And I'm happy to teach them. Like your grandmother."

He bent to gather his backpack while Luz untied Serena's rope and scooped her up in her arms so that she wouldn't have a hard time in the thick brush in the dark. As they walked, the sun lowered. Luz sensed that he was as aware of her presence as she was of his. He was a lot like Sully in his easygoing, midwestern manner, but he was completely different, too. Billy was an academic, like her grandfather, and she felt the tug and pull of a man completely secure in his career and intelligence.

"So, your grandmother raised butterflies," he said over the loud crunching of their boots on dry ground.

"Uh-huh. For as long as I've known her."

"It's great that your grandmother took the time to teach kids. I teach at the university, but I'm always out with kids at schools or helping them learn to tag. Kids get it. They're so eager to learn and help. They're the future."

"I think that's why Abuela did it, too. But it's also part of her culture. She was raised in Mexico in a village near where the monarchs migrate every year. Her family reveres the monarchs and welcomes their return."

He seemed to focus in on this. "Oh yeah? Where about?"

"It's a small town, I doubt you've heard of it."

"Try me."

"Angangueo."

He turned his head, a crooked grin on his face, and studied her with a look of bemusement. "No kidding? I'm heading that way later this week."

Luz didn't know whether this was just one of those weird coincidences you looked back on in life and knew it was meant to be, or karma. After all, how many people could be heading toward Angangueo?

"Talk about synchronicity," she said with a soft laugh. "So what takes you to Angangueo, of all places?"

"The monarchs, of course. Part of my job is to scout out the overwintering colonies to observe and catalog them. I love research and teaching, but I'm a field researcher at heart. Being in the mountains tracking the colonies, that's what I love to do most."

She could imagine him in the mountain forests tracking butterflies. A roaming scientist with his backpack and net, more a Dr. Livingston than an adventurer.

"Are you flying?"

"No, I'm driving. I have a lot of equipment."

She perked up at this, eager for a firsthand account of border crossing. "I heard it was dangerous to cross the borders now."

"Could be. But I've been doing this every year for the past ten, so I know my route pretty well and don't veer from it."

"Maybe I'll see you there," she added, throwing it out there like a challenge.

He cocked his head and skewered her with his eyes. "Don't tell me."

"Yep."

He chuckled incredulously and tugged at his mustache. "When are you heading out?"

"I'm on my way now, which was why I was curious about crossing the borders. I don't want to run into any banditos. This is just a stopover. I dropped off a friend who needed a ride but I have to get back on the road. I need to get there by the Day of the Dead."

"Are you traveling alone?"

"I hope not. My plan is to have my aunt go with me."

"That's good. Never a good idea to take a trip like that alone, you being a pretty girl and all. Just make sure your paperwork is in order, get your car insured, and stick to the main roads. You'll be fine."

Luz felt better getting encouragement from someone who'd actually driven the trip.

Billy looked off at the tree draped with monarchs. "I've been chasing butterflies for ten years and one thing I've learned is that what we call coincidence is more expected than unexpected. Many scientists and theologians believe that everything that occurs can be related to a prior cause or association. Look at all those monarchs," he said, lifting his arm to indicate the hundreds of monarchs hanging in dense masses, showing their dull gray underwings. "Each one sets out on this journey alone. Yet along the way it hooks up with other butterflies all heading in the same direction, to the same place, at the same time, forming a river of monarchs flowing across the sky. And at night, they cluster together in trees to form roosts like this."

"So you're saying that we're both here because we're both chasing monarchs, and it's not so weird that we met."

"Cause and effect. It decreases the odds."

Luz chuckled. "But not by much."

"No," he agreed, laughing. "There are millions of monarchs. And only you and me. But here we are."

You and me. Luz thought his comment rang with a vaguely intimate note.

"Maybe you called it right the first time," he said in conclusion. "Synchronicity. Life isn't a series of random events at all, but rather an expression of a deeper order." He smiled. "In other words, maybe we were meant to meet."

Her heart fluttered as she studied his face for signs of flirtatiousness. He simply smiled in that paradoxical manner of his she couldn't interpret. She doubted he meant anything by it, but she suddenly became aware that she was a young woman alone in a field out of shouting distance. And it was getting dark. She knew better than to be flirtatious under such circumstances, especially with a man she was clearly attracted to. Yet, despite the warnings her brain shot out, she didn't feel afraid of Billy McCall.

She looked down at Serena. She stared up at her, her eyes bulging from the sockets, a clear sign she was alert and ready to go.

"I guess we'll leave our meeting in Mexico to chance, then. Or coincidence."

Billy caught the signal in her voice and looked over his shoulder at the sky. The sun was slipping away, turning the sky the same brilliant orange of a monarch's wings.

"We'd better go. It's going to be a cold night. Those butterflies were smart to hunker down."

There was an awkward pause as they became silhouettes in the dark. She wondered if he'd ask for her phone number, or the address of where she'd be staying in Mexico. He didn't ask for either and she felt the stab of disappointment.

"Do you know your way out? I could walk you to your car."

Luz looked around her. She spied the peaked gable of Mrs. Penfold's roof over the purpling line of trees. "No, I'm okay. I'm just beyond those trees. And I've got Serena to protect me."

"Well, take care, Luz. I'll keep my eyes open for you when I get to Angangueo."

She smiled, girlishly grasping at the thread of encouragement. "Thanks for the tagging lesson."

"No thanks needed. I taught you for a reason. With your skills, I expect you to be out and tagging next fall. We need all the volunteers we can get."

That sounded to her ears like a tolerant teacher's admonishment of his smitten student. Luz's cheeks flamed and she blessed the darkness as she waved farewell, then turned and walked away from Billy McCall and the cluster of trees with Serena in her arms. She stole a quick glance over her shoulder. Billy walked in his easy gait in the opposite direction. She wondered if she'd ever see him again. She hoped she would. Probably wouldn't. Regardless, she'd never forget today.

As she walked out of the field, she reflected on how all the negative thoughts and despair she'd felt earlier had dissipated with the day's light. Butterflies always had the power to make her feel happy. Abuela used to tell her that it was impossible to be unhappy when a butterfly was in sight. She used to point out people to her in the park and say, *Look there! Watch them. See how people smile when they see a butterfly? They can't help themselves. Butterflies are joy with wings.*

Luz smiled at the memory as she walked. Crossing the field, she felt the scrape of the tall grass against her jeans and Serena's warmth in her arms. She heard the crunch of her own footfall in a silence that enveloped her. Night deepened around her. Yet in her heart she felt a small flame of joy that flickered bright and lit up her spirits as she made her way along the unfamiliar path.

Eleven

The weather presents many dangers for monarchs on their journey south. If it is too cold, they freeze and are unable to fly. Too hot, they get overheated and are unable to fly. Too much wind, they wait. If the butterflies linger in one place too long, they won't be able to complete the journey.

L uz's mind was filled with thoughts of Billy and butterflies as she walked Serena along the softer gravel path to the parking lot. She was surprised to see the silhouette of a woman standing beside her car. As she neared, the woman waved and called out.

"Luz? There you are! We've been looking for you!"

"Margaret?" Luz came closer and recognized the slim silhouette and pale hair of the general manager of the garden center. "I was just walking Serena in the field." Then she thought of Ofelia and her heart rate accelerated. "Is everything okay? How's Ofelia?"

"She's fine," Margaret replied in a reassuring tone. "They admitted her. Don't worry; they just want to keep her for observation."

"Can I go see her?"

"The doctors want her to rest. Mrs. Penfold stayed with her and got her settled. She said to tell you that Ofelia is sleeping and that we should all get some sleep."

Luz hesitated. Where was she going to spend the night?

Margaret must have noticed her uncertainty because she asked, "Do you have a place to stay?"

"Well, we came straight here. We'd expected to stay with Ofelia's aunt." She idly scratched her head, considering her options. "I'll figure something out. If worse comes to worst, I can always sleep in the car. Would it be okay, here in the lot?"

"Oh, no," Margaret replied. "It's not safe. I'm not even sure it's legal. There's a hotel near the hospital," she offered.

"Is it expensive?"

"A bit, yes. But there are lots of discount motels not too far away."

Luz nodded and brought her hand up to twirl a lock of hair. "Do they take dogs?"

Margaret looked down at Serena with a puzzled expression. "Can't she stay in the car for a night?"

Luz sighed with resignation. "I don't think so. She's so little and she's already gone through so many changes and I promised Ofelia I'd look after her. No, I couldn't. Hey," she said, "really, I don't mind sleeping in the car for one night and I'm pretty sure I won't get in trouble if you let me sleep in the lot."

Margaret shook her head, then released a short huff of annoyance. "I won't sleep a wink worrying about you out here, and Mrs. Penfold would have my head on a platter if I didn't take care of you. You can stay at my place. It's not far. I have a pullout sofa in the den you can sleep on." She looked at Serena. Imitating the Wicked Witch of the West, she added, "And your little dog, too."

"Thank you," Luz said, somewhat surprised, even stunned by the offer after the way Margaret had acted earlier. "That's really nice of you."

"Thank God you don't have a St. Bernard. Little dogs, little poops, right? But if she pees on my carpet . . ."

"I'll watch her," Luz promised, relieved beyond words she wouldn't have to sleep in the car. She lifted Serena into her arms to nestle her face against the fur of her neck, hiding her smile. Luz just knew the carpet would be beige.

The following morning Luz awoke to the grinding hum of a lawn mower outside her window. She yawned noisily and pushed back the comforter. Serena popped her head up, her large, round eyes questioning why Luz had disturbed her sleep.

The pullout sofa had a thin mattress on a weak frame of springs and it tilted downward at a dizzying angle. So Luz was surprised that she'd slept so well and had vivid dreams. They were mostly about Sully. She threw her arm over her eyes, grasping at wisps in her mind, but the dream was gone. She dragged her arm off her face and lay looking at the ceiling, filled with an aching longing. She'd tried to call Sully last night. She'd wanted to hear his voice because she'd felt a little guilty about flirting with Billy. But her phone battery was dead. She glanced over to the bedside table to see the phone plugged into the charger. She'd have to remember to call Sully before she got back on the road. She wanted to hear his voice, even if that voice told her to come back home. Truth was, every day she woke up wanting to do just that.

Serena whined and scratched at the door. Luz leaped after her and scooped her in her arms, terrified the dog would pee on the carpet. "You stay put and don't move a muscle," she ordered Serena while pointing a finger at her. Not taking her eyes off the dog for fear of an accident, she hurriedly slipped back into the jeans and top she'd worn the day before.

She slowly opened the den door and peeked out to see if the coast was clear. Morning light flowed in through Margaret's picture window, drenching her beige carpet, walls, and sofa. The sleek and modern room looked like what Luz imagined those girls in sexy heels in magazines lived in. Luz had always lived in rooms filled with color and memories. Bureaus overflowed with letters and papers, photographs cluttered desks, and religious icons adorned the walls. From the looks of the apartment, all of Margaret's interests and connections were neatly organized and boxed up, hidden from view.

Outside was more of the same. While Serena did her business, Luz peered out at the great expanse of uninterrupted lawn that stretched far out to a small man-made pond. A large rider mower was systematically cutting grass, back and forth, leaving parallel tracks across the green. Margaret's condominium was one of four identical three-story buildings that sat in cookie-cutter fashion overlooking the pond, unbroken by shade tree or flower bed. Luz found it bereft of any of the wild symmetry she'd seen in the prairie yesterday.

Once back inside the apartment she heard the tinkling of water from the faucet and dishes clanging. She followed the noise to the small kitchen with stainless steel appliances and granite counters. Margaret was standing at the sink wearing a long, white cotton robe and slippers. Her hair was damp and pulled back in a neat knot. Luz looked self-consciously down at her rumpled, worn clothes and felt like wadded-up tissue compared to all that freshness.

"Good morning!" Margaret exclaimed in a cheery voice. She

had a shiny silver teakettle in her hand. "I hope I didn't wake you. I'm an early riser. Always have been."

"Me, too," Luz mumbled, longing for a shower.

"You went out?"

"I took Serena for a walk first thing. I wanted to grab her bag of food and my toiletries. I, uh, would love a shower."

"Oh, of course. Help yourself. The bathroom is down the hall and I laid out a fresh towel."

"Thanks." Serena whimpered and looked at Luz meaningfully. "I'd better feed Serena first. Uh, Margaret, I hate to ask, but do you have an old bowl or cup you don't care about that I could use to feed Serena? We've been improvising with Styrofoam cups but it doesn't really do the job." Visions of shredded Styrofoam across the car floor flashed through her mind.

"I suppose," Margaret replied with reluctance. She reached into the cupboard and pulled out a plastic tub with a lid. She handed it to Luz. "Keep it."

While Luz fed the dog, Margaret pulled a china bowl from the cabinet, a spoon from a drawer, and a cloth napkin from another and placed them on a cheerful white mat trimmed with embroidered strawberries. Luz wondered if she was going an extra step for her, or if someone like Margaret used cloth napkins and place mats for breakfast every morning.

"I've got homemade granola," Margaret offered. "It's a specialty of mine so I think you'll like it." She put the tin on the table, then turned to open the fridge. Standing before the open door, she checked out the supplies and said, "There's yogurt, whole wheat bread for toast, peanut butter, milk—nonfat only, I'm afraid. And"—she pulled open the fruit and vegetable crisper—"some blueberries. I can make eggs if you like."

Luz hadn't had such an offering for breakfast since before Abuela died. Except Abuela had never cooked with whole grains or nonfat anything. Over Margaret's shoulder she stole a glimpse inside the fridge. It was sparkling clean. On the shelves—not overly stuffed or shoved in haphazardly—was a single row of frosty water bottles, a few wedges of cheese, jars of fancy jams, select condiments in the rack on the door, and Pyrex bowls with neatly written labels on the lids that showed the date. Luz felt an unexplainable desire for an organized fridge just like that one day.

"The granola sounds great, thanks. And maybe some berries. Please?" Luz added, remembering her manners. Then, feeling a throbbing in her skull, she asked, "Do you have any coffee?"

Margaret scrunched up her nose in distaste as she carried milk and cereal to the table. "No, sorry. I don't drink coffee. Or anything with caffeine. I'm making a nice pot of herbal tea. It's great with honey."

Luz smiled and nodded, but inside she groaned. She'd woken up to the smell of Abuela's dark, rich coffee all her life and started drinking it at age twelve with lots of warm milk, cinnamon, and sugar.

"You wouldn't happen to have any hot chocolate?" she asked hopefully.

"No, sorry. All that sugar . . ."

Resigned, Luz tied Serena to the leg of a chair and escaped to Margaret's immaculate white tiled bathroom. She took a quick but luxurious shower, then dressed in clean jeans and a soft white cotton sweater. Feeling more herself, she returned to the kitchen. Margaret was dressed in her uniform shirt and khakis and had pulled her hair back into a tight ponytail.

While they sipped herbal tea and ate, they tentatively exchanged general information about their places of birth, educations, and jobs. Margaret didn't seem the same cool and indifferent woman Luz had met at the office the day before. This morning, Margaret was warmer and, though not chatty, she'd let down her guard.

Luz learned that Margaret was not a pampered debutante. She'd graduated from the University of Kansas with a degree in horticulture, then went on to graduate school in business, all on her own. She accomplished this by working part-time and earning scholarships, plodding forward with dogged determination. After graduation, she worked for the university before she was offered the job at Hidden Ponds. Over the years she'd saved enough to make down payments on her own condo and car. Luz listened, hanging on to every word. That kind of independence spoke to Luz of a life she'd imagined for herself.

"Were you always interested in horticulture?" Luz asked.

Margaret nodded. "My father was an entomologist, and my mother taught science in elementary school. They taught me the scientific names of plants and insects from the get-go. How could I not love gardens?" She laughed lightly, her fingers tracing the edge of her cup. "Oxeye daisy were two of my first words."

"They must be very proud of you."

Margaret's face went still before she said, "My father is. My mother died before I graduated. I like to think she would be."

This one admission made Luz feel a bond with Margaret. Did the fact that both of them lost their mothers qualify for a sisterhood moment? Like discovering they both belonged to the same sorority or came from the same town? She felt this truth ran a deeper course and hinted at private emotions that couldn't be easily explained. It was akin to stealing a look into Margaret's fridge. What was inside was personal. It revealed secrets.

"I lost my mother, too," Luz told her.

Margaret's eyes went soft and Luz knew that she felt the bond, too. Margaret offered a small smile and asked, "How old were you when she died?"

"Five."

"Oh, so young."

"I hardly remember her."

"I'm sorry. I can't imagine. At least I had my mother for twenty-one years. I was a woman when she passed. But I still miss her." Margaret's smile was bittersweet. "Sometimes at the strangest moments I'll see or do something and think Mom would've liked that."

Luz tightened her grip on the cup. She'd never know what her mother might have liked. She didn't have even that much. "So, you must love it at Hidden Ponds, then," she said, clumsily changing the subject. "Being a horticulturalist and all. It's an amazing place."

"I do," Margaret replied, but her voice was tenuous and she looked out the window.

"I hear a *but* . . ."

Margaret held back a smile and poured herself more tea from the pretty floral china teapot. "But somehow I got stuck in the office. I'd always thought I'd end up in the nursery, experimenting, maybe testing new plants. Anything outdoors."

Margaret straightened in her chair, physically collecting herself as though she'd suddenly realized she'd divulged too much. "Don't get me wrong. It's a very good job," Margaret said with emphasis. "And Mrs. Penfold needs me. She's a wonderful woman and has the gift of a green thumb." She cleared her throat and added, "But she can be impulsive."

Luz thought of Abuela's words. "Impulsive?"

Margaret nodded. "Especially when it comes to spending. Look how she was with Ofelia. You know she's going to pick up the hospital bills, and help her get a start. No one knows better than me that she really can't afford it. She can't seem to help herself. I'll have to help her through the muddle she'll no doubt get herself in."

Luz sat back in her chair. The woman was able to turn on a switch that changed her personality from warm to frigid, she thought.

Seeing Luz's thunderous expression, Margaret rushed to add, "Not that it's Ofelia's fault, of course."

Luz swallowed the toast that seemed stuck in her throat. She waited a minute, letting the words digest. "You call Mrs. Penfold's giving impulsive." Then, envisioning Abuela's face, she smiled. "My grandmother would have called it kindness."

"Well, I . . ."

"Hey, I get what you're saying," Luz said. "Sometimes I'd get frustrated with Abuela, especially about how she gave so much of her time to the neighborhood children. Every summer she taught them how to hunt for the tiny butterfly eggs in her garden. She'd let them gather fresh milkweed leaves and feed the caterpillars. They'd hang around all summer, playing in the garden and begging for more cookies or juice. You know how kids are." She leaned back in her chair, remembering. "We never had two dimes to rub together. I was working at a job I hated and I'd get frustrated to come home and see her doling out more snacks I paid for when I didn't have money to go out for a beer. I sometimes complained we were running a summer camp.

"Abuela used to just smile at me in that wise-woman way she had and tell me kindness was like the sun and the rain. If you were miserly with it, your world would wither up. But the more you gave, the more you reaped. Well, at her funeral, I was surprised when a number of older boys—young men—came up to me to tell me those summers with La Dama Mariposa, that's what they called her, kept them from the streets." She paused, holding back a rush of emotion that again threatened tears. "Hearing those words were a revelation. They made me feel both contrite and grateful for all the years I had with Abuela." Her lips eased into a soft smile.

"So, I think that Mrs. Penfold is a lot like my grandmother. She's full of the sun and the rain. One look at her garden tells me all I ever need to know about her."

Margaret tightened her robe in silence and looked pensively out the window.

Luz gathered her napkin and dishes and rose to put them on the counter. "I guess I'd better gather my things and check on Ofelia. Breakfast was great. You were kind to take such good care of me. Thanks."

"So, where do you go from here?"

"Well," Luz said, leaning back against the counter, "after I see Ofelia, I'm off to San Antonio. And then, if all goes well, I'm continuing on to Mexico."

"Mexico?" Margaret said, surprised. "That's a long drive. Are you going to visit family?"

"Yes. My aunt lives in San Antonio. I'm hoping she'll come along to see the rest of the family in Michoacán. It's a long story, but there's a tradition in my family to greet the monarchs when they return to the mountains in the fall, around the Day of the Dead. My grandmother died recently, you see, so I want to be there when the monarchs arrive."

Margaret straightened and leaned forward with interest. "You're going to Michoacán?" she asked. "To see the sanctuaries?"

Luz was surprised she knew about the sanctuaries. "That's the plan."

Margaret seemed at a loss for words. "You're talking about the monarch sanctuaries? Up in the mountains?" When Luz nodded, Margaret's eyes danced with excitement and she set her elbows on the table, cupping her chin.

"I've read about them. And seen videos on television. I'm always so amazed that those fragile creatures can make such an amazing journey. Miraculous, really. I think I still have the *National Geographic* magazine my parents got back in the seventies when they first discovered the sanctuaries. It was a huge find; everybody was talking about it. Until then, nobody knew where the butterflies went."

"Except the villagers, of course," Luz added wryly.

"Well, yes. Of course. But not the scientific community," Margaret replied, and it was clear from her tone that in her opinion, this was the group that mattered. "My parents collected moths and butterflies. They had an impressive variety of species. For them, the discovery of the monarch sanctuaries in Michoacán was as exciting as Neil Armstrong's walk on the moon. They used to talk about all of us going to the sanctuaries one day. They even bought tents and sleeping bags and planned out the trip. It was our dream. My father is a typical German—he loves detail and outlined our adventure to the minutiae, even the clothes and equipment we'd need to pack. He especially loved the tiny flashlights, the compass, and, oh yes"—she chuckled softly—"the Swiss Army knives. He even designed our observation notebooks." She smiled at the memory.

Luz smiled, thinking to herself, *like father like daughter*.

"But we never made it."

Luz caught a flicker of regret in Margaret's eyes. "You still can go," she said.

"What? Oh, no. Dad's not well. He has a heart condition and would never make it to those high elevations. And of course, Mom . . ." She pinched her lips. Margaret picked up the teacup again. "No, we missed our chance," she said. Then she sighed and her face softened. "But imagine, seeing millions and millions of butterflies." She sipped her tea slowly, her eyes lost in thought. "You're lucky to be going."

"Hardly luck," Luz said. "I missed my chance to go with Abuela, too. I've had a lot of time to think in the car and one of the questions I've been preoccupied with is, How many people lose opportunities to spend time with loved ones before it is too late? Abuela and I talked about this trip for as long as I can remember. But we kept putting it off and putting it off. There was never enough time or money. And now . . ." She shrugged, feeling the weight of remorse in her shoulders. "Anyway, I'm going now. It might not be the way Abuela had planned the trip, but at least we're making it together."

Margaret's face turned wistful. "My mother used to tell me that we make our own luck." She set down her cup, rose, and wrapped her arms around Luz in a heartfelt hug. "I admire your courage," she told her.

Luz was surprised by the sincerity of the impulsive gesture. She felt Margaret's slender arms around her and hugged her back, feeling even more strongly that sisterly bond.

The moment was broken by the phone ringing. They both pulled back and looked at each other with wide eyes, thinking at the same time that it was news about Ofelia. Margaret dashed for the phone on the kitchen counter. Luz was right behind her.

"It's Mrs. Penfold," she mouthed, waving Luz closer. Holding the phone from her ear, she punched the speakerphone key. A second later, Mrs. Penfold's voice could be heard, ringing with excitement.

"Oh, my dears!" she exclaimed. "Tell Luz to come quick. Ofelia is having the baby!"

"Oh, Ofelia, she's beautiful. A perfect, pretty-in-pink darling!" Luz said, looking at the sweet innocence of the baby.

The hospital's birthing room was decorated in floral chintz, like a big, cozy bedroom. Ofelia lay in bed propped up against pillows, sipping ice water. She looked more herself this morning. Someone had given her a new pink cotton robe and she'd applied pink lipstick that made her smile a vision of glossy joy. Her happiness was so evident that it overshadowed the dark bruise around her eye.

"She is, isn't she?" Ofelia replied with pride. "*Ay,* Luz," she said dramatically. "I was so worried when they told me she was coming. I kept saying, 'No! It's too soon.' I was so afraid for her. But look at her! Here she is and the doctor—who's a saint, I tell you—she says she was only like two weeks early and that wasn't too much."

Luz tore her gaze from the baby to look at Ofelia. "But I thought you weren't due for another month!"

Ofelia shrugged with a smirk. "Yeah, well, my math was never too good."

Luz rolled her eyes and they both laughed at the absurdity of that statement. It felt good to laugh in a safe place with the baby born and healthy. "Hey, it doesn't matter," she replied. "We made it. Maybe you didn't get to Mexico, but this might be as far as you were meant to go. Karma and all that." She looked at the pink perfection of the infant's face. Then she walked to Ofelia and placed the swaddled baby in her arms. "I'd say you made it straight to heaven."

Ofelia took the baby in her arms hungrily. "Luz, thank you," she said in a softer voice. "I wouldn't be here, in this safe place, without you. All I ever wanted was a family. That's why I tried so hard to make it work with Angel. But there was nothing there. I was scared and trapped. You saved me, you know that? The first time I saw you I knew you were special. It must've been those crazy blue eyes of yours."

Luz chuckled but the words fell sweet on her ears. "You saved yourself."

"No, but I'll tell you this!" she said with typical Ofelia bravado. "I found my strength again when I laid eyes on my daughter. She's everything to me. I love her so much I want to eat her up. Now I know I have all I ever wanted. She *is* my family." Her dark eyes narrowed and she said in almost a snarl, "And I'll kill anyone who tries to hurt her."

Luz felt a tremor at hearing the ferociousness of a mother's love. "Abuela used to say that goddesses are everywhere. Looking at you, I see she was right."

Ofelia lowered her head to place a kiss on her infant's forehead. "All mothers are goddesses."

"She used to tell me a story about the goddess who became the mother of all things beautiful."

"Tell me that one," Ofelia said with a yawn, settling back against the pillows. The excitement of the morning was at war with her physical exhaustion. She shifted her weight to rest her arm on a pillow and cradled her baby. "Tell us both a story."

Luz relished the thought of taking on Abuela's role of storyteller.

She sat in the comfortable armchair beside Ofelia's bed, remembering how she used to listen to Abuela's melodic voice. She could paint a scene so vividly that the story would come alive in Luz's imagination. And there were so many stories.

Luz began her favorite, the tale of the two goddesses who sacrificed themselves for mankind. As she told of how Little Nana courageously jumped into the fire, she felt akin to the meek goddess who in the end exalted in glory for bringing light to the world. And when she embellished the details of Xochiquetzal's selfless decision to be the mother of all things to come, she felt her usual longing for her own mother, especially as she watched Ofelia cradle her infant daughter. Did my mother gaze at me in that way? Luz wondered.

When she was finished, she looked up. Ofelia's full mouth was turned down in a frown of confusion.

"Didn't you like it?" Luz asked.

"No, I love that story. It's one of my favorites, too," Ofelia replied. Then she shook her head. "But you got one part wrong. It wasn't Xochiquetzal who brought the flowers and butterflies to earth. It was Quetzalpapalotl."

Luz's cheeks flushed with indignation. "Abuela told me this story a million times."

Ofelia shook her head. "We learned all this Aztec culture stuff in school back in Mexico. Mexicans are really into insects, especially butterflies and moths. I get a lot of them mixed up but I remember *her* because she was kind of kinky. Xochiquetzal is the goddess of beauty and pleasure. She followed the warriors to the battlefields and made love to them at the moment of death—with a butterfly in her mouth. I mean, really. You don't forget something like that, right? It had something to do with her giving them courage and how, if they died, they'd go to her secret garden high in the mountains in the afterlife.

"Quetzalpapalotl is the god of butterflies. In fact, that's even the name the Aztecs gave the monarch butterflies. He has this bird-butterfly temple in Teotihuacán that I went to when I was a kid. It's really beautiful. You should go there when you're in Mexico."

Luz sat back in her chair and shook her head in confusion.

The baby made soft grunting noises that immediately riveted Ofelia's attention. Ofelia removed her from her swaddling, checked her diaper, then, finding it dry, clumsily tried to swaddle the baby again. After much mumbling and fumbling, Ofelia just wrapped up the baby any way she could and held her close. When she settled, Ofelia puffed a hair out of her face. She looked over at Luz and offered a mollifying grin.

"Hey, Luz, it's like a fairy tale, eh? Everyone changes a story a little for her own child. Maybe Abuela wanted you to have butterflies and goddesses. I like that better myself." She looked at her baby. "Don't you, *mi amor*?" Ofelia bent to kiss her baby's forehead. Then she laughed a tired laugh. "Besides, who can ever get those Aztec gods' names right? There's so many of them—fire, rain, flowers, sun, butterflies—Xochi this and Quetzal that."

Luz didn't reply. It was impossible to even consider that Abuela got her story wrong or that she would have deliberately changed it. But Ofelia seemed so sure.

The door opened and Margaret poked her head in. Her blond hair fell like water. She looked anxiously at Ofelia, then Luz. "Sorry to bother you. The nurse said we only have a few minutes before we have to leave. I was wondering, hoping rather . . . Can I see the baby?"

Luz felt a sudden chill in the room and glanced at Ofelia. It looked as if a cloud had darkened her brow. "Margaret let me stay with her last night," Luz told Ofelia, letting her know that things had changed.

"Oh yeah? That's nice. Uh, sure, come on in," Ofelia said, but her tone remained wary.

Margaret approached with hesitation, her gaze fixed on the baby. "She's so little," she said in an awestruck voice. "And so beautiful."

Ofelia's guard lowered and she smiled despite herself, turning her gaze to her daughter. "Six and a half pounds," she said proudly. She sized Margaret up, then reluctantly offered, "Want to hold her?"

Margaret was stunned by the offer and back-stepped. "Me? I've never held a baby before. Not one so little."

"You're kidding, right? Well, it's easy. Put your arms out," Ofelia instructed, waving her over.

Margaret came closer, walking stiffly.

"Take it easy. She won't bite. She doesn't have any teeth!" Ofelia gently laid the baby in Margaret's outstretched arms. "Now support her head. Careful! That's right."

Margaret stood in icy composure, holding the baby stiffly. Luz shot Ofelia a look that asked, Are you sure it's safe?

Ofelia only shrugged with a knowing smile, then returned her sharp gaze to her child. "Do you want to sit down?"

"No," Margaret choked out. "I'll just stand."

Margaret stared quietly at the baby's face. As the seconds ticked, Luz watched in amazement as she witnessed a small crack in Margaret's brittle composure. It was what she imagined a crack in an Arctic glacier must look like, a deep fissure, ice streaming as it thawed. Suddenly, Margaret's eyes welled with tears.

Ofelia chuckled sweetly. "Yeah, she has that effect on everyone."

Luz didn't know what to say, so she said nothing, embarrassed to witness such a personal moment.

Margaret sniffed and gently returned the baby to Ofelia's arms. "Thank you," she whispered. Then, embarrassed by her runaway emotions, she mumbled her good-bye, turned, and hurried from the room.

Mrs. Penfold came in as Margaret left. Her face appeared troubled as it followed Margaret's hasty exodus.

Ofelia's face flooded with joy at seeing her. "Mrs. P! She's had her first feeding!" Ofelia exclaimed.

"Really?" All worry fled from Mrs. Penfold's face as she rushed to Ofelia's side. She lifted the baby into her arms and made soft clucking noises, enraptured.

"So, what are you going to do now?" Luz asked Ofelia. "Will you stay here in Kansas or head south to your aunt in Florida?"

Ofelia's face froze in indecision and she swung her head to look at Mrs. Penfold.

"Oh, she'll stay here for a while," Mrs. Penfold spoke up. "We'll take good care of her and this sweetums, won't we?" Her eyes danced as she gazed at the baby. "Oh, yes we will!"

Luz watched Mrs. Penfold hover over the baby like a mother hen and knew that Ofelia would be taken care of. She could leave. It was a bittersweet moment and she rose reluctantly from her chair. "I better go," she said.

Ofelia leaned forward, reaching out to grab Luz's arm. "You're not leaving, like really leaving, are you?"

"You know I have to get back on the road. I've got to make it to Mexico by November first."

"Oh, Luz, I can't stand that you're leaving."

"Don't cry!" Luz admonished with a short laugh. "It'll spoil your makeup."

"See? You're my best friend!" Ofelia gave a hiccupy laugh. "My only friend! What am I going to do without you?"

"You'll be so busy taking care of that baby you won't even miss me," Luz replied, but she hoped Ofelia would miss her, as she knew she'd miss Ofelia. Then a thought jumped into her brain that so surprised her she put her hand to her cheek. "Oh! I almost forgot. What should I do with Serena?" Just saying the little dog's name filled Luz with sadness that she'd be leaving this new friend, as well.

"Serena?" Ofelia said, her face creased with worry. "I don't know! *Ay,* how could I've forgotten my other sweet baby? What should I do? It'll be hard enough to take care of this one baby. And I don't even have a place. I love her, but what am I going to do with a dog, too?"

"Don't look at me," Mrs. Penfold said with her hands up. "I have cats."

Luz licked her lips. Her mind was screaming for her to be quiet, but her heart screamed louder. "I'll keep her."

Ofelia released a short laugh of disbelief. "You? But you don't even like her."

"Maybe not at first, but she kind of grows on you. We get along fine now and she's good company. Really," she confessed. "I'd love to have her."

Ofelia laughed again with surprise and nodded. "I don't think I could have given her to anyone else. She's a good little dog. Sweet, but a little bossy sometimes."

"Sounds like someone I know."

Ofelia held out her arms in a typically dramatic gesture, teary once again. Luz stepped into her embrace.

"Promise you'll visit?" Ofelia said.

"I promise. Kansas isn't so far. And I've a new liking for road trips. But you have to promise to send pictures."

"*Yo prometo*. Be careful," Ofelia said, squeezing her tight.

"Be happy," Luz replied.

Luz pulled back and put on a brave smile. Wiping her eyes, she headed toward the door.

"Wait!" Ofelia called after her. She reached over to the bedside table and grabbed a pair of small pink booties. "I made these. They're not very good, but I tried hard. Please, take them. They're for Abuela. For her *ofrenda*."

Luz took the crocheted booties, deeply moved. They looked impossibly small in her hand. She looked at the baby squirming and making soft mewling noises in Mrs. Penfold's arms.

"I never asked! What did you name her?"

Ofelia reached up to smooth a lock of dark hair on her infant's head with her finger. When she looked back at Luz, her smile was smug.

"I named her Luz, of course."

Twelve

During their long migration, monarchs must stop to rest, feed, and drink. They also seek protection and roost during storms or other adverse conditions. When conditions improve, they fly!

Luz was in the driveway of Margaret's condo building, packing her suitcase into the trunk of her car, when Margaret came from the garage carrying a cooler.

"Chilled water and some fruit for your trip," she said, drawing near. "And in here"—she lifted a blue and green paper bag with the name of a local bookstore emblazoned across it—"is some trail mix, gum, and a candy bar. Oh, and a fresh pillowcase for your pillow. And don't let that dog sleep on it. It's not healthy."

"Hey, thanks. Now I won't have to make a stop." Luz took hold of the cooler, taken aback once more by Margaret's thoughtfulness. When she opened the car door, Serena promptly jumped in, looking smart in the new pink beribboned collar with matching leash that Mrs. Penfold had purchased for her. The Chihuahua sniffed the backseat, searching until she found the box of ashes under the pillow. She proceeded to dig into the pillow till she deemed it comfortable, then walked around in a circle and nestled in, resting her chin in her paws.

"Hopeless," muttered Margaret.

Serena looked up at her with her round eyes unblinking.

Luz pushed the front seat back into place. Spread out neatly on the seat was one bottle of water, her maps, her purse, her phone. "Well, I guess that's everything."

"Wait, I just thought of something." Margaret ran back to her open garage. A moment later she returned lugging two green parcels.

"What are these?" asked Luz.

"My tent and sleeping bag. Remember I told you that my dad bought them for me years ago? Well, here they are, like brand-new. I've never used them. It's time somebody did."

"I can't take them."

"Take them," she said, thrusting them into Luz's arms. They smelled slightly of mildew, but still had the tags. "You never know, you might need them. They're only collecting dust here. Besides, I've always wanted to go see the butterflies. At least my tent can make the trip." She tightened her lips and looked away with an embarrassed laugh.

Luz put the tent and sleeping bag in the trunk and paused with her hands resting on the dusty plastic. She looked up again at Margaret, who was standing with her arms tight around her chest, like she was trying with all her might to hold herself together. Luz blew out a plume of air, closed the trunk, and climbed into the car, wondering at the sadness she'd seen in Margaret's eyes. Abuela used to say that a person's sadness was like a well. Nobody knew how deep it went.

She didn't know Margaret. There was something about her when she'd first met her that made her feel chilled—it wasn't only that she looked bright white with her sculptured features and air of superiority. But today Luz had been surprised to discover that

Margaret wasn't a stereotype after all. Behind her marble features beat a heart that had known pain and loss and was capable of acts of real kindness. If only she wasn't so buttoned up and locked down, Luz thought. If anyone needed to hear the call of Xochiquetzal, Margaret did.

Luz hesitated, her hands on the wheel, and recalled the words *Who will bring light to the world?* She took a deep breath.

"Margaret? Why don't you come along?"

Margaret swung her head to look at her, shocked. "What?"

"Come with me. I have room and you said you wanted to see the monarchs."

"Me? I . . . I can't just go! I've got my job. Responsibilities."

Luz thought of Abuela's words to her. "Your work will always be there. Come on, Margaret. Jump in."

Margaret shook her head and took two steps back. "No, no, I can't. Mrs. Penfold depends on me, especially now with Ofelia. I have to find a job for her, an apartment. Then there's the end-of-season sale coming up. There's so much to do . . ." Her voice trailed off.

"Okay, then," Luz said, feeling a little guilty for the whisper of relief she felt. The offer had been an impulsive act on her part, but hadn't Abuela said impulses that came from the heart were good? "Thanks for everything." Then, with nothing more to say, she started the engine. "I'm off!"

Margaret lifted one hand, almost like a salute. "Good luck!"

Luz turned her head to meet Margaret's gaze and held it. "We make our own luck."

Margaret's face went still.

Luz rolled down the window and waved a final good-bye. "Okay, Abuela. We're on our way again." She shifted into reverse and rolled back into the street. She'd just shifted into first gear when she heard Margaret's voice shouting.

"Luz, wait! Stop!"

Luz jerked her head around to see Margaret running after the car, arms flailing in the air. Luz hit the squeaky brakes, ground the gear into reverse, and drove back to the driveway.

Margaret ran to the door and clutched it, breathing hard. "I've changed my mind," she said in a choppy cadence. "I want to go with you! Can I?"

"Yes!" Luz blurted out with surprise at the wildness in Margaret's eyes. Luz had seen that desperation in Margaret's eyes at breakfast when they talked about her mother. And again when she held the baby. Something must have just snapped in her. "What changed your mind?"

"Everything," Margaret said.

Once Margaret composed herself, she fell into character and created a long to-do list to tackle before she could leave on the trip. First on her list was a call to Mrs. Penfold, who took the news of her intended leave of absence without any problem. She even encouraged Margaret to take her time and enjoy her adventure. So much for Mrs. Penfold not being able to get along without her, Luz thought with a smothered smile. Then Luz's smile faded to openmouthed admiration when she overheard Margaret offering Ofelia her condo to live in until she got back. That gesture nudged Margaret up several notches in Luz's esteem.

But she slipped down again when she suggested to Luz that they take her sedan to Mexico instead of Luz's Volkswagen.

"What? No!" Luz cried, recoiling at the thought.

"Be reasonable, Luz. My car is way better than yours," Margaret replied. "I, uh, I mean, newer," Margaret amended. "Yours might not make it."

"Didn't your mama ever tell you to think before you speak?"

Margaret tsked and crossed her arms over her stomach. "I'm just calling it as I see it. Your car is ancient and it's a long trip. My car has got to be safer. And honestly, Luz, no offense, but it's pretty darn ghetto. I mean, look at the rust and dents. It's not safe."

This had been Luz's own reaction when she'd first seen the VW. She remembered Abuela's face when she handed Luz the keys, so excited, so full of promise. It may not have been the best car in the world, but it was the best that Abuela could afford. And that was good enough for Luz.

Luz teased back, "Nah, the ol' boy has a lot of character. Besides, Abuela bought me this car. It might sound crazy, but I feel her presence in it. Taking your car would be like leaving Abuela behind."

"We'd take her ashes, of course."

"Nope," Luz said, standing firm. This was *her* odyssey. Hers and Abuela's. "Look, Margaret, if you want to take your car, go ahead. You can follow me. But I'm driving El Toro."

Margaret scrunched her face. "El Toro?"

"Yes," Luz replied defiantly, eyes lit. "That's its name. Every car should have a name."

"Mine doesn't."

"And it's all the sorrier for it. This car might be little but it has the heart of a bull."

Margaret's mouth turned in derision. "It looks more like an ox."

"Ox, steer, bull—they're all the same."

"FYI, an ox is a neutered bull, fit for pulling carts. I think that applies here."

Luz patted the hood affectionately. "Don't you listen to her, Señor Toro. She's just jealous."

Margaret laughed, rolled her eyes at the tiny car, and threw up her hands. "Fine, you hideous beast. El Toro it is!"

Luz watched Margaret's efficient packing with awe. Abuela had called Luz practical and careful, but she was a piker compared to Margaret. "You're like a Girl Scout with all of this stuff," she told Margaret. "What's that motto? 'Always prepared'?"

Margaret stuck her head out from the backseat, where she was arranging the pillow and box of ashes. "As a matter of fact, I was an Ambassador."

Luz could picture it, her sash ablaze with patches. "I'll just bet you had tons of merit badges."

Margaret climbed out from the car and reached up to tighten the loose hairs in her ponytail. "Sure did. But these are just your everyday, practical measures for safety," she said with precision. "No offense, El Toro, but we're heading through some pretty remote areas where there won't be a handy tow truck to save us. If the car breaks down, we could be stuck for hours. Or more, God forbid."

Luz stood a moment to survey the car. She kicked her tires. She checked her watch. Reaching up, she slammed down the trunk. Then, digging into her jeans, she pulled out the keys. "Well, I think we're ready now. I don't think we can squeeze another thing in, and all this put us back. It's already two o'clock. Time's a wasting! Hop in, girlfriend. I want to get some miles under my belt while there's still daylight."

"Wait! I just have to grab some glue and markers."

Luz cursed under her breath. "What for?"

"For Abuela!"

Aerial photos and topographical maps that Margaret had pulled up on the computer before they left showed the Kansas landscape as a beautiful patchwork quilt of color and texture. "Very Van Gogh," as Margaret put it. And it was true. There were moments of breathtaking beauty. The Midwest was the land of rivers.

Luz regretted being on a strict timetable. There wasn't time to take an exit and see what was beyond the monotonous highway. Someday, she'd like to slow down and see more of the sights she was passing by—the rivers, universities, churches, small, friendly towns and bucolic farms with grazing animals. But Luz knew that, like the plucky monarch, she had to be in Mexico in two weeks.

The landscape was classic midwestern farmland, not unlike what she was used to seeing in Wisconsin. Here and there the tedium of open fields was broken by enormous grain silos, a picturesque, bright red barn, and modest frame houses, most of them white with green roofs.

An armada of steel-colored clouds gathered over the land, heralded by the growl of thunder. Luz turned on her headlights in anticipation of the storm. While she drove, she wondered what it would be like living in one of those farmhouses, married to a man not unlike Sully, with a few kids, a dog in the yard, a cat. She smiled, enjoying the scene in her mind. She tried to imagine herself milking cows, collecting eggs from chickens, waking up early to the call of a rooster. She chuckled. That was more of a stretch.

"What's so funny?" asked Margaret, turning her head from the window. She'd been silent for miles, taking in the blur of scenery.

"Oh, I was just wondering what it would be like to live in one of those houses out there. On a farm." They passed another house. This one was a pretty Cape Cod surrounded by stately pecan trees. It was an island in the middle of acres of fields. "They're miles away from their nearest neighbor. I wonder if they get lonely."

"They're pretty isolated," Margaret answered. "But I've found that neighbors in a rural community are more in touch with each other than neighbors who live next door in a city. There are lots of groups to join in a farming community. It's a small town. Everyone knows everyone's business. Everyone knows your name. In the city, there are so many people it's easier to get lost. Besides, is anyone really isolated anymore? Everyone is connected by phones and the Internet. Social networking. Online, I have people I hardly know commenting on my mundane daily activities. It's kind of like having a neighbor calling out from the window, 'Hi! Sunny day today, isn't it? Think I'll hang some laundry.'"

"But it's not the same as a real face smiling at you, or the touch of a hand," Luz argued. It struck her how she'd made two new, completely different friends on this odyssey across the country—without a phone or WiFi. She'd done it the old-fashioned way—meeting them face-to-face. Margaret, with her discipline and intelligence, and Ofelia, with her teasing humor and blunt honesty, were not people she might ordinarily have connected with. They were different ages, and had different lifestyles and different goals. But she was finding out she had more in common with them than not.

Thunder cracked loud and fierce and lightning lit up the sky. Margaret startled and jerked her head to peer through the window. "We're about to get drenched."

As though on cue, the sky opened up and a thunderous downpour hammered their car like tom-toms. Rain came down in sheets, and even though her windshield wipers were going full speed, Luz could barely see the road ahead. She slowed to a crawl while the wind pushed and rattled the small car.

Margaret and Serena sat tense and wide-eyed in the passenger seat. Margaret's hands were clenched but she remained silent. Lightning seemed to surround them and the road looked like a lake. Luz was terrified of hydroplaning. She leaned forward over the wheel and squinted. Up ahead she saw an overpass.

"I'm pulling over," she told Margaret. "I think we should sit this one out."

"Good idea." Margaret's relief was evident in the long sigh she released when Luz pulled off the road and turned off the engine.

Once they were nestled under the overpass, the percussive pounding ceased. They sat in a relatively blissful silence. Beyond the protective lair, the storm raged, spitting pellets of rain and renting the sky with lightning and thunder.

"Good ol' El Toro did a good job keeping us dry," Luz said.

"I don't think it will be a long wait. It's a fast-moving storm."

They opened bottles of water, ate candy bars, and sat for a while in silence as the storm blew around them. Serena daintily hopped to the backseat and curled up against the pillow. Luz closed her eyes and leaned back, listening to the increasingly muted thunder as the clouds rolled farther away.

"I was thinking of what we were saying," Margaret said finally.

Luz opened her eyes and turned her head to face Margaret. "About the Internet?"

Margaret nodded. "And being isolated. Truth is, most nights I sit in my room alone and troll through the social networking sites, just seeing if anyone commented or sent pictures. Or even just said hello." She sighed again, a sad sound that whistled through the small space. "It can get pretty lonely, no matter where you live."

Luz looked at the woman beside her in the passenger seat in skinny black jeans and thin layers of black Capilene. In her lap she carried two books: one on wildflowers, the other on butterflies and moths. She'd spent a great deal of time writing notes in the observation notebook that her father had designed for her years earlier. Yet even with all her scientific prowess, she didn't exude the personal confidence or sparkle that could make a plain girl pretty.

"Margaret," Luz ventured cautiously. She didn't want Margaret's protective shield to pop up again. "What made you change your mind about coming on this trip? Really."

Margaret put a piece of paper in her book to mark her place, then closed it and rested her hand on the cover. "It wasn't just one thing. It was more a buildup of things over time. There was a time I had such ambition. I wanted to be top of my class so I could get a scholarship. My father used to tell me to look on my left, then my right. I had to work harder than both those people to succeed. So I did. I worked, worked, worked. I won my scholarship, then a fellowship, and after that I got an internship at the university. When the job for Hidden Ponds came up, I knew I was younger than what Mrs. Penfold advertised for, but I went after it and"—she shrugged with a short laugh—"I got it."

"That's amazing," Luz said, feeling admiration. To think she achieved all that on her own. "Look at all you've accomplished. You have a great job, your own condo, a car."

"Right." Margaret's voice was flat. "And when I go home to that condo, I bring my work home—all my files and notes. Only now I don't really want to work on them. Most nights I don't even open my briefcase. I don't read my journals. I seem to have lost my spark and fallen into a rut. Lately, it's begun to hit me that I've worked so hard and with such focus, I didn't notice that the phone stopped ringing."

Luz licked her lips. She understood that loneliness. "You must have friends?"

"Oh, sure," she said quickly, heading off any pity. "Friends from college, mostly. But they're all married now and have children so, well, you know. They don't have a lot of free time, and frankly, my life is so different from theirs it's like we're living in separate worlds. More and more I find I'm going out by myself, and sometimes, I just can't bear to eat out alone so I take carryout home and watch TV. I watch a lot of TV . . . Sometimes, while I'm watching, I feel this panic well up inside of me, like I'm frozen and can't move. I just keep watching and it doesn't even matter what's on."

She turned and asked with genuine concern, "Do you think I'm addicted?"

"No," Luz answered quickly. "Maybe a little depressed."

"Hmm . . ." Margaret's face was troubled as she reached for her bottle of water. She took a long sip, staring at some fixed point in the distance.

Lightning lit up the clouds. Their mottled purple and yellow coloring reminded Luz of Ofelia's bruises. Luz recalled the intimate conversations they'd shared in this car and here she was again, now privy to Margaret's confession. She recognized this as one of those rare moments of intimacy between friends that demanded honesty. She adjusted her seat to lean against the door and face Margaret fully.

"I get a little depressed sometimes, too," Luz confessed.

Margaret tilted her head.

Luz took a breath. "I work in a foundry in Milwaukee."

"Uh-huh," Margaret said.

"I hate my job but we needed the money. So I quit school and got the job that paid the most money."

"You quit school?" Margaret asked. That bit of information elicited more indignation than shock. "Didn't you have any choices?"

"Not really. Abuela was let go from her job and she was too old to find another. I couldn't leave her to fend for herself. She spent her life savings taking care of me and there was no one else. Besides, I loved her." She shook her head. "There was no question of my responsibilities. So I quit school and got a job. I kept telling myself it was only temporary. That I was going to save my money and go back to school. But the days just flew by and the next thing you know, a year goes by. I feel stuck in a rut, too."

"How can you be stuck in a rut? You're twenty, right?"

"Twenty-one."

Margaret shook her head. "What was your major?"

"Well, it was a technical college," Luz explained. "I was in a Human Services Associate program for a degree as a social service worker. I'd like to work in a community outreach program, to do sort of what Abuela did with neighborhood kids. She made a difference. I'd like that, you know? To know my life had meaning." She laughed with derision. "I ended up working with machines."

"I think you'd be great working with people, Luz. You're a good listener. You can't just give up, that's not like you. You can still go to school. You should."

"How?" Luz said dejectedly. "I don't have any money."

"Oh, come on," Margaret replied with a hint of exasperation. "If you want it bad enough you can find a way. I did. There are a lot of programs available. You just have to know where to look. When we get back, I'll help you."

It was a simple offer, made almost offhandedly, but Luz grasped it, feeling the first rush of hope for what the next phase of her life might be. She'd been traveling on this journey, believing in her heart that it was a personal odyssey, but she'd not considered what she'd do when she returned home. It didn't have to be more of the same. And here was Margaret, kicking her butt, forcing her to see how her life *could* change.

"Which brings me to the second reason I'm going on this trip," Margaret continued, screwing the top back on the water bottle. "*Time*. I don't see many babies. My girlfriends have them but I don't see them much. To be honest, I never really wanted to. Usually they stay home with a sitter when we go out. So this morning when I held Ofelia's baby, I stared down at this beautiful infant, all pink and sweet-smelling, and it hit me—like a slap against the skull—that I'm probably never going to have a child of my own."

"Oh, come on, Margaret. You're not that old." Luz studied Margaret. She was slender and her face was smooth, even without makeup. Only faint crow's-feet marred her milky skin. "How old *are* you?"

"Thirty-seven," she replied thinly.

Now it was Luz's turn to scoff. "You make yourself sound ancient. That's still young."

Margaret gave her a recriminatory look. "Like I said. My phone isn't ringing. I'm good at a lot of things, but I'm not good at small talk and flirting and all those feminine tricks for attracting men. Never was. I can sit at a table and talk shop till the cows come home, but ask me to hold a drink and charm a guy and I'm bored out of my mind. Every once in a blue moon a friend hooks me up with a man." She shrugged. "I'm not willing to settle just to be with a guy and get married."

Luz looked at her bottled water. "Sully wants to get married.

Just the idea of it makes me nervous. I thought girls were supposed to be excited and happy at the prospect. I wish I was."

"Maybe you don't love him."

"That's the thing. I *do* love him. But do I love him for who he is, or for the security he offers me? He's strong and steady. For someone like me, without any family, that offers a lot." She thought of Billy with his Bohemian lifestyle, his intellect, his ease of speech, and his tantalizing smile. "Or do I want someone completely different? Someone with passion and surprises? Oh, I'm not sure," she said with a heartfelt sigh. "I don't want to settle, either."

"Just don't say 'I do' until you know the answer to those questions."

"I know," Luz replied soberly. "I've got a lot to figure out about myself before I can commit to any man. I love Sully but I'm confused. I don't know what's best for *me* right now."

Margaret nodded emphatically. "I spent so much time working for my future, I don't know myself either. Do you know what I think? The only time that matters is right now." She raised her water bottle. "This brings me to my final reason why I jumped on board this trip." She peered at Luz. "*You.*"

"*Me?* What did I do?"

"It's what you're doing! You're going to Texas, and then Mexico, even if it means risking your life in this old jalopy. When I see you I see a girl with a passion. A girl who's lost her mother and grandmother. I see a girl like I used to be and want to be again." She turned her head to look out the window. "You started off, leaving me behind, and then you uttered my mother's words to me. Something inside me clicked. I just knew I had to go. I think that's what my mother meant when she said I had to make my own luck. I had to trust my intuition. Like you, I'd missed my chance to go with my mother, but that adventure we'd dreamed about is still there. I'm alive, I've got my health. What was I waiting for?" She turned back to face Luz, smiling. "Does that answer your question?"

Luz reached over to pat Margaret's hand. It was a rush to think she'd helped Margaret see the light, as she put it. What Margaret didn't realize was that she'd done the same for Luz. "Kindred spirits. I knew it."

Luz peered out the window. The storm had blown past and the rain was a steady drizzle. "We should go," she said, reaching for her safety belt. Luz fired up the engine, turned on her signal, and guided the car safely back onto the highway. El Toro's engine sputtered as it struggled to gain speed and the girls laughingly called out, "Go, go, go!"

The sky was clearing over the vast acres of farmland and great shafts of light broke through purple clouds. Luz smiled as she gazed out the windshield at a road that appeared bathed in glittering light.

Thirteen

Monarchs begin the journey as individuals; however, they will gather in number in different places and at different times. No one knows if the butterflies seek each other out and fly together on purpose, or if they just happen to be heading in the same direction to the same place.

An hour later they were somewhere in Oklahoma and the sky was turning dusky as the sun lowered in the west.

"I'm starting to wonder when an exit is coming up," said Luz, chewing her lip.

"With a motel," Margaret added. "I haven't seen an exit sign for miles. We should be coming close to Oklahoma City. If I could just get connected on the Internet I could get us a reservation somewhere."

"Something will turn up," Luz said.

Margaret lifted her phone near the window. "I can't even get a cell phone connection out here."

Luz glanced at Margaret, her thoughts turning to Sully. "I knew I forgot something! My phone charger. Damn."

"You can pick one up."

Luz mentally kicked herself. She could see the charger sitting on the desk in Margaret's den. "I'm guessing my phone is dead."

"If you need to call someone, you can always use mine."

"Yeah, thanks. I'd like to leave a message for my boyfriend. Just so he knows I'm safe."

"When was the last time you called him?"

"I haven't since Chicago."

"Oh."

"It's not that I don't want to call him. I'm just not sure I want to hear him tell me how I should turn around and come back home."

"Why is he—"

The silence was suddenly rent by the resounding blare of a horn. Margaret yelped and Luz jumped, clinging to the wheel. In her rearview mirror she saw an enormous RV coming up fast, its headlights bearing down on them. The bus looked like a whale about to eat a minnow.

"Go around, jerk!" Luz shouted, and waved her hand out the window. She swung her head to look out the window as the behemoth roared close in the left lane. It was a huge RV painted with wild purple psychedelic swirls. Two guys in the front, long-haired and bearded, pointed at El Toro and laughed before the RV changed gears and pushed past them, belching fumes and rattling the VW as if it weighed no more than a leaf.

"I don't believe it!" Margaret cried. "I think I just got mooned!"

"Really?" Luz squinted out the front windshield but the RV was already too far up the road. "I'm sorry I missed that."

"Don't be," Margaret said with disgust.

Luz didn't know which was funnier, the mooning or Margaret's reaction. No matter where they were, or what the speed limit, cars and trucks passed them by. El Toro never pushed beyond fifty-five miles per hour. But Luz had to admit, this was ignominious.

Luz patted the dashboard. "That's okay, Toro. Don't let them rattle you. You just keep plugging along. Let *them* get the ticket."

"I doubt there's a policeman within fifty miles of here. We're really in the middle of nowhere. We need to find a place soon." They pushed on a little farther, and in answer to their prayers, the next road sign showed the distinct KOA campground letters.

"Let's get off here," Margaret said, pointing.

Luz took a quick glance. "A campground? You're kidding, right?"

"No, it's safe. I've been camping lots of times in the Girl Scouts."

"But where do we sleep?"

"We've got the tent!"

"Yeah, okay," Luz replied, remembering. Luz was a city girl and had never been camping before. Sully was always asking her to go camping with him in Wisconsin but she never understood the lure of sleeping outdoors on the cold ground when there was a warm bed available. "Are there toilets? That flush? I don't want to dig holes in the dirt and make offerings to the moon."

Margaret chuckled. "Yes, and yes. There's hot water, too. Look," she said more seriously. "It's almost seven thirty and the office will close soon. We're beat and you can't drive much farther. There might be a motel up the road, but who knows how far. Let's just go in and get the scoop. We can always get back on the road. Besides, this is an adventure, right?"

Luz flicked the turn signal and took the exit. They followed the narrow, rutted gravel road bordered by tall trees that blocked the day's final pale rays of light. Dry leaves skittered noisily across the gravel. Luz pulled up in front of a pretty gabled wood cabin with a wide porch bedecked with flowers. A neat arrangement of dark green shrubs bordered the walkway, and behind it, a large yellow sign emblazoned with a green and red tented KOA emblem read CAMPSITE REGISTRATION.

"Lock your door," Luz ordered as they stepped into the lot. Serena jumped up to stare out the window, whining to join them. "I'll only be a minute," she told the dog, and hated the pleading she saw in her eyes. The temperature had dropped to the low sixties, comfortable enough, but she felt moisture in the air and frowned up at the sky. Gravel crunched beneath their feet as they walked toward the cabin. Suddenly the bell over the front door jingled and a stocky, middle-aged man in a USMC cap emerged, carrying a big bag of ice.

"Evenin', ladies," he said in a southern drawl, holding the door as the two walked in.

Inside, the cabin was designed as a lobby. Heavy wood chairs covered in red plaid fabric sat around a low table made of logs and glass. Brochures and a photo album of the campground invited you to sit and browse. To one side, a small store lined with shelves looked picked over at season's end. On the opposite side was a long wood registration counter, behind which sat an unusually thin, elderly woman with short, red hair almost as bright as the fabric on the chairs. She was watching a small TV tucked in the corner and turned with reluctance to greet them in a tired voice. Luz couldn't blame her. It was almost closing time.

"Hey there." She hardly took a breath before she launched into a rote description of the campground and all its amenities, which were many. Apparently, it being midweek and postsummer, they were lucky. If it were summer, she assured them, they might not find a space available just waltzing in without a reservation. Things being what they were, however, she could offer them a very nice site just a short walk to the bathrooms and showers for twenty-five dollars for one night's stay. She ended with an apology that the pool had just closed for the rest of the season, but instead, she'd offer them some wood for their campfire, free of charge. "Seeing as you're the last customers of the day."

Maybe all those years pinching pennies with Abuela rubbed off, because a hot shower and a cheap place to stay was all Luz needed for convincing. The caretaker handed them a map and some bound firewood, then shut and locked the cabin door after them.

The girls followed the map past the playground and swimming pool, beyond a cluster of Kozy Kabins, to lot number 315.

"It's cute!" Luz declared when she caught sight of the picnic table and a fire pit at their assigned spot. As soon as Margaret opened her door Serena weaseled out from the back and began scampering off, her nose to the ground. Luz rushed after her, stepping on the leash, jerking Serena to a stop. The dog looked back at Luz with accusation.

"You're a city girl like me. I don't want you to get lost," Luz said, stroking under the dog's chin. She yawned and stretched her arms far out, looking around. The park was nearly empty. Only one neighbor was visible in a nice spot under a maple, aflame with color. It was a small, white RV, the kind pulled by a car. A blue awning was pulled out and under it sat an elderly, white-haired couple on two matching blue canvas chairs. The two of them sat watching them without expression. Luz smiled and waved. Neither responded. They just kept watching.

"Never mind them. Let's go find the showers before it gets too dark," Margaret said.

The small cinder-block bathroom building had narrow vent windows near the ceiling, two sinks, two toilets, and two shower stalls. She'd seen the empty bucket and mop near the entry and caught the faint scent of bleach, but seeing the silverfish in a corner and the cracks in the tile, Luz wished she'd brought some flip-flops. The night was chilly so Luz wasted no time undressing and stepping under the downpour of hot water. While she scrubbed, she heard a woman singing some Widespread Panic song in a neighboring stall. She had a lusty voice that went so off-key on the high notes that Luz almost choked on the water as she laughed. She showered in record time and, shivering, dried off and changed into fresh underwear, jeans, a hoodie, and thick socks while Margaret took her turn. The woman in the second stall was still singing when they left.

By the time they got back to their site, the sky was dusky. Their neighbors had a nice fire going and were sitting at their picnic table. The aroma of grilled meat wafted their way. Luz's mouth watered as she and Margaret took the gear from the trunk and set it on the level graveled spot where they hoped to erect a tent.

"You've put up a tent before, right?" Luz asked Margaret. "Since you were an Ambassador in the Girl Scouts and all."

"Actually, we slept in cabins," she said sheepishly. "What about you?"

"Me? No! I'm from the city. I've never been camping."

"Well, how hard can it be, right?" said Margaret cheerfully. "If little kids can do it, so can we."

While Margaret read the directions, Luz tried removing the tent from its bag, cursing a blue streak. It was like stripping the casing off a sausage. Together they figured out they had to first spread out the thin bottom tarp on the ground.

"Fluff it up like a sheet first," Margaret instructed, then got on all fours to smooth it out. "It's so wrinkled," she said in dismay.

"We're not going to iron it," Luz said, giggling when Margaret jokingly stuck out her tongue. "Besides, it goes under the tent, so you won't have to look at it."

Margaret pulled out a flashlight as the sky was getting grayer by the second and the temperature dropping with it. She read the next step. "Seems easy enough. All we have to do is spread the tent over the tarp, then put in the stakes."

Unfortunately, the ground was so hard that they couldn't get the stakes into the ground without a hammer. And they didn't have a hammer. Shoes, boxes, and rocks wouldn't get the job done.

"Do you think they'd have one?" Margaret asked in frustration, indicating their neighbors.

"I'm not going to ask them." Luz stepped closer and whispered, "They're watching us like we're on TV. It creeps me out. Let's just put the poles in first. Once we're in the tent, we won't need the stakes anyway. Our weight will hold it in place."

Luz went to the supplies and pulled two sectioned poles out of a nylon bag. They were each folded multiple times at joints and opened to a long, wiggly pole.

"They look like those nunchakus," Margaret said, fiddling with it.

Luz started laughing. "I wonder who translated this. It says here to push the pole into the hole."

Margaret giggled and tried weaving the legs of the pole into the seam at the opposite side. The wiggly poles kept falling over, again and again. Margaret cursed the poor translation and tossed the directions to the ground. She crawled under the tent and tried holding it up in the middle while Luz tugged the corners taut and tried again to pound the stakes into the graveled ground with her shoe.

Over and over the tent toppled over, and each time it fell over, Luz and Margaret laughed harder. Finally they collapsed on top of the tent, laughing until their sides hurt and tears flowed from their eyes.

"You girls are either filming for *America's Funniest Home Videos* or you could use some help."

Luz followed the southern drawl to see a curvaceous girl in her twenties walking on the path in tight black jeans, red cowboy boots, and a jean jacket ablaze in rhinestones. She was a flash of sparkles in the dim light. Her platinum-colored hair was damp and pulled up in a high ponytail showing dark roots. Her heavily lined, dark blue eyes scanned the scene with mild amusement.

Luz thought she looked like an angel of mercy. "Do you know how to put up a tent?"

"Better than you two, I reckon." She lowered her enormous purple leather bag to the ground. A few hair products fell out and Luz figured out that she was the soprano from the shower. "What's your name, honey?"

"I'm Luz."

The girl cut a cursory glance toward Margaret, who stayed back, frowning. "I'm Stacie." She released a loud, staged sigh and surveyed her nails. They were big hands with long, ruby-tipped fingers. "Lord, I just pray I don't break a nail. I just had them done."

It turned out Stacie knew what she was doing. In short order she laid out the gear. "First off, you girls were putting your tent up in the wrong spot. See, that's real important. Take it from me." As she spoke she tightened the links of the poles so they formed single, long poles. Then she easily slipped them through the seams and like magic, the tent stood.

Seeing that the process required little more than simple common sense, Luz felt her cheeks burn. She cast a sideways glance at Margaret, whose lips were pursed with chagrin. Stacie had them move the tent to the flattest section of their lot, kicking bits of rock with her boot and scouring each section of it with the flashlight.

"The trick is not to set your tent on any rocks, sticks, or hills. One time a buddy of mine at Bonnaroo set his tent up on this hill of red ants. Them's aggressive little bastards. Sting like hell. Once that nest was disturbed, they attacked. See, when that first one bites, it sends out some kinda smell that acts like an alarm going off for all the others."

"Pheromone," corrected Margaret. When Stacie looked over her shoulder with a puzzled expression, Margaret explained in a teacherlike voice, "The ant released a pheromone. That's the scent that causes the other ants to swarm. They sting en masse."

"In what?" Stacie asked, scrunching up her face.

Margaret rolled her eyes. "It means all at once."

"Yeah, yeah, that's what happened," Stacie said, nodding. "My friend's leg blew up like a balloon and he was howling like a banshee. Didn't kill him, though. Just wished it did, it hurt so bad. So, you don't want to be putting your tent on no ant hills. Or gravelly spots, neither, on accounta you'll never get the stakes to go in."

Luz and Margaret shared a look.

With Stacie's help the girls secured the tent with the stakes in short order. Luz thought Stacie looked especially pleased with herself.

"I don't know about you girls," Luz said, "but I'd love to start a fire and have a glass of wine."

"Great idea," Margaret said, making a beeline for the car. As she opened the door, Serena came bounding out straight into Stacie's arms. Stacie cooed over "the precious li'l thing" till Margaret came back from the car with a bottle of red in one hand, a bottle of white in the other, some plastic cups under her arm, and a worried expression. She turned to Stacie. "You wouldn't happen to have a corkscrew, would you?"

A slow smile eased across the girl's face, carving deep lines at the corners of her eyes. "Of course. I never travel without the necessities of life."

"If you've got a corkscrew, we'd be happy to share," Luz said.

"Tell you what, girls. I hitched a ride with a group of guys up the road a piece. They're good ol' boys from Georgia and been nothin' but gentlemen. But they're freewheeling, if you know what I mean. They're following the Widespread Panic tour."

"Oh my God," Margaret exclaimed, grabbing Luz's arm. "I'll bet those are the guys who mooned us."

Stacie giggled. "Sounds like them. Like I said, they're fixed on having a good time. They've started in on drinking and smoking and Lord help me, they're getting high as kites." She crossed her arms and twisted on one heel. Though she appeared relaxed, Luz recognized a flash of desperation lurking in the girl's eyes. "If it's all right with you," Stacie said, "I'd be real grateful if I could get my gear and stay with you tonight. I've got peanut butter to share." Her ruby lips turned up in a teasing smile. "And a corkscrew. What do you say?"

"Yes," Luz answered without hesitation.

Margaret's silence was too resolute for Stacie not to notice; she quickly surmised it was Luz who made the decisions, and she flashed her a megawatt smile. "Well, okay, then! I'll just go get the corkscrew and be right back." She handed Serena to Luz and walked off, following her beam of light and disappearing into the darkness.

"Are you crazy? We don't know her," Margaret said, rising to grab the firewood. "She could rob us blind."

"First of all, I doubt she'd do that," Luz replied, tying Serena to one of the tent stakes. "Second, I didn't know you that well either before you hitched a ride."

"True," Margaret admitted. She'd crouched before the fire pit and begun neatly stacking the firewood. She rose, wiping her hands on her pants. "But I didn't dress like a Vegas showgirl."

"You also didn't know how to put up a tent, Miss Girl Scout. You should be kicked out of the corps. And third, Margaret, what do we really have to steal?"

Margaret laughed and her cheeks flushed. "But I can make a hell of a fire. Watch this."

She struck a match and bent to light the pyramid of logs in the circle of rocks. The flame sparked. Margaret bent on all fours and blew soft plumes of air onto the flame. Soon the underbelly of the wood glowed an infernal red. Margaret came back to sit on the wood bench beside Luz. She slapped the dirt from her knees and hands with a satisfied air. "There. Not bad for a geek, huh?"

"You were a geek?"

"Yeah," she said, bending to lean her forearms against her knees. "What did you expect? I collected insects." She laughed in a self-deprecating manner. "I had glasses as thick as Coke bottles. I got my eyes zapped when I was thirty and now I've got twenty-twenty vision. I wish I'd done it sooner. But I didn't do it because I wanted to be prettier," she added. "I had laser surgery because I wanted to see better on field trips and not have to fool with glasses."

Luz smirked with wonder. "You never fail to amaze me."

"I live to amaze you," she replied with a laugh.

Luz paused and looked anxiously at Margaret, who was staring at the fire. "Do me a favor? Lighten up on Stacie."

Margaret turned her head to face her. "I just don't trust her."

"That's just because she doesn't dress like you."

"To put it mildly."

"I think you'd look good with a few rhinestones and some color."

Margaret snorted and glanced meaningfully at Luz's rumpled clothes. She crossed her arms, then fixed her gaze on the path that Stacie had walked down. "You know," she said in a sincere tone. "I have to admit, sometimes I imagine what it would be like to dress like that. Flashy and sexy. A vixen. It takes a certain physical confidence, don't you think?" Then she turned her head and her wistful expression vanished. "I mean," she said self-consciously, "I could never wear clothes *that* tight. It's not me."

Luz thought of Margaret's plain beige uniform, her colorless, magazine-decorated apartment, and realized that Margaret might have pushed that flamboyant side of herself down too deep. "Oh, I don't know," she said. "I think there's a little sparkle in all of us, just waiting to shine out."

"You think?" Margaret laughed and shook her head.

They sat for several minutes watching the fire gain strength. The snaps and cracks of the burning wood spiraled to a sky as black as a woolen blanket. Soon, too, the ubiquitous high hum of the mosquitoes hovered near their heads, prompting them to dig out the bug spray from their bags. Seeing Margaret's phone, Luz remembered that she hadn't yet called Sully. She borrowed Margaret's phone and punched Sully's number. Gazing at the starless sky above, she listened to the phone ring and ring until his message clicked on.

"Hi, this is Sully. Leave a message and I'll get back to you."

"Hi, Sully, it's me. Luz. Hey, where are you?" she said as a gentle tease. "I'm in Oklahoma now. Should make Texas tomorrow. I'm camping, can you believe it? And I'm not traveling alone anymore. I'm with two girls I met on the way. They're really nice. Listen, I know I haven't called but I left my charger behind and my phone is dead. So I borrowed this phone and just wanted to check in and tell you I'm okay and not to worry. Love you. Bye."

"All set?" Margaret asked, taking back her phone and tucking it into her bag.

"Yes, thanks. I feel better. I guess I did all I could."

Margaret hesitated, setting her purse back on the ground. She crossed her legs at the ankles. "You know, you could've bought a charger at any one of the gas stations we passed along the way."

Luz bent her head, forced to acknowledge what she'd pushed to the far corners of her mind. She stretched out her legs beside Margaret's and stared at the flames licking the logs.

"I told myself I just didn't want to spend the money. It's a valid enough reason. I don't know what's coming up on the trip and it makes sense to me to be frugal and not spend on anything I don't absolutely need."

"A phone isn't something you don't need. At least not on a trip like this."

"I thought I'd wait till I got to San Antonio." Luz paused, heard the lie in her own words. "No. There's another reason, but"—she sighed heavily—"I didn't want to think about it. I've got enough to deal with right now."

"What reason was that?"

Luz collected herself and forced the idea from the nether regions of her thoughts. "I didn't want to talk with him."

There was a short pause and Margaret said, "Oh. Well."

"I told myself that I was trying to stand on my own. To make my own decisions and not always depend on Sully."

"There's nothing wrong with that."

"Not if I hurt him. I don't want to hurt him. He's a great guy. I'm just . . . not sure of my feelings and I know if I talk to him he'll just hammer at me to come home and right now I don't want anyone telling me what to do. This is the first time I've taken a trip like this and I'm thinking just about me and what I want. I don't want to worry about anything but the journey. I don't need the pressure." She flicked a glance sideways at Margaret, searching for affirmation. "Is that selfish?"

"No, it's not selfish. You're just trying to find out who you are. That doesn't mean that Sully is a bad guy and doesn't want what's right for you, either. It's just sometimes you need to figure that out on your own."

A scuttling noise drew their attention to the gravel walkway that led to their campsite. Stacie was walking up, lugging her enormous purple bag over her shoulder. When she reached their campsite she dropped it with a heavy sigh of relief. She put her hand on her hip and surveyed the two women huddled by the fire in close conversation.

"What's the matter, you two? Did someone die? You look like a coven of witches by the fire there."

Margaret patted Luz's arm, rose, and stretched her arms. "No one died," she replied. "But we could use a glass of wine. You brought the corkscrew, I hope?"

Stacie dug into her purse and handed the simple, dollar-store-variety corkscrew to Margaret. "I couldn't find mine so I borrowed this one from the boys. And *this*!" Stacie moved her hand from behind her back, proudly waving a bottle of rum. "They've got so many they'll never miss it."

Margaret grabbed the bottle of white and peeled off the foil. Then with finesse, she quickly uncorked the bottle, poured liberal amounts of wine into the plastic Solo cups, and handed one to each of the girls.

"To sum up," Margaret began, "Luz's boyfriend is worried about her and wants her to come home. She needed to check in with him but isn't sure how she feels about that." She glanced at Luz. "Did I get it right?"

Luz nodded with a smirk.

"Girl," Stacie said, holding out her cup like a pointed finger. "You're too young to be worried about checkin' in with some guy. Unless he's your husband. And even then it don't really matter if you're with your girlfriends. You got to keep your priorities straight. Right now you don't need to be worrying about nothing but number one. So here, let's drink our wine and eat some of this gourmet peanut butter and liven it up around here. I brought some music and I feel like howlin' at the moon."

The scent of cold ashes permeated the frosty air. Luz could smell them in her hair and taste them in her mouth. Their tent billowed in the wind, making flapping noises like a wet sheet. She shivered and burrowed deeper in the sleeping bag. It had rained during the night. She didn't hear it but felt the moisture in the air, and the dampness stained the edges of their tent.

Prying open a sandy eye, she saw Margaret cuddled beside her, her pale hair strewn against the pillow and her thin lips pursed open as a guttural, unladylike snoring bellowed out. Beside her, Stacie lay facedown on a rolled-up towel. Luz rose slowly, her head pounding from too much alcohol and too little food. She managed to sit cross-legged, shivering in the chilly morning air. Serena grumbled at having had the warmth of the sleeping bag removed and curled tighter in her ball. Luz put her fingertips to her throbbing temples as she struggled to recollect last night's campfire party.

She didn't remember ever seeing the bottom of her cup, there was always somebody pouring. There was a lot of dancing, too. A soft chuckle escaped her and she looked again at Margaret. She was still wearing Stacie's rhinestone jacket. At one point Margaret had put on Stacie's jacket and stood up, belting out lyrics to a Widespread Panic song that Stacie had taught her.

A muffled groan sounded as Margaret slowly opened her eyes.

"Well, if it isn't the dancing queen," Luz said.

"My mouth tastes like ashes."

"That's because it *is* ashes. The fire went out."

"Now I know why I'm freezing!" Margaret pulled the sleeping bag back up over her shoulders.

"I'd kill for a cup of coffee. Do you think they'd have coffee at the front desk?" Luz asked hopefully.

"Don't mention eating or drinking," Margaret moaned. She put her arm over her eyes, then moved it to peer out at Luz. "Dancing queen? Was I really that bad?"

"You were better." She laughed and said teasingly, "The butterfly has emerged!"

Margaret brought her hand up to cover her face with another, louder groan.

"No, you were great!"

Margaret chuckled softly, then moaned again. "It hurts to laugh. Don't make me laugh."

Luz fell back against her pillow like a dead weight.

"I had a good time last night," Margaret said in a soft voice.

"Mmm . . ."

"No, I mean, I really had a good time. I've never danced like that." She paused, then asked, "Do you have to be drunk to do that?"

"No. But it helps."

"I'd hate to think I'd always have to get drunk to have a good time. 'Cause I don't think I care much for hangovers."

"Nope." Luz smacked her dry lips. "We need water. I'll bet they sell bottled water at the store. Maybe they'll have coffee, too. I'll go check it out."

"Yes, you should."

Neither woman rose.

They heard a loud sigh of exasperation as Stacie dragged herself up to her elbows.

"What a bunch of lightweights. *I'll* go. I got to pee anyway." She rose easily, sans groaning. In fact, Luz thought she looked too darn perky as she reached up to redo her ponytail. She was wearing Margaret's wool peacoat, an interesting fashion statement with her cowboy boots. Stacie reached down to grab her leather bag.

"You girls think you can hold down the fort till I get back?"

After a hurried breakfast of coffee and peanut butter sandwiches, Luz took off on a walk with Serena while Margaret went in search of wildflowers to add to her observation notebook.

Serena trotted jauntily at Luz's side with her head down, sniffing exultantly. The day had begun cold and damp with a gray, overcast sky but the sun was struggling to break through the clouds. Luz relished the occasional shaft of light that sliced through the gray to shed a bit of warmth on her skin, like a gift. The night's rain had left several puddles in the rutted dirt road. They reflected the sudden bursts of sunlight to sparkle like Stacie's rhinestones.

Rounding a bend, she stopped abruptly with an intake of breath. Five monarchs clustered around a large puddle at the side of the road. Farther ahead, more groups congregated at several of the small black pools.

"There you are," she breathed, coming to a halt. She'd wondered when she might see more butterflies. They'd probably roosted in these trees the night before and were just now coming out with the sun.

She knew that on sunny days after a rain, butterflies gathered around the edges of mud puddles to sip salts and minerals from the soil. It was called puddling, but Luz rarely saw it. Abuela used to leave a small dish in the garden to collect water, but more often Luz would spy a butterfly sipping a drop of water from a flower after a rain. Luz knew these butterflies would drink their fill, then pack it up, catch a warm breeze, and be on their way south.

As should she, Luz thought, and tugged at Serena's leash. Once again, the butterflies had given her the sign she needed. She felt filled with hope for the next leg of her journey. "Let's let them drink in peace," she said to Serena, leading her away from the monarchs.

A short time later, she and Margaret were packing up the car when they heard a familiar, high-pitched voice calling to them. Serena barked with excitement and strained at the leash tethered to the picnic table.

"So," Stacie said, sauntering close, her ever-present purple satchel hanging heavily from her side, overflowing with clothing. She bent to pet Serena, who was shivering with joy and licking her face. "You're taking off."

"On the road again," Luz replied, tossing the sleeping bag into the trunk.

Margaret emerged from the backseat with the pillow in her hand. Her face was still chalky from being hungover, but her slack jaw reflected her surprise to see Stacie again.

"You're headed to Texas, right?" Stacie asked.

"That's right. San Antonio."

Stacie dropped her purse and absently scratched her chin with her fingernail. "I'm from Austin, you know."

"Oh?" There was something pending in her tone that had Luz wondering what was coming.

"Sooooo," Stacie said, and she held her hands together in a pleading, prayerlike gesture. "I was wondering if I could catch a ride with you girls."

From the corner of her eye, Luz saw Margaret discreetly wave her hands and shake her head no.

"But, you said you're headed to L.A.," Luz replied. "San Antonio isn't anywhere near L.A."

"It's south, isn't it? And L.A. is in Southern California. At least I'm headed in the right direction. I've got all kinds of connections in Texas. I'm sure I can help you girls out."

Luz was left to wonder if Stacie had ever really looked at a map of the United States. If she had, she'd know that if she went to San Antonio, she'd overshoot her mark. "Your plan doesn't make sense, Stacie. We're headed way out of your way."

"Come on, Luz, let me tag along. Truth is, I don't want to ride with those guys anymore. They live like pigs and they're all horny as hell. I swear to God they don't have enough weed to make it worth my while. You'd be such a lifesaver. And I'd pay my way and help with gas. Please just take me a little ways so I can find me some new options. I can't get stuck here with those guys. I think us girls got on real good."

Luz liked Stacie, with her exuberance and willingness to take whatever fate threw at her. Maybe both she and Margaret could stand to let a little of that rhinestone attitude rub off on them. Besides, how could she say no? In the end, they were all just following the call of Xochiquetzal.

"Sure," she replied. Luz looked over to see Margaret slump against the car with her face in her hands. "We're taking off. You got everything you need?"

"I got everything I need right here," Stacie said, lifting her enormous purple leather purse.

Fourteen

Texas is the funnel through which most migrating monarchs must pass on their way to their overwintering grounds in Mexico. Texas is also the first stop on their northward journey, when they seek out both nectar and host plants for eggs for the next generation. Thus, Texas is of critical importance in the migration of the monarch butterfly.

Stacie took a turn at the wheel and drove with the assurance of a truck driver. "Honey, if you'd grown up on a ranch like I did, you'd learn two things before you can walk. First is how to ride a horse. Second is how to drive a tractor. Plus on the road, I've driven everything from an RV to a vintage Corvette. If it's got wheels and an engine, I can drive it."

She knew the scenery, too, talking a mile a minute about anything and everything they passed. When they crossed the Red River into Texas, she honked the horn and let loose with a piercing whistle. "That's the Red River, baby!" she shouted, leaning on the horn. "Woowee! That's home!"

Luz wore an ear-to-ear grin and waved at the passing cars that honked back at them as they crossed the bridge. She'd really left the confines of her home state, she thought, giddy. She was seeing America!

Texas was a big state, however, and they had long hours of driving ahead of them. They made a pit stop for gas, to pee, and to grab a few candy bars, bottles of water, and a phone charger. Luz took the wheel back after cities and towns gave way once again to endless miles of flatness. It might have been dreary except that the roads were lined with countless wildflowers—goldenrod, Margaret informed them as she wrote in her notebook. When the wind gusted, it cascaded across the tall flowers like a wave rolling across a golden ocean.

Yet Luz's attention was skyward and she kept craning her neck to peek up through her open window.

"What are you looking for?" Stacie asked from the backseat.

"Butterflies," Luz replied. "Monarchs, actually. Now that we're in Texas I thought I'd be seeing loads of them. Where are they?"

"You'd have a better shot at spotting one if you looked along the side of the road. Most of the time I see them flying around the flowers down there," she said, pointing at the large swatch of wildflowers that banked the highway. "Or getting smashed on the windshield." She snickered.

"You think that's funny?" Margaret hissed.

There was a tense silence in the small car. Luz glanced in the rearview mirror to see Stacie slump back and look at her nails.

"I didn't mean anything by it," Stacie said at last.

"That's okay," Luz said. "I wondered about that myself. I'll die if we hit one."

"Truth is," Stacie said, "I really love butterflies on account of my granny loved them. She never sprayed her flowers with pesticides or nothin' because she said that'd kill the butterflies and ladybugs. She liked ladybugs, too. Then she took sick and the Lord called her home. We had a real nice service. At the cemetery, the minister was reading from the Bible when suddenly I seen a monarch butterfly land right on her gravestone! It stayed right there for the whole service. But the really weird thing is, now whenever I get sad and start missing her, I see a butterfly! You know what I think? I think those butterflies were my granny come from heaven to let me know she's all right. So that's why they're special to me." She glanced over at Margaret with reproach. "It's the God's truth."

Margaret looked unconvinced.

"I believe you," Luz said with heart. "I guess, then, you won't think it's weird that I'm chasing butterflies, believing they're signs from *my* grandmother."

"No friggin' way!" Stacie leaned far forward to bring her face closer. "You know what?" she asked, her eyes bright. "I'll bet we were meant to meet each other."

Margaret snorted.

"Things like this happen more often than you'd think." Then Stacie asked Margaret pointedly, "*You* got a butterfly story?"

"No," Margaret replied with a sniff. "I'm simply interested in observing the migration phenomenon and seeing the overwintering grounds."

Stacie smirked. "Figures."

Luz listened to the two argue about whether butterflies—or any animal—could be messengers from spirits. To her mind, it was a matter of faith and could never be proved. You either believed or you didn't. She looked up at the sky again.

"Where are they?" Luz said again.

Margaret looked out her window. "I don't see any butterflies at all. You'd think the monarchs would be passing through in big numbers about now. October is peak season."

Stacie scooted to lean over and peer out at the sky.

"Well, it's a big sky," Luz answered with a light laugh. "And they fly high."

"What makes them migrate?" Stacie asked.

"Instinct. They're all following a map that instinct put in their brains and in the fall they all start traveling in the same direction at the same time. By the time they reach Texas it's like our highways at Thanksgiving. It gets crowded."

"I got that map in my brain, too," Stacie said, settling back in her seat. "I keep trying to get to L.A. but I always end up right back here in Texas."

Miles rolled beneath them as Luz shared stories about the sanctuaries, the traditions of the Day of the Dead, and of how they were decorating the box of ashes as a small altar for Abuela.

Meanwhile, Margaret was taping to the box the marigolds and food-wrapper flowers that Ofelia had made. Stacie hung over the seat and watched every move that Margaret made. Occasionally she pushed her arm through the narrow seat opening and pointed with her long, scarlet fingernails where Margaret should tape something. Margaret's lips were tight and Luz thought she looked like a boiling pot about to blow its lid.

To Ofelia's collection Margaret added the yellow and red receipt from the KOA park, pinned baby Luz's pink booties onto the ends of the rope, and tied it back around the box.

"There!" Margaret said, looking at the box with thinly concealed pride. "I think our *ofrenda* is coming along nicely."

"Oh, no, it needs color!" Stacie stated her opinion from the backseat. "It's too bland with all that brown."

"I happen to like brown," Margaret replied thinly.

Luz's lips twitched.

"Let me have it," Stacie said, reaching for it.

Margaret brought the box closer to her chest and glared.

"I'm a really good artist," Stacie said coaxingly. "Did you see all those psychedelic swirls on the guys' RV? I did that. Pretty good, huh?"

"You did?" Luz asked.

"Yep. And the letters, too." Stacie wiggled her fingers for the box.

"But, this box is so small . . . ," Luz hedged. She wasn't sure she wanted a purple, psychedelic *ofrenda*.

"At least let me write her name. That's my specialty."

Margaret swung her head around with impatience. "Can't you take a hint? She said no."

"No, she didn't."

"Wait," Luz interjected, throwing water on the flames between the two women. "It's all right. Go ahead and give it a try. But be conservative, okay? Nothing too weird. That's my grandmother in there."

"Don't you worry," Stacie said in all seriousness as she took hold of the box. Immediately, Serena jumped up from the car floor where she'd been lying on a pillow and commenced sniffing the box. Stacie nudged the dog back onto the pillow and offered her a bit of her cookie for distraction.

"I loved my granny," Stacie said. "I wouldn't do anything that'd make her embarrassed."

"Has she seen that tattoo on your ass?" Margaret asked over her shoulder.

"Thanks for noticing," Stacie quipped, chin up. "At least you didn't call it a tramp stamp."

Margaret turned back to face the road, muttering that she'd never even heard of that expression but it sounded about right.

"Since you asked, no, she didn't see it," Stacie added with a twinge of hurt in her voice. "My granny passed two years ago and I got that tattoo for her. It's a butterfly. And not a day goes by that I don't miss her."

Luz caught Margaret's eye and shook her head in silent censure. She glanced in the rearview, chewing her bottom lip as Stacie worked on the box. Margaret turned back to watch, at first to police the work, but as Stacie drew, she was temporarily silenced by the obvious talent. Stacie wrote the name *Abuela* in a swirling, hippie kind of calligraphy. The letters seemed to fly across the box along with the drawings of monarch butterflies traveling from one side of the box to the other. Then she filled in the letters with the muted colors of autumn. Finally, she rearranged the rope and the paper flowers in an attractive pattern around the box.

"It's beautiful," Luz said.

"It's a start," Stacie replied modestly.

"Honestly," Margaret said with a modicum of surprise, "you did a good job." She fell into silence while her fingers tapped her observation notebook in her lap, then cleared her throat. "Maybe . . . ," she began hesitantly. After a pause, she continued more assuredly, "My father taught me that scientific observation should be impartial. Just an honest recording of what was observed. Maybe part of what I need to learn on this trip is to not always jump to make snap judgments about something, like whether butterflies are messengers from heaven, or . . . about people."

"We could all stand to learn a little of that," Luz said, eyes on the road.

Margaret took hold of her notebook and carefully ripped a page from it. The page was filled with her neat, vertical handwriting.

"What are you doing?" Luz asked, surprised that she'd do such a thing. Margaret had studiously pored over her notes since the beginning of the trip, religiously filling in page after page.

Margaret turned around and handed the paper to Stacie. "That's what I'm trying to do on this journey and I'd like to dedicate it to Abuela. For the *ofrenda*."

A hesitant smile bloomed on Stacie's face as she accepted the paper. Stacie sat back against the seat and neatly folded the paper into a small square revealing Margaret's script. Then she taped it to the side of the box. Around it, she drew an elaborate gold frame and filled it in with embellishments. "There," she said with finality. "Now that looks right."

The car lapsed once again into silence. This time, however, Luz didn't sense the fractiousness she had earlier. Instead, she experienced a soft glow; she'd been fortunate to share so many stories with these interesting yet so different women. Maybe Stacie was right and they were all meant to meet one another. Her maps and carefully laid-out plans for the trip—outlining exactly where she'd stop and at what time—lay scattered on the floor at Margaret's feet. Probably where they belonged. She thought of Billy's words to her that magical night of butterflies. *Life isn't a series of random events at all, but rather an expression of a deeper order.* When you looked back at them all, Luz thought, they made perfect sense, like chapters in a story.

Luz glanced in the rearview mirror. Stacie had her head back against the seat with her eyes closed. Her mascara had smudged to look like bruises under her eyes. Luz turned to look again at Margaret. Her face was serene as she gazed out at the scenery, and Luz didn't perceive any sadness in her face. She imagined Ofelia with baby Luz in her arms.

Luz sighed as she reflected on how this trip was taking so many unexpected turns, dangerous curves, dead ends, road blocks, and U-turns. Straight roads were boring, anyway. In the end, she just had to read the signs.

Luz was grateful for a turn in the backseat with Serena in her lap and Abuela's ashes by her feet. Her left leg ached from pushing in the clutch for so many days. Outside, the day was sunny and warm. The car's air-conditioning didn't work so they rolled down the windows and let the October breeze cool their cheeks and whisk through their hair. Luz lay her head against the backrest, letting it loll lazily to the left as she looked out at the miles of dreary, straw-colored landscape broken by occasional trees, apartments, or strip malls. Here and there was the ubiquitous water tank that stuck up from the flat earth like a token on a game board. The road construction had narrowed the highway to one lane and it seemed to be going on forever. Her eyelids drooped and Serena whimpered in her sleep.

Stacie looked out over the horizon and shook her head. "Where I grew up is a sight prettier than this stretch here."

"I thought a lot of Texas was like this," Margaret said.

"Oh, no," Stacie replied emphatically. "Everyone thinks Texas looks like it did in the movie *Giant*. Just remote, dry land full of cattle and oil rigs. Texas is big, honey. Some of the prettiest land on God's earth is right here. You just wait. I want to see your face when you roll into the Hill Country."

"Is that where you're from?" asked Margaret.

"I'm from Austin. But I wish you could've seen my granny's ranch. My daddy worked the place while my granny lived, but she wasn't cold in the ground before he sold the ranch and moved us to a brand-new house in a nearby town. Mama was happy, but it near broke my heart. I don't know if I can ever forgive them for selling it. It was like they up and sold our family history. I learned I could live in wide-open spaces, and I could live in big cities where I rubbed shoulders. One extreme or the other. But that in-between stuff—towns and suburbs—no way. Not for me. I up and left and I've been moving around ever since. But Lord, I miss that ranch still. There's nothing like sitting on a grassy hill in the summertime, looking over water. Or in the fall, seeing shade trees tinged in gold. Everything I remember from my childhood is from that one place."

"It's funny what you remember from being a kid," Margaret said. "We weren't a demonstrative family but—"

"You weren't what?" Stacie interrupted.

"We didn't hug or kiss much," Margaret answered without rancor. "But there was a lot of love. I'm sure my parents fought from time to time, but I don't remember it. I only recall the happy moments, like us sitting under the tree at Christmas, or blowing out candles on birthday cakes. My folks were academics so we never had the money for a big vacation, but some of my happiest memories were just going hiking and hunting for plants and insects."

"Sounds like a blast," Stacie said with unveiled sarcasm.

"No, I get that," Luz said from the back. She rested her hand on Abuela's box of ashes. "It's not the big holidays or the big presents that mean the most. We couldn't afford vacations either, but I never felt deprived. This is my first time out of the Midwest."

Stacie glanced at Luz in the rearview mirror, her eyes wide. "Girl, are you kidding me?"

"Me, too," chimed in Margaret.

"*You* I can believe," Stacie added with a wink.

Luz laughed, preferring the gentle teasing between the two over the pointed jabs. "My happiest memories were in my grandmother's garden when we released a brand-new butterfly. I loved to watch it test its wings, fluttering them slowly back and forth, so fresh and velvety. I must've released a thousand butterflies but each time felt like the first."

"Well, I never released a butterfly or went hunting for bugs," said Stacie. "Can't say I'm sorry about that. And I don't remember no big vacations or birthday presents, either." She paused and stuck one arm out the window, her fingers wiggling as though trying to catch the breeze. "What I remember are the trees," she said. "The ranch had lots of them—oak, mesquites, pecan, cedar. There ain't no tree on God's good earth that smells like cedar. It announces its presence before you see it, like my granny's perfume. No matter where I am, whenever I smell cedar, I close my eyes and think of Texas. It's—" Stacie's voice dropped an octave. "Oh, that's not good."

"What?" the other two cried in unison. Luz jerked up, waking Serena.

"The warning light just went on! It's flashing red. What does that mean?"

The girls looked at one another, a sinking feeling in their guts.

"There's smoke coming out of the engine. You have to stop the car!" ordered Margaret.

"I can't! There's nowhere to pull over!" Stacie pointed to the orange construction cones.

"Just wait," Luz said, scooting up on the seat so she could look over Stacie's shoulder and see the dashboard. El Toro was old and didn't have all the fancy signals newer cars did. The red light didn't give a clue to what was wrong. Serena picked up on the tension and began barking.

"I knew it! We're going to die in this piece of junk!" cried Margaret.

Stacie and Luz swung their heads to look at Margaret, shocked by her outburst.

"Well, *I'm* not dying on this godforsaken road," Stacie said, peering far over the wheel in search of an exit. "It'll be like *never* before someone finds us."

"Okay, girls," Margaret said, sounding like Mrs. Penfold. "Let's think. There's got to be a manual in here somewhere." She jerked open the minuscule glove compartment and began skimming through the papers she found inside.

"Do you really think this piece of shit has a manual?" Stacie asked. "That manual went out in the seventies back with the upholstery."

"Hey, at least I'm trying to do something!" Margaret shoved the papers back into the compartment but they wouldn't fit. She rammed them in and pounded the door closed with her fist, over and over, but it wouldn't close. "Just pull over," she barked. "I don't think you're supposed to drive with the red light on."

"Look!" Luz cried, pointing over Stacie's shoulder. "There's an exit. Just take it!"

Stacie pulled off onto what appeared to be the loneliest-looking exit any of them had ever seen. The construction fencing was cracked and dusty, the earth alongside the road was parched, and there wasn't a tree or blade of green in sight. The breaks squeaked as they came to a stop at the end of the dusty exit ramp.

Luz tightened her hands on the back of the seat, afraid that El Toro was breaking down again. Only this wasn't a big city, it was the middle of tumbleweed nowhere. There were only two buildings as far as she could see. One was a ramshackle gas station with three ancient-looking pumps, and the other a vacant Dairy Queen, its white shingles falling off. The engine rumbled beneath them and for a moment they were silent as they stared out at the desolate scene.

"I think we're in the Twilight Zone," Margaret said.

"Nah, we're just in Texas," Stacie said, and shifted into gear. "Girls, I'm singing hallelujah! This gas station might not be much, but it's what's here. I suggest we pull in, unless y'all want to travel down the road a mile or so to where that water tower is. This here's ranch country and the spreads go on for miles."

"Let's pull in," Luz said.

Stacie obliged, driving into the Wilbur Less Gas Station. The sign proudly announced: WHERE LESS IS MORE.

Stacie pulled up beside a pump and turned off the engine. It rattled a second, then sputtered to silence. Margaret and Luz climbed out from the passenger side with Serena in tow. Stacie pulled lipstick out of her bag and artfully applied a fresh coat of fuchsia, then looked around. Except for a man fueling his pickup truck pulling a U-Haul, the place looked deserted.

"Well, girls," Margaret said dryly, looking at the broken air pump, the filthy windows of the store, and the hand-painted sign. "I'd say this was a time when Less is not more."

Stacie stretched her arms over her head. "Nope. For sure, Less is less."

Luz started laughing. Suddenly the ridiculous all seemed hysterically funny. "You could say he lived *down* to his name."

Margaret burst out laughing, too, so hard she had to hold on to Luz's shoulder for balance.

Stacie watched the two with a puzzled frown.

Luz finally contained her laughter, feeling a hundred times better for the release. After taking Serena for a quick walk to the brown grass, she went to the dusty hood of the car and pried it open; it let out an angry squeak. She reached out to check the oil and leaped back with a yelp.

"You can't touch it!" Margaret exclaimed. "You need a rag or something. Stacie, could you grab some of those paper towels?"

Using the paper, Luz was successful in pulling out the burning-hot dipstick while the other two women watched. Thanks to Sully, she'd learned how to do this. *Someday you'll get stranded and I won't be there to help,* he'd told her, and it turned out he was right. Pulling out the dipstick, Luz saw that the oil was pretty much gone. She mentally kicked herself for traveling so far without checking.

"It's dry as a bone. We need oil," she told the girls.

"Well, that doesn't sound so bad," Stacie said. "I mean, we can fix that, right?"

"Right." Luz went to the glove compartment and pulled out the now torn and scrunched-up papers. Biting her tongue so she wouldn't say anything and get them all riled again, she pulled out the sheet of Sully's instructions.

"Wait here," she told them, giving Margaret the leash. "I'll go in and buy some oil."

"I'll go with you. It's my turn to pay," Margaret said, handing the leash to Stacie.

Inside the station everything looked old, including the thin, grizzled, gray-haired man behind the counter. He sat far back in his chair with his yellowed straw hat down low over his eyes. Luz wasn't sure he was awake until she stepped to the counter. He reached up to push back his hat, revealing rheumy blue eyes rimmed in red.

"Yeah?" he asked in greeting.

"Hi," Luz said. "I need to fill up with gas. And I need a can of"—she checked her paper— "10W-40 oil."

"Sorry. Ain't got none."

"What? Gas or oil?"

"Look for yourself, missy." He lifted a skinny arm and pointed, revealing dark-rimmed nails. "I got 10W-30. I got straight thirty-weight. I even got that new stuff, twenty. But I ain't got 10W-40."

"But that's the kind I was told to get." She glanced at the dusty shelf with its assorted dusty cans of oil. "Will one of those other oils work? I'm driving a VW Bug."

"Reckon you could try and see."

The old coot seemed to be enjoying her discomfort. Luz swallowed a lump of indignation. "Is there another gas station nearby?"

"Yeah," he drawled. "Up the road a piece."

Margaret drew back her shoulders. "How far is 'a piece'?"

"Don't know exactly."

"Roughly."

"Two, maybe four miles."

Luz looked at Margaret, despair flickering in her eyes. "We could try and drive. Or walk?" She turned to the man behind the counter. "You couldn't maybe drive us?"

"Nope. Can't leave the store."

Luz closed her eyes and pinched her lips. There was no use

telling the man he wasn't being the least helpful. "I'll call Sully," she told Margaret. "*He'll* know what to do about the oil," she said louder than she had to. "Can I borrow your phone? Mine's still dead."

The old man lifted his chin, indicating the phone. "Might not get that fancy phone to work out here."

Luz scowled at him, then dialed Sully's number only to discover that she couldn't get reception. Hoping to get a better signal, she went outside with Margaret right behind. Once again, there was no reception. Feeling dejected, they walked back across the dust and dirt to the car and stared helplessly at the engine, reassessing.

Stacie was leaning over the hood of the nearby pickup truck, her ample bottom swaying from left to right, deep in conversation with the man filling his tank. Serena stood at her ankles, staring back at them with pleading eyes. When the man was finished with the gas, Stacie came sauntering over, leading her new friend as though he, too, were on a leash.

"Hi, girls," she sang out. "I brought someone who might help us damsels in distress." She looked up and smiled sweetly into the man's face. "This here's Wayne."

"Ladies," he said, touching his hat. "You look like you could use some help."

Stacie flashed them a smug smile.

"Well, sir," Margaret began, "my friend here forgot to change her oil and so the red light came on. We figured out we need oil, but the guy in there says he doesn't have the right kind. We're not sure what to do next."

"Mind if I take a look?"

Wayne bent over the engine and checked the oil, clearly wanting to get his own read. He whistled and shook his head in disbelief when he saw the dipstick. "You girls should be glad your engine didn't seize solid," he said. "What kind of oil do you think you need, and what kind do they got in there?"

"Sully says we need . . . well, here," Luz said, handing the paper to the man.

Wayne looked at the list, nodding in that way men did that told everyone they understood the situation perfectly.

"See, oil has different viscosity," Wayne began, speaking slow like he was speaking to children. Mentally challenged children. "Never mind about all that. Come on in the store and I'll point out the right one to get."

Wayne bought them all Cokes and they sat in the shade and chatted while the engine cooled and their thirst slackened. He filled the oil tank and wouldn't take a penny for his time. "Just be sure to check the oil every time you buy gas," he told them.

"He's a real knight in shining armor," Margaret said, looking after him as he walked back to his truck. "I didn't think guys like that existed anymore."

"Oh, there's lots of guys like that in Texas," Stacie said, a hint of pride in her voice. "Ain't nothing a Texas boy loves more than to come to a girl's rescue. 'Specially if she's pretty."

"That so? Then why are you going to L.A.?" Margaret asked her.

"It's my destiny," she said, and smiled that megawatt smile of hers. "Speaking of which . . . it's time to say good-bye to you girls. I'm hitching my star to Wayne."

Luz was shocked and her face showed it. "You're what? Stacie, you only just met him!"

"He's nice. I can tell."

"I know we didn't hit it off right away, but . . . ," Margaret began.

"Oh, Lord, no," Stacie exclaimed with a light laugh. "You might've been wearing your britches too tight, but that's not why I'm going. I was talking to Wayne and he told me he's heading straight to L.A. and he offered to give me a lift. Hey, it's the way I roll. Wherever the whim takes me. So I thank you for your hospitality. I really hope you make it all the way to Mexico and find all you need to find."

She stepped forward to hug Margaret. "Keep it real." Then she moved to Luz. "I just know my granny would have loved you. She liked a girl with a lot of heart." Then softly in her ear she added, "Thanks for saying yes."

Stacie stepped away and dug through her bulging purple bag. She pulled out some papers and thrust them into Luz's hands.

"This is for Abuela's *ofrenda*," she said. "I loved her stories, too. Whenever I see a butterfly, I'll think of her. And you!" She turned on her heel and hurried off in her signature hip-rolling walk to Wayne's pickup.

Luz looked in her hand and saw the label from the oil bottle crumpled up with a twenty-dollar bill. She lifted her arm to wave the label in an exuberant farewell.

Stacie stuck her platinum head out the window as the truck pulled away and shouted, "You might not know where you're going, but in the end, you get to where you're supposed to be!"

Luz and Margaret waved and watched the back of the U-Haul as it spit gravel and dust and disappeared up the entrance ramp to the highway.

"Words to live by," Margaret said dryly.

Luz laughed and slammed the hood shut. "Come on, Margaret. It's just you and me again. Let's get back on the road and get to where we're supposed to be."

Fifteen

When the caterpillar has become too large for its skin, it molts. Monarch caterpillars go through five stages of growth called instars and grow two thousand times their hatch size before forming a chrysalis.

Mariposa brushed the palomino until her golden brown coat gleamed and her pale mane was free of tangles. She'd put her back into it, brushing till her arms ached and sweat dampened her flannel shirt. When she was finished she smelled worse than Opal, but now she was satisfied there wasn't a speck of dirt left on the horse's tawny hair, from the white stripe down her face to her flank.

She lowered her arms and tossed the soft bristled finishing brush into the basket. Opal shook her head and leaned into Mariposa with her weight.

"You want more, do you?" she said with a soft chuckle, reaching up to run her hand across Opal's neck and ears. "Greedy girl."

When she'd first started taking care of Opal, she'd felt terrified whenever the big horse leaned into her. Now she understood that the gesture was a sort of nestling, even if Opal's weight made it cumbersome. Mariposa rested her head against Opal's neck and closed her eyes. The heat of the horse seemed to come from her core. Inhaling, Mariposa smelled the fresh hay she'd laid and that horse scent that always calmed her. She had come today to settle in her mind the question of calling her mother. She hadn't yet heard from her and Mariposa didn't think she could keep on waiting, wondering.

"I missed you," she said against Opal's neck.

"We missed you, too."

Opal jerked her head back, startled by Sam's voice, but Mariposa had grown accustomed to Sam walking up quietly. She found his company comforting. She trusted him in a way she hadn't been able to trust a man in many years. Mariposa continued petting Opal's neck with smooth, firm strokes.

"Easy, girl. It's all right, Opal," she said in a soothing voice as she turned to look over her shoulder. He'd stopped at the threshold and leaned against the gate, crossing his arms. It was a gesture meant to give her space as much as the horse and she appreciated it.

"I didn't mean to startle you," Sam said.

"You didn't."

"Opal looks good."

Mariposa nodded, pleased.

"How are you?" he said.

It was a common expression of greeting, but Mariposa heard the deep concern embedded in the words. She turned to face Sam. His hat was off, his dark hair was damp at the temples, and his bronze skin glistened with sweat after working the horses. But it was his eagle eyes that always caught her attention. They were searching her face, looking for signs of pensiveness or sadness.

"Conflicted," she replied, opening herself to a discussion that, to her surprise, she wanted to prompt. Immediately Sam's attention focused, as she knew it would.

"About what?"

"I've been thinking a lot about our last conversation. Back at the lake. You asked why I didn't call my mother myself. I've been asking myself that question, a hundred times a day. And I don't have any decent answer, other than that I'm afraid." She turned to stroke Opal's long neck, feeling comfort in the feel of her soft hair against her palm. "I've been haunted wondering why they haven't called me back. That's more torture than just picking up the phone and calling."

"What's the worst that can happen if you call?"

Mariposa closed her eyes. "She'd hang up on me."

Sam reached out to put his hand over hers on Opal's neck. Mariposa flinched but he didn't move his hand away. Instead, he tightened his hold.

"Then we deal with it," he said.

Mariposa looked at his hand over hers. "We?" she dared whisper.

"You won't be alone. I'll be there with you." He moved his hand from hers to bring it to her face. He found a tear tracing a dusty path down her cheek and gently wiped it away. "That is, if you want me to be."

Tentatively, she looked up at Sam. His face was so close to hers that she could see his pupils pulse. She looked away from his bruising intensity. His sincerity frightened her, more than any menace she might've found lurking in that darkness. Cruelty she'd learned how to deal with over the years. She doubted goodness when she found it, or someone who wanted to help her for nothing in exchange.

She was shivering and Sam didn't move. He knew to give frightened animals space and time in order not to spook them. Slowly, tentatively, Mariposa moved her shaky hand from Opal to let it rest against his chest. It felt like a very great distance to move.

Sam closed his eyes and she heard him slowly expel a long breath. She hadn't realized he'd been holding it.

"I want you to be with me," she said, lifting her eyes to his. "I'm ready to make the call."

Mariposa glanced over her shoulder as she pushed her apartment door open wider to allow Sam to pass. "Come in," she said, hearing the tremor in her voice. It wasn't because Sam was a man who made her nervous, though that played a part. Sam was the first person she'd ever brought into her sanctuary. Watching him cross the threshold was the breaking down of another boundary she'd set up.

Mariposa had always thought hers was the apartment of a nun. Spare and tidy and chaste. It was the caretaker's studio in the basement of the upper-class condominium building. Her entrance was down a short flight of dreary cement steps from the garden to a bulky and unattractive bolted door. But inside there were large windows that allowed copious amounts of light to drench the small space. The paucity of furniture suited her. A twin bed covered in a white matelasse coverlet was pushed against the back wall and near the windows sat a small, dark wood table and two mismatched wood chairs painted a bright green. Dominating the room was a long shelf constructed of lumber and cinder blocks. The lower shelves were crammed with books but along the top were several ten-gallon aquariums.

She went directly to the sink and began making coffee. She needed to keep busy. As she poured water into the coffeepot, she was intensely aware that Sam was idly walking around her space. He would not miss an iota, she thought, but she shook off her unease, for there was nothing in here that she was ashamed to reveal. While she measured coffee into the pot, she saw Sam walk by her bed and pick up the book left open on the bedside table. It was a used, worn copy of *The Encyclopedia of Insects.*

"A little light reading before sleep, huh?" he said.

"It's my bible."

He set the book down and walked to the aquariums. He bent to inspect and saw the dozens of bright yellow and black monarch caterpillars of different sizes, all ravenously eating the milkweed leaves set in glass jars.

"Look at them go," Sam said, bending low to watch the caterpillars more closely. "They're eating machines."

"That's all they do. Eat and grow."

"And poop."

She laughed, acknowledging the truth in that, and came to his side. "Nearly as much as they eat. We call it frass."

"I'm always amused at all the names we give animal excrement— mutes, guano, dung, cow pies."

She laughed again and moved to the third tank. These caterpillars were bigger, over two inches in length. One was wandering across the glass wall, leaving a barely visible streaky trail. "These guys will wander about till they find the right spot to go into chrysalis," she said, lowering to her knees to look up at the top of the lid.

"Come see," she said, urging Sam to scoot lower. "There are two caterpillars hanging from the top. See how the head curls up to look like the letter *J*? My mother used to say it was an upside-down question mark and the caterpillars were asking, *¿Qué sigue?* What's next?" She smiled at the memory. "They hang there for hours, aerialists without a net."

Sam obliged, going down on one knee, leaning on the other as he bent his head to look. His leather jacket creaked and he made a soft grunting noise as he found a comfortable spot on her hard-wood floor. She hid her smile, even as she felt her body coil at his close proximity.

"Oh, look, Sam! That one is changing to a chrysalis! Can you see that small patch of green there, on the one on the left?"

"Yes," Sam replied, his voice tinged with surprise. "I've never seen that."

She looked over at his face, delighted that he took an interest in a subject that meant so much to her. His was a strong face, tawny colored with sharp angles. The faint stubble of a five o'clock shadow grazed his chin and she could catch the faint scent of soap and leather that always lingered on his skin.

"I'd better check on that coffee." Mariposa rose to her feet and went directly to her galley kitchen to gather two mugs.

Sam went to the chair and sat, setting one polished boot on his knee. "My people have a lot of myths about butterflies," he said. "The butterfly is the totem of transformation and change and a symbol of courage. That should be your totem."

"Courage?" she asked, setting a mug of steaming coffee on the table. She went to gather cream and sugar and placed these on the table with two spoons. Then she took the seat across from him and poured a liberal amount of cream into her mug. "Is it courage to change when you don't have much choice in the matter?"

Sam didn't reply, and brought his coffee to his lips. His dark eyes glittered, watching her over the rim.

"My sobriety was no act of selfless courage, Sam. I was forced to quit drugs by a judge when he sentenced me to three years for trafficking. I was sent right into treatment and though it was the hardest thirty days of my life, in the end I was grateful for it. Looking back, I'm ashamed to think of all the things I've done as an addict. I was as low as a caterpillar, driven only by an insatiable appetite."

"Symbolism can be an important ally," he argued, setting his mug back on the table. "The lowly caterpillar changes into a creature of great beauty. It's a powerful image."

An enigmatic smile played on her lips as she gently shook her head. "Why does everyone always think only of the butterfly as beautiful?" she asked him. "It's the change itself—the metamorphosis—that is the true wonder." She lifted her hand to indicate the aquariums filled with caterpillars. "No one stops to think of how the caterpillar must shed its skin five times before it forms the chrysalis. The caterpillar doesn't just change. It completely transforms. The old form dies and the new is reborn. That's the miracle that gives us hope."

Sam leaned back in his chair and put his tanned hand on his knee. His large turquoise ring caught her eye. An eagle was carved into the silver.

She turned to look into the tanks again, feeling an overwhelming urge to explain herself so that Sam would understand.

"When I first came out of treatment, I was like that first tiny caterpillar out of the egg. I had no idea of who I was. My senses were numb. All I could do was eat and exist. I was afraid—all the time—but I had to keep going forward. Each phase was like bursting out of an old coat. Over the last few years I went through these phases again and again. It takes great courage to go into the darkness, to face your demons. Yet, it's not so much courage that keeps me going. It's more a fear of falling back into the darkness."

Mariposa took a sip of her coffee, savored the richness of it, then slowly lowered the mug to the table. She looked up at Sam. "But I'm not afraid now. I'm ready for the next step. I'm ready to make the call."

It was only because he'd given his word to Luz that Sully went to her bungalow. The moment he stepped inside, his heart fell. Abuela was gone and so was Luz. The house felt as cold and empty as the great hollow ache in his chest where his heart used to beat.

Sully methodically set the mail on the front table, mostly circulars and junk mail. Then he walked down the hall to the kitchen, his footfall echoing loudly. Of all the rooms, this one felt the most desolate. When Abuela was alive, there was always music and food and laughter. He didn't sense anything of her spirit left here. Perhaps Luz was right after all. She'd flown off with the butterflies.

Luz . . . He shook his head. Hell, he was thinking so much about her, now *he* was even starting to believe stuff like that. He filled the watering can at the sink, then one by one dutifully watered Abuela's plants. He couldn't let them die, no matter what was—or wasn't—going on with him and Luz.

He'd loved that old woman. She never said a mean or rude word to him, or to anyone else. She always greeted him with a warm smile and something to eat. She treated him like a prince in these walls, used to tease him that her life's mission was to "fill out his bones." They'd had a special bond, or at least he liked to think so. In all honesty, he enjoyed the trips to pick things up with her. She'd tell him stories about Luz from before he'd met her, things Luz would never tell him herself. Like how she sang to the trees and flowers, how her favorite food was ice cream, and how she hadn't let go of Abuela's hand for days after her mother died. Often at the end of the errand, when he dropped her back home, Abuela nudged him in his ribs, winked, and said, "So, when are you going to marry my granddaughter, eh?" He loved her for that. It told him she approved, and Abuela's approval had meant a lot to him.

Sully put away the watering can and went down the hall. He paused at the threshold of Luz's bedroom. The lavender and pink room was the room of a child, but he knew Luz had been a woman with a woman's responsibilities for several years before her time. He respected Luz for giving up school to get a job, knowing how much she wanted to study for a degree in social work. That's when he'd first seen her. Leaning against the locker, one foot on the wall, her nose deep in her book. He had to cough three times to get her to look up. One look in her pale blue eyes fringed with all those black lashes and he was gone.

But he loved her most for her heart. She was a lot like her grandmother, only she didn't see it. For whatever reason, she didn't have a lot of self-confidence. She was always criticizing herself—she was too heavy, her face was too plain, her hair too thick. She didn't fit the model's bony profile, as if he'd ever wanted that. No matter how many times he told her how beautiful she was, she'd shake her head no. She had this crazy idea in her head that she'd never be as beautiful as her mother.

After Abuela died, he worried that Luz was going to have a breakdown. She imploded, sort of like the way he'd read a black star did. All the light she carried was sucked into some dark place.

Sully ran his hand through his hair, feeling the ache in his heart expand and contract. Since she'd left on this crazy trip, he'd had a lot of time to think. He could see now how much she'd needed to take this trip. He just wished he could've taken it with her.

But why didn't she answer the dozen messages he'd left on her cell phone? All he got in the past few days was a single message from her telling him that she was fine, that she'd lost her phone charger, and that she'd call when she bought another. That he was not to worry. How the hell was he not going to worry? That was like telling him not to breathe!

Suddenly the sound of the telephone ringing rent the stillness of the house. He tensed, hope springing to life in his heart. Maybe it was Luz leaving a message, he thought. It rang five times before the answering machine clicked on. He stepped closer to the machine on the desk, listening intently. At the beep he heard a woman's voice.

"Hello? Hello? *¿Estás aquí? Por favor.* Please answer!"

Sully stood frozen. He didn't recognize the voice.

"Mami, it's me. I know it's been a long time. What can I say? There are no words to erase all the years. But I'm sorry. *Perdóname,* Mami."

Sully heard the heartbreak in the voice and was unsure whether to answer the phone and take a message. He hovered over the phone in indecision.

"Mami, if you are not there, please call me." She left a number and Sully scrambled to find paper and pencil in the desk drawer to write it down. "I beg you, even if you call only to tell me never to call you again. Please, call me." The woman's voice broke.

Sully lurched for the phone, but it was too late. He heard the fast busy signal of disconnect. He slowly set the phone back into the cradle. It had to be Luz's aunt, the one she couldn't reach. Luz hardly ever talked about her family, but he knew Luz was going to

San Antonio to visit her aunt. Her *tía* Maria in San Antonio. He remembered because he'd helped Luz search this desk for the address and telephone number.

"Shit," he muttered. This was the woman Luz needed the phone number for. He should have grabbed the phone sooner. He picked up the paper and dialed the number he'd written. After two rings, the same voice answered.

"Hello?" The woman's voice was hesitant, cautious.

"Uh, hi. This is Sully Gibson. You don't know me, but I'm a friend of Luz." He heard a quick intake of breath. "I-I heard your message. I wasn't listening in or nothing. I was just here watering the plants for Luz. Collecting the mail, that kind of stuff, while she's gone. I couldn't help but overhear and I thought I should call you back."

"Luz is gone? I don't understand. Where is she?"

"She's on her way to San Antonio right now."

There was a moment of shocked silence. "Luz is coming here?"

"Yes, ma'am. She's driving there. But the problem is she doesn't know your address. The phone number Abuela had is no longer in service. Luz was hoping to find it once she got into town. I know it sounds crazy, but Luz can be pretty stubborn when she wants something. So if you give me your address, then I'll pass it on to her."

"Yes, of course. Are you ready?"

Sully wrote down the address, feeling a bit smug that Luz would be very happy to get it and grateful to him for thinking on his feet.

"Do you know when she's arriving?" the woman asked.

"Any day, I'd think. She's driving, so I can't be certain."

"*Dios mio*," the woman muttered. "Do you want Maria's address, too? Just in case?"

Sully was momentarily confused. "You're not Tía Maria?"

"No. I'm . . . her sister. Luz's mother. Mariposa."

Sully squeezed his eyes shut and lowered his head. That news floored him. Luz's mother was alive? Hell, Luz sure didn't know that. He had to wonder if Abuela did. His heart began to pound as he thought about Luz, naively on her way to San Antonio. She was looking for her aunt Maria. She had no idea what was coming.

"I'm pretty sure she isn't going to see you, ma'am. She's looking for her aunt Maria's house." He cleared his throat. "Luz thinks you're dead."

He heard another sharp intake of breath. "Luz thinks I'm dead?" she asked, her voice ringing with shock and accusation. "That's what she told her? That I was dead?"

"Yes."

"Please," she said, sounding flustered. "Is my mother there?"

"You mean, Abuela?"

"Yes. My mother. Esperanza Avila. May I talk to her, please?"

Sully's mind went blank. This kept getting weirder. Shit, shit, shit, he thought to himself, hating to be the one to have to tell this woman the sad news about her mother. What was the right thing to say at a time like this?

"Hello?"

"Yeah, I'm still here. Mrs. . . ."

"Avila. Miss Avila."

"Uh, yes, Miss Avila." He cleared his throat again. He had no choice but to man up and tell her the truth. "I'm sorry to be the one to have to tell you this, but Abuela, that is, your mother, is dead."

"No!" He heard rapid breathing, then she blurted out with disbelief, "When?"

"A few weeks ago. It was a heart attack. She died quickly. There was nothing anybody could do. I'm sorry. We all loved her." He paused, hearing nothing.

"Hello? Miss Avila? Hello?"

"Thank you. Good-bye."

Sully heard a click and once again, they were disconnected. He stared at the receiver a moment, then put it back in the cradle. His hand rested on it, stunned. He shook his head in disbelief, his mind still trying to make sense of all that he'd learned in the past few minutes, more than Luz had known most of her life. In his mind he saw her driving in that ridiculous old car, the box of Abuela's ashes in the backseat, heading straight toward shock and heartbreak. His strong-hearted girl.

Sully's jaw clenched as he grabbed the paper bearing the address and phone number of Luz's mother and raced out the door.

Mariposa stood clutching the phone to her breast. It buzzed angrily but all she heard was this young man's voice in her mind saying, over and over, *Your mother is dead.*

"Mariposa? What's happened? What did she say?" asked Sam, moving quickly to her side. He took hold of her elbow and gently turned her to face him.

Mariposa looked into his eyes, seeing only the blackness of his pupils.

"Tell me what happened," he said in that low voice of his.

It was his calm that reached her. She opened her mouth to respond but the words would not come out. She turned away from him and stared, openmouthed and eyes wide, at her neat little room. Her gaze swept the kitchen, the bed, the aquariums bustling with life. Everything appeared to be in the same place it was a few moments ago, but nothing was the same or ever would be again.

Her mother was dead. She would never again see her face, hear her voice. It was too late. She would never be forgiven. Mariposa felt the panic erupt in her chest, sudden and violent, scorching her with blinding pain and remorse. She gasped for breath.

Sam had his arms around her and held her to his chest. She felt the coarseness of the fabric against her cheek as she swallowed gulps of air. Nothing erupted, no tears, no cries, just this tremendous ache. "Sam," she choked out, pulling back to take refuge in his gaze. She took a shuddering breath and spoke as if in shock. "My mother is dead."

His arms tightened around her. "I'm sorry."

Gasping, she pushed from his arms and fled through the door. She heard the rushing of blood in her ears as she ran, ignoring the couples sitting on the patio, around the building to her garden. She ran directly to the patch of tilled soil she had been working on, and dropping to her knees, she pushed her hands into the black, crumbling soil. She gathered great handfuls of earth and squeezed as tight as she could, breathing hard. Then, throwing back her head, she opened her mouth and a cry ripped from her soul out to the heavens.

"Mami . . ."

Sixteen

*When she's finished growing, the caterpillar stops eating and leaves
its host plant to wander in search of a safe place, protected from the
weather and enemies, where she can pupate. Once she finds a suitable
spot she spins a silk mat and a small white knot and rests. Her time as
a caterpillar is almost over.*

The landscape markedly changed as they moved farther
south into the Texas Hill Country. More and more Luz saw
the trees that Stacie had reminisced about—in tight clusters
on a vast plain or standing alone and dramatic, like a silent sentry.
Everywhere she looked she saw signs of fall, more subtle and more
varied than in the north. It was as if the scorching heat of the Texas
summer had leached the bright summer colors from the earth. For
as far as she could see, the hills rolled in an intricate tapestry of
muted greens, browns, rusty purples, and pinks.

There were so many wildflowers and native plants along the
highway that to Luz they became a blur of color. But Margaret
jumped up in her seat whenever she spied a new variety, excitedly pointed it out, then hurriedly scribbled the name down on
her list or checked it in the volume in her lap. The Latin names
rolled off her tongue: *Gaillardia, Liatris, Rudbeckia, Solidago.*
Luz had long since stopped asking what the common names were.

Margaret had told her it made more sense for her to learn the scientific names in Latin.

"Common names of a plant often change with location," she told her. "It can get confusing. The scientific names are always correct."

Luz nodded politely, but in her heart she wondered why Margaret would want to stumble over those long names that didn't make a whit of sense when they could just call the flower by a name picked for what the flower looked like: Indian blanket, gayfeather, black-eyed Susan, goldenrod. Most of all, why would she prefer to twist her tongue around *Asclepias* when *milkweed* did the job?

Margaret was in seventh heaven at seeing the native wildflowers along the highway. "We have Lady Bird Johnson to thank for all this," Margaret told her. "She's the patron saint of native plants and wildflowers, in my opinion. Look at all that goldenrod blooming out there. Did you ever see anything so beautiful? I'd be happy to accomplish a fraction of what she did in her lifetime. I just have to figure out how. Maybe I'll find out on this trip. Do you think?"

"Absolutely. A wise woman once told me that we're supposed to find out where we're supposed to be."

Margaret tossed her head back and laughed heartily, from her belly. Luz glanced from the road to look at her. Margaret was blooming. She had a new look of determination in her eyes, a new perked-ear alertness, like Serena had when she caught a scent.

"Hey, slow down and pull off to the side a minute," Margaret exclaimed. "I want to make a stop."

"What for? Is something wrong?"

"No, just do it!"

Luz slowed El Toro and came to a stop on the shoulder. She held on to Serena as Margaret hopped out and walked into a roadside field brilliantly lit by countless vivid orange flowers. She walked through the stalks with the carefree joy of a child playing in the field. When she bent to pick a handful of blooms, her hand rose to idly chase away a bug, and when she stood up she was beaming. The sun shone on her face and she seemed to absorb the brilliant colors that surrounded her. She's in her element, Luz thought as she watched her walk back to the car with her flowers.

"What's that for?"

"Well, I know they're cosmos, not marigolds. But I thought it could be a contribution to Abuela's *ofrenda*," Margaret exclaimed, her flush almost as bright as the flowers.

An hour later, just as the sun was setting, Luz caught her first glimpse of the outline of the city of San Antonio. Looking out, Luz understood why so much fuss was made about the Texas sky. Poets, writers, painters, grandfathers telling stories—they all struggled to put words or color to what they couldn't fully capture. Seeing a Texas sunset stretch out to infinity in reds and oranges so surreal they defied description made Luz believe that there had to be a higher power. Only God could paint like that.

She felt a shiver of nervousness, wondering what awaited her in this city that had been the first American home of her great-grandparents. She was the fourth generation passing through, her lineage as tied to this city as it was to the small mountain village in Michoacán. Yet, as she approached the vista of tall buildings on the horizon, she felt as if she were nothing more than a tourist seeing it for the first time. She'd been on the road for a week and knew nothing more about the family that had settled here generations ago.

They chose a modest motel on the outskirts of the city. There were a few to choose from but their budgets were tight, so they selected the cheapest clean one with a room available. As they stepped in, the air felt close, and the multicolored polyester fabrics on the beds and drapes looked like they were put up in the 1970s.

"Even then, they should've shot the decorator," Margaret declared. Everything was minuscule—a mini white refrigerator, a mini Mr. Coffee machine, a minidresser that served as a stand for the small television, and in the bathroom, teeny-tiny bottles of shampoo and conditioner.

After camping, however, it felt like a five-star hotel. Luz grinned as she washed her hair with the shampoo. The hot water sluicing down her body had never felt so luxurious. She took her time applying lotion to her dry skin, careful to leave some in the teensy bottle for Margaret.

The mirror was fogged when she was through. She took a washcloth and wiped the condensation from the mirror. As she swiped, her reflection gradually appeared in the filmy glass. Her hand slowed, then dropped to her side as she stared at her own reflection.

Her body was still full at the breasts and rounded at the hips, but now she saw the definition of strong bones and sharper curves. When did she get such a pronounced waist? She turned to the side. How much weight had she lost? she wondered. She'd noticed over the past week that her jeans were looser, but she'd been too preoccupied to give it much thought. Even after years with Sully, she still felt self-conscious about her full hips. She often strategically braced half her weight against the chair armrest when she sat on his lap so he wouldn't think she was too heavy. Or snapped at him when he pinched the soft rolls on her side or lay his hand on her belly. The rolls were gone now.

Her grandmother's death had shocked her with its suddenness. The funeral and grief had taken its toll on her and the trip had its unscheduled stops. Luz realized she'd missed a lot of meals. She leaned forward and with her fingertips gently traced the sharper contours of her cheeks, the bridge of her nose, down to her lips. Her eyes seemed larger in her face. The youthful pudginess of her cheeks, the girlishness in her expression, had given way to a new maturity that wasn't there before. She marveled at how the changes she felt occurring inside herself were reflected outside as well.

She was curious to see her aunt Maria. Did she have Abuela's nose, her cheekbones, her laugh? Would Maria look at all like her mother? What new stories could Maria tell about Mariposa and Abuela?

Luz emerged from the bathroom eager to find her aunt's address. Margaret was sitting at the desk in front of her computer, thrilled to be back online and reading up on the sanctuaries. She sat with one leg curled beneath her and dipping french fries in ketchup. The smell of the fast food in the greasy bag made her mouth water. Serena was curled up on the bed, her pointed nose resting delicately on her forepaws. The moment Luz grabbed the bag of food, Serena leaped up and began whining. Luz fed Serena part of her hamburger and ate the rest as she began flipping through the address book.

As she had before, Luz methodically went through all of the entries written in the well-worn pages. The penmanship was old-school, taught by the nuns. Every letter was well formed in her feather script. Luz's index finger scrolled down each page. Her grandmother had been neat. Several entries had been crossed out and new ones added over the years as her aunt moved. Luz took a breath, then picked up the phone and dialed the last number listed for Maria Avila. It was the same number that she'd dialed before the funeral. The phone rang twice. Luz heard the same announcement that the number had been disconnected.

"Any luck?" Margaret asked.

"No. I didn't really expect an answer but I hoped. Next, the phone book."

Undaunted, Luz pulled out the bottom drawer of the bedside stand and found a phone book for San Antonio. Pulling it up to the bed, she opened it, eager. Moving Serena back, Luz began to search for her aunt's name in earnest. She gasped when she saw how many there were.

"There have to be at least fifteen Maria Zamoras in San Antonio!"

"I know. I checked the Internet. It's about the same. At least it's not fifty."

"I guess I'll just have to call each and every one. Maybe I'll be lucky and hit the jackpot on the first try."

"Maybe, but it's getting late. It's nine o'clock already. You don't want to get people angry. Why don't you start tomorrow when you're fresh? It's been a long day, and I don't know about you, but I'm exhausted."

Luz sighed and closed the phone book and set it on the floor. She felt her enthusiasm pall in the wake of apprehension. "What if I can't find her? What if she's not even living in San Antonio anymore?"

"We keep on going," Margaret replied, not missing a beat. "This isn't our final destination, you know."

Luz looked at the resolution on Margaret's face. At the moment, her determination would have to be enough for both of them. For Margaret, the end of the journey wasn't San Antonio, but the butterfly sanctuaries in Mexico. This was just a stopping point. Luz knew her own journey could end in this city if she didn't find her aunt.

She went to rummage through her suitcase and pulled out Abuela's photo album. It, too, was made of soft leather with edges dulled from use. She brought it back to the bed. Folding her leg under her, she began to leaf through the familiar pictures.

"I love photo albums," Margaret said, abandoning her computer to sit beside Luz on the mattress. She leaned forward, squinting. "Is that Abuela?"

"Yes," Luz replied, her heart pumping with affection. Abuela stood straight, dressed in a traditional white ruffled dress heavily embroidered with brightly colored flowers. Her black hair glistened, wound in braids and gilded with fresh flowers. "That's on her wedding day to Luis, her first husband."

"I thought she'd look like that," Margaret said softly. "Kind, but strong. A wise woman."

Luz felt again the aching heaviness in her heart that came whenever she saw a photograph of Abuela or got lost in thoughts about her. She tried not to dwell on her grief and for most of the day she'd succeeded. Now, night had fallen and Luz felt the darkness keenly.

Margaret reached over and handed Luz a paper napkin. Luz wiped her eyes and blew her nose.

"And who's that guy holding the machete?" Margaret asked with a laugh, trying to add levity.

Luz chuckled. As they sat shoulder to shoulder, Luz focused again on the photographs while the tightness in her chest loosened. "That's Luis Zamora, her first husband. From what I could tell he was a character but a real hard worker. He came to America as a *bracero*."

"I don't know what that is."

"During World War Two, a lot of men in the States were in the military overseas and worker shortages were becoming a problem. So the U.S. government began recruiting workers from Mexico, mostly for agricultural jobs. They called these men *braceros,* which means laborers. After that it was back and forth, always sending money back home. He'd be gone six to nine months of every year and Abuela told me how lonely it was for her. She raised her children almost alone. Two daughters and a son."

"Two daughters? I thought your mother had a different father."

"She did. Abuela had a second daughter with Luis but she died soon after she was born. I think about that sometimes, about how afraid she must've been to be alone at a time like that. I've always wondered if that wasn't why Abuela came all the way from Mexico to Milwaukee to help my mother when I was born. She didn't want her daughter to be alone for the birth, like she was."

There were more pictures of Esperanza with Luis and their children Manolo and Maria. And more of their extended families. Luz was embarrassed that she didn't know the names of all the cousins she'd never met.

"He's handsome," Margaret said, pointing to a photograph of Mariposa standing beside a young, tall, blond-haired man in front of a fountain.

"That's my father," Luz said dispassionately. "I don't know him. He's not a part of my life." The words fell cold from her mouth. She couldn't muster any feelings for him.

"At least I know where you got your blue eyes from."

"Not completely. My grandfather Hector has blue eyes." Luz pointed to a photograph of a clean-shaven man wearing round, wire-rim glasses and a suit and tie. His light brown hair fringed his collar and he had thick sideburns in the style of the 1960s. "He was a professor at the university. There's a lot of European ancestry in Mexico. You've got the Spanish, the French, and the German. Mexico is a nationality, not an ethnic group."

"What color are Sully's eyes?"

"Blue. Why?"

"Just trying to figure out the odds of your kids having blue eyes."

Luz jabbed her playfully in the side and turned to the next page. This held a crumpled photograph of Abuela standing beside Mariposa, who was holding a baby.

"Is that you?"

"Yeah."

"Look at you. You were so cute. And look at all that hair!"

Luz studied the photo that she'd found in Abuela's hands when she died. It had been Abuela's favorite. In it, a slender Mariposa with long, softly flowing brown hair that fell nearly to her waist held chubby-faced baby Luz wrapped in a white lace blanket. Mariposa was gazing at her daughter with adoration. Luz had removed the photograph from Abuela's hands, carefully smoothed it out, and taped it into the album. Whenever Luz looked at this photograph it sparked a desperate yearning for her mother.

"So that's your mother?"

"Yes."

"She's beautiful."

Luz halfheartedly smiled. "Everybody says so."

"You don't remember her?"

"I'm not really sure if what I remember is from my own memories or from these few photographs. And, of course, from what Abuela told me about her."

"How did she die?"

Luz stared at the picture, feeling the fog slowly slide into her head. Whenever she asked herself that question she felt a tight ache in her stomach. Was her mother murdered? Did she jump off a cliff? What happened to her?

"I don't know," she said softly.

After a pause, Margaret asked with disbelief, "You don't know? You mean you don't know what the illness was?"

"No. It was an accident. In Mexico. But I don't know anything more. My grandmother refused to talk about it. She was devastated. If I even mentioned it she got upset. I didn't want to hurt her, so I learned early on to stop asking."

"I had an uncle Phil who died. My mom's brother. Whenever I asked how he died my mother just shook her head and said, 'It's none of your business. Run along and play.' I knew they were covering something up. He was the dark family secret. I found out years later that he killed himself."

Luz drew back, appalled. "Jeesh, Margaret. What are you saying?"

"No!" Margaret reached out to touch Luz's sleeve. "I'm just saying that sometimes parents have a way of deflecting questions they don't want to answer, for whatever reason. Kids pick up the undercurrent when something's off. If they don't get the truth, what they imagine is sometimes worse."

Luz nodded her head, tentatively letting the argument sink in.

"Luz, doesn't it strike you as odd that you don't know the details of your mother's death?"

She was about to say an automatic no, but instead, she chose to open up and remain honest with her friend. "Yes. I tried to Google her name a few times but nothing ever popped up. It happened in a remote area of Mexico. Abuela said it was difficult to get information."

"You don't need a newspaper clipping at age five, but by the time you were twenty-one, you'd think your grandmother would've heard some details."

There is much you don't know about Mariposa.

"I wonder if that's what she wanted to tell me when we were on this trip. Right before she died, she kept telling me how there was a lot I didn't know about my mother. She was going to tell me more during our trip."

"That's cryptic."

Luz shrugged, frowning. "I don't want to make more of this than there is."

"See what I mean? If you don't get the truth, you can imagine some pretty wild things."

Luz felt herself shutting down and didn't answer. She closed the photo album, brought her knees close, and wrapped her arms around her legs. In her mind, she saw the images of her relatives in all the photographs. "I wonder what other genes I carry. Whose laugh do I have? Does anyone else like to cook like I do?"

Margaret yawned and rose from the bed. She walked toward the bathroom, grabbing a towel en route. "I guess you'll find out tomorrow."

Thunder rumbled in the late night sky. Luz lay in her bed, her blanket clutched in stiff hands. She hadn't been afraid of the thunder for years, not since she was a child. She blamed the photographs and talking of family secrets for eliciting these old feelings of longing and the gale of insecurity.

She stared at the ceiling while the thunder clapped and flashes of light lit the room. She wondered if her desire to reach out to her family hadn't morphed into something more than familial obligation. She wanted to know who she was and where she came from. She wanted to belong to a family.

As Aunt Maria was her only living female relative, it fell to her to take Luz to the mountains to see the monarchs, as generations of women had done before her. Would Tía Maria feel any obligation to her niece? Would she be angry that she'd shown up unannounced, or be grateful and help bring Abuela's ashes home? What if Luz couldn't find her?

Thunder clapped loudly overhead, so close that the motel's power flickered. Luz yelped and curled into a ball, bringing the blanket over her head. When she was a child Abuela used to hear her cries and come to her bedside to find her shivering in a cold sweat. She'd gather Luz in her arms and let her cling tight and her face burrow in her soft breasts. Abuela stroked her back and her hair, curling locks around her ear in a soothing rhythm while she told her stories of the Aztec gods of rain and thunder. In time, Luz would hear only the words as they resonated in her chest, feel her grandmother's arms around her, and forget the storm outside.

Ah, querida, *you remember how Little Nana leaped into the fire to become the sun? She was so radiant in the sky. A marvel to behold. The gods knew that for this resplendent sun to survive for eternity they would have to give the sun their own blood. So the gods sacrificed themselves and with a tremendous roar the god Ehecatl created a powerful wind that blew the gods back into the spiritual world. He blew again and the great wind pushed the sun and it began to move in the sky and the earth began to rotate around it.*

For many, many years the Aztec people made sacrifices to the gods to repay them for the blood they gave to the sun. They wanted to woo the gods to come back down to earth. Foolish people. The gods already existed among us. They abide in the natural forces. We cannot see them, but they are here. We can feel their power.

So do not be afraid, mi niña. *When you hear the roar of thunder, you hear the voice of Ehecatl making his presence known. He comes in his crown of clouds and carrying rattlers to shake up the sky and make thunder and bring wind. He comes with the great god Tlaloc, who brings the rain to nourish the earth. Shhh . . . listen now. Do you hear the pitter-patter of rain on the roof? Each drop is a gift from the gods. A sign of renewal and rebirth. Shhh . . . sleep now, and listen to the music of the preciousness of life.*

Thunder rumbled low in the far distance as the storm passed. Outside Luz's window, the rain beat a soft and rhythmic beat. With memories of Abuela fresh in her mind, Luz nestled Serena closer against her and surrendered to sleep.

Seventeen

The milkweed that monarch caterpillars eat contains toxins called cardenolides. It is a poison stored in the adult monarch's abdomen and acts as a form of defense from would-be predators. The brilliant colors of the monarch butterflies and caterpillars advertise their toxicity.

The metal slop bucket rattled as Mariposa pushed it down the hallway. She washed the lobby floor of the four-story condominium building every Monday and Thursday with hot water and vinegar. The pungent scent triggered memories of her mother scrubbing the wood floors of their home early every morning. Mariposa rested against her mop and closed her eyes as a fresh wave of regret burned so sharp that she felt her shoulders curl like a leaf caught in a flame.

She took a long, shuddering breath and forced herself to keep working. She couldn't afford to lose this job. It was menial but honest, and given her record, she was grateful to have it. Her duties included sweeping, dusting, and cleaning the general areas of the building. In exchange, she was given the caretaker's garden apartment and a modest salary.

The lobby door opened. She heard the tip-tapping of high heels and the clickety clack of dog's nails on the floor. Mariposa turned her head and said, "Good afternoon, Mrs. Barrett."

"Hello, Mary," the woman replied in an absentminded manner.

Mariposa had greeted Mrs. Barrett daily for two years, yet Mrs. Barrett never called her by her full name. Mariposa had corrected her many times early on, but Mrs. Barrett insisted on calling her Mary, as she insisted on being called Mrs. Barrett, despite the fact that she was divorced. Hearing herself called by the wrong name grated on Mariposa, but she'd stopped correcting her.

Mrs. Barrett was a middle-aged executive at an insurance company. Mariposa knew she had to be successful because she always wore the most beautiful shoes and bags. Today she wore a bright yellow silk dress and black patent leather heels that Mariposa thought must've cost more than she earned in a week. She breezed past Mariposa toward her mailbox with hardly a glance. Her expensive shoes and her corgi's big muddy paws left dirty prints across the damp floor. After riffling through her mail, Mrs. Barrett noticed Mariposa waiting, mop in hand, staring at the floor. She looked down.

"Oh," she said with a scrap of surprise. "Bootsie, you bad girl," she said to her dog. "Making such a mess." She looked at Mariposa with a perfunctory smile. "I guess it's a good thing you're still here with your mop! I'll just get out of your way. Come along, Bootsie." She walked off to the elevator without another word, trailing more mud.

Mariposa felt dead inside and immune to the slings and arrows of people who did not matter to her. She simply dragged the mop across the floor again in a monotonous pattern. When she was finished she hoisted her bucket, heavy with dirty water. She grimaced as she lugged it down the hall to the custodial closet, where she dumped the dirty water, panting with effort. Mariposa put her hand to her lower back and rubbed the sore spot.

She was only forty years old but she had aches like an old

woman. Then again, she'd lived twenty of those years hard. Drugs, poor diet, smoking—they took their toll on her muscles, skin, and hair. She saw the changes every time she looked in the mirror.

Not that beauty mattered to her any longer. There was a time when she was accustomed to the attention of men and the envy of women. That seemed so long ago. She'd made a lot of mistakes in her life and learned some hard lessons. She didn't want to make any more. Day by day, that was her mantra. She had to hold it together, to somehow get stronger so she could face her daughter. Luz's forgiveness was all she wanted from life now.

She rinsed the buckets and neatly put away her tools. As soon as she was finished she removed her dirty apron, let her long hair free from its elastic, and went directly to her garden. The small, walled garden that bordered the patio of the condominium building was her refuge. She'd received permission from the owner to plant the garden at her own expense—as long as she maintained it. Local Mexican landscape crews befriended her and helped her out, delivering soil and offering their strong backs to till it. In exchange, she shared her knowledge of horticulture and gave them young plants that she'd started from seeds in her makeshift greenhouse. Her garden had been worth all the work and expense and soul she'd put into it. It had been her salvation.

There were moments in the past three years of recovery when she felt such despair that she didn't think she could make it past another day without using. Moments like now. At these low points when her hands shook and her gut roiled, she'd go to the garden and put her hands deep into the earth. Ungloved and bare, she'd dig down deep and squeeze the dirt between her fingers, breathe in its pungent smell, and feel rooted to a profound source that connected her to a greater whole.

Her mother had often told her that when she dropped to her knees and worked in the garden, she found peace and strength. Esperanza had given this power a name—God. Mariposa, however, had lost faith in her mother's kind and benevolent God, but she could not deny the existence of a greater power. So she'd created a garden as her sanctuary, her temple. Each flower she planted, each knotty weed she pulled, each butterfly she released she offered as a prayer, with the same innocent heart that she had as a child lighting a candle in church. Today, her offerings were to her mother.

Mariposa saw the butterflies that flocked to her garden year after year as a sign that she'd been heard. The monarchs especially, these great messengers to the goddesses, allowed her to cling to the slim hope that although her mother was gone, soon she would reunite with her daughter.

She heard the squeaking of the garden's iron gate opening and closing. It was cocktail hour and people from the condominiums were coming to the garden to socialize. Mariposa couldn't bear the idle cheerfulness during her mourning. She quickly gathered the pile of weeds into a bag, eager to flee.

"Mariposa?"

Mariposa was startled to hear Sam's voice. She looked up to see him standing at the edge of the garden. He wore his customary blue chambray shirt open at the top and tucked neatly into his jeans. His large silver belt buckle was of some Native American symbol.

She rose slowly, her breath catching in her throat. Sam had stayed with her for hours after she'd heard the news of her mother's death. He'd brought her back indoors from the garden, not leaving until sometime late in the evening when she was asleep. She'd been vaguely aware of him helping her wash the dirt from her hands and sitting by her bed while she wept inconsolably. She hadn't seen him in the two days since and despite her despair, she had missed him.

Sam smiled and raised his hand to tip his hat. Then his gaze swept across the garden. She saw his lips curl up slightly in appreciation before he turned his attention back to her. "It's a beautiful garden," he said.

"Thank you."

"You missed your riding lesson," he said, calling across the garden in a loud voice.

"I couldn't come. You know why."

"Opal doesn't know that. She missed you."

"I missed her, too," she said in a ragged voice, feeling another gush of grief rise up to spill from her eyes. Mariposa tugged at her garden gloves, taking them off slowly, calming herself. Just breathing hurt. She felt raw, like an open wound that hadn't had time to heal.

"Mariposa, are you going to join me here on the patio or would you rather I came out to you, because what I have to say to you I'd rather not shout out across the garden."

"I'm coming." She cut a path through the echinacea and asters to stand a distance away from him in the shade of the patio. She was grateful none of the tenants were around, so they could speak privately. She reached up to wipe the moisture from her brow, aware that her jeans and shirt were damp and soiled from her work.

He closed the last few feet between them in two steps. "How are you?"

She heard the deep concern embedded in that common expression of greeting. She raised her gaze, seeking comfort in his dark eyes.

"I'm afraid."

"What are you afraid of?"

"That I can't handle this. It's too hard."

"The death of a loved one is one of the hardest blows for us to deal with," Sam began, his voice calm and easy. "But you have to take it one day at a time."

"I don't know if I can make it. I'm hanging on by a thread."

"And what's that thread?"

She exhaled a long, shuddering breath. "Luz." Just hearing herself speak the name aloud was like a soothing caress to Mariposa. "Knowing she's coming, that she's in a car somewhere on her way here, is the only thing that's keeping me from running away."

"And using."

Mariposa wrapped her arms around herself and nodded curtly.

"I'm here," he told her, putting his hand on her tight shoulder. "Opal's here. And soon, your daughter will be here."

"I want my *mother*," she cried, slapping her hands to her face.

Sam took a deep breath. "I know."

Mariposa wiped her tears from her cheeks in quick, angry strokes. "Luz thinks I'm dead," she said. "Maybe it's better off that way. She doesn't know me. She doesn't love me. Maybe I *am* better off dead."

"Is that what you want?"

Mariposa closed her eyes tight and nodded.

"But you're not dead. That was a lie. I don't know why your mother told her that. I expect she had her reasons. But that doesn't make it right. You owe it to yourself and to Luz to face the truth. How she handles it is out of your control. You can only control yourself. The way ahead is in facing and living the truth."

"And what's that truth?" Mariposa asked.

"You're Mariposa Avila, a recovering addict."

She turned her back to him and fixed her gaze on a small spigot from which water was slowly dripping.

"Think a minute about Opal," Sam said firmly. "You can't just call and tell us you're not coming. It doesn't work that way. Not because we need your help. We can take care of our animals. But because you need to be consistent with Opal. She depends on you to feed her, to brush her, to walk her. You've become an important part of her life. And she yours.

"What worries me is that you're falling into your old pattern. You're isolating yourself again. Setting up a spiral for relapse. Once the spiral begins your clever mind will seek out ways to spark self-loathing. Once that happens, you set off a sequence of failures that will lead to more depression and despair, and ultimately, to what was your goal all along—alcohol and drugs."

Mariposa stared harder at each drop that fell with extraordinary slowness from the spigot. She felt numbed by his perfect analysis.

Sam's voice softened and he reached up to gently cradle her chin. "Come on, Brave Face," he said, using his nickname for her. "You're strong. We'll get through this."

His support filled the black hole she'd felt opening. She knew her impulsive behavior was at the crux of her addiction. She was good at playing this old game. Her mother had delighted in comparing her flighty behavior to that of a butterfly. Excuses were made for what they called her "spontaneity." It was a kind of suicide.

"How do I change?"

Sam reached into his pocket, pulled out some tissues, and handed them to her. "I think you're doing a good job right now."

Mariposa took the tissues and blotted her eyes. "Right. I'm doing great."

"Look at yourself, Mariposa. You're doing your job. You're back in the garden. You're keeping up your routine. You aren't only in your head. That's all good." He took the tissues from her hand and wiped a tear from her cheek. "Think of it as keeping one toe on the edge of the cliff."

Mariposa looked up at him with the stirrings of reborn trust.

"Today is going to be hard," he told her. "Tomorrow is going to be hard. And the day after that. And after that. You know how this works. You knew it wasn't going to be easy. But you've come a long way."

She nodded.

"And," he said, "so has your daughter."

Eighteen

Once the caterpillar securely hooks her rear legs to the silk button,
she will rest in a J position for many hours. Inside, a chemical change
has already begun. As the chrysalis forms, the old caterpillar skin is
forced off. She twists and turns, securing her hold and shaking off the
remnants of her old caterpillar skin. The chrysalis stage begins.

T wo days later, Luz lay in her bed in the motel and wondered how, in this day of instant communication, at a time
when people complained about lack of privacy, she could
not find her aunt Maria.

She had diligently called every number on her list. Some she'd
reached immediately and they'd told her with varying degrees of
politeness that they were not her relation. In cases where she got
an answering machine, she called back at different times of the day
and into the evening.

That morning, three numbers still did not answer the phone.
Luz dropped Margaret off at the River Walk to do some shopping while she drove to the remaining addresses. At the first
house, the person who answered the door informed her that
this Maria Zamora, no blood relation, had died since the publi-
cation of the phone book. At the second address, the party had
moved. The third location looked deserted. No one knew her

aunt Maria, neither by the name Zamora nor her old married name, Garcia.

Dejected, Luz returned to her cheap motel room ready to drown her sorrows in a hamburger and a milkshake. As she stepped into the room, Serena raced up to her, whimpering with joy.

"Look at you, so excited to see me," she said, feeling buoyed by the dog's boundless affection. Her whole body wagged, not just her tail, and Luz could swear the little dog was smiling. "You'd think I'd been gone for a year, not just an afternoon."

Looking up, she saw several shopping bags on the floor, and strewn over the beds was an eclectic collection of shirts, pants, scarves, and dresses on hangers. They were in the prettiest soft hues of pink, blue, and lavender. Margaret was standing in front of the mirror wearing a burgundy silk dress that clung to her body enough to reveal her feminine curves without flaunting them. She tilted her head as she studied her reflection, seemingly transfixed as she pivoted on her heel for a view of her left, then her right side, a Mona Lisa smile on her face.

"You look beautiful," Luz breathed.

Margaret twirled around and when she stopped she giggled, covering her mouth like a little girl. But her face was suffused with pleasure. She hooked her hair behind her ear and asked shyly, "Do I?"

"Absolutely."

"It's different from anything I've ever worn before. It even feels pretty."

"What *is* all this?" Luz asked, indicating the assortment of clothes on the bed. "Did you rob a store?"

"No," Margaret replied with a chuckle. "I just raided my savings account." She added a quick skip to her walk as she crossed the room and opened the small fridge. Pulling out an opened bottle of white wine, she lifted it in the air and announced, "I discovered color!"

Luz laughed and bent to scoop up Serena, who was clawing at her legs, begging for attention. "All right, you greedy mongrel," she said, giving the dog a kiss on the head.

Margaret was pouring wine into a glass and refreshed her own. "I had the best time shopping. Did you know there are people who do an analysis of your skin color, hair color, eye color and match it up with a season? They know what colors you should have in your wardrobe." She handed Luz the glass of wine.

"That's been around for ages," Luz said incredulously. She was distracted by Serena, who was trying to nose into her glass, and set the dog back on the floor. Serena sneezed her displeasure and promptly began jumping up on Luz's leg again.

"Well, I'd never heard of it. I'm a summer," Margaret said, and stepped back to survey her numerous purchases. "And these are the colors I should wear."

Luz felt a little giddy from the wine and Margaret's happiness. She walked around the bed littered with clothing, taking in the soft hues of summer. Margaret chose styles that were more sleek and chic than clothes Luz might have picked out for herself. She was still stuck in the college-girl look. As she held up a crisp pale peach blouse, a tweedy straight skirt, high-heeled pumps, Luz thought maybe *she'd* look nice in these more sophisticated styles, too.

Luz reached down to pick up a hand-painted scarf in brilliant shades of red. "Now this one speaks to me," she said, letting the silk slide through her fingers like water.

Margaret walked over and, reaching down, picked the scarf back up and handed it to Luz. "I'm glad you like it because I bought it for you. See how you were naturally drawn to it? That's because you're a winter," she informed her. "Red is your color."

Luz hurried to the mirror to wrap the fine silk around her neck. The brilliant ruby hue set off Luz's creamy skin and contrasted with her glossy black hair. "Oh, Margaret. I've never had such a beautiful scarf."

Margaret grinned with affection. "I thought you could use a little color, too."

Luz felt ashamed of her earlier thoughts about all Margaret's beige. "Actually, I don't have a lot of red clothes. Abuela wears . . . *wore* red a lot. And she always looked beautiful in it." Her voice drifted as she stared at her reflection. She'd begun wearing her hair bound in the traditional long braid that fell down her back, like Abuela had done. Today, in this gorgeous color, she caught glimpses of Abuela staring back at her.

Margaret set her glass down and began folding her purchases with the expert precision of a sales clerk and stacking them neatly back into the bags. "I thought you might wear that scarf to dress up that plain black dress you plan to wear when you meet your aunt."

Luz felt all the joy of the moment fizzle, like air escaping a pin-pricked balloon. "*If* I meet my aunt." She took a long sip of her wine and turned away from the mirror.

"No luck, I take it?"

"I can't believe it's a dead end." Luz sat on the edge of the bed, feeling again the hopelessness of the day's defeat. "I honestly, truly believed I would find her. I can be so naive."

"I don't know. Optimism isn't necessarily the same as naïveté. San Antonio is a big city," Margaret replied, stretching out on the mattress beside her. "It doesn't mean she isn't here somewhere. I was thinking. A lot of people don't use landlines anymore. If she only has a cell phone, the phone book wouldn't list her."

"Oh, God," Luz groaned. She'd not thought of that possibility but it made sense. "If that's the case I'll never find her without hiring a detective. And I sure don't have the money to do that." Luz felt the weight of her failure. "I can't even afford to keep looking. I'm burning through my cash in this city."

Margaret turned on her side and held her head up on her palm. "Here's a crazy thought. What if we admit that we can't find her and move on?"

Luz sipped her wine. She didn't reply.

"Now seems like the right time to bring this up," Margaret began, pulling herself into a sitting position. She tucked her legs beneath her and leaned forward with intent. "We spent two days here and admittedly, we've gone through all the possibilities. Since we didn't find your aunt, I'm thinking we should leave El Toro here and fly to Mexico." She put her hands up to stall Luz's objections. "I know you don't have much money, and I'm not rich either, but I do have enough to buy two round-trip plane tickets to Morelia. I did a little research on the Internet and the fares aren't so bad from here. And there are several flights a day."

"But," Luz began hesitatingly, "we'd still have to rent a car when we got there. It's not like there are tours to Angangueo."

"Actually, yes, there are. Straight to the sanctuaries. I think it's the way to go. Once we're in Morelia, we could arrange a trip to the sanctuaries with a tour guide. It's all aboveboard, organized, and it's safe."

"Yeah, but for how much?"

"For both of us, a couple thousand dollars."

"What? I don't have that much money!"

266

"But it covers everything—transportation, hotels, food, fees."

"I don't have that much," Luz repeated. She shook her head dejectedly, feeling the day's failures press in on her. "I just don't."

"Luz," Margaret said with some exasperation. She poured more wine into Luz's glass, filling it to the top. Then she replenished her own glass. "We're both committed to this trip. It's do or die. So I say, let's pool our money and get her done. It doesn't matter how much each of us puts down. I'll make up the difference. If it weren't for you, I wouldn't be going on this trip in the first place. So let's just do it. What do you say?"

Luz moistened her lips at the prospect. She turned the plastic glass in her hand around and around. She hadn't expected this. Margaret made it seem so easy. So reasonable. But why did every instinct in her body scream no?

Perhaps because for her, this wasn't just a trip to see the butterflies. For her, the purpose of the trip was to bring Abuela's ashes home. This journey had crystallized her goal to include meeting her extended family, to honor Abuela, and to sit with them at her gravesite on the Day of the Dead.

And her most secret wish was so ethereal that she didn't dare admit it to Sully or Margaret, even to herself. In the deepest corner of her heart, she believed, as her ancestors had believed for centuries, that the spirit of her grandmother would return in the form of a monarch butterfly for the Day of the Dead. She held tight to her faith that she would feel Abuela's presence when the monarchs came through her village. What was faith but belief in something unexplainable?

Luz set down her wineglass and clasped her hands together. "Margaret, first, thank you," she said sincerely. "It's a really nice offer and I appreciate it. But, for me this trip is about more than going to see the butterfly sanctuaries. I'm bringing Abuela's ashes home." She brought her hands up in a gesture of exasperation. "But without my aunt, I don't know how I can do it. I've just got to find her." She stood up and, overwhelmed with the frustration of her failure, threw the address book on the floor. "Where is she?" she cried.

"Wait. What's that?" Margaret asked, staring at the floor.

Luz turned around and followed Margaret's gaze. The address book had fallen open to the back page. "What?"

Margaret stretched clumsily from the bed to reach out and grab the book from the floor. Then she pulled herself back onto the mattress and swung her legs around to sit up and look carefully at the page. "Look at this," she said, pointing to a number scribbled at an angle across the last page of the book. "Right here. What's this number?"

"I don't know," Luz replied with a shrug of dejection. "There's no name."

"But it has a San Antonio area code."

Luz's attention perked up and she stepped closer to look at it again. She tamped down the spark of hope in her chest. "So? Abuela was very neat. She'd have put the number down in the right place."

"Hey, I'm neat and organized, too. But when I'm in a hurry I jot down a number on anything I can find. Backs of envelopes, scraps of paper . . . you should see my desk at the end of a day. When I have time, I put the numbers in my address book. Sometimes, it's days later and I can't remember whose number it is."

"Do you think . . . ?"

"What have you got to lose?"

Luz stared at the number and mustered the courage to try again.

Her hopes had been dashed so many times, and people could be very rude when they thought their privacy was being invaded.

"Luz? What are you waiting for?"

Luz climbed across the mattress to the phone. She took a deep breath and dialed the number with quick, jabbing motions. It rang once. Her mind ordered her not to get her hopes up. It rang again. She looked over at Margaret. She was sitting at the edge of the mattress and, meeting Luz's gaze, gave her a thumbs-up. On the third ring, a woman answered the phone.

"Hello?" The woman sounded a bit breathless, like she'd run to answer it.

"Uh, hi. This is Luz Avila," Luz began as she had fifteen times before. "I'm—"

"Thank God."

Nineteen

*The chrysalis appears to be at rest but in truth a dramatic
transformation is occurring within. Sudden movements are observed
if they are disturbed but otherwise, movement is limited. They are
well camouflaged, since they have no other means of defense against
predators.*

Luz tried not to have too high expectations as she drove to a
suburb just outside the city limits. She was nervous enough
just to meet her aunt and tell her the sad news of Abuela's
passing. She had no idea how Tía Maria would react and she only
hoped she wouldn't kill the messenger. She glanced back at the
box of Abuela's ashes.

"I'm doing what you asked," Luz said aloud. "Help me say the
right thing."

Serena sat primly in the passenger seat. She'd had a bath and
her nails trimmed. Her large eyes were wide in a state of alert. "You
know something's up, don't you?" Luz said. Serena looked at her,
yawned, then faced the windshield again.

After a half-hour drive, Luz pulled up to a modest, one-story
white stucco house with a low, red-tiled roof in the popular south-
western style. She parked at the curb and climbed slowly out of
the car. She couldn't shake the feeling she was being watched. Luz

had taken great care with her appearance. She'd ironed the hated black dress, polished her black pumps, and even bought a pair of nylons for the event. She especially hated nylons and rarely wore them, thinking it was one of the perks of having tawny skin. But she wanted to make a good impression on her aunt, and more, she wanted to show her that Abuela did a good job raising her. Margaret had wound her hair into a braid and she wore Abuela's silver and pearl earrings. "Don't forget your scarf," Margaret had told her. "You don't want to look like you're going to a funeral."

From the look of the front yard, it was obvious her aunt did not inherit her mother's love of gardening. It was a mournful, thirsty bit of land choked with weeds. Serena promptly peed on it. They walked along the cracked cement sidewalk up to the front door. Here, at least, someone had taken a broom to the porch and placed a cheery orange mum by the front door. The price tag was still on the colored paper. Luz smiled, touched that her aunt had made the effort.

It took her nine days and over twelve hundred miles to find her aunt. Driving the half hour from the motel to this front door was the hardest leg of the journey. But she'd done it. She adjusted her grip on Serena and reached out for the doorbell, but before she could push it, the door flung open and Luz saw a smiling face and a sea of red.

"Oh! *Mi sobrina*, Luz! You're here! Let me look at you. *Ay, mira! Mira!*" Tía Maria brought her hands up to her tear-stained face. "You look so much like my mother!"

Her aunt flung her arms out for a heartfelt embrace. Luz could see no course but to step into it. Maria was a large woman, robust and full breasted, and while she pressed Luz to her cheek, Luz was pleasantly surprised to discover she smelled of maize and vanilla, like Abuela. That scent triggered a surge of emotion and Luz blinked back tears.

"Come in! Come in!" Maria exclaimed, and stepped back from the door.

"Thank you," Luz said, firmly holding the photo album and Serena as she crossed the threshold. "I'm sorry I had to bring my dog. Is it okay for her to come in? I couldn't leave her at the hotel and it's too hot to leave her in the car. She won't pee. I'll hold her."

"I love dogs!" Maria said, and made a beeline for Serena, bending over to smile sweetly into the dog's bulging eyes. "A Chihuahua!" she exclaimed, clasping her hands together in a gesture very much like Abuela's. "Oh, she's a beauty. A fawn. My favorite color. Come here, baby," she said, reaching out to take Serena into her arms. Luz thought Serena would cringe from the woman with the big voice, but she went eagerly into Tía Maria's arms, her tail wagging, and commenced licking her face.

"She's so sweet!" Maria was completely captured by the dog. "I used to have one, too," she said wistfully. "Cha Chi died a year ago. Eighteen years I had her. I haven't had the heart to get another one yet. But aren't you the prettiest girl?"

Luz studied her aunt as she crooned to Serena. She had Abuela's dark eyes and possibly her nose, but in stature and features, she appeared to resemble her father, Luis, more.

"*Ay,* I can't get over how much you look like Mami," Maria said again, shaking her head with a sad expression. "Except for the eyes, of course. Those are from your father." She sniffed. "But your hair, your face. Your body! You even move like her. *Es increíble.* Give me your jacket, and sit, please!"

Luz held her hands tightly in front of her and looked around the small living room. A large, overstuffed tan faux-suede sofa too big for the room was crammed up beside a huge red recliner placed in front of a large television. Beyond the living room was a side room used as a dining room and beyond that, a wall of sliding glass doors that presumably led to the patio. It struck Luz as odd that the heavy red drapes were drawn, making the inside dark and closed in. Luz sat on the edge of the sofa with her hands clasped on her knees.

"Do you want something to drink?" Maria asked. She seemed anxious to serve. "I have coffee, juice, wine, water."

"No, thank you," Luz replied, tugging her dress hem over her knees.

"If you're sure." Maria walked to the red chair and lowered herself into it. Once seated, she began stroking Serena's back, settling her into her ample lap. If Serena were a cat, Luz thought, she'd be purring.

"So you drove here? All the way from Wisconsin?"

"Yes."

"Such a long way! You know my mother, your *abuela,* drove even farther when you were born." She tilted her head. "You are a lot like her in heart, too, I think."

Luz plucked at the hem of her dress, inordinately pleased. "Thank you. Any comparison to Abuela is a compliment."

"I can tell how much you love her."

Luz squeezed her hands together, aware that in the space of a few minutes she'd have to deliver shattering news to her aunt about her mother, and it made her mouth so dry that she wished she'd asked for water. "Tía Maria?" she began, licking her lips. "There's something I have to tell you. I have some sad news about Abuela."

Tía Maria's face fell and she looked suddenly stricken with

sadness. "*Ay,* you sweet girl! You don't have to tell me. I know my mother is dead. God rest her soul." She brought her hand to her chest. "My heart is broken."

Luz swallowed hard, confused. "But . . . how?" she stumbled. "How did you know? I only just arrived. I brought her ashes."

"Her ashes? You brought them?" Maria brought her hands to her cheeks, seemingly overcome. She gazed at the floor by Luz's feet. "Where are they?"

"In the car. I'll get them." Luz began to rise but Maria put her hand out to stop her.

"Wait, wait. Don't hurry off. We can get them later." Maria seemed somewhat unsure as she looked back over her shoulder at the sliding patio doors. When Luz settled back on the sofa, tears began to fill Maria's eyes. "You're so kind to have brought them. I . . . I felt so sorry to have missed her funeral. I still can't believe it. Mami dead. It doesn't seem real. It seems like I just talked to her."

Luz watched the tears flow down her aunt's face, but she couldn't put things to right in her mind. She scooted forward on the sofa. "But, Tía Maria, how did you find out? If I didn't tell you . . . who did?"

Maria's face stilled and her eyes widened. Then she exhaled and said in a serious tone, "This is where it gets complicated." She turned her head once more to look back at the sliding glass doors.

Luz followed her gaze and thought she saw a shadow of movement outside on the patio. There was a person out there, she realized. More than one. She looked at her aunt with puzzlement.

Maria put Serena on the floor, patting her head, then reached over, stretching past Luz's knees to take hold of her hands. She gave them a quick squeeze. "My dear, we are all family here. We care about you and we are here for your support."

Luz looked into her eyes, pulsing with meaning, and all she could think was, *we*?

Her aunt looked at her with a troubled gaze. She seemed to be struggling to find the right words. When none were forthcoming she sighed lustily and released Luz's hands.

"I think there is someone you should meet."

Grabbing both arms of the chair, Maria slowly pulled herself to a standing position. She paused, took a breath, then said kindly, "Wait here, *querida*."

Luz was baffled by the subterfuge. Clearly there was more family waiting to meet her on the patio. Her cousins, probably. Why the drama? Was there such tension between Abuela and her daughter that they thought Luz wouldn't want to meet them?

Maria walked around the coffee table, through the alcove dining room, and navigated the tight space around the wrought-iron dining table to the sliding glass doors. She dug through the folds of curtain fabric to find the drawstring, then began yanking on the cords. A few short, jerky pulls and the curtains opened. Light poured into the room, spreading over the red plush carpeting. Squinting, Luz could make out three figures standing behind the glass doors. Maria walked over and with another soft grunt, the reluctant door rattled open.

Luz's eyes focused on the first person to step into the room. A tall man . . . a baseball cap, short brown hair. She felt her heart freeze and she gasped in recognition.

"Sully!" she exclaimed, leaping to her feet. Her mouth hung open in surprise as she watched his progress toward her in a hesitant gait, his hands dug deep into his pockets. He wore new khaki pants and the brown plaid shirt she'd given him for his birthday. His usually unruly hair was freshly trimmed. He stepped forward to hug her tight; then, releasing her, he stepped back awkwardly. His blue eyes were troubled and unsure. It frightened her.

"What are you doing here?" she sputtered.

"I came here to see you," he said simply.

"But . . ." She was speechless with confusion. That didn't explain why he was here, at her aunt's house. Now. She had so many questions to ask but her attention was caught by the two other people who followed Sully into the room. One was a tall man of Native American descent. His skin looked like leather and his eyes were the rich brown color of the earth. He was clean-shaven and neatly dressed in a suede jacket. When he stepped into the room he removed his cowboy hat and held it in his hands. He was the only one not looking at her. His gaze was on the tall, slender woman at his side.

She was a wisp of a woman, so frail it looked like a gust of wind could blow her away, yet there was a tensile strength in her straight-backed carriage, like that of a dancer. Her soft, brown hair was long and fell in waves almost to the waist of her dowdy, blue floral dress. There was something familiar about her features. Luz thought she had to be some relative and she offered a small smile. The woman seemed surprised by it but her eyes lit up and she returned a shaky smile.

The tension in the room thickened as everyone stood in awkward stillness, staring at Luz with uneasy smiles on their faces. Luz felt her muscles bow up in the undercurrent. These two clearly were too old to be her cousins. Maybe an aunt and her husband? She looked to Tía Maria, expecting her to make introductions, but her aunt stayed in the background with her eyes glued to the other woman in the room.

The tall man put his hand on the woman's shoulder and

squeezed it. The woman startled slightly and looked back at him. Then she nodded and, with her gaze on Luz, walked a few steps toward her. Instinctively, Luz took a step back. The woman stopped advancing. Her eyes were filled with apprehension as her gaze swept over Luz's face, as though memorizing each detail. She seemed to tremble with the effort.

Meanwhile Maria, unable to stand the tension a moment longer, rushed to the other woman's side. "She looks like Mami, doesn't she?"

The woman's smile was bittersweet and she nodded her head.

Luz's attention sharpened on the word *Mami*. "You knew my grandmother?" she asked her.

"Very well," she replied. Her voice was calm and easy on the ear. "And you, of course, are Luz."

"Yes."

"*¿Me conoces?* Do you know who I am?"

The voice, the expression . . . Luz sensed she knew the answer, but she couldn't quite grasp it. She shook her head tentatively. "No."

Disappointment flickered in the woman's eyes, replaced as quickly with understanding. "Luz," she began, then hesitated. "Luz, I'm your mother."

Luz heard the words but they didn't make sense. "What?"

"It's true," Tía Maria interjected. "Honey, this is Mariposa. Your mother."

Luz shook her head. "No," she blurted. "No, that's not possible. My mother is dead."

"No, I'm not dead," the woman said. "I'm here."

Luz could only shake her head in denial. She felt like her head was spinning. The woman reached out to her but Luz recoiled, stepping back. "What's going on here?" she cried accusingly. "Why are you saying that?" Her gaze swept from this woman, to her aunt, and finally to Sully. "Why are you doing this? Abuela told me my mother was dead!"

Everyone started speaking then, giving explanations that sounded to her ears like a garble of noise swirling around her. *Mariposa, mother, Luz, true* . . . Luz put her hands to her ears and closed her eyes. Everyone began pressing closer. Hands were touching her.

"Stop!" she shouted, squeezing her eyes tight. Immediately the room fell silent. Luz opened her eyes and saw everyone looking at her with expectant expressions. It was all too much. She turned on her heel and ran to the front door. She had to get away, to get some fresh air. She fumbled with the handle, but she couldn't get the door to open. She pounded the wood and cried, "Let me out of here!"

Sully ran to her side. "Give us a minute," he ordered everyone, putting his arm out to ward them off. "I've got this."

Sully turned the handle and opened the door. Luz rushed out, escaping the madness, gulping huge mouthfuls of air as she ran to the curb. She ran to El Toro, where she could hide and feel safe. She yanked the door but it was locked. Her purse was in the house. Defeated, she wrapped her arms tight around herself and bent over, ravaged by the fulcrum of shock and pain that raged inside of her.

Then Sully was there. His arms were around her, familiar and strong, pressing her close against his chest. She'd forgotten how safe she felt in his arms and clung to him. He didn't talk. He didn't need to. He held on to her, an anchor while she gasped for air, adrift. She didn't know how long they stood there, but in time she quieted enough to notice that his hands were stroking her hair. She heard his heart beating steadily in his chest.

Her lips moved against his shirt. "Sully?"

"Yeah, babe."

"What's going on? What are you doing here?"

"Oh, man, Luz." He sighed. "Where do I begin? It's been a crazy couple of days. But first, how are you? That's what matters most."

She gave a short laugh. "I don't know."

"Okay. Fair answer." He paused, then began again. "A couple of days ago I was in your house doing the stuff you asked me to do when your phone rang. At first I thought it was you and listened in. Then I heard this woman talking on the answering machine, saying 'Mami.' It wasn't long before I figured out she didn't know that Abuela died. I thought she was your aunt, so I grabbed the phone, right? But she'd already hung up. So I got her number from the phone ID and called her right back.

"It wasn't your aunt. But when she said she was your mother it didn't make any sense. You told me your mother was dead. That's when I knew something was out of whack. All I could think of was you driving out here and hell, Luz. I didn't want you walking blind into all this. All alone. But I couldn't reach you. So I did the only thing I could think of. I got on a plane and came down here."

"To be with me."

"I told you. I'd be here if you needed me. Wherever you were."

She paused, letting that sink in and feeling the strength of his love for her warming the chill in her heart.

"So," she said, then swallowed. She couldn't push the words out. "So, that woman is my mother?"

"Looks like it."

She brought her fist to her mouth. How could her mother be alive? Her mind wouldn't accept it. Abuela had told her she was dead. All these years . . . But even as she denied it, a small voice cried from deep within, trembling with hope and wonder: Could it be possible? Joy at the possibility, fear that it could be true, swirled inside of her, making her feel dizzy.

She leaned back to look into Sully's face. He returned her gaze, his blue eyes steady and sure. He had her in his arms again and was not letting her go. Again she rested her head on his chest.

"My mother is alive," she said more calmly. Saying the words aloud, hearing them, helped her accept the truth.

"Yes."

"But, Sully, where has she been all these years?"

"I think that's something you should ask her."

Luz shook her head, feeling a panic rise up in her chest at confronting the woman. "No. I don't want to talk to her. I'm not ready yet. I don't know what to say!"

He patted her shoulder consolingly. "I can understand that," he said. "But if it's any consolation, I think she's more afraid than you are. Luz, think. You've always talked about how much you missed your mother. How you wanted to know more about her."

"I thought she was dead."

"But she's not! She's alive. All you ever dreamed about is standing in that room."

Luz turned her head to look across the scrubby, weed-strewn yard to the house. The distance seemed too far.

"I'll come with you," he said, cajoling. "You won't be alone."

She hesitated, feeling a stubborn anger that wanted to dig in, to turn her back on the woman who had turned her back on her.

"Just for a little while."

"Maybe just for a little while," she said reluctantly. "I have to get Serena."

"You can leave whenever you want. Just give me the word and we're outta there." He released her and took a step back. He held her shoulders and gave her a gentle shake. "Are you ready?"

She nodded and straightened, smoothing out her hair. Sully wrapped an arm around her and they began walking toward the house, so close that they were bumping hips. When they reached the front door her hand paused on the door handle and she looked up at Sully.

"It was *you* who told them that Abuela died."

"Yeah. It was hard, but I did it for you."

All conversation ceased when Luz walked back into the room. She felt Sully's strength beside her even as he let his hand slide from her shoulder so she could stand alone. Tía Maria sat in the great red chair, stroking Serena, who was perched on the cushion of her belly, her nose delicately resting between her paws in repose. She didn't jump up when Luz walked in, but merely raised her gaze and watched.

The tall man, whose name Luz still didn't know, stood beside the woman she now knew was her mother. Luz took a moment to look at her, to search her face and features for anything that might trigger some memory.

It was her age that had fooled her. In the photographs Mariposa was a dewy, exuberant young woman. She had Abuela's high cheekbones, as Luz did. But Mariposa's other features were softer, more European, like those of her father, Hector. It occurred to Luz that it was only the photographs she could refer to. No personal memory of her mother came to mind. None at all. That harsh reality struck her as suddenly very sad and she felt her eyes moisten.

Luz also saw Mariposa's fragility. She looked like she was holding herself together by a very slender thread. Luz didn't know what had happened to her mother during all those years she was gone, but it was clear that she was wounded.

But so was she, Luz decided, and lifted her chin in indignation. "Where were you?" she demanded.

Mariposa straightened as though struck, but she sucked in her breath and moved closer, grasping at the opening to a first conversation. She clasped her hands tight before her, seemingly gathering her words. "That is a very long, very difficult story," she began. "One I'm not proud of."

"I'm not a little girl anymore," Luz said, cold as ice. "You left *her* a long time ago. I'm grown up now. I can handle it."

Mariposa's hand shook as she brought it to her neck.

Tía Maria spoke up. "Luz . . ."

The tall man reached out to put his hand on Tía Maria's arm, silencing her.

Mariposa said, "It might be true that you can handle hearing it. But I'm not sure I can handle telling it. Of course, I'll try." She paused, then brought her head up to look Luz in the eyes. "I left you because I am an addict."

Luz cringed at the word. It conjured up sordid images in her mind that she shied away from.

"I have been clean for five years. Three years in prison, and two since I got out."

"*Prison?*"

"Yes."

Luz put her hands to her face, feeling numb, letting her fingers slide down her cheeks to clasp tightly at her chest. She couldn't believe what she was hearing. The mother she'd envisioned in her mind, the perfect woman of her dreams, the good mother Abuela had told stories about . . . this woman was a drug-addict ex-convict?

"Luz," Mariposa said, coming closer.

Luz dropped her hands and returned a guarded look, unaware she had stepped back.

"Will you take a walk with me?"

"Why would I want to take a walk with *you*?"

"Because we need to be alone," Mariposa replied in an even voice. "And because I always find my mind is clearer when I'm outdoors. Please?"

Luz resented that she'd discovered something that she and her mother had in common. She glanced up at the others, all of them watching intently.

"Okay," she agreed warily.

Her mother reached out to her but Luz jerked away. "Don't touch me."

Immediately, Mariposa withdrew. "I'm sorry. Okay, I won't."

Nervously, with trepidation, they retraced the steps Luz had taken moments earlier, out the front door to the sidewalk, where they began to walk. Autumn had painted the old oaks that lined the street of the neighborhood. The sidewalk wasn't wide but they walked side by side, their shoulders occasionally bumping. Each time she felt the brush Luz tightened her shoulders and drew away.

They walked in silence, allowing the pieces to settle in their minds like the leaves floating from trees to the earth. Despite the anger Luz felt toward this woman for leaving her all those many years ago, she couldn't deny the girlish wonder she felt at the realization that the woman walking at her side was her *mother*. It seemed impossible. Unreal, like she was walking in her own dream.

Mariposa had a long stride but she slowed to keep pace with Luz. "You've grown up to be a lovely young woman," she told her.

"You can thank Abuela for that," Luz replied crisply.

"I wish I could."

"You could have if you'd bothered to call her. It's too late now, isn't it?"

Mariposa walked in silence several steps before she answered raggedly, "I know. I have to live with that."

Luz refused to feel sorry for her. Yet she realized in that moment that she had power over this woman. Each word was a land mine.

"Why were you in prison?" Luz asked.

"For trafficking drugs."

"Trafficking? You didn't just take drugs. You sold them, too?" she asked bitterly.

Mariposa didn't flinch. "Technically, I carried them. Across the border. I was what they called a mule. I've done all sorts of things, most of them unpleasant. Do you want me to tell you all of them now? Or is it enough to say an addict does whatever she has to, to get the drugs? I deserved to go to prison. I served my time. I've been clean for five years."

Luz stopped walking and clenched her fists at her sides. "Why didn't you come home?" she cried. "Abuela would've helped you. We both would have."

Mariposa stopped and closed her eyes. "There's no way I can explain to you the irrational savageness of addiction. I . . . I didn't see the way out."

"But you said you were clean now?"

"Yes. After I got out of prison, I went directly into therapy. It took me a long time just to get through a day without using. A day turned into a week. A week into a month. A month into a year. When I felt strong enough, I tried to contact you."

"Why bother?" she said bitterly. "After all those years?"

"To ask . . . no, to beg for your forgiveness."

Luz wrapped her arms around her chest and looked away. Her jaw was locked in fury. There was no way she could forgive her. How dare she ask her to? Did she think it would be so easy? Luz refused to feel sorry for this woman—Mariposa. She would *never* call her mother again. A part of her wanted her to suffer even a fraction of the pain she'd caused her and Abuela.

Abuela . . . A new thought came to Luz, sudden and piercing. "Did Abuela know you were alive?"

"I don't know."

"Why would she tell me you were dead?" Luz cried. The possibility of Abuela's betrayal ravaged her more than anything else and sent her emotions skyrocketing. "Why would she lie to me?"

"She didn't lie!" Mariposa cried in defense of her mother. Color flooded her face. "She didn't know! That was the hell I put her in. All those years, she didn't know if I was alive or dead. I'm sure, knowing her, she didn't want to put you in that same hell of not knowing. You were just a little girl when I left. She needed something to tell you. And later, as the years went by, she must have believed it to be true."

Luz turned her head to fix her gaze on some point in the distance. She could believe that about Abuela. It would be like her to protect her. Abuela's strange behavior before she died, her determination to come to San Antonio, her cryptic words—*There is much you do not know about Mariposa*—came back to Luz now.

"Did she ever know the truth?" she asked, not looking at Mariposa. "That you were alive?"

"I think, just before she died, she did. I asked Maria to call her for me. To tell her that I wanted to see her. I thought it might come easier that way, but it was more that I was afraid. While she was on the phone with Maria, you came into the room. Mami—Abuela—didn't want you to hear the truth on the phone like that so she took Maria's number and told her she'd call her back. But she never did. I thought it was because she didn't want to talk to me. But now, I think she died soon after that call."

Luz saw in her mind's eye the scribbled phone number in the back of the book and it all made sense now. Abuela had to have written the number down in haste when she'd walked into the room. The sequence of events was falling into place. "Abuela never told me Tía Maria called."

"None of that matters now," Mariposa said in a broken voice. "I should've called. If I'd had the courage, I might have had the chance to hear her voice. Once before . . . I could have asked her forgiveness."

Luz turned her head to see Mariposa standing with her head bent, her face twisted in unspeakable agony. In all her dreams and imaginings, she'd never wondered what her mother would look like crying. She couldn't bear it.

"Mariposa," she said, using her name for the first time. "Abuela would've forgiven you. I know she loved you. She spoke of you with such tenderness. She was your mother. And there's nothing stronger than a mother's love." She felt a sudden stab of hurt and couldn't help herself from adding, "Or, that's what I hear anyway."

Mariposa wiped her eyes. "I deserve that."

Luz looked at her feet as the seconds ticked by, feeling bad for the dig. She didn't like kicking someone when she was already down. "What I meant was I *know* she would have forgiven you. Or already did. Abuela was coming to see you."

Mariposa's head shot up and the eagerness in her wet eyes was painful to behold. "She was?"

Luz nodded. "*She* was the one who wanted to come on this trip. Not me. You should've seen her. Right after the phone call from Tía Maria she was like a woman possessed, making all these plans, getting maps. I'd never seen her so hell-bent on doing something. She even bought the car! Spent every dime she had on it." She snorted. "She'd saved money under her mattress."

A laugh burst from Mariposa's lips. She shot her hand up to cover her mouth and from behind her fingers Luz saw the first real smile blossom across her tear-streaked face.

"Car? What car?"

"That one," Luz said, pointing down the street. "See?"

Mariposa craned her neck, eager to find it. "Which one?"

"The orange Bug."

They began walking quickly back toward the house, Mariposa scanning the cars, going on tiptoe for a better look.

"I see it!" she exclaimed, laughing like a girl. She ran directly to El Toro.

"Yeah, that's it."

"It's a Vocho!" she exclaimed, wonder glowing on her face. "That's what we call these ol' VW Bugs in Mexico. She used to talk about the one she had with Luis. It was her first car. And this one, it's orange, like hers was. She called it La Monarca."

Luz grinned at hearing this new bit of information about Abuela. "I call this one El Toro."

A tender look of memory eased across Mariposa's face. "For Ferdinand."

"You know that story?"

"Of course. Ferdinand the Bull. It was your favorite. You used to ask me to read it to you almost every night."

"I remember the book," Luz said. Then, shying away from the tender moment, she added, "But not you reading it to me. I almost named it Ferdinand but I wanted to give the car something to live up to. It turns out it's more a Ferdinand. It doesn't go fast and breaks down from time to time. But it's got a lot of character."

Mariposa laughed lightly at the vision. "It likes to sit and smell the flowers."

"Yeah," Luz said, begrudgingly enjoying the shared memory. She reached out to lay a hand on the hood. "Sometimes I just sit in there to think. I feel Abuela's presence in there."

Mariposa's face became suddenly serious. "You do?" She peered in the window. "Can . . . can we go in it? Please? Just for a minute?"

"I guess so." Luz patted her purse and found the keys. She opened the door and watched Mariposa climb into the passenger seat. She puffed out a plume of anxiety at going into this close space with her mother as she rounded the hood and climbed in. She cracked open her window to let fresh air into the close space. For a few minutes they sat in an awkward silence. Luz tapped her fingers on her lap, and stealing a glance from under lowered lids, she saw Mariposa sitting rigid, with her hands flat over her thighs.

"She was really going to come see me?" Mariposa asked, turning her head to face Luz, her eyes revealing her vulnerability.

"Yes. The day before she died, I found her in the garden standing like a statue, wringing her hands. It was early in the morning.

She wasn't in the kitchen, where I'd usually find her, and her bed wasn't made, so I knew something was wrong. When I found her, she was still in her nightgown." She paused, seeing Abuela in her mind's eye. "She looked so sad," she said softly. "So worried. She kept saying, over and over, how we had to go to San Antonio right away. Then we were supposed to go to see the family in Angangueo. I thought she was in a hurry to get to Mexico by November first for the Day of the Dead celebration. Now I know she was in a hurry to see you. She said how there were things I needed to know about you. How we'd have time to talk in the car on the drive down. But she died the next day." Mariposa paled as she listened with her brown eyes wide. "If Abuela had lived, she'd be here now."

Mariposa's lips trembled and she brought her hand up to still them, looking away.

"There's something I want to show you." Luz turned and stretched to reach into the backseat. She found the box of ashes and carefully carried it to the front. She smiled with affection at seeing the ragtag collection of their offerings: Stacie's wild and brightly colored letters swirled across the box along with the dozen monarchs she'd painted. Fast-food papers and candy wrappers made into flowers, the wilted marigolds and cosmos, the oil can wrapper, a page of Margaret's observations, and a pair of knitted pink booties.

Mariposa looked at the box with a puzzled expression.

"This is Abuela's ashes."

Mariposa's mouth fell open in a gasp. She stared at the box, frozen for a moment, before her face collapsed in tears. She reached out with trembling hands to take the box into her lap. "You brought her ashes?" she said in a choked sob.

Mariposa took the box and could no longer contain the myriad, turbulent emotions that she'd managed to hold in check. Tears flowed freely down her face, and though she bent her head, she couldn't stop the wrenching sobs that broke from her heart. Mariposa reached out in a rush to wrap her arms around Luz. Luz stiffened in resistance, but with Abuela's ashes between them, she was swept up in the tide of emotion and at last gave in to her own tears as well.

"I'm sorry," Mariposa said, moving her lips against her daughter's head. "I'm so sorry."

As the sun lowered in the autumn sky, Luz sat with her mother's arms around her and her grandmother's ashes in her lap. In the cragged branches of the oaks overhead, birds sang evening songs in their nests. Luz's heart answered as she listened to the soothing, infant love songs of a mother to her child.

Twenty

The final stage of metamorphosis is called the imago. Before the butterfly emerges, the chrysalis appears black. But in fact it is transparent. On close inspection, one can see the black monarch's wing with a glimmer of orange.

The peaceful, dove gray light of dawn colored the austere hotel room walls when Luz opened her eyes. She felt drowsy, filled with the restorative calm of a good night's sleep. Waking, she felt Sully's arms heavy around her body, blanketing her with his warmth. She breathed deep and smelled the heady scent of skin and sex.

She smiled a slow, sultry smile, thinking of Ofelia's tale of the goddess Xochiquetzal and how she'd made love to the Aztec warriors with a butterfly held between her lips. For their sacrifice in battle, she promised them eternal life far off in her mountain garden. Sully had come to do battle for her, she realized, reaching to stroke the soft hairs on his arm. What could she promise him in return?

Her mind was spinning with all that had happened. In the quiet peace of this fresh day, she could give her mind free reign to piece together the events of the tumultuous day before. It was still hard to accept that her mother was alive. Even now, she wondered if she'd dreamed it.

When she and Mariposa had returned to the house after their walk, there had been an awkward silence. Once everyone in the room sensed that the two women had made at least a start at reconciliation, the relief was palpable. At last the identity of the man who had stood in stoic silence beside Mariposa was revealed. His name was Sam Morningstar and he was introduced as her friend. Though from the way he looked at Mariposa, Luz thought Sam's feelings went far beyond the bounds of friendship. Throughout the rest of the evening Sam's gaze returned again and again to Mariposa, gauging her fatigue or her reactions to a comment. It was the same with Sully for Luz.

It was a relief when Tía Maria came in from the kitchen, drying her hands, to call out with what Luz now understood was her aunt's typical bossy cheerfulness, "Let's eat!"

In the end, it was the sharing of Abuela's recipes that had brought the women together. Luz figured out that Tía Maria had inherited Abuela's talent for cooking. It was her passion, as it had been Abuela's, and her glorious kitchen, fully half the small house, was so much like Abuela's in color and function that Luz had to stand and gape, blinking back tears, when she stepped into it. Fresh herbs grew in terra-cotta pots at the window, a pestle and mortar sat beside a bowl filled with avocados, a pork butt was braising in the Dutch oven, three different sauces were simmering on the stove, and from the oven Luz recognized the unmistakable scent of tamales.

Luz had breathed in the scents of the foods of her culture and felt the tension in her shoulders dissipate. She felt at home here.

Tía Maria turned out to be a diva of chilies and spice. She gave Luz an apron and orders to stir the sauces. Luz warmed to the task and took pride when she saw her aunt's raised brows of surprise when Luz tasted the verde sauce and added a few more spices.

"What are you doing?" Tía Maria asked.

"It's too bland."

"Too *what*?"

"Abuela always said a weak sauce is like a weak man—no good for a strong woman."

Tía Maria threw back her head and laughed till tears came into her eyes. "*Ay*! I had forgotten that one!"

Once it was clear that Luz knew the family recipes, they'd staged a mock battle over the correct seasonings to put in Abuela's secret mole sauce. Mariposa, on the other hand, had two left hands in the kitchen. She couldn't chop a pepper or pit an avocado. She even dropped an egg on the floor. But she did remember how her mother's recipes tasted and she acted as judge and jury, tasting each sauce. Maria made jokes about Mariposa's inability to cook, but Mariposa gave back as good as she got, teasing Tía Maria about the sorry shape of her lawn.

Luz chopped and stirred, chuckling as she listened to the sisters' banter. She quietly observed how Abuela's different talents—her DNA—were handed down to her daughters—cooking to Maria, gardening to Mariposa. As they cooked, the sisters shared with Luz their stories of how, at fifteen, each had journeyed with Abuela to the Sacred Circle high up in the mountains of Michoacán to pay witness to the monarchs that gathered there. Luz listened and watched the myriad emotions flicker across their expressive faces as they described, with their eyes shining, their feelings at seeing millions of butterflies dancing before them. Luz could not even imagine the experience, but it was clear that it had been a pivotal experience for each of them. It was, literally and emotionally, their coming-of-age.

It had been an amazing night, Luz thought with a sigh. Lying in bed with Sully as a new day dawned, Luz replayed in her mind each word, each gesture, and each glance of that important evening. By the time Sully awoke, a bright shaft of light had sliced through the narrow opening of the curtains.

Sully yawned noisily and stretched his arms over his head. Then he rubbed his eyes and stared out, frozen. Luz held back a smile, knowing that he was figuring out where he was. He glanced at her and his face softened with recognition. He brought his arm back around Luz and squeezed her.

"Good morning," he said, kissing the top of her head.

"Good morning."

"It's nice waking up with you in my arms."

"Mmm," she replied.

"You okay?"

"Yes," she replied honestly. "But confused. Reeling. I'm still trying to believe it all really happened. The only place I feel safe right now is in your arms."

"It's where you belong."

"I'm so glad you came. Thank you."

He moved to kiss her nose. "My pleasure," he replied with a glint in his eye.

"I was thinking. Maybe I should go home with you today. I can give the ashes to Maria and Mariposa now. She was their mother. They can decide what they want to do next. It's their place."

"What about going to Mexico?"

"All Abuela really wanted was for me to meet my mother. The rest was just a ruse. I understand that now."

"I don't know about that."

"I've gone through so much in the past few weeks. You don't know."

"Bad?" he asked, alarm ringing in his voice.

"No. But I'm not the same person I was when I left. I don't know who I am anymore. And I'm tired, Sully. I miss my own house in Milwaukee, my own kitchen, my own bed. I want to go home."

He squeezed her and held tight. He was so strong that he didn't realize he'd squeezed the breath from her, but to Luz it still felt reassuring.

"Luz, you can't quit now. You've got to keep going."

"But you're the one who said the trip was too dangerous. That I shouldn't go on and I should come home."

"That was before."

"Before what?"

"Before I understood how important this is. You need some time with your mother. To go home now would be quitting before your journey is complete."

She sighed, unconvinced. "I can come back."

"What was the reason you went on this trip in the first place?" he asked her.

"To bring Abuela's ashes home. But I did that."

"No, you didn't."

She lifted her head to look questioningly at him.

"She said she wanted to go back to Angangueo," he reminded her.

"But—"

"Think about it, Luz. Abuela was one smart old lady. If she knew your mother was alive, she knew you'd meet up with her here in San Antonio. She wanted you to take the journey up the mountain with your mother. Not her. It was never about Abuela going with you."

"She said she wanted to . . ."

"You're supposed to go with Mariposa."

Luz laid her head against his shoulder, feeling her heart beating faster as she wondered about what Sully said.

"What if she doesn't want to go?"

"Ask her. She'll go. I'd bet money on it."

She turned on her side and raised her head to her palm to look at him. "Let me get this straight," she said. "You're telling me that I should ask Mariposa to go to the Sacred Circle with me. In Mexico."

"Right."

She stared at him, agog. "Who are you and what did you do with my boyfriend?" she teased. Her loving eye swept over his morning face. She loved the way his tawny hair lay disheveled and spiky against the pillow, and the thick stubble that framed his cheek. This early in the morning she could see the vulnerability of the boy in the man. He gazed back at her in his usual taciturn manner, chuckling softly at her joke.

Luz reached up to trace her fingers gently from his forehead to his chin. "I'm sorry I didn't call again. I lost my phone charger, but that really was just an excuse. The truth is I didn't want to talk with you. I thought you were going to try to talk me out of going, like you did before. I didn't want to fight with you again. Especially since there were times when I didn't think I could go on. I just—"

Sully put his finger to her lips. "Shh . . . I know. I can't lie, it hurt. But only because I was afraid of losing you. I was a bull-headed ass. I should've encouraged you. You needed to go. I see that now. So no apologies. From either of us." He kissed her softly. "But you should go to Mexico."

"Come with me!"

"I can't. Even if I wanted to, I don't have a passport."

Luz exhaled a plume of air, defeated.

"But there is one thing you can do for me," he said.

She smirked and cast him a sloe-eyed glance. "I thought I already did."

"Well, yeah," he said smugly. "But I was thinking of something else. Since I spent all that time fixing up El Toro, maybe you wouldn't mind giving me a lift to the airport?"

Luz laughed and slipped her arms around his neck. "Of course. But first, let me tell you the story of Xochiquetzal and the warriors."

Mariposa stood staring at the door a half hour before Luz was scheduled to arrive. Her mind went through the long list of chores she'd hurriedly created last night after Luz had agreed to stop by her apartment. She slept very little, imagining all the conversations they might have. In her drowsy, half-conscious state she imagined quite a lot. Mostly she drifted back to the one pure memory that had sustained her through so many years of depraved conditions. She could see Luz's small, chubby hand in hers when she was a toddler, still unstable on her feet. She'd depended on her mother to guide her and not let her fall.

Mariposa was wide awake now and fully aware that sharing tender mother-daughter memories was not likely to happen. She had to guard against being such a fool and remember that she had let go of Luz's hand when she was a child. More likely today would be a self-righteous grilling, a lot of questions that began with *Why did you* and *How could you.*

She wrung her hands while her gaze swept around the room for the tenth time in as many minutes. The old green Formica kitchen counter was dated but it gleamed, the linoleum was curling in a corner but the floor was spotless, and the aquarium glass sparkled. She filled a vivid green Fiesta jug with cheery fall-colored mums. Beside it on the table was a spice cake with cream cheese frosting and two Fiesta mugs. Sniffing, she caught the scent of the freshly brewed coffee with cinnamon, the way her mother made it.

Mariposa slid into a chair and folded her hands on the table. All was ready, she thought as her gaze turned again to the door. She leaped to her feet at the sound of knocking. Putting her hand to her heart, she took three deep breaths to calm herself, then walked to the door and swung it wide.

She didn't think she'd ever get over the rush of love that swept through her every time she saw her daughter's face. Her little girl was a woman now! She searched her face for traces of the little girl she'd last seen so many years before. Her eyes were the same shining blue color and looked at her with that same beguiling combination of curiosity and stubbornness. But her cheeks were thinner, her lips full, her legs long . . . Luz had her mother's hair, shining, thick and black as midnight. Seeing her wear it in the same traditional long braid moved her. Part of her mother still lived in her daughter.

"Luz," she said in welcome, and held out her arms.

"Mariposa," Luz replied succinctly, and stepped forward to stiffly accept her mother's embrace before quickly stepping away.

Mariposa told herself not to be hurt that Luz did not call her *mother*. It was too soon and, she reminded herself, she'd have to accept that Luz might never choose to use that endearment. "Come in," she said, stepping aside. "I'm so glad you came."

She held herself tight as Luz walked in and examined her small apartment. It wasn't the posh apartments of the rest of the building, she knew. But neither was it the dreary, dark basement apartment it could have been. It was small and spare, to be sure. But the walls were painted the lovely warm tangerine color that Abuela had loved, and she'd hand-painted the yellow and green stencils along the ceiling. She was glad Luz had come just as the late afternoon sunlight poured in from the angled windows.

"It's a nice place," Luz said politely.

"Thank you," Mariposa answered, pleased because it sounded like she meant it. She watched Luz walk straight to the aquariums and look inside.

"You still have cats," Luz said. "Ours all pupated and the butterflies flew off weeks ago."

"If these fellows hurry, they'll catch up. Mami taught me how to raise butterflies. She must have taught you, too?"

Luz absently nodded and turned from the aquariums without another comment. Mariposa wondered if Luz was holding back from sharing with her any of her life with Abuela, as a kind of punishment. Or maybe she was like so many young women her age and didn't care for caterpillars or butterflies or nature in general. Girls seemed to be interested only in shoes and clothing and the antics of starlets.

"You see the black one," Mariposa said, walking to one aquarium. She pointed out a black chrysalis to Luz. "This one should emerge tomorrow."

"I know," Luz said succinctly. "I've seen that lots of times with Abuela."

Luz was shutting her out, not allowing her to take Abuela's place in her heart. Mariposa said, "Abuela once told me something that I keep close, like a talisman. She used to say, 'Just when the caterpillar thought she was at her darkest moment, she became a butterfly.' Every time I see a butterfly emerge, I'm reminded I've been given a second chance. It gives me hope that even someone who has messed up as badly as I have can start over."

"But we're not butterflies, are we?" Luz lashed out. "We're people."

Mariposa drew back. "Yes," she said tightly, nodding. "Of course."

"You can't make it all sound so simple. So easy," Luz said angrily. "A butterfly flies off and it's no big deal. That's her nature. But you were my mother. You left me when I needed you. I thought you were dead!"

Mariposa cringed, waiting for the deluge of angry words to hit, knowing Luz had to say them.

Tears glistened in Luz's eyes. "That's *not* okay," she said heatedly. "You had a mother. I didn't! I needed you. And now you're back. Why should I care? How can I trust that you won't run off again? How can you make up all that time?" She shook her head, tightening her arms across her chest. "Maybe it's too late to start over."

Mariposa took a breath, knowing this was an important moment. "I refer to butterflies a lot because it's hard for me to express myself. I identify with them and sometimes"—she shrugged—"it helps. What I was trying to say, in the only way I know how, is that when the butterfly emerges from the chrysalis, it's continuing in a new shape and form. So maybe we're not starting over. Maybe for us, it's enough to start fresh."

Mariposa turned and went to her galley kitchen to pour coffee. She knew she had to give them both a moment to regain their equilibrium. Luz's emotions were like tinder; the smallest spark could set her off.

"Please, won't you sit down?" Mariposa asked, pulling out a chair.

Luz walked over and reluctantly sat at the small table. Mariposa served mugs of steaming coffee, amused to watch Luz pour liberal amounts of cream into hers, as Abuela used to do.

"Cake?" Mariposa asked. "I made it this morning."

"Yes, please."

Mariposa served two generous slices of the cake, and with the hostess duties done, she spread her napkin on her lap and searched for a polite opening that was general and not an emotional hot button. Luz sat across from her, staring at the cake. They were each being tentative.

Mariposa picked up her fork. "Did you have any trouble finding the place?"

"No," Luz replied, picking up her fork as well. "Your directions were excellent. It's a beautiful building."

"The condos upstairs are beautiful, not tiny like mine. But I'm happy to have this place. It suits me." Mariposa tasted the cake, relieved that it was moist and not too sweet.

"You're the caretaker, you said?"

"That's right."

Luz ate a forkful of cake. "This is delicious," she said, making an effort.

"Thank you," Mariposa replied, grateful. "And your young man? Sully? Where is he?"

"He went to tour the Alamo." Luz smiled, recalling how excited

301

Sully was about touring it. "He said he couldn't go home without seeing it. Margaret went with him."

"Who's Margaret?"

"She's the woman I'm traveling to Mexico with."

Mariposa put down her fork. "Excuse me? Did you say you're going to Mexico?"

Luz's eyes widened and she looked like she was sorry she'd brought the subject up. She put down her fork and dabbed her mouth with her napkin. "Maybe. I'm not sure. It depends."

"Depends on what, might I ask?"

There was a brief silence.

Mariposa said, "I'm sorry. I don't mean to pry."

Luz lifted her gaze and Mariposa found herself pinned by her scrutiny. "It depends," Luz said evenly, "on whether I'm going to Angangueo."

"*Angangueo?*"

"Yes." Luz set her napkin on the table and sat straight in her chair. "Abuela's last wish was to go home again," Luz told her.

Mariposa went very still.

"She wanted to come here to San Antonio first, like I told you. But after here, she intended for us to drive on to her village. I think she knew she was getting old and she wanted to see her family again. And she wanted me to meet the people I knew only from the stories she told and the photographs in her album. I don't think Abuela wanted me to be alone when she . . . when she died."

Mariposa saw tears shining in Luz's eyes and her heart tightened. "Oh, Luz . . ."

"But she died before we could go. I think . . ." Luz tightened her lips to still their trembling. "This morning Sully told me that Abuela meant for me to come here to meet you. But she also meant for us to go on together to the Sacred Circle with her ashes. And I think he's right. It's about more than just me and you," Luz said belligerently. "It's about *tradition*."

Mariposa could only look at the strong, determined young woman and think what a wonderful job her mother had done raising her. Better than she could have done. Luz had just opened up a door wider than Mariposa ever could have.

Mariposa knew her silence was misinterpreted, because she saw a flash of disappointment in Luz's eyes. "You don't have to go," Luz said crossly. "I'll ask Tía Maria."

Mariposa was surprised by the spark of jealousy she felt at even the suggestion that her sister accompany Luz to the Sacred Circle. Luz was *her* daughter. *She* should be the one to take her.

"Oh, Luz," she said. "You speak of the tradition in our family for a mother to bring her daughter to the mountains at the brink of womanhood."

Luz nodded.

"There is a long history to this tradition."

"I know the myth about Xochiquetzal."

"Well, yes. That is the Aztec myth. All children learn about Xochiquetzal, the goddess of love, pleasure, and beauty. She lives in a flower garden on a mountaintop, high above the heavens."

"The place all good soldiers go."

Mariposa laughed. "You know *that* story, do you?"

"I know a lot of stories. But I didn't learn that one from Abuela."

"But, Luz, our tradition has deeper roots than that. We are Purépecha, a people as ancient and proud as the Aztecs. But today, the old customs are dying out. In Mexico, when a young girl turns fifteen, *quince años,* a great party is thrown to introduce her to the world as a young woman."

"It's like a sweet-sixteen party. Mexican girls do it here, too. I know all this," Luz said impatiently.

Mariposa continued. "The dusty, rocky land of Michoacán is a land of hard-won farms, of goats and sheep, adobe and wood, fire and fish, bees and butterflies. There, the myths of the ancient gods—the gods of the sun, the sky, mother earth, death, rain, and fertility—still resonate in our souls.

"Luz, I have been gone for more than fifteen years. I was not there for your *quinceañera*. I failed you in every way possible and I know that you would have preferred to make this journey with Abuela. Even Tía Maria."

Luz averted her gaze.

"But, for all that, I am your mother."

Luz's gaze darted back up to meet Mariposa's expectantly.

"It would be my duty, my honor, and my privilege to take you on this journey. Will you allow me to accompany you? *¿Por favor?*"

Luz turned her head to look at the aquariums. The chrysalis was black and inside, the imago was waiting to emerge. "Maybe not start over," Luz said, turning back to Mariposa. Her smile was tentative but held a hint of hope. "Maybe just a fresh start."

Twenty-One

Migrating monarchs spend much of their time gliding to conserve energy and reduce wear and tear on their wings. Like hawks, they soar by catching thermal after thermal, rising to high altitudes. When they begin arriving in the vicinity of the overwintering sites, they are seen as a high-flying, butterfly-filled sky.

Luz stood beside El Toro, holding the box of Abuela's ashes and looking at the road buzzing with traffic outside their motel. She was about to embark on her trip to Mexico. She was filled with apprehension at what awaited her on this next leg of her adventure. She'd learned from the first that nothing on this journey went as planned. Rather, it was a series of unexpected experiences. She looked at the box of ashes and smiled. Abuela would have loved it. Each stop was a new story.

"I still think this is crazy!" Margaret exclaimed. She tossed the final bag into El Toro's cramped trunk, then turned to Mariposa. "Come on, you're her mother. You know better than to let us drive across Mexico in this heap of tin."

Mariposa's lips pursed as she shared a commiserating glance with Luz. "You're talking to the wrong mother."

Luz opened the door of the driver's side and tapped the roof of the car. "Stop complaining. Get in! We're making a run for the border!"

The weather was clear but slightly overcast, perfect for traveling. El Toro was filled with gas, the oil was checked, the tires were full, and there was plenty of water to drink. Sully had gone over the car before he returned to Milwaukee, and though he still suggested that they rent a four-wheel drive, he'd declared the Bug sound.

Once Mariposa had offered to go along on the trip, all the pieces came together. Mariposa had driven the trip to Michoacán many times, though not always to see the family. Luz wasn't naive. She knew that a drug cartel infested the thick forests of that state in Mexico.

Tía Maria chose to stay behind. "Oh, honey, I'm too out of shape to make that climb," she'd told Luz when she asked her to come along. "It's nine thousand feet up. I wouldn't be able to take a step without losing my breath. Besides, I've been there before. I don't need to go again. And there's no way I'm squeezing into the backseat of that little car!"

It turned out to be a blessing in disguise, because Maria gleefully agreed to take care of Serena. The last Luz saw of the Chihuahua, she was nestled against Maria's ample bosom while being fed a bite of kibble.

Luz watched Margaret climb into the backseat. For all her worries about El Toro, Margaret was a good sport. Luz was lucky to have found a friend so conscientious and someone who had her back. It shocked her to realize that Margaret was in fact closer in age to Mariposa than she was to Luz. They seemed worlds apart in experience, and Luz wondered how they'd get along. Margaret was very protective of Luz and Mariposa showed early signs of resenting the interference.

Next Mariposa settled into the passenger seat. In the forty-eight hours since they'd decided to make this trip together, they'd been exceedingly polite and spoken of little else but preparations for the journey. There was a lot to do and they were relieved to have a focus for all the pent-up energy bubbling under the surface. Luz was uneasy about where their conversations might lead in the upcoming days of close travel. They'd hit some bumpy spots and ruts, for sure. But, she thought with a sigh, there was no use wasting time worrying or whining about that now. She'd made up her mind and her path lay ahead. She only needed the courage to follow it.

"Okay, Abuela," she said aloud. "I'm taking you home." She handed the box of Abuela's ashes to Margaret in the backseat. Mariposa watched the transfer with reverence. When she turned back to the front she caught Luz's gaze and smiled. They both knew they were thinking of Abuela.

They talked about inconsequential things as they traveled from San Antonio through the lush Hill Country suburbs, past rolling farmland to a stretch of arid and scrubby soil. Three hours later they arrived in the small border town of McAllen, the final stop before they entered Mexico. The town was as Luz expected: a motley collection of storefronts with large signs where they could stop to eat, buy sundries, change dollars into pesos, and insure the Bug.

They decided to split up the tasks to save time and meet at the car in an hour. Margaret went to exchange dollars for pesos while Mariposa searched for maps. Luz tucked her purse securely under her arm and went to insure the car. There were two men waiting in line ahead of her. The man at the counter was Hispanic and wore a large white cowboy hat. Behind him was a familiar-looking tall man in a brown shirt and jeans. The back of his neck was sunburned under a worn field hat. He turned his head to check out the printed instructions pinned on the wall.

"Billy!" she called out.

Billy McCall turned around and, seeing her, a slow grin of recognition eased across his face. He laughed and shook his head in disbelief.

"Butterfly Girl!" he said. "See? I told you we'd meet up again. The more I do this the more I see what a small world it really is."

Luz chuckled, elated to see him again. "As I recall, you were the one who had doubts."

"Not really. But I have to admit, I'm surprised to see you here. So you're on your way."

It was more a declaration than a question, but Luz nodded. "At last. I thought you'd be in Mexico by now."

"Nope. I chased the butterflies to Texas and got lucky. Found an incredible roost not too far out of San Antonio. I was supposed to meet up with a colleague of mine here at the airport, but he got held up. So I'm going on south without him."

His turn came up so he turned to focus on the business at hand. When he finished insuring his vehicle, he paused as Luz stepped up to the counter. "Good luck to you, Butterfly Girl. See you around."

She was sorry to see him go. She had lots of questions she wanted to ask him about the trip but he was already out the door. She turned back to the attendant to complete her transaction. When she stepped out of the shop, she found Billy waiting for her.

He scratched the back of his neck in consternation. "You ever drive in Mexico before?"

"No."

He frowned with chagrin. "That's what I figured. If you've got a minute, I've got some maps and some recommendations of places to stay, stuff like that. You can't be too careful."

"Great!" she said, relieved beyond words. This had turned out better than she'd hoped. Mariposa claimed she knew the way like the back of her hand, but Luz trusted Billy more. She looked at her watch. "Where are you parked?"

"In the lot around the corner."

"Perfect. That's where I am. I'll walk you over."

They walked around the corner to the parking lot to find Mariposa and Margaret leaning against El Toro, waiting. They straightened, surprised to see Luz with Billy at her side.

"This is Billy McCall. He's with the University of Kansas. He's headed to the sanctuaries to do research and he's going to give us a heads-up on what to expect. Billy, this is . . ." She looked at her mother and stumbled for the word to use. "Mariposa Avila," she said, deciding further explanation was unnecessary.

Mariposa's smile was stiff and guarded. She didn't extend her hand.

"And this is Margaret Johnson. She's from Hidden Ponds. You might know her?"

Margaret smiled shyly and extended her hand.

Billy shook her hand and gave her his laconic smile. "Nice to meet you," he said.

A shadow crossed Margaret's face as she stepped back.

After introductions, Billy turned his attention to El Toro. "This is your ride?" he asked with a hint of incredulousness. His hand traveled to his mustache as he tugged it in thought. "I've got to be honest. I'm a little unsure about you all driving in that old car. There's some pretty rough terrain."

Margaret turned to glare at them with *I told you so* in her eyes.

"This car will make it just fine," Mariposa said.

Billy cocked his head and looked at Mariposa speculatively. "You think so? Well, I hope so. But it still makes me uneasy to think of you traveling alone in that car, or any car for that matter. It's not safe if you break down. Tell you what. Maybe we should caravan, given that we're all going to the same general area. Once we get to Angangueo, I'll head off on my own."

"Thanks, but we'll be fine," Mariposa said. She crossed her arms over her chest. "I know these roads, I know the language, and I know these old Vochos."

"Wait a minute," Margaret said, trying to lighten the dark cloud Mariposa just cast over them. "I think that's a really good idea. I don't mean to be rude," she said to Mariposa, "but I've driven in this car longer than you have and I've been in it when it broke down. I don't want to be alone out on some deserted Mexican highway if that happens again. So I say we take Billy up on his kind offer." She smiled at Billy, then cast Luz a pleading glance.

Luz looked at her mother. It was obvious from her tone and stance that she didn't want to tag along with Billy. But it was Luz's car and her decision.

"Thanks, Billy. That sure would give me peace of mind. I have to admit I was a little nervous." She patted the car's hood. "No offense, El Toro."

"Well, okay then. Here's what we'll do. We'll get in line, pay our toll, and go over the bridge to the Mexican side. If you're lucky enough to get the coveted green light, we'll keep on going. If one of us gets the red light that means you have to pull over for inspection. If that happens, the other car will just pull over on the other side and wait. Sound good?"

"Sounds like a plan," Luz replied.

"My car's parked right over there," he said, pointing to a battered white SUV a few cars away. "I'll pull out first and you can follow me." He turned to go.

"Excuse me! Billy?" Margaret called out.

Billy stopped and swung his head around.

"I don't mean to be pushy, but since we're going to the same place, and since the person you were waiting for didn't show up, would you mind if I rode in your car? I wouldn't ask, but it's pretty crowded in that backseat."

He scratched his mustache, amused. "Sure. Hop in."

Luz followed Margaret as she went to the car to pull out her bag.

"What are you doing?" Luz hissed.

"I'm following the example of St. Stacie. I'm hitching my star to Billy."

Luz felt an irrational tug of jealousy. "You don't even know him."

"Actually, I do. I took a class from him at the university. He just doesn't remember me." She looked over her shoulder and drew Luz a few steps farther from the others. "Seriously, Luz, I'm a third wheel. My being out of your car will give you and your mom a chance to talk privately. You need this time with her. And," she added with a smirk, "the fact that it will be a whole lot more comfortable in his car than in that backseat is a bonus."

Billy fired up his car engine and tapped his horn.

Margaret lifted her chin. "Be right there!" She hugged Luz tightly. "Hey, we're still traveling together, right? See you on the other side!"

Margaret trotted to the car with the eagerness of a child running toward a Christmas tree. Billy pushed open the passenger door. A blast of Mozart filled the air.

"*¡Vámonos!*" he called out.

They made it across the Pharr-Reynosa International Bridge without incident and only the usual delays. Billy led them through bustling border towns with dusty streets, elaborate plazas, and shop after shop burgeoning with tourist items. Street vendors approached their car at stoplights aggressively trying to sell trinkets "cheap, lady, very cheap!" Children peddled chicle gum. The towns emptied out into a long, deserted stretch of desert. Luz and Mariposa followed Billy's car in a deep silence, each lost in her private thoughts as they made their way through the hardscrabble terrain.

"How do you know Margaret?" Mariposa asked, breaking the long silence.

With that question, they began to talk. Luz began with Tía Maria's fateful phone call a month earlier and the sequence of events that unfolded that led to Luz's decision to bring Abuela's ashes to Mexico. She didn't leave anything out: the car trouble in Chicago, Ofelia and Angel, the baby being born in Kansas, picking up Margaret at Hidden Ponds, the chance meeting with Billy, and finding the scribbled phone number in Abuela's address book.

"All along, the one constant was that I felt Abuela's presence in the car with me," Luz said softly.

"I do, too."

"You do?"

"Without question. She's here with us."

"After Abuela died," Luz began in a soft voice, "I felt so alone. I didn't know how I'd go on. I prayed for her to give me some sign that she was still with me. The next morning, I discovered a monarch, just emerged, in her workroom. It was such a surprise! It was so late in the season and I'd completely missed the chrysalis. But there she was. And what was so amazing was that the butterfly didn't fly off when I brought her to the garden. She stayed with me, almost like she wanted me to pay attention. I had this overwhelming conviction that Abuela had come to me in the form of this monarch. It was the sign I'd prayed for."

Mariposa was silent.

"You probably think I'm silly."

"I don't think you're silly at all," Mariposa said. "Many, many people have told me similar stories—a butterfly appeared after the death of someone they loved. Or a butterfly sat on their shoulder when they were sad or depressed. Most moving to me was reading about the discovery of hundreds of drawings of butterflies carved into the walls of the children's barracks at the Majdanek concentration camp, probably with pebbles and their fingernails. Imagine those tender fingernails, carving dreams into their only canvas, a wall. For millennia, all around the world, there have been myths about butterflies. Personally, I whisper a message to the gods each time I release a butterfly. I don't think your story is the least bit silly. We have a special connection to them."

Luz smiled but kept her eyes on the road. "Well, anyway, that's the one constant in this Canterbury Tale. I'm following the signs."

"No one knows what signals the monarchs use to navigate their way. For you, it's Abuela."

"And for you?" Luz asked, glancing at her mother.

Mariposa settled back in her seat and closed her eyes. "I'm following you."

Mariposa took her turn at the wheel when the sky darkened. Luz let her head rest as the wheels hummed beneath them. She felt the rhythmic bump like a heartbeat.

She turned her head to look at the dark silhouette of the woman driving the car. Her hair was pulled back at the neck; her tan skin was untouched by makeup. On the left side of her face, a small, jagged scar traveled the length of her smile line. Who was she? Luz wondered. All her life she'd had an idealized version of her mother. The woman in the car beside her was a stranger. Luz wondered what her life would have been like if Mariposa had not left. What experiences would they have shared? Would they have been close, or would they have been like Maria and Abuela, loving each other but not getting along?

Mariposa turned to see Luz staring at her and smiled. "Are you tired?"

Luz blinked heavy lids. "Very."

"I hope he turns off for a hotel soon," Mariposa muttered, still not enamored with their guide. "Every fool knows it's suicidal to drive in Mexico at night. The stories I could tell you."

Luz turned her gaze back to the road. She wondered about those stories. Of all Abuela's stories, the biggest whopper was the one about her mother.

The following day they started out early after breakfast at their modest hotel of *chilaquiles*—delicious strips of fried corn tortillas simmered in salsa and served with cheese, eggs, and beans. Clouds were rolling in but the sky was blue, and they'd planned on a full day of travel. Mariposa took the wheel as they plowed up and over the Sierra Madres. She was like a trail driver of the Old West, urging a tired and struggling El Toro, grinding gears ruthlessly and using her tongue as a lash. As the incline steepened, the VW began to lose speed and the engine labored, groaning in a low octave.

"Come on, Toro. You bull! You can do it!" Luz shouted, rocking back and forth in her seat to help it along.

Mariposa laughed and joined in the chorus. "Go, go, go . . ." Luz knew that Billy wasn't laughing in his car, however. He kept pushing on far ahead, only to have to stop and wait for El Toro to catch up. If she were a betting woman, Luz would bet that Billy would rue the day he'd asked them to follow him.

The mountainous landscape was beautiful. They wound around verdant forests and overpasses with breathtaking views of the valley. Once things leveled out again, Luz took the wheel and they fell into an easy conversation.

"One of the girls I met on this trip, Ofelia, made me think of you," Luz told Mariposa. "She was really sweet and I loved her. But she had this mouth."

Mariposa turned to look at her from under raised brows.

Luz rolled her eyes and chuckled. "No, not that way. It was more that she was the same age you were when you had me."

"Was she the one who was abused by her boyfriend?"

"Yes. She was pregnant and alone in a city she didn't know. For you it was Milwaukee, for her Chicago. It made me wonder. Did my father beat you?"

Mariposa kept her eyes on the road and didn't reply for a full minute. "Well, honey, I've been beaten," she replied. "More than a few times over the years. One guy gave me this scar here." She pointed to the faint scar near her mouth. "And another a scar here." She reached up to open her blouse wider to reveal a thick, jagged scar high on her right shoulder that looked like a stab wound. "I've been beaten by women, too. It's not always just the men."

Mariposa shook her head, making Luz think she was brushing away memories that were still painful to recall.

"But Max, your father—it's odd how we never say his name—he never laid a hand on me. He hurt me much deeper than any physical scar when he left me."

"I don't know anything about him, other than what I saw in a photograph. I don't even know his last name."

Mariposa glanced at Luz, then turned her gaze back to the road. "It was Stroh. Maximilian Stroh."

Luz rolled the name on her tongue. It felt foreign.

"That's not *your* name. We never married. You know that?"

"Yes. Didn't you ever want to get married?"

An enigmatic smile played at Mariposa's lips. "I was eighteen. I don't know if the thought of marriage crossed my mind when I first ran off with him. Later, when I found I was pregnant, yes, I did want to get married. I even expected that we would. Demanded it." She paused and Luz waited, breathlessly, for her to continue. "Max did not."

"He really just left you?"

Mariposa nodded soberly. "I had a job as a waitress at a local club. One evening I came home from my shift and he was gone. He left a note and what little money he could. Pitiful, really."

"What did the note say?"

"Not much. It was a scribbled note on lined paper. It said 'I'm sorry.'"

"That's it? Nothing more?" Luz felt outrage against him. "What a bastard!"

Mariposa slowly nodded her head.

"How could you fall for a jerk like that?"

"Oh, he was charming," Mariposa replied. "Max was different from any of the other young men I knew at the university. He was a foreign student from Germany and he was so handsome with his white-blond hair, his blue eyes, and his smile . . ." She glanced at Luz and stopped.

Luz wasn't smiling. "Did you love him?" At the very least, she'd always thought her mother must have loved her father.

"Yes. Very much. For all that I knew of love at eighteen. I felt for him what I've never felt for another man before or since. He was my first lover." She paused. "I hope that doesn't shock you."

"Please," Luz replied with a short laugh.

"It would have shocked my mother."

Luz thought of Abuela and all the conversations they'd had about her and Sully. "Maybe not. Abuela was old-fashioned, but she was hardly a prude."

"She hated Max. There was no doubt about that."

"I thought she never met him!"

"She and my father met him when they came to visit the university. We had lunch. I remember Max drank German beer and my father drank Mexican beer. Mami thought he was a phony intellectual, vain, self-centered. All of which was true. She liked nothing about him, not even the way he held his cigarette. You know the way, between the thumb and index finger, like this." She lifted her hand and demonstrated his old European smoking technique. Luz had to laugh, imagining it.

"Why would she say she never met him?"

"Did she? Poor Mami. She either blocked him out of her mind or, more likely, hated him so much that she didn't want you to have any information about him, not even negative. Luz, he wasn't evil. He never beat me or abused me in any way. When we were together we laughed and had a wonderful time. But he was twenty and didn't want to be saddled with a wife and child. And by the time he left, we'd started arguing about money and the baby. So, like the spoiled little boy he was, he ran home to Germany. It's pitiful that I don't even know what town he was from."

"Good riddance."

"Yes. But I'm ashamed to admit he broke my heart. But what was worse, he broke my spirit. Some might say it was good I got my comeuppance. But carrying his child with him leaving so unceremoniously, with no support—it was humiliating. I was devastated."

Luz nodded her head and lowered the window, taking a breath. "That's enough for now," she said in a soft voice. She looked out the window at the scenery passing by and thought that knowing this about her father didn't change anything in her world. She didn't have any desire to seek him out or to meet him. He left nothing of himself behind, not even his name. In contrast, Luz was hungry for more information about her mother's life—her decisions, reactions, emotions. She felt a visceral connection to her that she couldn't understand, especially since she'd left her, too.

"This boyfriend of yours," Mariposa said. "Has he ever abused you?"

"Sully?" Luz cried, incredulous. "No! Never. He never would."

"Good." Mariposa ran her hand through her hair with a sigh. "You know, that was the one thing I never could reconcile about the monarchs. I love just about everything about them, except the way the males treat the females. They're bullies. The males don't use pheromones to attract a mate, like other butterflies. When a male monarch sees a female in the air that he likes, he knocks her from the sky and mates." She looked at Luz. "I hope that you choose your mate for love. Sex without love means nothing. Your young man, your Sully. Do you love him?"

"Yes. I do."

Mariposa turned her head and her eyes studied Luz's face. "Good."

It started to rain when they reached the modest hotel that Billy frequented in the small town of Maravatío. It was a colonial build-ing on the charming town square. The innkeepers, a kindly elderly couple, ran the inn with their children. They greeted Billy like a prodigal son.

It rained all night, a soft, nourishing rain that made music against the tin roof. They woke up to an overcast sky; the rain had stopped and the winds were pushing the clouds out. Billy was ready to roll early, eager to get to his destination.

"Keep an eye open," he told them as the caravan took off. "It's a good day for monarchs."

By midday Billy turned off the main highway and took a narrow, rugged road that cut through the rural landscape. As they drew closer to Angangueo, Mariposa expected their conversations to turn to the jagged personal landscape of their histories. Luz had been quieter than usual since their conversation about her father the day before. Mariposa knew it was a lot for her to take in and she had yet to process it. Sam had spoken to her at length about allowing Luz the opportunity to ask questions, no matter how awkward or painful they might be to answer. She wished Sam were here with her now. She missed his quiet, steadying hand on the reins.

But Luz didn't ask dangerous questions. She sat quiet, even tense, anxious about meeting her extended family in Angangueo.

All morning they'd been spotting more monarchs. Two here, three there. In the past hour they'd begun to appear more and more, one after another. Luz kept her eyes on the sky.

"There's another one!" Luz cried excitedly, pointing at the sky.

"I can't see it, unless you want me to drive off the road. I'd better keep my eyes straight ahead."

Luz continued to cast quick glances into the sky.

Mariposa saw that Billy had flicked on his turn signal and was pulling off to the side of the road. She hit the brakes, muttering with disgust, "What's he doing now? That man is driving me crazy. He's always stopping to look at something. And Margaret eggs him on, pointing out this plant or that flower. They're two peas in a pod."

"Well, it is his job, after all. They're both researching."

"I know it. I'm just getting testy. I'm anxious to see the family and we're so close. Each stop is an aggravation."

By the time Mariposa pulled over to the side of the road, Billy was already out of the car and standing at the edge of a precipice, looking at the sky with his binoculars. Margaret was rounding the truck, looking up at the sky under the shield of her palm.

Luz grabbed her binoculars from the back of the car. "What are you looking at?"

Margaret pointed to the sky.

Luz saw a monarch fly by at eye level, her ragged-edged wings pumping the air. "A monarch!" she exclaimed.

Mariposa came from around the car to her side. "I saw it. And there are another couple over there," she said, pointing. "We're going to start seeing more."

"Hey, ladies," Billy called out, lowering his glasses. "What are you doing? Look up!"

Mariposa and Luz looked again into the cloudy sky. What looked like the front edge of a dark cloud was moving faster than the others across the sky. Mariposa lifted her hand, shielding her eyes and squinting. Way up in the sky she saw the unmistakable shape of dozens of butterflies, flying under the dark cloud. She smiled and glanced at Luz. She saw her jolt and whip her hand into the air, excitedly pointing. "Oh, my God!" Luz cried out.

Mariposa craned her neck to look to the sky again. At that moment the sun moved from behind a cloud and the sky overhead seemed to explode in orange glitter.

That was no cloud.

"Woohoo!" Luz cried exuberantly, jumping up and down like a schoolgirl.

Mariposa laughed aloud, exhilarated at the sight. Above them were thousands and thousands of monarchs riding a current across the sky. It was impossible to guess exactly how many there were. She felt humbled watching them. These fragile, heroic voyagers, each following an age-old instinct, formed a magnificent river of purpose flowing across the sky.

For a brief moment, Mariposa remembered the caterpillars. Each egg that hatched to an eyelash-size caterpillar survived the odds to grow and be resurrected as a butterfly. Each metamorphosis was a miracle. And here they were—thousands and thousands of them, jubilantly flying to their sanctuary. She felt awash with hope.

Billy was standing at the edge of the road, looking out across the vista. His face was lit up like a boy's as he pointed to a distant hillside carpeted with yellow flowers. The dew from the earlier rain glistened in the sun. "That's El Cerrito, the Little Hill. That'll be their first stop. They'll fill their tanks before they head up to the sanctuaries for the winter. Let's go!" He sprinted back to his car.

Mariposa called him back. "You go ahead. That's in the opposite direction. We're going straight to Angangueo. Our family is expecting us." She looked at Luz, to confirm that she agreed with the plan. "Okay?"

Luz nodded in agreement, then looked to Margaret.

Margaret walked over to Luz and took both her hands in hers. "Hey, I get why you're going straight on to town," Margaret said. "But this is the fork in the road for me. I've always wanted to work in the field, and Billy is giving me that chance."

"But Margaret! To go off like this with Billy. It's so . . ."

"Spontaneous? God, I hope so. I'm tired of waiting on the sidelines, taking the safe route."

"But . . ."

"I'll be fine. Billy's great and we work well together. We think the same. Hey, don't look so sad. Be happy for me. This is the adventure I've been waiting for."

"Will I see you in town?"

Margaret shrugged her shoulders and offered a good imitation of Billy's lopsided grin. "I don't know. But you'll hear from me. You have my cell number and I'll call you. Don't worry!" She pulled Luz in and hugged her tightly. "Thank you so much for letting me come with you. You're braver and stronger than you think. You've changed my life."

Margaret released her, hurried around the truck, and climbed in as Billy fired the engine. He stuck his arm out the window for a quick, spread-fingered wave. As he pulled back onto the road, a grinning Margaret stuck her head out the window and yelled, "I hope you get to where you're supposed to be!" Laughing, she slipped her head back inside.

Luz laughed and waved as she watched Billy's truck disappear down the road. Who knew, she thought, and her mind drifted to Sully.

"I know where we are," Mariposa said, her eyes gleaming as she climbed into the driver's seat. "Get in! We're almost there."

Twenty-Two

The Mexican holiday known as the Day of the Dead on November 1 and 2 corresponds with the arrival of the bulk of the monarchs to the overwintering sites in Michoacán. Locals consider the monarch butterflies to be the souls or spirits of departed relatives that have returned for an annual visit.

The small colonial town of Angangueo was nestled in a narrow valley, its tumble of colorful stucco houses terracing the mountainside. They passed small farms dotted with modest wood slat houses, goats and sheep, and majestic pine forests. El Toro whined as it climbed the rutted roads close to town, but Mariposa drove the old car like she was born for the task.

At last they reached the narrow town that seemed to stretch out along the winding, constricted main street. The white storefronts were topped with tile roofs and window trims as bright as the peppers and tomatoes sold in the open market. The town was decorated with festive streamers looped between the buildings, their plastic colored flags flapping in the breeze. Locals thronged the sidewalks, carrying baskets overflowing with orange flowers, bread, sweets, and traditional foods for the Day of the Dead.

Mariposa's fingers danced on the wheel as El Toro inched along the congested cobblestone streets. Looking out the window, Luz chuckled at the irony of the Corona beer sign blocking her view of the beautiful church in the square at the end of the street.

Mariposa pulled into a parking space before a white building with the name MERCADO on a large, hand-painted sign. A black cat sat on the windowsill in front of large flower boxes filled with flowers the colors of jewels. Luz looked up to see a hand darting back and white lace curtains fluttering in the second-floor windows.

Mariposa turned off the engine and El Toro rumbled, then stilled. "We're here," she said, and exhaled the stress of miles.

Almost on cue, the door of the grocery store swung open and a boisterous line of men, women, and children filed out, arms waving in excitement and shouting exclamations of welcome and joy.

Family, Luz thought. She felt frozen, unaccustomed to such a welcome from any family, much less so many! She knew that Tía Maria had telephoned her brother the day they'd left to give them notice of their arrival, but she hadn't expected them to be waiting with anticipation. Mariposa turned to smile encouragingly at Luz and pat her hand. Then she unbuckled her seat belt and lurched from the car. She ran like a young girl, her long hair flowing behind her, into the open arms of waiting women. A few of them looked to be of Abuela's generation. They wore dresses with cardigan sweaters and had the same terra-cotta skin and long braids. They drew Mariposa into their circle to pat her back, all crying with joy.

With a gesture, Mariposa indicated Luz sitting in the car. The older women's faces lit up at seeing her, and with a fluttering of hands, the matriarchs rattled off instructions to two of the younger women standing nearby in jeans and sweaters. The girls hurried to the car, opened Luz's door, and drew her out with great smiles, saying, "*¡Hola! ¡Bienvenido! ¡Venga!*" They led her toward the cluster of older women, who welcomed her with great hugs and kisses like she was a long-lost daughter, exclaiming, "*¡Que bonita!*" Their heads tilted toward one another as they spoke rushed words. Luz felt nervous but endured their scrutiny, her smile plastered across her face. She smoothed her hair, worn again in the traditional braid.

There was a stirring behind them and the women parted to make way for a barrel-chested man in an embroidered white shirt that matched his thick hair. He was an imposing man, clearly the patriarch. He stood with his broad shoulders back, assessing her with his dark eyes. Luz stared back, thinking this had to be her *tío* Manolo. He was a twin to Tía Maria.

Tears slowly filled his eyes. "You look just like my mother!" he exclaimed. He swept open his arms and lifted Luz into the air with a tight embrace as the women laughed and applauded. Luz was giddy with relief and joy at the hearty welcome, so much like his sister Maria's. Mariposa flew to his side and he wrapped one arm around her, too.

He spoke to Luz rapidly in Spanish, and nervous, she couldn't understand even a few sentences. She tried to shut out the noise of chattering around her and concentrate on the words. He had slowed down and she understood that he was asking her if she spoke Spanish. Luz's throat felt tight and her heart pounded loudly in her ears as she managed to choke out some words.

"*Un poquito.*"

Manolo stopped talking and turned to look at Mariposa questioningly. She only lifted her shoulders. He then turned back to Luz. "You speak a little, eh? *¿Un poquito?*" he asked, teasing her with her own words. "Spanish is the language of our people. Of your family. How could my mother not teach you?" he said in flawless English.

Luz was shocked at his fluency until she recalled that Manolo had spent years in the United States. In a flash, Luz recalled Abuela's face, imploring her to speak in Spanish.

"She tried," Luz replied. "I understand more than I can speak."

Understanding flickered in his eyes. "I speak English, but my wife, my children, all the family, they speak very little. But you will practice while you are here, eh? We will help you. Before long, you will be fluent!"

"*Voy a tratar de hablar en español,*" she said, grateful for this kindness.

"Good girl!" Manolo exclaimed, beaming with approval. "You were the light of her life, you know that? Mami was always talking about you, praising you. You could do no wrong." His smile fell and his expression grew tragic. "I cannot believe she is gone." He lifted his arm from Luz's shoulders to pound his chest. "It is empty in here. *Nada.* There's a hole I can't fill." He hugged his sister in a consoling embrace.

"Manolo," Mariposa said, wiping her eyes. "Luz has brought you a great gift. Go on, tell him, Luz." She looked at Luz with encouragement shining in her eyes.

Luz turned and walked back to the car. She didn't hurry, aware that every eye was on her. She opened the door and, moving aside bags, pulled the box of ashes from the backseat. The paper flowers were more raggedy than ever and petals of the brown marigolds flaked off and scattered in the wind, but to her eyes the box looked beautiful. She returned to her uncle, surrounded now by a tight cluster of women.

"Tío Manolo," she said. "Abuela's last wish was to come home. These are her ashes. I've brought her home to Angangueo."

Manolo's eyes widened, then his face shattered with heartbreak. He reached out and with great tenderness lifted the box into his

327

big hands. He held it before him with the reverence of a priest. He turned to Luz. Though tears overflowed from his eyes, his voice was strong and level.

"You could not have brought us a greater gift. You honor us. You honor our mother. You have great heart to make this long journey, Luz. It is no wonder that our mother loved you."

His wife, Estella, stepped forward. Her thick salt-and-pepper hair was pulled back tight from her attractive face, from which her bright eyes radiated warmth and intelligence. "We thank you for bringing our Esperanza home," she said in Spanish. "This is your home now, too."

Manolo turned to face his family, twenty strong. He raised the box of ashes higher into the air. He spoke in Spanish, but his words were slow, in the manner of a pronouncement. Mariposa came to slip her arm around Luz's waist as they listened.

Now that the spotlight was off her, Luz could relax and found she understood more of what her uncle was saying. She might have missed a word or two, but it was enough to understand that he was explaining how his mother had returned home. There were mumblings of excitement at this news. Smiling now, Manolo went on to say that this miracle had happened just in time for them to build the most beautiful *ofrenda* to honor her. This they would do in time to welcome her spirit home for the Day of the Dead!

While the family erupted in excitement and joy around her, Luz looked at the small box in her uncle's hands and felt a tremendous sense of relief. She thought, We made it, Abuela! We're really here!

❧

That night there was a great reunion. Though the weather had grown unexpectedly cold, family members walked or drove miles to reach the home of Manolo and his family. The large apartment took up the entire floor above the store, and this night it overflowed with men, women, and children, many of whom resembled each other. Beer flowed and the long, scrubbed wood table in the main room creaked with the load of the feast as each guest brought dish after dish to share. Estella had especially prepared local trout and fresh guacamole made from avocados grown on the tree in the back. There was much laughing and hugging and kissing.

Luz sat in a place of honor at Tío Manolo's left, and Mariposa sat on his right. They were not allowed to help in the kitchen or carry food to or from the table, as all the other women did. Instead they shared stories of their long journey, Mariposa translating for Luz when needed. Manolo relished the stories and his boisterous laugh began in his belly and rumbled out forcefully with his head thrown back. When he spoke, his booming voice dominated the room, and he shouted out greetings to anyone who came into his home to join the party, ordering his wife and daughters to hurry and bring more beer!

Estella was in her element at having the family gathered for such a joyous occasion in her home. She flitted about the room refilling glasses, directing the women, wiping a child's mouth. If Manolo approved of Luz, then she did, too. However, it gradually became clear to Luz that the affection Estella showed her did not extend to Mariposa. Estella was polite to her husband's sister, but not warm. In fact, she was noticeably cool. She treated her in the same manner she would any stranger in her home.

"And how is my darling sister, Maria?" Manolo asked Luz. "She should have come."

"She seems good, I think. She has a very nice house."

"She isn't lonely, living alone? It is sad her children moved away, leaving her alone. They don't come to visit. Can you imagine such a thing?" Then he glanced at Mariposa and his expression grew sheepish.

Luz swept past the awkwardness. "I don't think Tía Maria is lonely now. She's babysitting my dog. A Chihuahua. I think it was love at first sight."

"Good! This is good!" He smiled and it was filled with warmth. "You are an angel!"

Luz smiled, amazed she could do no wrong. Everyone kept offering her more food and more beer. The more beer she drank, Luz found, the more her tongue loosened. Before long she joined in the conversations, murdering the language, but no one seemed to mind. They all smiled at her, seemingly grateful at her effort. She was surrounded by people who looked like her and Abuela. Especially her sisters, Tía Rosa and Tía Marisela. They had Abuela's wrinkled, vibrant face and dark eyes, sparkling with joy at Luz's homecoming. Luz's heart lurched when they clasped their hands at their chest in a gesture so like Abuela's. But there was so much family! When introduced Luz smiled and repeated the names and hoped she would get better at remembering them all in the days to come.

Mariposa and Luz were given a spare bedroom in the back of the apartment overlooking the garden. Two narrow twin beds with wood headboards painted in brilliant blue, green, and red were separated by a small table covered with a lace cloth. A lamp warmed the room with soft light. There was no rug and only a flimsy covering of lace at the window, so Luz undressed quickly, glad for the large shade tree that scraped against the house. She slipped into thick wool socks and a sweatshirt, then unwound her hair and combed it with her fingers, in a hurry to climb under the thin blanket.

"It's so cold," she whispered, rubbing her feet together and shivering.

"You forget how cold it can get in the mountains," Mariposa replied. "We're so high up. Would you like another blanket? I could ask Estella."

"No, she's exhausted," Luz said, her teeth chattering. "I'll be all right."

Mariposa rose and walked to the closet, where she pulled out a wool shawl from the shelf. Luz was surprised when she came to her bed and spread the heavy shawl over her shoulders, tugging it up close to her chest. Luz felt the warmth immediately.

Mariposa paused with her fingertips resting on the shawl. "Good night, Luz," she said softly.

"Good night."

Mariposa smiled slightly, then reached over to extinguish the light. Luz thought she was about to smooth her hair or kiss her cheek but thought better of it. She could hear her move on her mattress, settling under the blanket. The moon was bright outside their window and filled the room with a soft, gray light. Luz lay on her back with her eyes open, trying not to move noisily from side to side on the thin mattress. She could smell the musty wool and remnant spices from dinner still wafting in the cold air. Closing her eyes, she tried to empty her mind of thoughts, to settle on the soft wind blowing outside the window, but once again her brain returned to the conversations of the evening. Faces from her large, extended family—Manolo, Estella, Marisela, Rosa—appeared in her mind, each leaving an emotional imprint.

But none more than the woman in the room with her. This was the third night they'd shared a room and she still could not grasp the reality that the faceless silhouette of the woman lying in the bed across from her was her mother. Was she really here? Or was this like her dream? If she reached out to touch that faceless visage, would she vanish again?

Mariposa awoke as the first rays of dawn broke on El Día de los Muertos. She rose from her bed and dressed quietly, careful not to disturb her sleeping daughter. The air was chilly and even though Luz slept in her sweatshirt under the blanket and shawl, she was curled up like an infant. Mariposa gently removed the shawl and took the blanket from her bed and laid it over Luz.

Mariposa gazed at her daughter, soaking in her features. How many years had she dreamed of just such a moment? Yet, although Luz was a grown woman now—so strong and independent, more than she knew—when she slept she still looked like the little girl Mariposa remembered. She let her fingers gently graze her daughter's hair, smoothing it from her face. Then she bent and softly kissed her cheek, pausing to inhale her sweet scent.

Luz stirred and sleepily waved her away. Mariposa held her breath and stepped back. When Luz was quiet, she went to the closet. The door squeaked on its hinges. She froze and glanced back at Luz. She opened it fully and very quietly pulled the box of Abuela's ashes down from the shelf where Luz had put it. Mariposa smiled when she saw all the adornments Luz and her friends had taped to the box. Young girls could be so silly. She knew they meant no harm, but she thought pinning all that garbage onto the box bordered on the disrespectful. She intended to fulfill her obligation as a dutiful daughter and create a beautiful altar at her mother's gravesite today, one that respected their traditions. It would be the most beautiful *ofrenda* in the cemetery, worthy of her mother.

Quickly and without making a sound, Mariposa tore off the paper flowers, labels, cards, and booties and tossed them into the trash basket. Then, grabbing her purse, she slipped from the room with the ashes, closing the door soundlessly behind her. She made her way down the dark back stairs to the kitchen at the rear of the house. Here the fire was burning and she found her sister-in-law, Estella, with her hands already molding a firm ball of masa flour in her hands.

"Good morning," she said in Spanish.

Estella glanced up from her work, then as quickly returned her gaze to the table. "You're up early. There is coffee on the stove."

"Thank you." Mariposa helped herself to a mug and poured a cup of the steaming black, rich coffee. She took her first sip, sighing with pleasure. "Mmm . . . good," she murmured. "We talked too much last night. We'll be sleepy at the vigil tonight!"

"We'll be fine."

Mariposa resigned herself to her sister-in-law's frostiness and quietly sipped more coffee. She could feel the adrenaline flowing stronger than the caffeine. Being home again invigorated her as she planned all that she had to accomplish today.

Estella pounded the flour in her hand, left to right. "I'll have tortillas made soon. There is some juice. Oranges. Sit down. Breakfast will be soon."

"I'm not hungry. I have to get going. I've got so much to do before tonight."

"You can't work all day on an empty stomach."

"I'll eat. Don't worry. Where can I find the lumber and a hammer?"

"Manolo gathered all that you need and put them in the pushcart. It's in the shed out back. If you wait a few minutes he'll be down to help you bring it to the cemetery."

"I've pushed a cart before. I can do it again. I'll let you know if I need help."

"Manolo and Luz will not be happy you went without them."

"They will understand why I need to do this."

Estella harrumphed and pounded the masa flour on the table. "He had the hole dug for the ashes. It is ready." She paused and looked at the box in Mariposa's hands. "Is that them?"

"Yes."

Estella made the sign of the cross. "God be with you today."

"My daughter . . ."

"Do not worry. We will take care of her. You do what you must do."

"Thank you," Mariposa said fervently, meaning it. She swallowed her sister-in-law's shunning with her coffee. She was restless, determined to start her day. She rinsed her cup and headed out without delay.

The sky was a soft gray and the air was damp and chilled. She wrapped her heavy shawl around her shoulders and headed across the yard. Though the building was in the heart of town, the yard was spacious and dominated by an enormous, spreading avocado tree. A few other fruit trees she couldn't identify were scattered around the several older outbuildings that were in need of repairs.

One was the chicken house. When the hens spied Mariposa they trotted in their straight-legged manner and scratched the earth, demanding a meal. She knew the hungry girls would follow her into the shed, so on finding the can of food, she tossed a handful of pellets to distract them. They skittered off and began pecking.

Mariposa found the wood cart in the shed behind the building as Estella had promised. The shed was tilting with age but solid on the inside. Manolo had all the supplies she needed to build an *ofrenda* neatly piled into the pushcart. She mentally thanked her brother for this kindness. There was so much to be done by nightfall but she could do it on her own. She had to. It was the least she could do to honor her mother.

The town was eerily quiet so early in the morning. The cart creaked loudly as she pushed it through the dimly lit streets. The only lights shone from the local mill, where the sound of constant chugging could be heard from machines grinding the corn. Pairs of women silently walked toward the mill for their day's masa flour to make tortillas. They smiled and waved as they passed. From off in the distance she heard the crow of a rooster. Mariposa wondered about her extended family living on the farm outside town. They would be waking now, the women making tortillas, the children helping with chores before school. She felt a sudden, intense rush of love for them. They were her family—uncles, aunts, cousins. Good, honest people who loved her. She had to remember her connection with them and gain strength from it.

Mariposa felt the whisperings of the past as she walked through the town that had been her playground as a child, and the birthplace of her mother and her mother's mother. How many times had she walked down this very street with her mother holding her hand tight? Never as a child in braids and ribbons did she imagine how she would let go of her mother's hand and run so far away. Or how desperate and depraved her life would become. Throughout the long, hard days of recovery she'd always believed that at the end of her trials, if she could just persevere, she would find forgiveness. She'd dreamed of holding her mother's hand again and hearing her mother's voice telling her once again that she loved her. This dream had filled the black hole of emptiness inside of her for so many years. And now it was gone.

Her despair stopped her. She bent over and sucked in the cold air, the pain was still so fresh. Sam had told her how memories were stored in the body. To stir bad memories up was dangerous. He warned her not to let them pollute the new life she was creating for herself. Mariposa picked up the wood handles of the cart and concentrated on moving forward, one step after another, using all her strength to push the wobbly cart along the cobblestone street. Her hands felt raw but she continued to push up the hill.

The church was at the end of the road, and the cemetery just beyond. She swerved to the side as a truck ambled past. Inside were two men in jean jackets holding farm tools, and a large, mangy dog sat in the back. They lifted a hand in greeting. She responded in kind.

Last night Manolo told her that Maria had telephoned as soon as she'd learned of Esperanza's death. He'd wept as he told Mariposa how they'd all grieved. Their mother's death had come so unexpectedly for everyone. Too many years of silence could not be reclaimed.

Manolo and Estella had already created a fine *ofrenda* for their mother in their home. Knowing they would, Mariposa had telephoned before she'd left San Antonio and begged her brother to allow her to build an altar at the gravesite alone. At first Manolo had refused, stating that it was the right of all the family to do this together. But Mariposa had explained in tears how she needed to do this as repentance for all the years of suffering she'd caused their mother. Manolo at last relented.

In her heart, Mariposa knew that the altar was only a symbol of her despair and regret. She was not fooled into believing it would earn her forgiveness. But this gesture was all she had to offer.

Mariposa arrived at the deserted cemetery. She pushed the cart to her family site and found the grave prepared for Esperanza. Manolo had spared no expense and placed a tall stone cross to mark the grave. The black dirt was freshly dug, waiting for her ashes.

Mariposa was unprepared for the shock of seeing the gravesite. The reality of her mother's death chilled her to the bone. She stared at the grave and felt the blackness of the earth open up to drag her down into its depths. She dropped to her knees and dug her hands into the cool soil, breathing deep and gathering her self-control.

Then she began to build.

Twenty-Three

*Female monarchs are capable of producing and laying more than five
hundred eggs in a lifetime. The eggs' expected survival rate is as low as
1 percent, which would mean only five of the five hundred eggs survive
to become a butterfly.*

Luz awoke on the morning of the Day of the Dead groggy
from all the *cervezas* she'd enjoyed the night before. She lay
in bed for a moment, capturing images of the party.

After most of the guests had left, Tía Estella and Tías Marisela
and Rosa had clustered around the table and discussed the extensive family festivities for the holiday while the men sat at another
table and played cards. Luz had watched Mariposa especially.
She'd never seen her so animated. From the moment she'd set
foot in Angangueo her reserve dissipated and she was a different
person. She talked with animation, laughing and opinionated,
giving Luz a peek at the flirtatious, flighty young woman she
once was. The family treated her with the respect afforded to the
child of the deceased. Especially her brother. She and Manolo
shared a bond that she didn't have with Estella. There the ties
were strained. Yet it didn't mar the evening. Mariposa didn't
drink alcohol but her eyes glittered and her face was flushed. In
retrospect, Luz wondered at the dramatic swing of Mariposa's

emotions. The excitement seemed to be burning at too high a pitch.

Luz yawned and looked to her mother's bed. It was empty. She was surprised to find it already made. She'd had a hard time falling asleep, but once she did she must've slept soundly, because she hadn't heard Mariposa dress or stir about the room. Luz pushed back the blankets, seeing that the heavy shawl was gone as well. Then, shivering, she dressed quickly in jeans, a new red sweater she'd purchased in San Antonio at Margaret's urging, and matching thick socks.

She made her way down the narrow stairs to the kitchen. She paused at the threshold. Her three aunts were working in the kitchen preparing mountains of food before a small clay stove. The room smelled of burning wood and spices. The women dressed alike in dark skirts and sweaters, with their hair pulled back into braids. Their hands were busy as they spoke, intent on their work, but all talking stopped when she walked in.

"*Buenos días,*" Luz said with an awkward smile.

"Luz! Come in! Did you sleep well?" her aunt Estella exclaimed in Spanish. She hurried to grab a cup and poured steaming coffee into it, then offered it to Luz.

"*Gracias,*" Luz said, keeping her promise to try to speak in Spanish.

Her aunt muttered something to the other women and they giggled. Luz felt her cheeks color.

Using her hands to indicate the food, Tía Estella spoke with exaggerated slowness so that Luz could understand that she was offering her breakfast.

"*Sí. Yo comprendo. Gracias,*" she replied, and inwardly groaned. It was going to be a long day.

After a hearty breakfast of beans, rice, and eggs, Luz went alone into the living room. It was empty now, scrubbed clean in preparation for the Day of the Dead festival. She prowled listlessly, stopping to admire the bright green pineapple pottery on the side table, feeling a bittersweet twinge in her heart as she remembered the one just like it that Abuela had so carefully pieced back together. Paintings of calla lilies, photographs of the family, and an icon of the Blessed Virgin filled the walls.

Dominating the room was an elaborate altar under a wooden arch completely covered with the big orange marigold heads that Ofelia had told her were called *cempasuchitl*. There were more of them in vases surrounding the altar. Bananas, apples, pumpkins, and candy filled pottery bowls. Several sugar skulls lined the back of the table; to the right was a metal incense burner, to the left were tall, white candles. The altar table was covered in a white tablecloth, and under a large, brightly painted crucifix was a gilt-framed photograph of Abuela.

Luz walked closer and admired the beautiful young Esperanza photographed looking like a plumed bird in her colorful native dress, standing against a white stucco wall. Her glossy black hair fell down over her shoulder in a braid. It was a young woman's face, full of hope and confidence. Luz reached out to touch it.

"You look like her," said a voice behind her.

Luz turned to see a young woman about her age standing at the door. She was a beautiful girl with large eyes and the family's sharp cheekbones. Her dark hair was cut short and tucked around ears studded in gold. Her eyes shone with warmth as she smiled beneath thick bangs. She was slight in build and carefully dressed in pressed jeans and a black sweater under a leather jacket. Luz remembered meeting her the night before, but couldn't remember her name.

"I'm Yadira," she said, coming closer. "Your cousin."

Luz felt a rush of relief that she'd met someone her age who spoke English. "I'm Luz."

"I know. My mother, she is your mother . . ." She paused in thought. "Half cousin," she said in careful English. "*¿Comprendes?* I think that make me your half cousin. Or something." She laughed. "*¡Yo no sé!*"

"I never had any cousins of any kind before so I'll take what I can get."

"We live at a farm. Not far. I come to say hello. I can practice English, no? It is not so good."

"It's great," Luz said, grateful for her attempt.

Yadira smiled with relief. "Today is busy," she began. "Many work to do."

"I know. I can see that. I tried to help. I kept asking Tía Estella over and over if I could help prepare food but she kept saying no. Finally she said to me"—she laughed—"and I think I translate this right, 'You can help me by not asking me how to help!'"

Yadira laughed and rolled her expressive eyes. "*Sí.* This is Tía Estella. She has big voice but, *cómo se dice?* She has big heart, too."

"It seems to run in the family," Luz said with another laugh.

Between Yadira's broken English and Luz's broken Spanish, they were able to patch together enough to carry on a conversation. Yadira pointed out the items on the altar and explained to Luz what they meant, giving Luz her first lesson in the traditions of the Day of the Dead. And there were many.

"This year is special because Esperanza, she die. Everybody is very sad and want to make a present to the altar. Today many family they come to bring food or gift so that she feel welcome. My mother, she gave me this to bring." She lifted a plastic bag and pulled out an intricately crocheted black shawl. She carefully laid the shawl across the base of the altar. The long fringe was showy against the white cloth.

"It's beautiful."

"It was made by your *abuela* for my mother on her wedding day. Tío Manolo he want everything to be good for his mother," Yadira told her. "His heart it is broke, you know? Now come. Mami wants for us to bring tortillas to Mariposa. She is at the cemetery."

"What's she doing there?"

"She is making the *ofrenda para tu abuela.*"

"Another one?"

Yadira laughed. "*Sí.* We make *ofrenda* for the grave, too. Mariposa, *tu mamá,* she want to do this alone. She go to cemetery this morning very early."

Luz held her tongue and stared at the photograph of Abuela on the altar. She felt a stab of betrayal that her mother would go to the cemetery to build an altar for Abuela without her. Wouldn't it have been a bonding experience for them to do it together? Luz tried to tamp down her hurt. She didn't want to judge. After all, she got to spend all of her life with Abuela. She was there the day she died. Mariposa had lost so many years. Maybe she just needed some time to be alone. She was Abuela's daughter, after all.

But, she thought as she glanced back at the photograph of Abuela on the altar, didn't she realize that Abuela was a mother to her, as well?

"Come. We go now?" asked Yadira.

Luz buried these resentments as she told herself that everyone dealt with grief in her own way. One thing she'd learned about the Day of the Dead—it was not a mournful day. It was a day to remember the departed with a joyful spirit.

She looked forward to nightfall. Today, November first, was the day the souls of the children returned. The vigil of adults would begin tonight and she was excited to participate in the festivities.

Yadira and Luz walked side by side through the streets of town, already crammed with people in a festive mood buying last-minute food, candy, and trinkets for the holiday. Flowers were everywhere, especially the fat orange marigolds that Yadira told her the Aztecs had used to honor their dead.

"My family grow these flowers on our farm especially for this holiday. It is good money for us, no?"

Luz thought it had to be, seeing that everyone—men, women, and children alike, were carrying bunches of them. Luz bought a bunch, too, to freshen up her own *ofrenda* later before she presented the box of ashes to the family. She felt all her earlier resentment vanish as she remembered that she had this most important contribution to offer to the family altar tonight—the box of Abuela's ashes that she'd carried all the way from Milwaukee to Michoacán.

Yadira loved to laugh and, linking arms with Luz, she led her from one booth to the next, eating sweets and making jokes about all the humorous sugar skeletons they saw. Luz couldn't resist and bought a toy skeleton that moved when she pulled the string.

At the end of the road they reached the impressive Catholic church, the focal point of the town. Luz stared agog at the church's entrance. It was completely covered in a dazzling display of fresh flowers. If she hadn't known they were flowers, she'd think she was seeing a stained-glass window. Women wearing traditional dark shawls over their heads were scurrying like ants carrying armfuls of even more flowers into the church. In the square before the church there were colorful stands selling fruit, pottery, arts and crafts, and flowers. Musicians performed while children danced and played games of hide-and-seek.

"This way," Yadira said, leading her through the throng in the square to the large black iron gate of the cemetery. Children were selling water from big, white buckets.

"Why are they selling water?" Luz asked.

"So visitors can wash the gravestones," Yadira explained in a low voice. "We prepare the graves for the spirits' return."

As they entered the cemetery, the mood was at once respectful. It was located on a dramatically high point overlooking the valley. Looking out, Luz felt that stirring of introspection she always did when faced with the majesty of a vista. A mist seemed to cloak the mountains in a somber shawl.

Many locals were already gathered at the graves, preparing them for the long night's vigil. Women wrapped in shawls and men in serapes carried their offerings with reverence to the graves of their deceased relatives. Others were busily scrubbing and cleaning the headstones. Luz smiled at a bored little boy sitting patiently beside a gravesite while his mother worked.

"Wait till tonight when you see the candles lit. It is most beautiful then," Yadira told her.

Luz thought it was all so beautiful now. As she walked through the cemetery she admired the decorations on the graves. Each was different, yet unique. Some were elaborate and others simple Indian crosses. A mangy dog crept up to an *ofrenda* and stole a piece of bread from a basket. She chuckled and turned to tell Yadira but stopped short when she spotted Mariposa.

❧

Mariposa raced against the sunset. She'd worked at a feverish pace since dawn but her *ofrenda* was not quite finished. She'd kept her eye on the neighboring *ofrendas* as the families worked, checking out their scale and scope. Hers had to be the most impressive, the most beautiful altar. Nothing less would do to honor her mother.

The sun had shone warm on her back as she'd scrubbed the stone clean and constructed the large wooden frame for the flowers—the largest in the cemetery. As she hammered nails and painted, she was consumed with memories of the many festivals her mother had celebrated with her, right here in this cemetery, to honor their deceased relatives. All day she'd heard her mother's melodious voice in her head. As the sun lowered, the voice in her head grew louder.

Mi niña, *look! Listen! We make first a cross for the head of the grave. For our people it is the symbol of the four elements of nature, eh? This is our way. First we put corn on the altar, for the earth. Sniff it,* querida. *You know that smell, eh? Maize is the aroma of our harvest. It will feed the souls when they return.*

Water is next. We place a container here to quench the thirst of the soul after its long journey. Now we put the paper. See how thin it is? This is so it can move with the wind to honor it. And last is fire. Each soul we welcome is represented by a candle. And one more for the forgotten soul, eh? Tonight we will light the candles so that our beloved ancestors can find their way home.

The forgotten soul. That would be her, Mariposa thought morosely. When she died, would Luz light a candle for her?

Mariposa could hear the music in the square and the increasing volume of voices, so festive. The sounds of their laughter spurred her on to a feverish pace. In her rush, she scratched a nasty streak down her arm, ripping her shirt and drawing blood. It's no matter, she thought to herself. It's a blood sacrifice. Her ancestors would approve. She ignored the cut and kept working. She had to finish in time before nightfall. The family would be here soon.

The family . . . they were kind to her. She was grateful. They meant well. But she knew what they were thinking. Especially Estella. There was no face for a woman who abandoned her child. No soul. When Estella looked at her, Mariposa saw the scorn. In Estella's eyes, Mariposa did the worst thing that a woman could do. Unthinkable for a mother like Estella. Unforgivable.

When the sun began to lower and the sky darkened, Mariposa at last stood back and surveyed her altar. Her chest heaved from exertion and her hands were cut and coated with mud. It was beautiful, she thought, satisfied. She'd created a large square-shaped tower divided into six open spaces representing a star—the symbol of the universe. On top of this was a large cross. Every inch of the extravagant wood construction was covered with orange marigolds and hand-painted paper monarchs. Ears of red corn and gold trinkets hung down in the open spaces of the star like ornaments on a Christmas tree.

Her family would be proud. If she could reconcile herself with them, if she found forgiveness in their eyes, then perhaps she would feel a modicum of forgiveness from her mother. In her heart, she desperately clung to the belief that if she succeeded, her mother would come.

There was only one thing left to do. Mariposa wearily bent to grab hold of a bunch of marigolds. The blood rushed to her head and she teetered, dizzy. She'd not eaten and she was tired. Straightening, she took the stems in her left hand and with her right she tore the petals off and let them fall from her fingers to cover the earth.

"Forgive me, Mother," she whispered as she sprinkled countless marigold petals over the grave.

Each time she ripped the petals from the flower, she released its pungent smell. The twilight air was filled with its perfume. Handful after handful, Mariposa lay the petals down, enough to cover the grave in a golden blanket. Each effort was a prayer. With each tug of the petals, she hit her chest in a ritual for atonement.

"*Mea culpa, mea culpa, mea maxima culpa,*" she prayed, pounding her chest in deep sorrow.

Luz stood frozen a few feet from the grave. Yadira came to her side and clutched her arm, anxiously watching the woman at the grave.

Mariposa was swaying back and forth, ripping petals from the marigolds and casting them with an erratic thrust to the grave already covered with the golden petals. She was keeling, singing some words in a trancelike state.

Luz motioned to Yadira for her to remain where she was. Luz walked up carefully to Mariposa and gently touched her arm.

"Mariposa?"

Mariposa startled and swung her head around to face her. Her eyes were wide and rimmed red from tears. She stared back at Luz, wild-eyed. There were streaks of dirt across her cheek, her long hair was disheveled, and her sleeve had splotches of blood.

"It's me. Luz."

Mariposa blinked several times, focusing. Then she took a long, shuddering breath. She nodded her head in recognition; then, in a sudden movement, she lurched forward to wrap her arms around Luz.

Luz staggered back. She didn't know what to do or say. She stood stiffly, her arms at her sides, unwilling to return the sudden embrace. When her mother didn't release her, she reached up to gently pat her mother's shoulder, and then gradually disentangled herself from her grasp.

Mariposa stepped back and wiped the dirt and tears from her face. As she lowered her hands, her beautiful dark eyes looked out at Luz. Then her gaze slid over to see Yadira. She sniffed and ran both hands through her hair, pushing it back from her face as she took another long breath.

"I'm sorry," Mariposa said with a soft laugh of embarrassment. "This death stuff can get pretty emotional."

Luz felt her shoulders lower with a sigh of relief. She'd been spooked by the pendulum's swing in her mother's emotions. But it was normal, right? Her mother had died and she was filled with grief.

"We brought you something to eat," Yadira told her in Spanish. She stepped forward to tentatively hand Mariposa the greasy brown bag filled with food.

Mariposa looked at it with distaste. But she took it and smiled. "Thanks."

"You should come home with us," Luz told her in a coaxing voice. "You look exhausted and we all need to clean up for the festival tonight."

"Right. Right." Mariposa nodded her head. She looked back at the gravesite for a final look. "But wait! Luz, you didn't say anything about my *ofrenda*. What do you think?"

Luz was aware that her mother hung on her every word. She

made a show of stepping back, putting her hands on her hips and taking her time to peruse the altar. It was without question the largest and most impressive in the cemetery and overflowed with copious flowers and decorations. It was a beautiful spectacle. But . . . she couldn't help but think that Abuela might have preferred something more like herself. Something lush, small, and simple.

"It's amazing," she told Mariposa. "It certainly makes a statement."

Mariposa grinned wide and heaved with relief. "It does, doesn't it?"

"Oh, wait. I've got something for it." Luz opened her bag and retrieved the funny skeleton that she'd purchased. Abuela used to love silly toys and Luz knew she'd get a kick out of this one. She walked up to the grave and laid the skeleton down near the gravestone.

"Luz, no," Mariposa said, coming up behind her. "That's a plastic toy. I only want natural things on the grave." She bent to pick up the toy and handed it to Luz. "You can put this on the *ofrenda* at the house."

Luz stuffed the plastic skeleton back into the bag. Her hands rolled up the paper, squeezing it tight.

Twenty-Four

High in the oyamel forests, when the sun goes down the butterflies rush to the trees to secure a safe place to roost for the cold night. The microclimate created by the thick forest protects them against drops in temperature. Loss of the surrounding buffer zone allows penetration into the core sanctuaries by wind, rain, and snow. This can be deadly to the monarchs.

The sky was black and a cold wind whistled through the trees. Inside their room, Mariposa and Luz dressed for the Day of the Dead celebration. Estella had lent them traditional shawls so they would blend in with the local people at this important festival. They'd eaten a simple meal and showered, and now felt refreshed. Mariposa was calm and seemingly back to her normal self, but Luz still sensed she was in a state of hyperawareness. Mariposa's eyes glittered as bright as the stars.

Before they'd left on this trip, Sam had taken Luz aside and asked her to keep an eye on Mariposa.

"She's still fragile," he told her. "So much is happening all at once. She is not really ready for this trip."

On this eve of the Day of the Dead celebration, Luz would present her *ofrenda* to the family. She knew the offerings she'd made for the box of ashes might be seen as childish, but Yadira had explained to her how, when the family gathered together for the gravesite vigil, they each took turns sharing stories. Luz's intention was to tell the story of her journey to Angangueo. She'd practiced telling a story about each of the seemingly silly offerings and explaining how they represented important milestones of Abuela's journey home. She felt a glow of satisfaction as she imagined their faces while they listened, sometimes smiling at her humor, like when she told of the car breaking down, sometimes solemn, as when she related how she'd met her mother at Tía Maria's house in San Antonio. She also planned how, when she was finished, she would offer to them—her newfound family—the gift of the cardboard box holding Abuela's ashes.

Luz wanted to do it properly, with a quiet respect for tradition and decorum. She dressed in jeans and a plain black sweater and went to stand before the mirror hanging over the bureau. She carefully wound her long hair into the traditional, single braid of the women of the village. Next, she wrapped several ribbons of bright colors through the braid in a fashion Yadira had taught her. Finally, she wrapped herself in a heavy red-and-purple-striped wool shawl. She looked at her reflection and thought that if Abuela's spirit came home tonight, it would be pleased.

From out in the streets she heard the sound of guitars playing music in the distance. Voices and laughter signaled that the villagers were starting to gather for the celebration. The festival was beginning! Her heart skipped with excitement as she went to the wardrobe closet. The door was loose on the hinges and she was careful opening it. There was no light switch, so she reached up and let her hand search the top shelf for the box of ashes. She pushed back an extra pillow but the box was not where it had been. Concerned, she stretched up on tiptoe and, batting her hand to reach the back wall, discovered that the box was gone.

Her heart began to beat in panic. Where could it be? She pushed back the few clothes hanging in the wardrobe and scanned the floor. She saw her black dress shoes, her backpack, Mariposa's boots, and a trash basket. A piece of bright paper, oddly familiar, caught her eye. She pulled the basket out from the closet and brought it into the light. She stared into it with uncomprehending eyes. There were the adornments that she and her friends had made for the *ofrenda,* tossed into the trash as nothing more than junk. How did they get there? she wondered. She reached in and pulled out one of the baby booties. The tiny bit of pink cotton was soft in her hand. Who would do this?

In an instant, she knew.

Her temper skyrocketed as she turned on her heel and went to the bedroom door. "Mariposa!" she called out.

Mariposa hurried in from the next room. She looked stunningly regal in a long, black skirt with a thick navy and black woven shawl wrapped around her shoulders and neck. She, too, had pulled her hair back into a traditional braid, but she refrained from using the bright ribbons of a young girl.

"Luz, what?" she asked, rushing in. "Is anything wrong?"

"Where are the ashes?" Luz demanded.

Mariposa's face froze. "What?" she said.

"The ashes! Abuela's ashes, where are they?"

Outside, the church bells began their somber tolling, calling the villagers to the cemetery. Mariposa clutched her hands together and looked to the window, distracted. When she faced Luz again, she'd regained some composure. "Why, we had to put them in the grave, of course," she said emphatically. "That's where—"

"Who did? You?"

"Well, yes."

"Why didn't you ask me?" Luz cried. "They were mine!"

Mariposa looked over her shoulder and silently closed the door. "Shhh . . . Luz, don't shout. You don't want the family to hear."

Luz tightened her lips to keep herself from saying she didn't care who heard. She was too angry and hurt to care.

"It's all very simple," Mariposa began. "There's nothing to be upset about. Manolo prepared the grave for the ashes and I simply put them into the grave for tonight's festivities. You were sleeping, Luz."

Luz was furious. Mariposa admitted that she took the ashes and she wasn't the least bit sorry. "You could've woken me up! Those were my ashes to give!"

"Don't be ridiculous, Luz. They weren't *your* ashes. They belong to the family."

"You tore off all the decorations! You threw them in the trash! How could you do that to me?"

Tía Estella called from downstairs in Spanish. "Come! We're leaving! The parade has begun. Hurry!"

"We'll talk about this later," Mariposa said.

"I want to talk *now*."

"Luz, please. We can't make the family late. Come along," she said urgently. "We'll talk about this later." Mariposa turned to open the door and with a final pleading glance at Luz, she hurried downstairs to join the family.

Luz looked at all the offerings that she and her friends had made for Abuela's *ofrenda* lying crumpled in her hands. In her mind she could see the smiling faces of Ofelia, Margaret, and Stacie, all singing out, *It's for Abuela!*

"Luz! *¡Vámonos!*"

Luz grabbed her purse and stuffed the offerings into it. The music of the parade drew closer and she could hear the laughter and singing in the streets rise to a crescendo. Clenching her jaw and flicking off the light, Luz went down the stairs to join the festivities, her heart as cold as the night air.

A full moon illuminated the misty sky, and in the cemetery below, hundreds of candles, each a meter tall, mirrored its glowing countenance. The hazy smoke of the copal incense hung heavy in the foggy air, tasting of pine and blending with the fragrance of the flowers.

Luz sat alone near Abuela's headstone, wrapped in her heavy shawl. She keenly felt the sting of Mariposa's thoughtless betrayal. She seethed in silent anger as she stared out, huddled in the cold, at the flickering flames of the candles. As she breathed in the scents, she prayed to Abuela to come tonight.

The Zamora family clustered close around the family plot and passed hot *atole,* a sweet drink made with corn flour, to help warm them against the deepening cold of the night. The family slipped into roles with Manolo as the head of the family, Estella in a place of honor beside him, and to his left, Mariposa. The rest of the family, a dozen or more, found a comfortable place to sit around the grave. Everyone made exclamations at how beautiful the *ofrenda* was, congratulating Mariposa on creating such a magnificent tribute.

Mariposa basked in their approval, thanking them for welcoming her back home.

"You brought our mother home to us," Manolo said with tears in his eyes. "She came home with the monarchs. Sister, we thank you for this."

"It wasn't only me. Luz helped," Mariposa told him, and she turned to Luz, smiling.

Helped? Luz's hands squeezed the shawl tight around her. Mariposa came to sit beside her, carrying a glass of steaming *atole* for her to drink. She smiled at Luz, her eyes luminous in the candlelight.

Luz grabbed her purse and rose without a word. She moved to the opposite side of the grave, taking a place on the ground next to Yadira.

Mariposa, stricken, drew her shawl close around her neck and looked at the ground. Estella's sharp gaze missed nothing and she tilted her head questioningly when she met Luz's eye across the grave, but Luz merely looked away to stare at the flickering flame of a candle. Yadira earned her place as a kindred spirit when she draped her heavy shawl around both their shoulders and linked arms with Luz in sisterly camaraderie.

As midnight approached, the church bells began tolling, guiding the souls home. The candles flickered in the darkness, lighting their way. Luz looked around her as more candles were lit around the cemetery. Soon it looked like a fiery island in the darkness.

Manolo stood and the murmuring of family voices hushed as heads tilted to listen. In a sonorous voice that went from bass to tenor, Manolo recited what sounded to Luz to be an epic poem or a prayer. The family members closed their eyes as they listened, occasionally joining in to recite a refrain.

Luz leaned toward Yadira and whispered, "What is he saying? I can't understand any of the words."

Yadira leaned her head closer. At that moment Luz felt that Yadira was her closest ally. "He is speaking Purépecha," she explained. "He speaks about death . . . the mystery, the rebirth. It is a very old language. Many of us do not understand it, too. But Tío

Manolo, he is an elder of the village and he does. The language, it is kept alive because of people like him in Michoacán. They carry the history of our ancestors in their stories. We do not wish to lose our culture."

When Tío Manolo finished his recitation, there was a long silence. He sat solemnly beside Estella, who patted his arm consolingly. Then the family began the feast. The men shared a bottle of *caña,* a potent alcohol made from sugarcane. The women in turn lifted the embroidered linen from the baskets of prepared food and shared the bread and tamales. With great ceremony, Estella offered the first plate of dinner to Esperanza and placed it on her grave.

"May you partake of the vitality of the food we offer you," she prayed to Esperanza's soul.

While they ate and drank, the stories began about Abuela. A soft buzz of hushed voices created a hum throughout the cemetery. As she listened, Luz pieced together the early history of her grandmother and her life as a young girl, and later as the wife of her first husband, Luis, and the mother of his children, Manolo, Maria, and Luisa. Their lives, and those of the entire village, were changed forever when the mine closed. Luis joined other men to work in the United States for nine months of the year while Esperanza single-handedly raised their children while working in the family store. It was during that time that she lost her youngest and buried her in this same cemetery. Luis saved enough to bring his family to America but a year later died in a farm accident.

Luz listened to the stories and understood how her family could believe Abuela's spirit had returned to join them by the fire. Yet Luz knew a different Abuela. A woman who'd lived a whole other story after the chapters of this one had been closed. She'd married again, had a daughter and a granddaughter. If Luz learned anything from the Day of the Dead ceremony, it was that life and death were part of one big cycle that repeated itself as the seasons repeated themselves, over and over.

Luz huddled under her shawl, feeling Yadira's warmth beside her, and longed to tell the story of her journey from Milwaukee to this moment, as she had intended. Her fingers touched the papers in her bag, but her heart wasn't in it. It didn't matter, she told herself. The story was written in her mind and in her heart.

After two in the morning most of the family members left to return home. Yadira hugged Luz and left her the blanket so she could keep warm. Only Manolo and Estella stayed with Mariposa and Luz. The voices in the cemetery hushed as the night grew bitterly cold. Luz wrapped the blanket tighter around her shoulders and huddled near a small brazier burner. Her lids grew heavy and at some point in the next hour she fell asleep.

She awoke to the sound of voices. Yawning, she opened her eyes to see dawn breaking as a dim gray light hung in the foggy mist. Around her she saw the silhouettes of women wrapped in shawls and men blanketed in their serapes rising and stretching, their faces weary. Somewhere in the distance a rooster crowed.

Estella came to Manolo's side. "Look, husband, the sun is rising. Your mother's spirit is leaving now, returning to her resting place. Now we must go to honor her at mass. Come."

Manolo set his jaw, his eyes glittering, but he complied, groaning with the effort of rising. Estella picked up her basket, then came to Luz's side. She bent to frame Luz's face in her cold, dry hands. In the dim light Luz saw the compassion shining in her eyes like flickering flames. Estella bent to kiss her cheek, then turned to assist her husband home.

Luz watched them join the other villagers as they left the

cemetery in a somnolent procession. Dawn's light blanketed the mountains and the cold damp of morning chilled her face. She glanced at Mariposa, wondering if she was leaving now, too. Mariposa's shawl had slipped low on her arms as she stood. The stricken look on her face alarmed Luz. Mariposa made her way to Abuela's grave and dropped to her knees. Rocking back and forth, she moaned in a low, anguished voice.

"Don't go, Mami. Don't go." She reached down to dig with her bare hands past the bed of flower petals into the earth.

"What are you *doing*?" Luz asked in horror. What Mariposa was doing seemed disrespectful to the grave, even sacrilegious. "Stop," she said, grabbing her arm.

"Leave me alone," Mariposa cried with emotion, swinging her arm back. She lost her balance and had to catch herself before she fell forward. "This is between me and my mother. It's none of your business."

"None of my business?" Luz exclaimed, rearing back. "None of my business?" A volcanic fury surged through her. All the anger she'd suppressed during the nightlong vigil, all of her rage at being abandoned, all the indignation at the destruction of her *ofrenda* spewed out like lava. This time, Luz would not be ignored. She tossed down her shawl and stood over her mother, glaring down at her.

"How dare you!" she cried. "Kneeling in the dirt in front of that ridiculous altar you made. It's so showy. Abuela would have hated it. Do you think that making that altar is going to make her forgive you? She's dead! It's too late. You had your chance and you blew it. No amount of stuff you put on that altar will change that."

"Don't . . ."

"She thought you were dead! *I* thought you were dead. You

left us and didn't bother to send a word. Not a *word!*" Luz sucked in air, panting with the effort. "You loved your drugs more than you loved me or Abuela." She spun around to look at the *ofrenda.* It looked garish in the morning light. "Look at all that shit," she cried. "You bought all that stuff. It means nothing to her. What did you give Abuela that meant something to her? What did you offer that meant something to you?"

Luz grabbed her purse, her heels digging in the soft dirt of the gravesite. She pulled out the offerings that had been torn from the box of ashes and discarded, then returned to the headstone. With deliberate movements she placed the booties down on the earth in front of Mariposa. "For Ofelia," she said. Next she set the torn cardboard covered with psychedelic lettering and painted monarchs beside the booties, saying, "For Stacie." The page torn from a book of observations she set beside the other items, saying, "For Margaret." Finally, she sprinkled the remnants of the wilted flowers and paper scraps over the grave and watched them land in a splayed pattern across the grave.

"Don't you touch them!" she hissed to Mariposa. "These were my offerings to Abuela and you threw them away like they were trash. Like you did to me. They aren't trash! I'm not trash!" she cried. "This was important to me. To *me!*" Her clenched fist pounded her heart and she felt tears burning her eyes. "You never once asked me about them. You never asked me how I felt about Abuela dying and being left alone. *I* brought Abuela's ashes home. Not you! This was *my* journey." She reached up to swipe away her tears. "I came here for her. These were meant for Abuela." Her voice broke at saying her name. "*She* was my mother. Not you. You're nothing to me. You're dead to me! Do you hear me? You're dead to me!"

Mariposa sat slump-shouldered on her mother's grave, surrounded by the sputtering candles. She stared up at Luz, her dark eyes vacant and her face ashen with shock.

Luz spun on her heel and marched blindly away, tripping over scattered offerings in her eagerness to escape. She swept up her purse and shawl, without looking back. She couldn't bear another moment in this cemetery.

The sun rose higher above the horizon. The aura of mystery and reconciliation that Luz had felt at sunset vanished like ghosts. The Day of the Dead was supposed to have been a celebration of love and a reaffirmation of life. All Luz felt as she ran from the cemetery was a crushing defeat and despair.

In the new light of dawn, all the dreams she'd harbored of her mother had been revealed as a nightmare.

Twenty-Five

Once settled in the sanctuaries, millions of monarchs spend much of their time huddled in endless roosts in the oyamel fir forests. When the sun shines they take flight. When a cloud covers the sun, the butterflies panic and rush back to roost. The sound of millions of flapping wings is like the wind in the trees.

Hours later, when the family had gone to mass to celebrate the joy of life, Luz remained behind, packing her suitcase. When she'd returned to the apartment she had gone straight to her room. No one spoke to her; they seemed to comprehend that she needed to be left alone. She stood for a long while under a hot shower, scrubbing off the dirt and letting the water warm her chilled body. When she'd dressed again and came downstairs, the house was empty and quiet.

Luz helped herself to a cup of black coffee and some bread. She felt tired and empty inside, drained of all her pent-up emotions. She went to the bedside table and picked up her phone, hoping for a message from Margaret, but there were none. She missed her friend. This was the trigger that made her cry.

She was bent over her suitcase, sniffling back tears, when she heard the door open. Luz closed her eyes while her hands stilled, instinctively knowing who it was.

Mariposa quietly entered the room. She didn't speak.

Luz gathered her resolve and turned to square off with her mother. Mariposa had washed the mud from her face and hands, and brushed and pulled her hair back into a tight ponytail, but she still wore the clothing of the night before. Dark smudges under her eyes and her chalky skin were evidence of the sleepless night. She stood quiet and composed, again the reserved woman Luz had met at Maria's house, holding herself together by a tight string.

"You're leaving?" Mariposa asked in a voice made hoarse with exhaustion.

"Tomorrow," Luz replied without warmth.

Mariposa considered this. After a moment she reached into the pocket of her skirt and retrieved a small woven drawstring satchel. She reached out and handed it to Luz.

Luz stared at it, not moving. "What's that?"

Mariposa tightened her lips and lifted the red bag higher toward Luz. "I meant to give this to you last night. But instead I made a mess of the evening, as usual. You were right. I thought only of myself and my own grief. I should have thought about yours."

Luz turned her back to the gift. "Whatever." She went back to her suitcase and resumed packing, wishing the woman would just leave her alone.

"Luz, I'm sorry."

"You're always sorry!" Luz said, spinning around. "It doesn't mean anything." She took a breath, determined not to lose her temper, then turned and tossed a shirt into the suitcase. "I'll pack and be out of here. I'll get out of your and everyone's way."

"I know you're angry. I don't blame you. But I promised you I would take you to the sanctuary."

"Forget about it. I don't want to go anymore."

"But you've come so far."

"It's not your problem, okay? I'm not a little girl anymore. I'll ask Tía Estella to take me. Or Yadira."

"Yes. You could do that." Mariposa sounded defeated. She looked around the room but her eyes didn't focus on anything. She took a step closer to Luz. "Here, you should take this with you," she said, offering the satchel to her again. "I put some of Abuela's ashes into this bag for you to bring with you to the sanctuary. I . . . I didn't feel her presence last night. I think if she were to be anywhere, it would be up there. With the butterflies."

Luz thought her heart had turned cold, but looking at the bag of ashes in Mariposa's hand, she felt a crack in the ice. She sucked in her breath.

"Those are Abuela's ashes?" she asked in a shaky voice.

"Yes. I'm so sorry I ruined your *ofrenda,*" Mariposa said in a rush. "It was thoughtless of me." She pushed her hand closer to Luz. "Please. Take this to the mountain so you can say your good-bye."

Luz reached out to take the woven bag. It felt heavier than she'd thought it would. She tightened her lips against the urge to say thank you.

"Luz, I thought a long time about what you said to me last night. You had every right to say those things. They weren't anything I hadn't already said to myself."

Luz turned to put the ashes on the table, a sinking feeling of shame in her stomach.

"You asked one question that I'd like to answer," Mariposa said.

Luz flicked a quick glance at Mariposa's face.

"You asked what I ever gave to my mother that mattered to me. I gave her you."

Luz took a step back and put up her hands against the onslaught of emotions. "I don't want to hear this now," she said. "I can't stand any more of it."

"You need to stand it! You need to be strong now, for me, for Abuela, and for yourself so that we can get past all this and move forward. Please, Luz. It's long past time for us to have this conversation."

"You're right. It's too late."

"You have no idea how hard it is for me to be with you."

Luz swung her head around, eyes wide with hurt.

"To see you every day and not feel ashamed and unworthy. I know I did the most terrible thing a mother could do to her child. I left you! Having a child, raising her to adulthood, this should have been my life's work. Instead, my life was filled with debased behavior I'm too ashamed to speak of. I was sick and ashamed, too ashamed to call. Don't you see? I thought it was better if you thought I was dead! I don't deserve my mother's forgiveness. I don't deserve you."

Mariposa walked to the window to look out through the lace. "There were many times when I wanted to end my life. Only the hope that I might see you again kept me going." She turned again to face Luz. "I know I can't take Abuela's place in your heart. I don't even want to try. I just ask that you let me guide you to the sanctuary, as we planned. You don't have to speak to me. I'll keep my distance. I promise."

Luz looked at the bag of ashes, confused. "Why did Abuela tell me all those lies about you?"

"No, not lies. Stories."

"What's the difference?"

"Ah, Luz, perhaps the young can't fully understand this. All myths and legends are nothing more than stories. Tales told by shamans, priests, mothers, and fathers since the beginning of time to try to explain universal truths. We take what we need from the stories, to give our lives meaning. Because each of us is writing our own story.

"Look at me, Luz. *Me.* I am not the story you heard from Abuela. I am not even the story that is forming in your mind now. Look into my eyes. For all my faults and weaknesses, I am your mother. You are my daughter. That is our story. I will take you to the sanctuary so that you can finish this journey. That much I can do for you. After that, I will abide by whatever decision you make."

"All right," Luz said begrudgingly. "I'm doing this for Abuela. Not for you."

"I understand," Mariposa said. "If you're ready, we can go now."

The rutted dirt road to the sanctuary was twisted and steep with precipitous climbs and drops. Mariposa drove El Toro past the remnants of the old mine. Abandoned conveyor belts, metal towers, and scaffolds were all that remained of one of the major silver mines of Mexico. They passed several small farms that dotted the mountains with fields covered with the remnants of cornstalks. She turned off at a small house built of wood slats and adobe, like the others they'd passed.

"We'll park the car here," she told Luz.

Mariposa had kept her word. She didn't talk and her manner was as formal as if she were a paid guide. Luz got out of the car and sullenly followed her to the door of the drab little house. It was a meager dwelling with neither plumbing nor electricity. A miserly trickle of smoke rose from the fireplace indoors. The dusty back area was a hardscrabble patch of earth enclosed by chicken wire attached to pieces of chopped timber. The fence swayed precariously but did its job of keeping in wandering hens and a few imposing turkeys. A tilting shed housed three sheep and a sweet lamb, all of which appeared content and well fed. A short, stocky man came to the door, tucking in his shirt. Mariposa quickly told him in Spanish of their intention to go up the mountain. His face revealed surprise that she wanted to go up the mountain today, during the holiday.

Luz listened to the rapid exchange as Mariposa told him who she was, using her brother's influence. She didn't mean to disturb their holiday and only wanted to rent two horses for the journey up the mountain. No, it had to be today, not tomorrow. Sorry, but they were leaving. The man insisted that they needed a guide and would not rent horses if they refused one. Mariposa argued with him but he held firm. Reluctantly, she agreed. Once the terms were agreed upon, he turned and called back into the house, "Pablocito!"

Moments later a painfully thin boy, no more than twelve or thirteen, with spiky, black hair appeared at the door. He glanced sullenly at Luz, clearly annoyed that he was called to duty on his holiday. After some terse and hasty instructions from his father, the boy stomped inside to return a few minutes later wearing a long-sleeved flannel shirt and an orange cotton scarf tied around his neck. He stepped outdoors without as much as a nod of acknowledgment.

"Go with Pablocito," the man said gruffly. "He will take you."

"Thank you," Mariposa answered with a slight bow.

The women followed Pablocito to the ramshackle barn, where he pulled two horses from their stalls. Mariposa took the large, spirited white one, Blanca. Luz got the smaller black horse with the sling back named Negra. After saddling them, the boy grabbed the rope to Luz's horse and gave a quick, impatient *Come along* wave to Mariposa.

Mariposa stroked Blanca's neck as she murmured a few words of assurance. The horse's ears twitched and she rolled her eyes back to inspect Mariposa. Then Mariposa climbed up quickly and settled in the saddle. Luz had never ridden a horse before and she felt sure the horse knew it. Pablocito came around, linked his fingers together, and bent to offer her a leg up. With his firm hoist, Luz clumsily slung her leg around the back of the horse, practically falling off with the effort. Taking a deep breath, she got comfortable in the leather saddle and picked up the reins. Pablocito grabbed hold of a rope and led her horse out from the corral at a leisurely walk.

With a click of her tongue and a gentle kick, Mariposa trotted ahead of Pablocito, making it clear that she was not about to let a boy lead her to her family's sacred spot. She looked elegant astride her large white horse, with her shoulders back and her chin up. She led them across the dirt road to a narrow opening in the dense foliage of the mountainside.

Luz's poor beast was as thin and rangy as the boy, but it thankfully moved at a steady pace, one hoof in front of the other along the narrow, dusty trail. Luz clung to the horse's mane with one hand and the saddle with the other, holding on for dear life. They slowly made their way up the rocky trail through the dense forest. The gray volcanic soil was so deep and powdery that Mariposa's horse kicked up clouds of dust on Luz and Pablocito. From time to time Luz's horse sneezed, and Luz felt guilty for riding above the dust while the boy leading her horse breathed it into his lungs. He was, she thought, no better than a boy in the coal mines.

They climbed higher and higher up the precipitous mountain. The air grew thinner and colder. It was a hard, uncomfortable ride, down steep paths where she leaned far back in the saddle, and up precipitous inclines where she leaned forward and prayed her horse didn't fall. Worst of all, the trails were so narrow at points that her horse's hooves sent cascades of stones tumbling down the rocky cliff. At such times Luz held her breath and looked up at the sky.

Then, on a breath, she saw a butterfly. A beautiful, big monarch floated on a breeze right past her. She felt the thrill of discovery and wanted to call out to Mariposa, but her grudge kept her silent. So she privately marveled at the single monarch—as if it were the first she'd ever seen in her life. Pablocito saw it and turned his head. Seeing her smile, he chuckled, digging deep crevices into the dust on his face. He pointed farther up the trail.

"*¡Más! ¡Muchas más!*" he told her.

He was right. More monarchs began flying past her, in groups of ten and twenty. When they passed what looked like a dry riverbed she saw hundreds of butterflies shooting past her and her poky horse, taking a shortcut straight through that path to the treetops. Luz laughed out loud with delight. Now she saw them everywhere, in the trees, on the ground, sipping nectar in meager patches of sunlight.

They'd climbed for almost an hour when the shaded path opened to an idyllic meadow. Like a deer stepping from the dark woods, Luz lifted her face and felt the warm kiss of sunlight on her skin. The soft, green grass was spiked with all kinds of wildflowers; purple, red, and yellow. Luz smiled to herself, thinking Margaret would be in heaven here, writing down the names of the plants and sketching them in her notebook. She would know them all. Monarchs on gossamer wings flitted about like dainty fairies, nectaring on the colorful blossoms and basking in the sunlight.

Mariposa stopped and dismounted; Luz followed suit. Her legs felt watery after the long ride and she stretched them while Mariposa spoke rapidly to the boy in Spanish. He nodded in understanding and led the horses to a spot in the shade.

"We'll walk from here," Mariposa told Luz. "Here." She handed her a bottle of water. Grateful, Luz drank thirstily. She'd not packed anything for this last-minute trek. Mariposa kept her word and remained silent. When Luz finished, Mariposa took the empty plastic bottles and put them in her backpack.

"Don't forget to bring the ashes," Mariposa said.

As if she would forget them, Luz thought to herself. Inside, she was torn between the resentment she held against Mariposa and her desire to share these amazing moments with her. She wondered if Abuela would have been able to make the climb, and what she might have had to share. Luz followed Mariposa's long strides, two silent women walking through the meadow.

The next section up was arduous as they climbed a steep mountain bank choked with vines. Luz felt her chest constrict in the thin air and her breath come short. She had to stop frequently to catch her breath, bending over like a winded old woman. The altitude didn't seem to bother Mariposa. She walked on ahead, quiet on her feet, and her long legs quickly outdistanced Luz.

Luz saw Mariposa stop in the trail to bend and pick up a butterfly. Catching up, Luz saw it lying still in her hands, but alive. Mariposa cupped the butterfly in both hands and, bringing it close to her mouth, softly blew a few warm breaths on it. She opened her hands. The butterfly shivered, flexed its wings a few times, and flew off into the air.

Luz looked at her mother with surprise. The woman was a series of contradictions. Restrained one moment, emotional the next. Cold, then hot. Destructive, then a savior. Luz was getting dizzy just trying to keep up.

Mariposa rose and slapped the dust from her hands. "Sometimes they get cold up here and fall in a stupor. They just need a little CPR," she added with a smile.

Luz didn't laugh, but she began looking for other butterflies that needed CPR.

"This last part is a little difficult, but you can do it," Mariposa said, her voice encouraging. "Just be careful not to trip on the vines. Ready?"

"Okay." Mariposa held out her hand and gave Luz a firm tug to help her up a rocky bank. They continued upward for another half hour of tough hiking, until suddenly Mariposa stopped at a ridge and stood motionless.

"There it is," she said in a soft voice.

Luz came to her side, looking around with curiosity. It all looked like the same forest to her. She followed Mariposa to an enormous fir, a granddaddy of the forest. Mariposa pointed. On its massive trunk were beautifully carved ancient symbols that Luz couldn't identify. Mariposa let her fingers glide across the wood carvings as myriad emotions flickered across her face. Then with a deep breath she grabbed hold of the trunk with both hands and in a flash rounded the massive base, descending to a lower ledge, and disappeared. Luz's breath caught. A few seconds later Mariposa poked her head around.

"Your turn," she said to Luz.

Luz balked.

"Don't be afraid. Women in our family have done this for

generations and we haven't lost one yet. Use both hands and swing your leg around. I'll help you. Careful now."

Luz licked her lips and looked beyond Mariposa's head to the steep cliff that seemed to drop to infinity. If she fell here, no one would ever find her. Did she trust her mother to catch her if she fell? She hesitated at seeing the muddy incline caused by Mariposa's boots.

From somewhere inside she heard Abuela's voice. *Courage!*

Luz suddenly thought of the story of Little Nana and how she'd stood bravely at the precipice while the gods commanded her to jump. Come on, Luz told herself. This is your moment. Taking a deep breath, she grabbed hold of the trunk with shaky hands. She mimicked Mariposa and swung around the base of the tree. Instantly Mariposa's strong hand was on her arm, guiding her around to safety on the ledge. Luz took a long, shaky breath and brushed the slivers of wood and moss from her jacket. Then she lifted her head.

All that she had read, all the stories she'd heard, all the photographs she'd seen couldn't capture the impact of experiencing this sacred cathedral of stone and trees. She stood on a cliff overlooking cragged mountains that climbed high into the clouds and between them lay a deep valley. The forest of giant oyamel trees, mysterious and mighty, stood with their boughs heavily laden with thick clumps of brown and gray leaves.

Only they weren't leaves. They were thousands—millions, an incomprehensible number—of monarch butterflies with their wings in closed position, clinging to the branches of trees in clumps, like beehives. She was so close to some of the branches that she could have reached out and touched them, but she didn't.

Mariposa spoke in a hushed voice at Luz's side.

"Abuela brought me to this same spot, as her mother took her. We believe that this is the temple of the goddess Xochiquetzal. It is said that she lives in a garden high up in the mountains surrounded by flowers. But what are butterflies if not flying flowers?"

She turned to face Luz with solemnity. Slowly, with purpose and determination, she breathed deep and straightened her back. Any weakness or excess emotion she might have shown the night before fled from her. Mariposa became otherworldly, her beauty ageless. She appeared as one with all the natural elements that surrounded them. Her high, sharp cheekbones were like the chiseled rocks of the mountains. Her hair flowed down her back, the same sienna color of stone. Her eyes glittered like obsidian, gleaming with mystery. She was a high priestess of this ancient and holy temple as she turned to face the great abyss. Her voice resonated with the rich timbre of conviction.

"This is the place, deep in the heart of the Mother of Mountains, the Sierra Madre, where monarchs have come for millennia following the call of the gods. This is the place where women in our family have come to offer them praise for generations. I call out to our mother, Esperanza, to join us here as we pay homage."

Mariposa took a deep breath; then, raising her arms in supplication, she began to sing. Luz's breath caught at the purity of her voice. She sang a song unlike any Luz had heard before. Though she recognized the language as Purépecha, she couldn't understand the strange keening of syllables and sounds. Yet in the universal language of music, Luz intuitively knew that her mother sang a song of women. As Mariposa stood at the precipice, her sweet voice sang of love and duty and heartache and commitment. The song pierced Luz's heart with its haunting melody, filling her soul with unspoken expectations of womanhood.

When Mariposa was finished, Luz reached up, surprised to find tears on her face.

Mariposa turned to face Luz and in the manner of ceremony, she reached out to clasp Luz's hand firmly in her own "My daughter, I pray that you are blessed with many children. That you have the strength to fight for them when needed. The wisdom to give good counsel. The heart to offer love and compassion. And the serenity to leave them in joy and peace when you are called to join the spirits."

Mariposa turned again to face the valley and called out in a ringing voice, "I stand here to humbly ask the Greater Spirit for your blessing. To help Luz in her transformation from child to woman. Grant her the gift of life and light. Give her wisdom to become one with you."

Mariposa turned and smiled benignly, almost shyly. She'd relinquished the role of high priestess as she released Luz's hand. "I'm going to leave you for a while," she told Luz. "I won't be far. Just to the other side of the ledge. You need to be alone now. There are times when words are a distraction. You must experience the moment in your own thoughts. Now you must listen to the butterflies." She leaned forward to kiss Luz on her forehead, lingered a second, then without another word turned to walk to a farther distance along the ledge.

Luz hadn't expected to be left alone. She breathed in the cool, moist air that tasted and smelled of pine. She thought of her mother's singing, feeling again the soul-stirring connection. Then she turned to face the fierce, cragged wall of sienna-colored rock that soared into the sky to pierce the soft, white clouds. Giant oyamel firs grew on the sides of the mountains, creating a canopy that protected the colonies of butterflies. She stared out at the forest, at its great quiet and stillness. The butterflies clung in tight clusters, appearing as hefty gray hives hanging from the branches.

Suddenly the sun broke through the clouds and in that miraculous moment the sky exploded in a burst of orange glitter. Cascades of monarchs took to the wing, dancing and swirling across the brilliant blue sky like orange snow. They were everywhere—over her, around her, in front of her. Seeing them, she was infused with a joy so intense and palpable that Luz felt her heart expand and grow with it. She opened up her arms to embrace the moment, filled with happiness, laughing out loud. The sound of a million beating wings filled the valley, echoing like the wind. She felt the fluttering of wings across her hair, her cheeks, her shoulders like kisses and heard the voice of Abuela sing out, *Dance,* querida*!*

Abuela's spirit filled her mind and heart and soul. Luz felt she was in the sky, dancing with the butterflies. There was no past. There was no future. There was only this glorious, glittering now. It was, she knew, what heaven must be like.

Mariposa stood alone on the precipice and looked out across the valley of her ancestors. She had fulfilled her duty, she told them. She'd brought her daughter to the Sacred Circle. Now she sent her prayer to her mother on the wings of the butterflies.

The sun burst through the clouds and in the space of a gasp the blue sky was afire with millions of flickering flames. In that instant Mariposa felt the spark of a small flame ignite within. It glowed and sent its dazzling light flowing through her bloodstream. With astonishment, she recognized this light. She knew this feeling! It had been so long since she'd felt it, or had even looked for it. She thought she'd extinguished this flame long ago.

She closed her eyes and meditated on the light, welcoming it back into her soul. As tears flowed down her cheeks. Mariposa understood in a burst of illumination that all this time she'd been seeking the forgiveness of others, but she'd never asked forgiveness from the most important person—herself. Without achieving that, she couldn't begin to change her life. One by one she peeled back the layers of her self-loathing, naming her weaknesses, forgiving them.

She felt the power grow within her. She opened her eyes and saw the blue sky aflame with orange fluttering. She heard in the rustling wings the voice of her mother, calling her. She yearned to be with her. She leaned forward. It would be so easy. All she had to do was spread her wings and fly and at last she would find peace.

"Mami!"

A voice pierced her thoughts, calling her back. She blinked and looked down at her feet, surprised to see that she was standing with her toes at the edge of the precipice.

"Mami!"

Was that Luz? At first she was stunned, and then her heart leaped wildly for joy. It was the first time her daughter had called her *mother.*

Mariposa looked out again at the butterflies dancing in the sky. Somewhere out there, she knew her mother waited for her. But beside her on the ledge, her own daughter called for her. She gave thanks to the Greater Spirit for answering her prayer.

Mariposa stepped away from the edge and walked to her daughter. She walked three feet, six feet—an immeasurable distance in light of that created between her and her daughter over so many lost years.

Continuity. Rebirth. Circle. These were the words Mariposa

would cling to. They gave her hope. Four generations of renewed promise created the marvel of the fourth-generation butterfly that, newly born, followed the call to travel thousands of miles to the Sacred Circle. Four generations from now, her great-great-granddaughter would make her journey to this same spot.

She found Luz standing absolutely still with a dozen butterflies on her arms, her head, her clothing.

"Mami, look!" Luz exclaimed, her face both beaming and amazed. "Isn't it a miracle?"

Mariposa smiled at her daughter and felt the flame inside of her flicker and glow brighter. "Yes. A miracle."

Luz reached out for her hand and Mariposa saw the little girl whose hand she had dropped so many years before. She leaped forward to grasp it now and held it tight as the butterflies took flight.

Luz reached into her backpack and retrieved the woven satchel that contained Abuela's ashes. She held it in her hands and recalled the long journey from their bungalow in Wisconsin to this mountainside in Mexico. She didn't feel sadness; rather, she felt free of her anger and confusion. She stood in glorious elation that at last she understood her grandmother and her grand passion for life. She stood at the precipice as the sun sent another burst of monarchs cascading to the sky.

"You're home, Abuela," she said, knowing she was heard. "Thank you!"

Luz handed her mother a handful of ashes and together they released the ashes into the air to mingle with the butterflies in their aerial dance of joy. It was here that Abuela's spirit resided; they both felt it. Mariposa and Luz stood arm in arm, basking in the light, each knowing that she would always remember this moment when they stood together in the Sacred Circle and witnessed a miracle.

Twenty-Six

The monarchs that survived the migration south and the long winter in Mexico will face similar dangers on their migration north in the spring. They fly out of the sanctuaries in search of milkweed on which to lay the eggs of the next generation. Each butterfly carries a microcosm of all the generations of the entire population. Thus, this remarkable cycle begins anew.

Luz sat in a window seat of the crowded plane and gazed out as she traveled north. It had been a tumultuous season of new relationships and good-byes. She'd said good-bye to Abuela. She'd met and said good-bye to her friends, her extended family in Mexico and in San Antonio. And her mother.

Luz closed her eyes and captured her last image of Mariposa. She was standing at the airport with her shoulders straight and a determined smile on her face. The roar of jet airplanes taking off and landing intermingled with the announcements on the intercom and the buzz of chatter. Conversation was nearly impossible. They were both trying to be upbeat and cheerful, but parting again, after having found each other, was difficult for them both.

On the long drive back from Angangueo to San Antonio, Luz and Mariposa had entertained the fantasy that Mariposa might come back to Milwaukee to live with Luz in the bungalow. When they'd returned to San Antonio, however, Sam had taken Luz aside and explained to her, in his clear, firm voice, that Mariposa was still in recovery. She needed her support group in San Antonio and her routine. Luz had to be the strong one now, he told her, because Mariposa would be unable to say no to her. She had to let Mariposa stay and return home alone. What he didn't say, but what was tacitly understood, was that Sam would be by Mariposa's side looking out for her. When Luz thought again of Mariposa's emotional highs and lows on the Day of the Dead, she believed Sam was right.

Mariposa's eyes had filled with tears when the final boarding call came. For a brief moment her tight hold on her composure slipped. She stepped forward and brought her hands up to cradle Luz's face and peer into her daughter's eyes.

"This isn't good-bye, *mi hija*," she told her. "Look for me in the spring when the days grow long and the sun warms again. I will fly north to see you. And in the fall, when the nights grow cold again and the leaves change, you will fly south to see me. We'll be like the butterflies, you and me."

Remembering these words, Luz smiled. The sentiment had settled in her heart and comforted her. It was the same feeling of peace she'd experienced when she was a child listening to Abuela's stories at night when a storm raged. The inherent truth embedded in these words resonated with Luz, and she no longer felt sad or afraid.

Luz bent forward and pulled out Abuela's photograph album from her carry-on bag. Leaning back in her seat, she opened it and began turning the pages. She gazed at the familiar photographs of her great-grandparents, her grandparents, her uncles and aunts. There was the favorite photo of her mother carrying Luz as a baby. Luz smoothed the curling edges.

Now there were new photographs in the album. Her lips curved at seeing the family portrait taken before she'd left Angangueo. Tío Manolo, Tía Estella, Tías Rosa and Marisela, Yadira, and other family members were gathered around Mariposa and Luz, squinting in the sun with bright smiles on their faces at Abuela's gravesite. She noted the strong family resemblance in many of their features, including her own. Obvious signs of shared DNA gave her a feeling of belonging.

This next photograph was taken at Tía Maria's house in San Antonio. Her aunt was sitting in her favorite plush red chair, smiling ecstatically with Serena poised daintily in her ample lap. Luz understood loneliness too well not to let Tía Maria keep the dog she adored. And it was never her decision, anyway. It was easy to see that Serena was in dog heaven and had chosen her forever home.

Luz finally understood how Abuela felt when she looked at the photo albums and told Luz stories about the living family members as well as the dead. They were all real personalities in her heart and mind, not meaningless names attached to faces in an album. Just as families told stories about their departed loved ones on the Day of the Dead, Abuela had kept her family close by telling and retelling stories and anecdotes, interweaving them with her stories about Mariposa and Luz to create one long, continuous thread.

Abuela had been right about so many things. Even El Toro, Luz thought with a chuckle. That little car had heart and had carried them all the way to Mexico and back. Luz had left the car with Mariposa. That little VW Bug had served her well. It had been her chrysalis on this journey and now she could leave it behind and fly home.

Home.

The truth was, Luz was eager to go home and to Sully. A month ago she couldn't wait to leave what she'd thought was a stale and uneventful life, one that trapped her. But in the light of her journey she'd realized it wasn't the place that had changed, but her heart.

During some of her loneliest moments on this epic journey she'd thought of the little bungalow on Milwaukee's south side with rooms the colors of oranges and limes. In her mind it was a place of refuge. Luz could decide in the future whether to keep the house or sell it. She'd talk to Margaret and apply for scholarships and grants so she could return to school. She had plans to make. The notion of starting this next phase of her life, free from obstacles, was empowering.

Maybe not start over. Maybe just start fresh.

In the spring her mother would fly in and together they would continue Abuela's garden. They'd plant milkweed and monarch nectar flowers. She would not spray pesticides or weed killer. Like her grandmother and her mother before her, she would raise the caterpillars to chrysalis. She would share the miracle of metamorphosis with the neighborhood children. And in the fall she would help tag the butterflies as Billy had taught her to do, and hopefully those monarchs would journey across the continent to the sanctuaries in Mexico.

Her little garden would be her own sanctuary and thus a vital cog in the butterfly's cycle of migration. After all, she'd stood in the Sacred Circle and danced with the butterflies. She could do no less.

She brought to mind the story of the goddesses who sacrificed themselves to bring light to the world. And her recurring dream of the faceless, floating goddess who she'd thought was her mother.

She no longer had that dream, but Luz understood that Abuela had wanted her to believe in goddesses.

And she did. Luz smiled, thinking of the three she'd met on this journey—Ofelia, Stacie, and Margaret. She imagined Margaret chasing monarchs with Billy in the mountain sanctuaries, diligently writing notes in her observation books. Stacie hitching a star to her next destination. And Ofelia, cradling her daughter at her breast, having found her family at last. Goddesses were everywhere, if you looked for them.

Abuela had told Luz the stories she thought a young girl should hear about her mother. But Luz preferred the real-life story of Mariposa. Her mother was a stronger, fiercer heroine than any naive fairy-tale princess for having suffered, fallen, endured the harsh realities of experience, and persevered.

And now Luz was free to begin her own story. She was no longer bogged down by missing chapters in her past. She wanted to write new pages that she hoped would include Sully and her mother. And her story would begin with the word *yes*!

Luz looked out the window at the landscape far, far below. She was retracing her route across the Great Plains states where she had chased butterflies and dreams. It seemed so long ago. She was no longer the uncertain young caterpillar. She felt as though she'd passed through the darkness of her chrysalis into a new world. Her spirit had been awakened. She understood that in every life there was death and rebirth and continuity. She accepted the challenge of her own transformation.

She was the butterfly. And she was flying home.